SHADES

An Evil Dead MC Story

By

Nicole James

SHADES

AN EVIL DEAD MC STORY

By

Nicole James

Published by Nicole James

Cover Art by Viola Estrella
Photography by Maciej Grochala
Image courtesy of Eksmagazyn
ISBN#: 9781530839728

AUTHOR'S NOTE

For those of you who have read the first and second book in the Outlaw Series, there are events that occur in the beginning of SHADES that overlap with events that occurred toward the end of CRASH. (But told from these new character's perspectives.) For those of you who have not read any of the others in the series, this is a stand-alone story. It is not necessary to have read the other stories to enjoy this one, although it may make it a richer experience to know some of the other characters' backstory.

He hadn't seen her in years and now here she was, the love of his life, riding back into his life…on the back of a brother's bike.

Fucking hell.

PROLOGUE

Skylar walked by her man's pretty black Harley, its chrome gleaming in the sun, and headed up the back stairs. She juggled two Starbucks cups and a bag containing a couple of blueberry muffins as she fiddled to get the back door of the second floor condo open. She tossed her head, trying to get her long dark hair out of the way, wishing she'd taken the time to put it up before she snuck out that morning. It was oppressively hot, something Atlanta was known for—heat and humidity.

She'd been in a hurry, wanting to get out and back before he woke up so that she could surprise him. He'd been so nice to her this week, surprising her by taking her out to celebrate her birthday a couple of days ago. They'd met up with his club brothers.

Rusty was a member of The Devil Kings. A motorcycle club. An MC. And one she should have known better than to get involved with, especially since she worked in the office of an attorney.

Eric would shake his head sadly if he knew; that or wring her neck. He'd been so good to her since she started working for him several years ago. Eric giving her a job had almost been charity. She wasn't a paralegal and had no legal knowledge—hell she hadn't even had any office experience. But she was smart and a fast learner. Maybe he had recognized those traits when he met her.

He used to come into the diner she'd worked at. It had been the only place she'd been able to get a job when she'd first hit town ten years ago. He'd come in every morning… well, he and his gay lover, Ben. The two of them were so cute together. Eric was the serious, level-headed one. Ben was the fly-by-the-seat-of-your-pants, fun-loving risk-taker. Eric was a big shot attorney. Ben was an interior decorator with—in his words—a flair for design and a boldness with color. Eric kept Ben's feet on the ground, and Ben pushed Eric out of his comfort zone.

She'd known the two of them for about a year, waiting on them every day when they came in, making sure their booth was always reserved, laughing at Ben's jokes, rolling her eyes with Eric when Ben's ideas got too outlandish. She'd even gone out to dinner with them on occasion.

It was one of those nights that Ben suggested that Eric hire Skylar for the receptionist position at his office. At first Eric was hesitant, but with a little arm-twisting from Ben, she'd soon found herself with a new job. One she was eternally grateful for. One she hoped they didn't regret giving her. She worked hard, always offering to help with extra tasks, always willing to take on more responsibility.

Which was how she found herself delivering legal documents the day she'd met Rusty. She'd been given paperwork that needed a signature. It had to be filed with the clerk's office by five that day, and Eric had asked if she wouldn't mind running them out to his client for the signature.

She'd found the place easily enough, parking in the diagonal spaces in front of the tiny storefront dental office that sat next to a tattoo parlor. Eric's client was a dentist who was embroiled in a messy divorce. When she'd parked her beat-up old silver Miata, she'd spotted the line of three bikes parked to her left, their chrome pipes gleaming in the afternoon sun. The sight of them immediately brought back memories of home and memories of the man that was her first love. She was drawn to motorcycles and the men who rode them. Always had been. She supposed she always would be. Every time she heard those machines coming, their pipes rumbling, announcing their approach long before she ever saw them, she would think of home. She would think of *him*, the man that had broken her heart. The man she had left behind all those years ago.

Shaking the wistful thoughts from her head, she'd adjusted her rearview mirror and looked at her blue eyes, checking her makeup. Satisfied, she'd gathered up her purse and the file and climbed from the car, pausing a moment to pull her black pencil-skirt down from where it had hiked up. As she'd yanked and tugged, her eyes had moved to the tattoo shop next door. There was no one out front, but she noticed a man standing just inside the door, watching her through the plate glass window. Mortified that he'd seen her shimmying down her skirt and checking her makeup, she'd hurried inside the dental office.

When she'd come back out with the signed papers in

hand, the man she'd seen through the window was leaning idly up against her car. She'd stopped short, her eyes trailing down his body, taking in the biceps of his crossed arms, his muscular build, the sexy way his legs were crossed at his booted ankles, and most notably, the black leather vest with the patches that proclaimed to the world his status as a member of an MC. Her eyes had skated back up to his attractive face.

"What are you doing?"

"Waitin' on you, darlin'," he'd drawled. "What's your name?"

"I don't think that's any of your business. Now would you move, please? I'm late."

"Nope."

"Nope? What do you mean, nope?"

"Not movin'. Not till you tell me your name, doll."

She'd let out an exasperated breath. "Skylar, okay. Can I go now?"

"Don't you want to know my name, Skylar?"

Her hand had landed on her hip. "Not really."

He'd grinned at that. "Feisty little thing, aren't you? My name's Rusty. Have a drink with me, Skylar. I'm not so bad when you get to know me."

"I've no desire to get to know you," she'd said, her eyes trailing over him again with undisguised appreciation of a fine male form. When her eyes lifted to meet his, she'd known he'd seen her words for a lie.

The corner of his mouth had lifted. "Bullshit. I think you'd like to get to know me real well, pretty lady." When she'd still hesitated, he'd pressed, "Nothin' to be afraid of, Skylar. It's just one drink. We don't get along, no harm, no foul. We go our separate ways." He must have seen from the way she'd bit her lip that she was actually considering it. Because that's when he pushed, "Come on, darlin', I'll be a gentleman. Cross my heart."

He'd actually reached up and made the slashing marks over his chest. And she couldn't help but smile. Maybe it was homesickness, maybe it was loneliness, maybe he was just a stand-in for the man she was *really* missing or maybe she'd just plain lost her damn mind because she'd actually accepted. And before long, Rusty had charmed his way into her bed.

That was five months ago.

Skylar shook the memory aside as she went through the back door. It was still quiet, so Rusty must still be asleep. She dropped her purse down on the small, round kitchen table, and her eyes fell on the item sitting on it. It was a circular wooden disk that served as a stand for an ornate jeweled dagger—a dagger that Skylar had admired one day when she and Rusty were in a shop. Rusty must have remembered how much she'd liked it, because he'd surprised her with it a couple of nights ago for a birthday present. He'd actually presented it to her at the bar in front of his club brothers and everything, not caring in the least about the ribbing they gave him.

Skylar frowned, wondering why the dagger was missing from the stand. She was sure they'd left it on the table the other night when they'd come back to his place. She walked out of the kitchen and into the living room where a front door faced the front of the building. She walked down the hall to her left, past the bathroom to the back bedroom.

When she walked through the doorway, she gasped, backing up into the opened door, slamming it up against the wall, the two Starbucks cups falling to the floor.

There on the bed, lying face up and unmoving, was Rusty. The jeweled dagger he'd given her stuck straight up out of his chest. There was blood everywhere, soaking the sheets under him.

Skylar's trembling hand covered her mouth, and her eyes filled with tears. Was he alive? Was he still alive? She moved toward him slowly on shaking legs and whispered his name. "Rusty? Oh my God. Oh my God. Oh my God." She chanted the phrase softly, over and over. Kneeling over him, she shook him and called again, "Rusty? Baby, answer me."

Reaching out a hand, she pressed it to his neck. His skin seemed cold, and she couldn't find a pulse. His chest wasn't moving, and he didn't appear to be breathing, but what did she know? Dashing back down the hall and into the kitchen, she dug through her purse trying to locate her cell phone. Pulling it out, she ran back to the bedroom and dialed 911 with shaking hands.

"911. What's your emergency?"

"M-maple Hill Condominiums. Number 246. A man's been stabbed. P-please hurry." And that's when she heard the roar of a pack of motorcycles pulling up. Dashing through to the living room and to the front window, she peered through the curtain. The Devil King's MC. His brothers. Rat, Reload,

Quick, Reno, and Bear.

Thank God they were here, maybe they could help him. Scurrying around the chair and ottoman, she headed to the door, flipped the deadbolt open, but paused with her hand on the knob.

Would they believe her?

Would they think she did it?

It *was* her dagger sticking out of Rusty, after all. Her *incriminating, identifiable* dagger that he'd given her in front of the entire club for her birthday several nights ago. Then she looked down at her hands, covered in blood from where she'd touched Rusty. *Oh my God.* When they come through that door and find that dagger and her with blood on her hands, they'll never believe her innocence. Making a snap decision, she backed away from the door.

And then she remembered. The duffle bag that had been on the nightstand—the one Rusty always kept close—was missing. She hadn't seen it. It hadn't been there. She knew he'd made a drop last night, and she figured it had to be full of money. Probably drugs and money. Not that she'd ever seen the contents. Not that she'd ever even touched it. But she wasn't stupid. And as much as Rusty kept her out of his business, she knew he protected that bag, and it wasn't because there was a change of clothes inside. Whoever had stabbed him must have done it to steal whatever was inside. Drugs, maybe. Money, more likely. Club money. Money, his brothers were probably coming to collect.

She could hear them trooping up the stairs. Her heart was in her throat as she tried to think what to do. Maybe she could talk some sense into them, convince them she wasn't involved. Bear would believe her, and Quick, maybe. But Reno, Reload, and Rat their VP…no way. If she didn't have answers, they'd beat them out of her, maybe even kill her.

Bang-bang-bang. One of them pounded on the door.

"Rusty, open the fucking door," Rat hollered.

Panicking, she backed into the kitchen, grabbed her purse, and pulled open the back door. As she went through, she heard them coming in the front. Closing the door softly, she dashed down the stairs and jumped in her car.

As she tore off out of the lot, the back door was thrown open, and Reload stepped out onto the wooden landing and yelled, "There she goes! She's gettin' away!"

Flooring it, she heard a shot fired and ducked, hoping to God that Reload got his name because he was a lousy shot. As she got to the highway, she saw two squad cars fly by and a paramedic ambulance heading in the direction she'd come, their lights flashing. She prayed the ambulance made it in time. She prayed Rusty was still alive, but she knew in her heart he was already gone.

Knowing it would only be a matter of minutes before she heard a hoard of bikes chasing after her, she drove as fast as she could, dodging in and out of lanes while her shaking hand dialed Eric. He was the only one who could help her now.

Her eyes on the rearview mirror, she hoped the police would be able to waylay the club before they were able to come after her, and she waited for Eric to answer his phone.

"Come on. Pick up. Pick up."

***

"You need to go to the police," Eric insisted, kneeling in front of her chair as she sat in his office twenty minutes later. It was Sunday morning, and she'd gotten him out of bed to meet her here.

She looked up at him with tears in her eyes and wiped her nose with a tissue, her hands still shaking. "You don't understand. You don't call the police on these people. It would only make it worse."

"What other option do you have? Go into hiding?" He frowned.

She nodded. "Yes. That's the only thing I *can* do."

"You can't be serious, Skylar. You have a life here."

"Eric, it'll only be a matter of time before they come for me. They may even show up *here*."

He pulled back at that. "This guy you were seeing, did you tell him where you worked?"

"No. But they know I work for an attorney. They know I delivered papers to Grayson Dentistry. It's next to the tattoo shop they all use. They know it's where Rusty first met me. That'll be their next stop after they hit my apartment. They'll question Dr. Grayson. It won't take them five minutes to get the information out of him. And then they'll show up here."

"Christ, Skylar. What did you get involved in?"

"I'm so sorry, Eric. I'm so sorry. I never meant to bring you any trouble."

"But… bikers, Skylar? What the hell?"

"He was charming and—"

"Charming? They aren't going to be so charming when

they show up here."

She looked up at him, panicked. "You can't be here when they come."

"I can't close my practice indefinitely."

"Then you have to tell them I disappeared. I never showed up for work. You haven't seen or heard from me. Oh God, I should go." She got up to leave, but he pushed her down.

"Go where?"

"I don't know. It doesn't matter."

"Yes, it does, honey. You think I'm just going to let you walk out the door? I couldn't live with it…and Ben would kill me." He tried to make a joke.

She barely cracked a smile. He dipped his head.

"Hey, look at me. I'll put you up in a hotel. Or better yet, you can stay in our Boca Raton condo."

She shook her head no. "I think I'm going to go back home."

"Birmingham?"

She nodded.

"Is there somewhere you can stay? Somewhere they won't track you?"

She looked down, realizing she couldn't bring this trouble down on anyone she knew.

"Do they know you're from there?"

"No. I never told anyone but you and Ben. You're the only ones they could get that information from."

"Let me make a call. I know someone in Birmingham. Maybe he can help."

***

An hour later, Skylar was driving down I-20 toward the hometown she hadn't seen in ten years. Eric had made a deal with a man who owned a second home he rarely used. He'd agreed to let Skylar stay there for a few months in exchange for use of Eric's condo in Florida. He was going to meet her with the keys. She had the directions in her purse.

Along with three thousand dollars.

Money that Eric had taken from his office safe and shoved into her hands, insisting she'd earned it and to consider it an early Christmas bonus. When she'd tried to refuse, he'd insisted, vowing Ben would "have his head" if he let her leave with no money. God bless those two men. What would she do without them?

***

Two hours later, she glanced at the directions once again as she drove down highway 119, south of town. "Over the mountain," as anyone from Birmingham referred to it. She passed mile after mile of tall pine trees, rolling hills with horses grazing behind split rail fences, and some very expensive homes. Slowing down, she turned right onto the driveway hidden in the overgrowth. It was barely visible from the road. If she hadn't been looking for it, she would never have noticed it.

About twenty yards off the road was an ornate iron gate, woods and bushes on either side. Parked in front was a black Lexus and a man leaning against it.

Skylar pulled her Miata up behind him and got out.

"You must be Eric's friend," the man asked, extending

his hand.

"Yes, sir. I'm Skylar."

"You must mean a lot to him. He really twisted my arm on this one."

"He's a good friend."

The man reached inside his pocket and pulled out what looked like a garage door opener. "This is the remote for the gate." He aimed it at the gate and pushed a button, and the gate began to slowly swing open. "I'd appreciate it if you kept it closed at all times."

She accepted the remote from his outstretched hand. "Yes, sir. Of course."

"Get in your car and follow me up to the house." He turned and headed to his Lexus.

Skylar looked at the gate and the long tree-lined drive that curved to the left, disappearing into the woods. What the hell kind of place had Eric made a deal for her to stay in? This seemed like a damned estate, not a house.

She followed him up to the house.

House? *Right*.

The drive had come up through the woods and approached the back of the residence, passing it on the left, then looped around to the side and ended in a circle in front of the home—complete with a fountain in the center.

Skylar climbed out of her car and looked up at the place. The home was huge. It was built of dark wood and stone work in sort of a Craftsman style that blended in with the rustic wooded setting. Stone steps led up to a large front porch. Skylar followed the owner up and waited while he unlocked the door. Then he turned and handed her the keys.

"Here's your set."

They stepped inside. He immediately stepped over to a security alarm. "The four digit code is one-four-seven-eight. It forms the letter L when you look at the keypad. The only way you'll remember it." He smiled.

"Thanks. That'll make it easy to remember."

He showed her how to set it when she was going to bed and how to set it when she left the premises. Then he gave her a tour.

From the entry, there was a living area on the left, complete with a stone fireplace. On the right was a gourmet kitchen and dining room. Dividing the space was a large open staircase straight ahead that led to the second floor. She followed him up, and he showed her the master bedroom that faced the front of the property. It was huge, with a giant four-poster bed and a set of French doors that led out to a covered porch.

There was a beautiful master bath, and two more bedroom suites in the rear of the second floor.

After making sure she had his number for emergencies, he left, instructing her that she had the place until November first. That gave her a little over six months to put her life back together. She'd need to find a job and another place to move when she had to give this place up.

She stood on the porch after the owner drove off. The home was on high ground. From the porch, she could see several mountain ridges in varying shades of blue-gray fading into the distance. Birmingham sat on the foothills of the Appalachian Mountain range, and it was quite beautiful. Just beyond some poplar and pine trees she could see a green pasture with horses grazing in the distance.

The house was set so far back from the highway she could just barely make out the sound of a car driving by.

Would she be safe here?

She couldn't be sure. And then her thoughts returned to Rusty. Although, she hadn't been in love with him, she had cared about him a great deal. He'd always been good to her. *God*, she prayed, *please forgive him his sins*. She hoped he was at peace. She'd prayed for his soul all the way from Atlanta. A tear slid down her cheek, and she brushed it away.

She turned and went back inside. She didn't even have anything in the car to unpack. She'd left town with the clothes on her back and her purse and what little she'd had in her car. She didn't even have her cell phone. Eric made her leave it, telling her they might be able to track her down if she used it. He'd instructed her to buy a disposable phone when she got to town and load it with minutes. Thankfully she had the money he'd given her. It would have to make due until she found a job and got an income.

The only thing she had going for her was that the club didn't know her last name. All they knew was that her name was Skylar. Eric planned to give them false information, if they ever came asking. A false last name and a false social security number, so if they ever did try to track her down, it would lead them nowhere.

Luckily, among the few things she did have was her laptop. She'd left it in her shoulder bag with all the files from work she sometimes carried around. It had been in her car, thankfully. She pulled it out now. The owner had said there was cable and internet set up, and he'd given her the password.

Opening her laptop, the first thing she did was close her Facebook account. She had no idea how technical any of the guys in the Devil Kings MC were, but she wasn't taking any chances.

Then she immediately stopped her mail. Thankfully, Eric had taught her to shred her mail daily, so she didn't think there was anything incriminating to be found if the MC searched her apartment.

If they questioned the apartment manager, they'd only find that the apartment was rented in the name of Eric Ramsey. Another favor he'd done for her when she didn't have the good credit to sign the lease. The electric was in his name, too. Although she paid all the bills.

Thank God for bad credit!

CHAPTER ONE

She rode back into his life when he least expected it...

Shades took a hit off his cigarette and looked up from the fire burning in the barrel in the backyard of the Evil Dead clubhouse. The Birmingham Chapter had just lost its VP and brothers were descending from all over the country for the funeral. Two bikes rode in through the back gate. Shades had to blink into the setting sun to be sure his eyes weren't deceiving him.

Holy shit.

Skylar.

He hadn't seen her in years, and now here she was, the love of his life, riding back into his life—on the back of a brother's bike.

Fucking hell.

Earlier that day...

Skylar drove through downtown Birmingham. It had been years since she'd been back home. She got off on 20th

Street and drove her little silver Miata through Five Points South. She had the top down, and the wind blew through her long dark hair. Stopping at the light, Skylar looked around her hometown. The place was the same, but the businesses had all changed. The fountain was still standing center stage on one corner—still attracting the hippie-homeless types. A couple of musicians were set up, playing, a guitar case taking tips. The restaurant on the corner with an outdoor courtyard had now become a microbrewery. The music hall where she'd snuck out to see her first concert was now a pool hall.

Following the directions she'd been given, she turned left onto a side street and parked half a block down. Climbing out of her car, she pushed her sunglasses on her head and looked up at the storefront window. *Lily Pad* was painted across in block letters. The trademark statue of a frog sat center-stage in the window. Smiling, she moved up onto the sidewalk and headed inside.

A bell tinkled over the door as she entered the shop. Skylar glanced around. Her best friend may have moved locations, but this place suited her. The floors were wood, the walls brick. Pottery, sculptures, and assorted art pieces filled the place. Recessed lighting from the ceiling spotlighted different pieces haphazardly arranged on upturned wooden crates. Brightly colored scatter rugs lay throughout.

The smell of incense permeated the place. Skylar had to grin though, knowing what it probably was an attempt to cover up.

She strolled toward the back, her heels clicking on the wooden floor. She was halfway to the back, when she spotted her—her best friend all through high school and the closest friend she'd ever had. So close, she felt more like a sister than a friend.

Although her back was to Skylar, she'd know the shape of her body anywhere—her thin shoulders and arms sticking out of the faded denim overalls she wore. A tube top was all she had on underneath. Her feet—as usual—were bare.

Her hair—now *that* was new. Her beautiful long golden brown hair now hung in long dreadlocks to her waist. The top of her head was covered in a blue bandana tied atop her head—the little triangle points falling in the back.

"Hey, girlfriend!" Skylar watched as she turned, her face lighting up.

"Skylar!" she yelled and launched into her arms, hugging her like an idiot. "You're here!"

Skylar hugged her back tight. "Letty, it's been so long. I've missed you."

Letty pulled back and wacked her playfully on the arm. "Then why did you stay gone so long, dumbass?"

Both women burst out laughing.

"Who's a dumbass?"

Skylar turned to see a big man standing in the doorway to the backroom.

Now the dreadlocks made sense.

The big muscled man had his own long dark dreads hanging to his waist. They were tied back in some semblance of a ponytail—as thick around as Skylar's arm. His skin was a smooth mocha brown.

Letty turned to look over her shoulder at the man.

"Relax, Ace. Come meet my best friend."

He strolled over, if a large muscled man could stroll and extended his hand. "Ace Luther."

Skylar studied him. He was bare-chested under his own pair of overalls. His eyes were a golden cat-eyed color. "Hi," she said, shaking the man's hand.

"Doesn't he have the most beautiful eyes you've ever seen, Skylar?" her friend asked, starring deeply into the man's eyes with adoration… and possibly love, Skylar noted.

"They are nice," Skylar admitted with a laugh.

Ace smiled, revealing even white teeth and nodded toward Letty. "Your friend's a goofball, but I guess you already know that."

Skylar laughed. "Sure do. It's why I love her."

***

Later that afternoon Letty and Skylar were talking near the cash register as Letty closed up. They'd planned to go out and have drinks and catch up on all that they'd missed in each other's lives. Letty had just changed out of the overalls and into a pair of low riding jeans, biker boots, and a halter top that left her belly bare. Both wrists held multiple strands of beaded bracelets, and there were more funky necklaces around her neck. The hippie-child look fit her, Skylar thought with a smile.

That wasn't Skylar, though. Never had been. Skylar always preferred something a little more subtle, a little more classic. Never wanting to fall into the cliché her upbringing made her feel destined for. Something she'd always fought against. Some things she'd never been able to control in her life, but her wardrobe was one thing she did have control over.

She, too, had low waist jeans, but instead of a halter top, she had a simple white racer-back tank that hugged her like a second skin. No biker boots for her—she wore a pair of black high-heeled sandals. Skylar always strived to have a bit of class to her look. Her jewelry showed it, too. The simple silver hoops in her ears and the matching silver cuff at her wrist.

The bell over the front door tinkled, and booted feet moved through the front of the shop. Skylar turned as two more faces from her past walked in—Letty's big brother, Crash and his best friend, Cole. Both were members of the Evil Dead MC, having joined up right after high school. They'd spent about five years with the Birmingham Chapter, before moving out to the West Coast where she'd heard they'd joined up with the San Jose Chapter.

They were both tall, broad-shouldered, good-looking men, both wearing the black leather cuts bearing their colors. The patches they bore on their backs with pride, declaring to the world their membership in one of the baddest MCs around—colors that struck fear into most.

"Crash!" she yelled, moving toward him for a hug.

He lifted her, squeezing her tight. "Damn, Skylar. Haven't seen you in forever."

"I know. It's been too long."

He released her, stepping back. "You look gorgeous as ever, squirt."

She grinned up at him, and then looked back at Letty.

"Same old Crash. Still calling me squirt."

Cole stepped forward. "Remember me, Skylar?"

She turned from Letty, and her eyes sparkled. "Cole!" She flew into his arms next. "I can't believe it. It's been forever!"

He laughed, hugging her back. When he released her, he reached up and ruffled the top of her head. "You coming to the party tonight, little sister?"

She looked back at Letty. "Umm, I don't know. I thought we were going out for drinks."

"She's going," Letty answered for her with a grin, then looked at Skylar. "What, there'll be drinks there."

"Club's having a wake for Bulldog. He passed away," Cole clarified for her.

"Oh, no. I'm so sorry to hear that."

Crash jammed his hands in his pockets. "That's why we're back in town. For the funeral."

Cole nodded. "You're welcome to come, Skylar."

She looked over at Letty, unsure. "I thought we were going out."

"We are. I just didn't tell you where. Didn't want to give you the chance to back out. I know how you are."

Crash pulled Skylar by the hand, stealing her away from Cole. "No backing out. Come on, squirt, you're on my bike. Sorry, Letty, but I'm not showin' up at the club with my own sister riding bitch."

"Yeah, yeah. I remember your stupid rule about that."

Cole grabbed Letty's hand. "Come on, girl. I don't mind you wrapping those long thighs around *me*," he teased.

***

Twenty minutes later, they rolled up to the clubhouse of the Birmingham Chapter of the Evil Dead. It was buried back in the poor neighborhoods that bordered the old steel plant. Skylar held tight to Crash as they rolled up several side streets, coming to a huge old two story clapboard house that sat, looming large, on a big corner lot. Skylar looked up at the building, remembering the times she'd been here with Letty that summer years ago.

Next to it sat an empty lot with overgrown grass. The two properties consumed the entire short block that ran between a couple of side streets. The back of the clubhouse was surrounded by a six-foot privacy fence and backed up to an alley that faced a junkyard on the other side. Across the street was a burned out house, and next to that, an abandoned house. Obviously, the neighborhood was not primo real estate, and she figured the club liked it that way. The fewer people and neighbors to mess with them, the better, apparently.

The front yard was overgrown, the sides overrun with tall bamboo and kudzu vines. There was a waist-high chain link fence around the front yard and a rusty gate she doubted anyone ever used. The metal mailbox out on the street was painted black with *Evil Dead MC* in white stencil across it. Up on the front porch in a chair by the door sat a skeleton holding a scythe like some leftover Halloween decoration, except for the Evil Dead support t-shirt it wore.

The bikes turned the corner and circled around to the alley, which led to the only entrance members used. There was a double wooden gate with the club name painted top-rocker style across it. One word on each portion of the swinging gates that, when closed, formed *Evil Dead.* Up on the back side of the house was a painted, winged skeleton holding a scythe, looking down at the back of the property as if guarding it.

Crash and Cole rolled through the back gate and into the large gravel lot that took up over an acre. The sun was sinking low on the horizon, its bright setting light hitting at a sharp angle and turning everything a brilliant golden. A bonfire had been started in an old oil drum in the center. About a dozen members were gathered around it, more members at picnic tables or milling around. The place was packed, the wake being a mandatory turnout. In addition to club members, there was also a strong showing of support clubs. A line of bikes three deep were parked around the outer edge of the property, backed up to the wood fence. Cole and Crash rolled along the line and backed their bikes into a couple of open spots.

Skylar climbed off the back and handed Crash the helmet he'd lent her. The men stashed the helmets on the ground, under the bikes. Crash looped his arm around Skylar's neck and led her toward the fire. Cole did the same with Letty, pulling her close.

Skylar stayed silent as they greeted several of their brothers, recognizing some faces from the old days. Others were new members they'd never met, but brothers just the same. Nervousness filled her. Her eyes darted around, searching. There was only one biker here that she feared running into. The one who had broken down all her walls, made her fall in love with him, and then ripped her heart out.

CHAPTER TWO

Shades watched Skylar walk toward him, another brother's arm around her, and his gut twisted. His mind drifted back to the first time he'd laid eyes on her. She'd been young then, eighteen, if he remembered correctly. At the time, he was just a prospect and had been ordered to guard the back gate for an all-day party the club was having.

Ten years ago—

Shades stood at the back gate and Boot, a full patched member, was standing next to him when an old Mustang drove up and parked in the adjacent grassy lot. It stopped in a cloud of dust, and Shades watched as two hot young babes emerged and strutted toward them.

"Who're they?" he asked.

Boot lit a smoke, looking over at the two girls. "That's Letty, Crash's little sister. The other one's her friend. And don't even think about it, Prospect. They're off limits."

The girls had smiled brightly at Boot as they'd breezed

through the gate. Shades' eyes skated over the first one—a pretty girl with dark blonde hair that hung to her waist—and moved on to land on the second girl. She was a knockout. Her silky dark hair also hung to her curvy waist exposed between her low-cut jeans and skimpy top. His eyes slid down over her body to a pair of very long legs encased in those tight jeans. She smiled at the two men as they entered, and Shades caught his breath when he got a close-up of her face. She had the most amazing vibrant blue eyes that stood out all the more in contrast to her dark hair.

Hot damn. She sure was a looker.

Almost unaware he was doing it, he murmured, "Christ, that girl's got it goin' on." His eyes followed her swaying ass as she walked away, and what a fine ass it was. Thoughts of how it'd feel to grab her by the hips and pull her back against his straining cock filled his head. The fantasy didn't last long before it was broken by a hard fist pound to his chest. He yanked his gaze around to see a stern expression on Boot's face.

"What'd I just say, Prospect?"

"Hands off. I heard you."

"Don't fuckin' forget it or Crash and Cole will both tear you up," Boot warned.

"Cole? What does he care?"

"Cole looks after that one like she was his own little sister, and since he's your sponsor, you had best just fucking steer clear."

"All right, old man. All right."

All through the party, he kept track of her, though. She

was definitely not at all like the type that usually caught his eye—bleach-bottle-blondes who dressed in trashy clothes, with piercings, tattoos, and a hard edge. This girl couldn't be further from that. She was dark-haired, long, and lean. Her skin was perfection with not a mark on it as far as he could see. Everything about her said clean, fresh, and soft. And damned if it didn't call to him.

And then finally she turned and met his gaze. He watched a shy smile form on her face that told him she knew he'd been tracking her movements. In return, he let a smile tug at the corner of his mouth, and he lifted his chin to her.

Once they'd made that initial connection, he kept catching her glances, and each time he'd smile at her, she'd return a shy smile back. Eventually, she walked toward him, and he couldn't stop the need that filled his gut as he watched her approach.

"Hey." She gave him another one of those cute-as-hell, shy little smiles.

"Hey, darlin'. How's it goin?" he answered, figuring a little small talk wouldn't get his ass in trouble, but still he glanced around the crowd, looking to see who was paying them any attention.

"Good party." Her eyes moved over the crowd as well.

"Yeah. Dead throw a good party." Taking a hit off his cigarette, he studied her. "You havin' a good time?"

She shrugged. "Parties aren't really my thing. I kind of got dragged here by my friend."

He flicked his cigarette, sending it sailing into the alley.

She looked him up and down. "Don't like parties either?

You're standing over here all alone."

Her voice did things to him. It was low and sexy and kind of shy. He couldn't keep his eyes from dropping to her breasts, and as he watched, her nipples pebbled in response. Wrenching his gaze back to her face, he stood in the entrance, fighting the overwhelming need to reach out and touch her, or if he was being honest, haul her into his arms. He shoved his hands in his pockets before he did something stupid in front of a yard full of club members. And touching her would definitely be a stupid move, especially when he'd been warned.

"Gate duty. Gotta make sure the uninvited stay out." He grinned and gave her a wink.

"Do you have to do this for the whole party?"

He nodded. "Yeah. Been here since about eight this morning, and I'll probably be here till two or three a.m."

"Wow. That's a long time."

"Life of a prospect, darlin'. Eighteen hours on your feet, standing at a gate, wishing for something to eat or just some fucking water. One or two hours of sleep a night. Surviving on Red Bulls, cigarettes, Starbucks, and ephedrine."

"Ephedrine? Like in diet pills?"

"Yeah, I know, but amphetamines give me headaches so…" He shrugged. "I stick with the cheap substitutes."

"That sounds rough. Don't they let you have a break?"

"Nope."

"Can I get you a beer or something?"

"Darlin', if I drank a beer right now, I'd fall asleep standing up. But I'd kill for a bottle of water."

She smiled. "Coming right up."

When she returned, he grinned. "Thanks, sweetheart. You're a lifesaver. I'm in your debt." He guzzled it down and watched as she pulled two more from her shoulder bag and set them on the ground by the wooden privacy fence.

"For later."

"What's your name, my beautiful angel of mercy?"

"Skylar. And you are?"

"Shades."

"Hi."

"Gotta tell you, Skylar, I've been warned off you."

"Why?" she asked with a frown, her eyes glancing around the back lot.

"Not just you. You and your friend. She's a brother's little sister, so…respect, you know?"

She nodded. "I see." Chuckling, she glanced over to where her outgoing friend was hitting on one of the brothers. "Not sure that's going to stop Letty, though."

A grin pulled at the corner of Shades' mouth. "Maybe not. But he's a full patched member. I'm just a prospect. They'd take my crossing that line a little more seriously I think."

"Am I going to get you in trouble by standing here talking to you?" Just then, Letty called to her and waved her over. Skylar turned to look, and then looked back at Shades as she began backing away. "Gotta go. It was nice spending time with you, Shades."

The soft way she said the last bit had his cock responding. He cleared his throat. What the hell was wrong with him? He held his own with some of the baddest of the bad every fucking day, and this little girl had him on the ropes. Fuck.

"Take care, Skylar. Thanks for the water."

He couldn't stop himself from watching the mesmerizing sway of her ass as she moved back toward her friend. And damned if she didn't turn and wink at him before she disappeared into the crowd.

***

Later that night, as the party was dying down, Shades was finally told he could knock off and go home. He made his way inside to say some goodbyes, and if he was being honest, to look for that little babe, Skylar, telling himself he just wanted to make sure she was okay.

About twenty minutes later, unable to find her, he fired his bike up, headed out the gate and down the street. He didn't get half a block when he spotted her. She was walking down the street. Alone. At 3 a.m. *What the fuck?* He let off on the throttle and coasted up beside her.

"Skylar. What the hell are you doing out here?"

She turned, almost jumping out of her skin. And then he could see her relax when she realized who it was.

"Oh, Shades. Hey."

"Babe, this is not a nice side of town. Why'd you leave the clubhouse?"

She shrugged. "Letty was my ride, and she hooked up with someone. And I couldn't find Cole or Crash."

"Climb on," he ordered, hoping she'd be quick so they could get out of there before someone from the club came along and spotted him with her. She didn't hesitate. He liked that. And he really liked the way her arms came around him, holding tight. He took off down the street, riding a couple of blocks away from the clubhouse before pulling over and asking her, "Where to, darlin'? Where do you live?"

"I was supposed to be spending the night at Letty's house."

"I guess that's out. I can take you to your house," he offered as he took his helmet off and handed it to her.

She took it and quickly strapped it on. "I can't show up now. It's 3 a.m. My foster dad will kill me."

"Foster dad?" he asked, frowning.

"I live in a foster home," she admitted softly.

"Really?" He twisted on the seat to get a better look at her, kind of shocked by her response. He'd never have guessed that. Not in a million years.

"Yeah." Her eyes looked away, and her chin came up, and he realized it was a touchy subject for her. He wondered why she'd admitted something so personal to him. They barely knew each other. A fact he'd love to remedy.

"Ok, home's out. Guess that just leaves my place. You can stay tonight and meet up with Letty in the morning. That work for you?" At the nervous look on her face, he added, "No strings, sweetheart. Just a place to crash, I promise. Besides, I owe you for the water." He grinned.

She nodded, and he hit the throttle.

He took Interstate 65 over the mountain and south of town, exiting on Route 31. It was late, and the streets were deserted. When they neared Shelby hospital, he turned off into a parking lot next to what looked like an auto repair shop. It was a cement block building that sat close to the road. It was painted gray with two bay doors. The parking area to the side and behind the building was gravel and surrounded by a privacy fence and gate. There were about four parking spots out front. He unlocked the gate and they rolled into the lot.

As they dismounted, a dog trotted over to them. “Hey, boy. How you doing?” Shades squatted down, taking the dog’s head in both his hands to scratch its ears. Skylar, who seemed a little uneasy around the large white pit bull, froze. Sensing her fear, Shades turned to her. “Hey, don’t be afraid. He looks tough, but he’s just a softy. Aren’t you, Toby?”

She hesitantly held her hand out for the dog to sniff, and then she looked up at the building, asking, “Where are we? What is this place?”

Straightening, Shades replied, “This is my shop. I have a small apartment upstairs. Come on.”

“Shop?”

“Auto-body shop,” he explained. “I also do a little mechanic work. Bikes mostly.”

He led the way inside, unlocking the glass shop door. The ceiling above them in the garage area was open. There was an office area ahead and a metal staircase that led to the second floor apartment that was situated over the office.

She followed him up the stairs, Toby trotting beside them. When they got to the second level, he watched her reaction as she looked around, taking in the space. It was indeed, as he’d said, small. There was a bed over by the windows that overlooked the main drag through town. A low dresser sat across from it. On the other side of the room was a small table with two chairs. A tiny kitchenette with a sink, mini fridge, and microwave. A door led to a small bathroom with a shower stall. The apartment was open to the level below in a loft style.

True to his word, he didn't touch her that night. They'd both crashed on the lone bed out of necessity, but they'd just laid and talked mostly.

"So, Skylar, how old are you?"

"Eighteen."

His head swiveled on his pillow, and he looked at her, his brows raised. "*Damn*, babe. Didn't think you were *that* young."

"How old did you think I was?"

"Twenty-one, at least."

She grinned, turning her head on the pillow. "Really? I look twenty-one?"

Instead of answering her, he stared at the ceiling and mumbled, "Fuck, this is wrong. Big time wrong. You're just a kid."

"I am not. Relax." She laughed at the worried look on his face.

"Jesus Christ, if the club finds out about this, I'm done for."

She reached up and made an X over her heart. "I won't tell anyone. Cross my heart."

"You do, and I'm a dead man, Skylar."

"And how old are you, Shades?"

"Twenty-three."

"So, you got an ol' lady, Shades?"

"Nope. And I ain't lookin' for one either."

"I see."

He went up on an elbow, turning to face her, his head resting on his hand. "Tell me about the foster thing." Her eyes went to him, and then looked away. The curtains were open, letting in the moonlight, and he studied her face.

"There's not much to tell." Her voice was soft in the dim light.

"How did you end up in the system?"

"My mother died when I was three, and I never knew my father." She shrugged. "I guess there was no one else to take me. I don't know. I was so little. I've never known anything else."

"So, you've been with this foster family your whole life?"

She let out a soft snort. "Hardly. I've been in six different homes."

"Six? You're shitting me." His eyebrows shot up with her stunning announcement.

"Nope. Not shitting you."

"Why so many? Did they abuse you?" He frowned down at her, wanting an answer, but realizing he was being an insensitive ass to blurt out a question like that the way he had. If her answer was yes, he didn't know how he was going to take it.

She shook her head slightly. "No, they just never worked out. I would act out or do something else that would make them give up on me, I guess." She let out a slight laugh. "I was kind of like the puppy that got returned to the pound. Over and over and over."

Shades listened to her try to make a joke out of it, and it broke his heart. "Babe…"

Her eyes came to his, and she interrupted sharply, "Don't." She shook her head. "Don't say how sorry you are, okay? Anyway, it's over now. I'm eighteen. And now that the Fullers won't be getting anymore government checks for my support, I guess I should count myself lucky that they didn't kick me out the door the day I turned eighteen."

"They can do that?"

She nodded. "They told me I had till the end of the summer to find a place."

"Christ, you've had a tough road. Amazes me how sweet and shy you seem to me." Hearing her story and everything she'd been through touched something inside of him, something he'd never felt before.

"Starting over a bunch of times will do that, I guess." She smiled, her eyes connecting with his. "But don't let it fool you. I can be tough when I'm backed into a corner."

He grinned and picked up her hand. Bringing it to his mouth, he brushed her fingers with a kiss. "The kitten turns into a tigress, huh?"

"Exactly."

"So, when the summer's up, you got a plan, tiger-girl?" he asked softly and watched her bite her lip.

"Not yet. But I'll get one."

"Can't you stay with your friend, Letty?"

She looked away, tugging her hand free. "I don't really want to talk about this, okay?"

He reached up and brushed a strand of hair back from her face. "Okay, sweetheart. You tired?"

She nodded. "You?"

He smiled at her, admitting wearily, "I'm beat." Then he pressed a kiss to her forehead and whispered, "Go to sleep, darlin'." He dropped to his back and within minutes they were both asleep.

***

The next morning he dropped her off down the street from her house.

Skylar stepped off the bike. Shades stayed seated, his booted feet holding up the bike, the motor still rumbling. He watched as she pulled off the helmet he'd lent her and handed it back to him.

"Thanks for the ride. And for last night."

Taking the helmet, he set it between his legs and pushed his sunglasses up on his head. "You're welcome, sweetheart."

"Will I see you again?"

"Club keeps me pretty busy." They stared at each other for a moment, and then he added, "You comin' to the BBQ next weekend?"

She smiled. "Maybe."

He nodded. "Then maybe I'll see you then."

"Well, thanks again." She started to back away, but he reached out, his finger hooking in one of her belt loops, stopping her. Her eyes came to his and got big as he pulled her toward him. Her hands landed on his chest, and he leaned in for a kiss, his mouth coming down on hers. He was soft at first, and then she opened to him and he deepened the kiss, delving in for a taste. When he lifted his head, her eyes were on his mouth, a look of wonder on her face, and he couldn't stop the grin that pulled at the corner of his mouth. What she said next surprised him.

"Your beard is soft," she murmured as if she hadn't expected that.

His grin deepened. "I see you've been wonderin'."

She smiled back, admitting, "Yeah, I guess I have."

He took her hand and brought it to his face, sliding her palm to his jaw, letting her touch him and feel the soft, close-cut beard that ran along it. Shades' hand slid to cup her nape and his eyes sank into the blue depths of hers as she followed the movement of her hand as it stroked his face.

Goddamn, he could get lost in those eyes.

And then all thought slid from his head as her thumb moved to brush gently over his mouth. Without conscious thought, he found his mouth parting and his teeth capturing the pad of her thumb in a soft nip.

Her eyes lifted to his, and he heard the quick intake of her breath. In that moment, when her eyes locked with his, he felt like a mule had just kicked him in the chest. Something zinged between them. He didn't know what it was, but he'd never experienced it with any other woman. It was like that soul-mate shit he'd heard people talk about. Shit he'd never believed in.

Until now. Until right this moment.

Something was happening between them, and it was freaking the shit out of him. He dropped his hand from her neck, breaking the spell, and she stepped back, somehow sensing the sudden change in him.

"I… um… guess I should go," she whispered, embarrassed now.

"Yeah, okay." He nodded.

"Thanks again, Shades."

He winked at her. "See ya 'round, Sky." As he watched, a smile formed on her face, and he knew she liked the way he'd shortened her name. Pulling his sunglasses down over his eyes and buckling the helmet on, he twisted the throttle, roaring away from the curb. Looking in his side mirror, he saw her standing where he'd left her, watching him ride away, and he smiled.

***

They saw each other over several parties that summer, and Skylar always made a point of coming over and talking with him. He could always get her laughing. And when she did, her face lit up. Fucking lit up. Absolutely fucking beautiful.

Usually, they were under the watchful eyes of his brothers, but occasionally, late at night, when it got dark and his brothers got drunk, they would find themselves alone for a few minutes. Sometimes he'd steal a kiss, but he wanted more. *Much* more. And he was finding that it was becoming more and more difficult to keep his hands off her. In fact, abiding by the hands-off orders he'd been given where she was concerned was becoming damn near impossible.

He found himself thinking about her often, even when he hadn't seen her for days or weeks. He was completely captivated by her, he could admit it. Fuck, he hadn't felt this way about a chick ever. But he knew he needed to rein his feelings in and leave her alone. Nothing was going to come of this—nothing *could* ever come of this, no matter how bad he wanted her.

And that was exactly what he told himself every week, until the next time she'd show up, and all his good intentions would go right out the fucking window.

One such night he was again ordered to stand gate duty. It was late, and everyone was starting to migrate inside as a light drizzle was starting up. Skylar had been sitting with a group at a picnic table under a tree in the yard. Shades, like he always did when she came around, was subconsciously keeping tabs on where she was.

He watched as some of the other girls she'd been sitting with made their way inside, complaining about the stray raindrops. He heard Skylar call after them that she would be along in a minute, after she sent a text.

And then they were alone, just the two of them left in the yard in the dark of night. He stood at the gate, his eyes on her as she sat in the dark shadows under the tree. The only light in the yard came from a dim bulb near the back door and the remains of burning embers in the fire pit.

Shades took a hit off his cigarette, the glow probably the only thing she could see by the darkened gate. But she was looking his way. He knew it. He could feel it. And then he watched her shadowy form stand and walk toward him.

As she approached, he tossed his cigarette, the glowing tip arcing as it flew into the alley. When she reached him, Shades barely let her get out a breathy greeting before he grabbed her by the hand, pulled her around the gate, and pushed her back up against the outside of the six-foot wooden fence as his mouth came down on hers.

When he finally broke the kiss, she stared up at him breathlessly. “Why did you do that?”

“Because I had to,” he replied, delving in for another one. When that kiss ended he looked down at her and confessed, “I watched you earlier, when you were dancing.” She’d been one of a group of girls that had started dancing when some good music came on the stereo that was piped into the yard. He’d been hypnotized by the way she’d moved to the music. “Were you gettin’ your ‘feel good’ on?”

“I was having fun,” she admitted.

“You were doin’ more than that, honey. You were driving me crazy. Me and every guy here.”

She grinned, her white teeth flashing in the moonlight. “Is that so?”

“You know it’s so. You can definitely move, girl.” He leaned in close again, nuzzling her neck. “You smell good, too.”

“So do you.”

He pulled back. “I do?”

She nodded, her hands running up the front of his cut. “Leather and wood-smoke and…you.”

He moved in closer again, promising, “One of these nights, girl. One of these nights, I swear.”

"What, Shades? What do you swear?"

"You and me, we're gonna find out just how hot this flame burns." He kissed her again, but broke off again, warning, "Your girls will be looking for you soon." He studied her mouth. "Fuck, what I wouldn't give for just a few more minutes with you."

The creaking sound of the back screen door opening carried to them. Shades released her, ordering in a whisper, "Don't move." He stepped around the open gate.

"Hey, Prospect, you seen Skylar?" Cole called out from the back steps.

"Nope. I think she left a while ago."

"Okay. You can go ahead lock up the gate and go home. You look beat."

"Thanks."

After Cole went back inside, Shades moved back over to Skylar, boxing her in against the wooden fence again.

"I just lied to a brother over you. Fuck, baby, what you do to me…"

"Shades—"

He cut her off with a kiss, moving in against her until their bodies were touching. His long fingers threaded into her hair holding her immobile as his mouth plundered deep. Eventually, they both had to come up for air. He broke off, his forehead pressing against hers, his breath sawing in and out.

"I saw you up at that shaved-ice place on Route 31 last week. You were standing out front when we all rode by."

Her voice came out with a breathy quality that told him

the kiss had affected her as much as it did him. "I saw you, too. Everyone did. There were a dozen of you, and we could hear those rumbling pipes coming a mile away."

"I rode past there three times this week, just hoping to see you there again, just hoping to catch a glimpse of you," he confessed, studying her reaction. "You know why I'm telling you this?"

She shook her head.

"Because you need to know where I'm at."

"And where is that?"

"Right on the edge, sweetheart. You've got me starvin' for it. Do you understand?"

She looked up at him and nodded.

He brushed his thumb across her cheekbone. "There's something in the way you look at me. In the way you're lookin' at me *now* that tells me you feel it, too. You gotta tell me, Sky, are we on the same page here?"

"Yes, Shades. I feel it, too."

"Little girl, getting messed up with you is the last fucking thing I need to be doing…" he broke off, shaking his head.

Skylar's hand came up and closed around his wrist. "Shades, I think about you all the time, every minute."

"Fuck, don't say that."

"It's true."

"Christ, if I had any sense, I'd send you right back through that gate." He bit his lip, shaking his head again. "But I can't. I fucking can't, Sky. You need to tell me no. Right now. Right fucking now, Sky."

She just looked up at him, refusing to do as he asked.

"You're still standing here."

"Yes."

"I'm starting to sense a stubborn streak in you."

Her chin came up. "Is that so bad?"

"Skylar, you know it's wrong—the things I'm gonna ask you to do if you stay."

"Ask me."

He stared down at her, his breathing heavy. "Come with me."

"Where?"

"Does it matter?"

She stared up at him.

"*Does it*, Sky?"

"No."

"Then come home with me. Back to my shop. Back to my bed."

***

Twenty minutes later, Shades was leading Skylar up the metal stairs to the tiny apartment above his shop. The light from the neon sign on the front of the building shone through the windows, illuminating the space in a soft blue light.

He turned to her, taking both her hands in his, and pulled her as he backed up to the low dresser where he planted his ass against the edge. Then he drew her between his spread thighs. It put her head a couple inches higher than his. They stood there, staring at each other a moment, and then Shades confessed, "I feel like I gotta be gentle and careful with you."

"Why?"

"Cause you're different. You're not like the others."

"You're right. I'm not. Is that a bad thing?"

Shades let out a huff, "Not hardly. It's a good thing. A very good thing."

Her eyes strayed to the bed.

"You havin' second thoughts?"

"No. Are you?"

His hand lifted to cup her face, his thumb moving over her mouth, his eyes following its movement. "This fire, baby. It could burn us both."

"Do you care?"

"I could get kicked out of the club for this."

"If Cole or Crash found out, they'd never let me up there again.'

"You willing to risk it?"

"Yes. Are you?"

"I'm standin' here, aren't I?"

"I am, too, Shades. I'm right here."

"You know they're gonna say we're bad for each other."

"How are we bad for each other?"

"They'll say that I'm no good for you. That I'll do nothing but drag you down. Are you gonna believe 'em?"

"No."

"Maybe you should."

"And if they tell you a girl like me will bring you nothing but problems, that I'm nothing more than a distraction, one you can't afford to have, are you going to believe them?"

"What do you think?"

"Say it."

"No, baby. I'll never believe that."

The words must have touched her, because she surprised him by stepping closer, her hands sliding under his cut to push it back over his shoulders and down to drop on the dresser behind him. She didn't stop there. Her hands moved to the hem of his t-shirt, and he helped her, reaching behind his head to grab two handfuls of fabric and pull it over his head. It fell to the floor as his eyes locked on hers, watching as her gaze moved over his shoulders, arms, and chest. They stopped on the rosary chain that hung around his neck. Her hand moved to the silver cross dangling over his cut six-pack. She picked it up, and he watched her study it. And then she asked, "Are you Catholic?"

A smile tugged at the corner of his mouth. "Not a very good one." He saw the confusion in her eyes. "It was my mother's. I wear it for her. Keep her close to my heart."

"She wanted you to be a good Catholic boy?"

The smile twisted on his face. "Obviously it didn't take too well."

She smiled back at him. "I don't think you're such a bad guy."

His hands slid to her waist, and he drew her closer. "Good to know, 'cause tonight you're gonna give in to me, Skylar."

"Am I?"

His brows came together in a confused frown. "Hey, if you're not feeling it, babe…" he broke off, standing up and starting to push her away, but she grabbed his arm, stopping him, more with her words than the hand on his bicep.

"No, I want this, Shades. I do."

Before he could stop himself, he stood and took her head in both his hands to pull her close. Burying his hands in her hair, he pulled her head back, tilting her face up to his as he looked down at her. There was something about the way she looked up at him with those innocent blue eyes that had him aching for her. He whispered, "Then close your eyes, babe, and we'll dive in the deep end together."

Her eyes slid closed.

He pressed his lips to hers in a soft gentle kiss, holding it a moment. And then he bent and grabbed her under her ass, lifting her and carrying her as he strode to the bed. And then she was down on her back, and he was on top of her, where he'd wanted to be all fucking summer, his hips cradled between her spread thighs. Goddamn that felt right. He brushed the hair back from her face and stared into her beautiful eyes.

"Shades?"

"Yeah?"

"I just don't want to get hurt."

Her soft admission gave him pause. The empty promise was on the tip of his tongue, but he couldn't bring himself to say the words. He wanted honesty between them. If this all went to shit, at least he'd know he hadn't reeled her in with a pack of lies. "I can't promise you that, babe. No one can." He could see he wasn't putting her mind at ease. "But I will promise you one thing. You let me in, Sky, I'll take good care of you."

"Will you?"

"Yeah, I will, and I'll make sure you have no regrets about tonight."

She grinned. "Is that a promise?"

"That's a guarantee." He dropped his mouth to hers, kissing her softly, and then he lifted again, looking in her eyes. "It's taken me all summer to get you here."

"Shades, I've been here before."

"Not talkin' about you bein' in my place or even in my bed. Talkin' about you bein' under me, like this." He rolled his hips to underline his meaning.

"Oh." Her answer came out in that soft, breathy voice he loved so much.

"That's not how I usually roll, babe. I've never spent this much time getting to know a woman the way I have with you."

"I don't want to hear about you and other women, Shades. Not now."

"I'm telling you this so you'll know. So you understand. This means something to me, Sky. You mean something to me."

"Shades?"

"Yeah?"

"Tell me everything's gonna be all right."

He knew better than to lie to her, but he couldn't stop the words she needed to hear from spilling out. Words he knew sure as shit were probably a lie. "Everything's gonna be all right, baby."

"I want you, Shades."

He smiled down at her, letting her words melt through him. "Feeling wanted feels good."

"I want to love you tonight."

"Gotta say, likin the idea of being loved by you, Sky." Her hands stroked softly up the bare skin of his back, and his eyes slid closed, and his jaw tightened as he felt himself grow even harder than he already was. And he knew there was no turning back now. He wanted his dick buried inside her. It was all he could think of, all he'd thought about all summer. No, not thought about—been *consumed* with. And there was one thing he knew wasn't a lie. He couldn't stop now if he wanted to. A muscle ticked in his jaw as he looked down at her. "I don't mean to scare you, baby…but… this is going all the way. Ain't no stopping now."

She stroked the hair back from his head tenderly, and then repeated the strokes several more times, while he stared down at her. "I don't want to stop you."

"No one's ever paid me attention like you," he confessed. "The gentle way you touch me, shit, you got my heart pounding. I don't think you realize, Sky, the way you affect me."

She grabbed his rosary chain and pulled him down, her mouth opening under his as he dove in. His body moved against her as he slid up a few inches and took control of the kiss, claiming her with his mouth as he pinned her to the bed.

After a few minutes, he went up on his knees, looking down at her, his hands going to the fastening of her jeans. While he worked at getting them down, she writhed on the bed, pulling her shirt over her head to toss it to the floor where her jeans soon followed. And then Shades sat back on his haunches and grinned as he took in her camouflage patterned bra and panty set. He chuckled. "Camo, babe, really?"

"I saw them at Wally World. I thought they were cute." She wiggled. "You don't like them?"

"Oh, I like, darlin'. I like. But I'd like them a hell of a lot more on the floor."

She undulated her body, and tempted, "Then maybe you should do something about that."

"Oh, I plan to." He hooked his thumbs in the fabric at her hips and began to slowly pull it down. Her panties joined the growing pile on the floor. Then he stretched next to her and eased one bra strap down her arm, pressing kisses along the edge of the bra. And then his hand was sliding under her to unhook it and toss it to join the rest.

His eyes roamed over her, his palm following along the trail of his eyes.

"No fair. You're still half dressed," she whispered breathlessly.

"You in a hurry all of a sudden?"

"No." Her voice panting, her chest rising and falling.

"Then let me take my time and do this right, okay?"

"Okay."

"Just relax. Let me set the pace." His mouth moved to her throat, a barely-there brush of his lips and facial hair before moving lower, trailing down to her breast.

"Okay." Her voice was a little shaky now.

He captured a nipple in his mouth and sucked hard,

liking the way she arched her back, begging for more. He growled and gave it to her, latching on to her other nipple with no mercy while his thumb and finger tormented the first. Fingers slid into his hair and clenched, holding him to her. His angel liked it a little rough. Good to know.

Pressing a line of soft kisses down her belly, he moved lower, drawn like a moth to a flame. Her scent called to him, pulling the deepest animalistic cravings from him.

He planted himself between her legs, his broad shoulders pushing her thighs wide, holding her open to him, and then his eyes traveled up over her body and locked with hers as his mouth sought her out. Her body jerked with the first stroke of his tongue, and then her head fell back, her back arching, her body seeking his touch. He didn't disappoint, his mouth moving over her, giving her what she wanted. And then he took it up a notch, two fingers moving inside her, hooking to find that sweet spot that had her suddenly frantic with need. He didn't let up until she was right on edge, and then he replaced his mouth with the pressure of his thumb, and she crashed over the threshold. Lifting his head, he watched the cascades of pleasure wash over her.

Beautiful. Fucking beautiful.

She lay panting as he slid up her body to pin her to the bed with his weight. He took her mouth, capturing her breathy moan. When he lifted his head, he rose up on his elbows, his biceps caging her in as his hands brushed the hair back from her face. The look on her face was dreamy and angelic and everything he'd hoped for. And he'd put that look there.

Her legs wrapped around him. "I want you inside me. Please."

"I'll be there soon, baby. When I know you're good and ready."

"I'm ready now," she pleaded.

"Not yet, baby. I say when." His body shifted to the side and his hand caressed down the soft skin of her belly to between her legs, where his fingers slid inside her. He captured the wetness that pooled there and spread it all around her, his fingers reigniting the flame that was just now starting to recede. "I want to see you come again, first."

"Shades, please, I don't know if I can."

"You can. You will." His hands worked their magic, and he soon had her writhing beneath him again, begging for release.

"Please, I need you. I…" her words broke off as a second orgasm swamped over her, and Shades smiled as she threw her head back, gasping. He slid from the bed to stand over her while he unbuckled his belt and let his jeans hit the floor. The look on her face as she took in his size and length had a smile tug at his mouth.

"Oh my God. There's no way," she objected in a breathy whisper, her chest still heaving.

He stretched out next to her. "It'll fit, sweetheart. I promise you." Taking his dick in his hand, he rubbed it over her, spreading her lubrication all over him.

She writhed, enjoying this new torture.

"Do you still want this, baby girl?" he growled as he stroked over the sensitized folds.

Her breath stuttered as she sucked in a lungful. "Yes. Yes. Yes."

He twisted, digging in his jeans for a condom. Once it was on, he moved over her, and lining himself up with her opening, he didn't hesitate to plunge in. He got about halfway and had to pause, poised above her. "Relax, baby. Take it all. I know you can."

She tried to open further, and he sank another couple of inches. "Shades, I can't."

"Shh, sure you can, honey." His mouth latched onto her nipple again and sucked hard, and she moaned. He pulled back and slid forward, slowly stroking, feeling a new rush of wetness ease his way. He hooked his arm under her knee and pushed up, opening her further to him as he slid in all the way to the hilt.

She gasped. "Oh God, Shades. You're so deep."

He kissed her. "I feel it too, baby. Lock your free leg around me."

She did as he ordered, and he began to thrust in earnest, pounding into her until he was slick with sweat, and his breathing was sawing in and out of his lungs. One hand was planted in the bed, his muscles corded as he held himself above her, the other arm was locked around her leg, holding her wide open. He knew he was being rough. He knew she'd feel every slam of his hips into her thighs tomorrow, and he didn't care. Nothing was going to slow him down or lessen his frantic movements. Even the throaty moans and whimpers she began to make didn't stop him. If anything, they drove him on, faster and harder until she clenched around him, driving him over the edge of restraint, and he went rock solid, coming hard as his body jerked with the most powerful orgasm of his fucking life.

As he came down, he released her leg and heard her moan as she dropped it down to the mattress. He lay stretched on top of her, slick with sweat, panting with exertion. With his dick still buried deep inside her, he rose up to look down into her eyes and whispered, "Hello, love."

She repeated it back with a look of awe. "Hello, love."

Present day—

The memory drifting through his mind cleared, and Shades watched his Skylar walking toward him, the arm of one of his brothers around her.

The years had been good to her. She'd been eighteen when he'd seen her last. She must be what, twenty-eight now?

She still wore her dark silky hair long, almost to her waist. Her slender body had always been on the athletic side, but her woman's body had filled out, the curves more pronounced since he'd last seen her. She looked more womanly than the girlish eighteen-year-old he remembered. Well, what did he expect? It had been ten years, after all.

His eyes couldn't help but run over those curves, before returning to her face. He'd forgotten how beautiful her blue eyes were, especially in combination with that gorgeous dark hair of hers.

Jesus Christ, he'd never thought she could get more

beautiful, but she had.

She sure as fuck had.

CHAPTER THREE

"Well, look what the cat dragged in."

Skylar looked at the man who had spoken. He was an older man with shoulder length gray hair, a beard, and wire-rimmed glasses that had always reminded her of Jerry Garcia. He came forward as they approached the group by the fire. The patch on his cut read *President*, just like it had ten years ago when Skylar had first visited the clubhouse.

First Cole, then Crash, enfolded him in a bear hug, slapping his back. "Butcher, good to see you."

"Cole. Crash. Wish it could have been under other circumstances."

"Amen, Brother."

His eyes moved to Letty, who was standing next to Cole, and he squinted, not quite sure for a moment. Then he turned to Crash. "This your *little sister*?"

The corner of Crash's mouth drew up as he fought a grin. "It's the dreadlocks. Wasn't too sure, myself."

She shoved his arm. "As if."

"Well shit, darlin'. I haven't seen you in years. Give me a hug, gal," Butcher exclaimed, pulling her to him.

She gladly went, laughing. "*You* haven't changed a bit, still trying to break my bones with your bear hugs."

He let her go, laughing, his palm patting her cheek. "Just because your big brother took off for that freak-land they call California, doesn't mean *you're* still not welcome, girl."

"Thanks, Butcher. It's good to see you. I'm so sorry about Bulldog. He was like an uncle to me and Crash."

Butcher nodded. "He was a good man. We're all gonna miss him." His eyes moved to Skylar who was standing back a bit, and he frowned. "Is that the girlfriend you used to always drag with you to our parties? The shy one?"

Letty turned, smiling. "Skylar? Yep, that's her. She's been gone for a while. I finally convinced her to come home."

"Good for you." His attention returned to Letty. "Don't be such a stranger, you hear?"

She nodded, grinning. "I won't."

Skylar felt Crash's arm sliding back around her shoulders. She knew she must seem a little off balance around his brothers, and she could tell he wanted her to feel at ease. She'd never been as outgoing as his sister. Skylar had always been more reserved. She felt his protective arm around her tighten, and he looked down at her and winked.

She stood silently as Butcher introduced Crash to a couple of new brothers that had joined up since he and Cole had moved away.

"This is Ghost," Butcher nodded to a young guy with

shoulder length brown hair, the top portion tied back and the rest left down. He had a beard and golden brown eyes.

Crash's eyes glinted with humor as he shook his hand. "Ghost, huh?"

Butcher grinned and filled in the details he knew Crash was wondering about. "Yeah, we never hear him coming. He's a sneaking son-of-a-bitch. Has a habit of appearing and disappearing like a fucking ghost."

Crash nodded. "I see."

Butcher stepped back, revealing the man next to him, and Skylar sucked in a sharp breath.

Shades.

She hadn't seen him standing there. She felt the blood drain from her face as she took him in for the first time in all these years. His light brown hair, shot through with gold, still fell just past his collar. His strong jaw was covered with a couple of day's growth of beard, not really a full beard, more like he shaved if and when he felt like it. He had a pair of aviator sunglasses on as he squinted against the glare of the setting sun.

"This is Shades," Butcher was continuing the introductions. "You remember him? He was prospecting when you left."

Crash's eyes narrowed at the reminder, and then his memory must have jogged, because he grinned. "Yeah, sure. Sorry I didn't get to stick around and vote you in, kid. I do remember giving you hell a time or two."

Skylar stiffened, and a tremble moved through her. Oh God, she'd hoped he wouldn't be here, and now she hoped he wouldn't recognize her or maybe, not even remember her. She noticed Shades' sunglasses move from Crash to her. Crash looked down at her, too, and she knew he saw the stricken look on her face. His eyes moved back to Shades, studying him. She could only imagine what he must be wondering, but she couldn't think about that. All she could focus on was Shades' face as he stared at her. A muscle ticked in his jaw, and it was obvious he was pissed.

Crash pulled his arm from around her and extended his hand to Shades.

Shades shook it, dragging his eyes from Skylar. "Good to see you man, it's been a long time." At the reference to time passing, his gaze slid meaningfully back to Skylar again.

She swallowed, praying he wouldn't acknowledge how he knew her. It was already apparent that Crash was picking up all kinds of vibes moving between the two. She was sure she reinforced it when she clutched his waist and practically hid up against his side as he released Shades' hand, and his arm settled back around her. She couldn't help it.

He wasn't the only one who caught the exchange and was frowning. She noticed the new guy, Ghost's eyes moving between his brother and her, obviously wondering as well what kind of history they had.

She hoped he never found out.

Butcher nodded toward the keg that sat over by the back door and said to Letty, "You and your friend go get yourselves something to drink while I catch up with your brother, okay, darlin'?"

Letty nodded and turned, motioning for Skylar to follow her. Crash's arm slid from around her, but not before he gave her a questioning look that asked without words if she was okay. She gave him a shaky smile, and the two moved off.

***

Crash turned to catch Shades' eyes following the girls as they walked away, or more specifically, Skylar. He'd caught the looks that had passed between them and more importantly, he'd felt the way Skylar had tensed up under his brother's scrutiny.

Butcher pulled Crash from his thoughts. "Your sister doin' okay?"

Crash grinned, knowing he was concerned by the dreads. "She's doing fine. She's got a shop down in Southside, and she's in love with some guy named, Ace."

"You good with that?"

Crash shrugged. "Just met the dude. He seems like a good guy, but I'll reserve judgment until I know him better."

Butcher chuckled. "I seem to remember no guy was good enough for your sister back in the day."

Crash grinned. "True."

Butcher turned as two more brothers walked up. He slapped the brother next to him on the shoulder and nodded to the man next to him. "You remember Boot and Tater."

Cole spoke up. "Hell, yeah. How are you boys?" They embraced, slapping each other's backs.

Crash did the same.

"Slick's inside. I know he's anxious to see you, but he's taking Bulldog's death the hardest."

They nodded.

Butcher lit up a cigar and waved it toward some other members standing off by the picnic tables and more near the back door. “Lot of new members since you left. I’ll have to be sure to introduce you both around later.”

They nodded.

“How are things going around here?” Cole asked.

Butcher puffed on his cigar. “Pushing a major membership drive. Gulf Coast Chapter just started up. Lost a couple boys to it. Sent ‘em down there to keep an eye on things.”

“Problems?”

“Some. But that’s a conversation for another time.”

“You short-handed?” Crash asked.

Butcher shrugged with a grin. “Not short-handed, per se, just pushing to be the biggest, baddest dog on the block.”

Cole grinned. “I see.”

Butcher looked between Cole and Crash. “Why don’t you boys come back home? Haven’t you had enough of that slick, West Coast life style?

Boot grinned around his smoke. “At least here you don’t have to deal with earthquakes, landslides, and wild fires.”

Crash laughed. “No. You’ve just got heat, humidity, and hurricanes.”

Butcher let loose a deep rumble of laughter. “True enough. True enough. But, seriously, give it some thought. We could use you two.” He looked between them. “VP position just came open.”

Cole gave a sad smile. “I know, Butcher. Sad you gotta

go through this. Can't see walking in that door"—he nodded toward the house referring to Bulldog—"and him not being there."

Crash added, "Between my granddad and that man, they're the ones who taught me what it means to be a man."

Butcher nodded and agreed, "He's gonna leave a big hole."

***

"Oh my God, I can't believe he's still here." Skylar whispered to Letty, her eyes connecting with Shades across the yard.

"Who?" Letty asked as she picked up the nozzle of the keg and put it to a red plastic cup.

"Shades." Skylar nodded back to the man by the fire, whose aviator sunglasses were aimed their way.

Letty glanced back over her shoulder. "Oh yeah. I remember him."

"Let's go inside. I want to get away from him."

Letty tossed the nozzle in frustration. "Sure. This keg is empty anyway." Then she looked up and took in Skylar's eyes, something clicking. "Wait! You mean you and him…and you never told me?"

Skylar looked away, and Letty suddenly put it all together. "Is that why you ran? It is, isn't it?"

Skylar nodded.

"All that time, I thought it was something I'd done or that the Fullers had kicked you out."

Skylar grabbed her by the arm and hustled her toward

the back door of the clubhouse. "Come on."

***

Shades used the excuse of needing another beer and moved off toward the clubhouse, intent on finding Skylar and cornering her while she was separated from Crash. He'd kept track of her out of the corner of his eye, and he knew the two girls had gone inside the clubhouse.

He went through the door and into the big open room, pushing his sunglasses up on his head. There was a bar against the back wall, and he spotted the two girls standing at the far left end of it. There was a hallway just around the corner from where she stood. That suited his purposes perfectly. Walking up behind Skylar, he surprised her by grabbing her upper arm. Turning to her friend, he snapped, "Excuse us a minute. The lady and I have some unfinished business."

Then he dragged a shocked Skylar around the corner, into the hall, and pushed her up against the wall.

"Remember me, sweetheart?"

She stared up at him, and he could tell she was scared to death. "Y-yes, of course I remember you, Shades."

Letty stuck her head around the corner. "You okay, Skylar?"

Shades turned his head long enough to snap, "She's fine. Go back to the bar." His gaze returned to Skylar to see her turn her head and whisper, "It's all right, Letty."

Letty gave another look at Shades, and he took a threatening step toward her, one arm still holding Skylar to the wall. Letty was a guest here in his clubhouse, and he didn't care whose Goddamned sister she was, no one questioned a club member in their own fucking clubhouse. He was about ready to growl at her again, when she backed down and went back to the bar.

His attention returned to Skylar, but now his blood was up even more than it had been. "Didn't expect to see *you* walkin' back into my life today."

"I'm not '*walking back into your life*', Shades."

"Where the fuck have you been all this time?"

"That's none of your business anymore, is it?"

"Maybe I'm makin' it my business." She wouldn't meet his eyes, and he pressed, "You with *him* now?" When she refused to reply, he shook her. "Answer me, Goddamn it. Are you his ol' lady?"

She glared up at him. "I'm not *yours*. That's all *you* need to know."

He punched a hole in the wall near her head and let out a roar of aggravation. Her body jumped in reaction. He knew the music and boisterous laughter that always accompanied these hell-raising wakes would drown out the sound of their argument. And he was proven right when no one came to investigate.

She stared up at him, fire in her eyes now. "I don't have to listen to this."

He took a deep breath and blew it out, some of the frustration he felt having been released into the crumbling drywall. His voice softened. "You always were a stubborn little thing."

"Maybe I've had to be."

His eyes took in her face. *Fuck.* Up close she was even more beautiful, and he felt the pull of attraction he'd always felt for her. It all came rushing back. His eyes moved over her face, down her neck to the cleavage exposed by the scoop of her white tank, and then he saw the chain and beads peeking out from under her hair and disappearing into that cleavage. And he knew right away what they were. Even before he found his hand lifting to pull it slowly out of her shirt.

Her hand flashed up to grab his wrist, but it was too late. The cross of his rosary was swinging from his clenched hand. The rosary she'd taken from him the last time he'd seen her. No, not taken. Stolen. Along with about a grand in cash he had stashed in his drawer.

"You *taking this*"—he held it aloft—"gutted me more than the cash you stole," he bit out, his eyes boring into hers. At least she had the decency to look guilty.

A shadow fell across them, and Shades looked up to see Cole standing two feet away.

"You okay, Skylar?"

"This isn't any of your concern, ol' man," Shades snarled.

"Back off, Brother, before I put you through the fucking wall," Cole warned with deadly quiet.

Shades shoved off of Skylar, turning to Cole. "I don't have to fucking back off. This is *my* Goddamn clubhouse, and I ain't a fucking prospect anymore, *Brother*." He said the last word as if Cole was no brother to him.

Cole's eyes snapped to Skylar, and he ordered, "Get

back outside to your ol' man."

Skylar gave Cole a confused look, but then hurried to comply, scurrying out from between Shades and the wall. Shades swore he heard her whisper a soft *thanks* as she passed Cole and disappeared.

"She's not yours anymore," Cole bit out.

"Yeah, you made sure of that, didn't you?" Shades glared at Cole, and then stalked off.

CHAPTER FOUR

Skylar crawled into bed. She stared at the ceiling, her teeth worrying her bottom lip. How could a day that started out so good, end up so bad? She'd been so excited to see Letty again after so long. Crash and Cole, too.

But the last place she'd expected to end up today was the Evil Dead clubhouse. Letty had been right about one thing—if she'd have mentioned that was the plan, Skylar never would have shown up. But with Crash, Cole, and Letty all staring her down, and then Crash immediately dragging her off toward his bike, it really hadn't given her a chance to come up with a way out.

She'd prayed all the way over there that she wouldn't run into Shades, hoping maybe he wasn't connected with the club anymore or had moved on. Or at least that he wouldn't really recognize or remember her. No such luck.

Story of her life.

And he had the nerve to think he could demand answers about where she'd been. Like he'd cared. After the way he'd ended things with her, she didn't owe him shit. Well, maybe that money, and she really should give him the rosary back.

She found her hand lifting to the necklace, her fingers absently moving over the beads. It comforted her, like it had for the last ten years. Whenever things got bad, she'd touch it and remember that one special summer she'd had with Shades.

Until it had all gone to hell.

Ten years ago—

Skylar snuggled up to Shades as he settled back against his headboard.

"Swear to Christ, you're gonna wear me out, babe."

She smiled and slugged him playfully in the ribs. "You have the gall to complain after that bout of really good sex we just had?"

"Really, *really* good sex," he corrected with a grin and pressed a soft kiss to her forehead. He pulled her closer, until her head was tucked up under his chin, her forehead pressed against his throat.

Skylar wrapped her arm around him. "I wish we didn't have to sneak around."

"Me too, baby." His voice rumbled through his chest under her ear. "When I get my patch, we won't have to do this shit anymore."

"When will that be?" she whispered.

His hand stroked up and down her bare back. "No tellin'. It's at least a year, sometimes two."

Her head popped up to look at him in shock. "That long?"

Shades' look moved between her eyes. "I've got no control over it, Sky." He shrugged. "It'll happen if and when they think I'm ready."

"And what will make them think you're ready?"

"Shit, I don't know. When they've tested me enough."

"What kind of tests?"

He shook his head. "Babe."

"Tell me."

"Baby, there's shit I *can't* tell you. It's just them makin' sure I'm gonna be loyal, you know? Makin' sure I've got my priorities in order, that the club comes first. That they can count on me."

"Haven't you already been in a year?"

"Be a year next month."

She rested her head back on his shoulder, and her arms squeezed him. "Then maybe we won't have to wait much longer."

"I hope not. But until then, they say jump, I gotta jump. You understand, don't you, Sky?"

"I understand."

"Doesn't mean you aren't important to me, you are. But I've wanted this for a long fuckin' time."

"I know, Shades. I know how bad you want that patch." She felt him press a kiss to her head.

"Let's get some sleep, babe."

Two hours later Shades' cell went off. Skylar lifted her head sleepily and yawned as he reached to the floor to dig it out of his jeans.

"Yeah?" he answered in a voice gravely with sleep. A moment later he was swinging his legs over the side of the bed. "Yeah, got it."

"Shades, what's going on?" Skylar sat up in bed as Shades tugged his jeans on and stood, turning to her.

"Nothing, Sky. I got called out again."

"Again? That's the third time this week."

"Life of a prospect, babe." He leaned down, cupping the back of her head and pressing a kiss to her forehead. "Go back to sleep."

***

When Skylar woke up the next morning, Shades still wasn't back. She found her phone and checked for missed calls. There was a text from him.

Had to make a run out of town
Can you get a ride home?

She texted him back that she would be fine and asked him to call her when he got back. He didn't reply. Gathering her clothes, she walked half a block to a fast food joint and called Letty for a ride home.

All that week, the only contact she had from Shades were a few brief texts saying he was busy with the club and would call her when he was free. And then finally, he texted, asking her to meet him at his place.

Twenty minutes later, she drove her beat-up old Pontiac into the lot. The closed sign was on the door, but when she pulled the handle, it opened. The bell tinkled above as she walked in.

"Up here."

She looked up to see Shades at the top of the stairs, leaning forward, his hands on the metal railing. He was in a pair of jeans, shirtless, and his hair was wet. She imagined he'd just got out of the shower. Walking across the garage floor toward the stairs, she noticed he didn't move. As she walked up the stairs, their eyes connected. There was no smile on his face, and she sensed something was wrong. "Are you okay?"

He gave a slight nod, as he continued to watch her ascend the stairs to him. When she got to the top, he stepped back, and then suddenly she was hauled into a tight embrace.

"I missed you," she murmured against his chest. He smelled like fresh soap, and her arms wrapped around his warm bare skin.

He didn't say it back, but she felt him stroking her hair, fisting handfuls of it as he held her tight to him. The next moment she was up in the air as he bent and lifted her. Her legs wrapped around his waist as he carried her to the bed.

She fell to her back on the mattress, and he came down on top of her. There was a sense of urgency in the way he tore at her clothes as if he couldn't fuck her fast enough. The buttons of her blouse went flying as he sat back and tore it open. She shimmied it off her shoulders, just as urgent to be with him. A moment later, she slid across the bed as he yanked her jeans off with a jerk. And then he stood to drop his pants while she unhooked her bra.

"Panties are mine," he declared as he kicked out of his pants. Her hands paused as she was about to push them down.

"Okay."

He put a knee to the bed, and his hands skated up her thighs. His fingers curled in the lace at her hips, and he slid them slowly down her legs at complete odds with the urgency he'd shown up until then. She kicked her feet free and writhed on the bed, staring up at him. Her chest rose and fell as she watched him bend over and shove her panties into the pocket of his jeans.

Oh my God, he was seriously keeping them. She let out a tinkling laugh. "You're crazy."

He stood there a moment by the foot of the bed, his eyes moving over her body, almost as if he were memorizing it.

"Shades?"

"Let me look at you. I want to remember this moment," he replied quietly.

At the serious look on his face, her smile disappeared. And she took a moment to take him in, her eyes moving over his gorgeous masculine form. She knew she'd remember the way he looked in that moment for the rest of her life.

And then he moved, crawling slowly up her body to come down on top of her, all hot, hard male. She pulled his head down to her and he kissed her, all that urgency returning as his warm hands roamed over her soft skin. He touched her everywhere. His mouth moved over her face, down her neck, her collarbone, her breasts. He slid down her body, pressing hot, wet open-mouthed kisses all over her. Skylar had never felt so cherished. And then suddenly, he was surging up, leaning over her and stretching to dig a condom out of a drawer. He tore open the packet with his teeth and rolled it on, his eyes connecting with hers, and then he was positioning between her thighs and surging inside her in one slick, urgent thrust that impaled her to the hilt.

She couldn't help the gasp that escaped her as he settled against her, his warm body pinning her down. His eyes connected with hers and held them the entire time he rolled his hips and thrust in and out and in and out. He watched her every response, her every expression, his eyes skating over her face, taking in her brows drawn together, her parted lips, the pulse beating in her throat. He missed nothing.

She clutched at him, her legs wrapping tightly around his waist as she began to climb that peak. His head dipped suddenly, his mouth capturing hers, and then, because they had to break apart to breathe, he pressed his forehead to hers as he continued to surge into her. All power and muscle and male dominance.

And she welcomed it, every aggressive thrust. She knew her thighs would be sore and bruised tomorrow, but she didn't care. She opened, taking the pounding he was giving, answering his unrelenting dominance with a feminine submissiveness, giving back a gentle softness that rose up to meet his demanding need.

She panted as an intense surge swelled up, and she felt herself milking him with overwhelming contractions as a powerful orgasm washed over her in wave after wave. Her body's response pushed him over the edge as he went solid above her, every muscle in his body flexing as he was rocked by his own powerful orgasm.

After a moment, his hard body sank down on top of her, and she relished in the feel of his heavy weight pinning her down. It felt right. It felt good. Her hands stroked over his back as if she couldn't get enough of him, as if she didn't want him to ever move from where he was, planted deep inside her.

But finally, after nuzzling her neck and getting his breathing back down to a normal rate, he slowly pulled out of her and went to take care of the condom.

When he returned, he hauled her close against his side, enfolding her in his arms. They were quiet for a long moment. He stroked his fingers through her hair slowly, over and over. And then he pressed a soft kiss to her forehead, holding his lips there for a long time. When he finally pulled away, he said, "Sky, we need to talk."

Her radar immediately went off. She lifted up to look at him. "About what?"

"About this. About us."

"What about us?" Suddenly he was pulling his arm out from under her and swinging his legs over the side of the bed. She slid her hand up his back to squeeze his shoulder. "Shades?"

He pulled away, standing up and yanking his jeans back on. That wasn't a good sign. He'd never pulled away from her after sex. Never. Unless he had a call out from the club.

"Shades, you're freaking me out. What is it?"

"I don't think this is gonna work."

"What's not going to work?"

"Us. You and me."

She couldn't have been more surprised by his answer. "What? Why?"

"It's not fair to you. I'm busy with the club all the time, and I found out I'm gonna be goin' out of town a lot."

She stared at him, trying to make sense of his words. It was like this wasn't the same man she'd been with just last week. "I don't understand."

"It's just not gonna work, Sky." His voice had a little more bite this time.

She could feel her face turning red with the heat of anger, embarrassment, and hurt. "And you waited until you fucked me one last time to tell me this?"

He ran his hand through his hair, looking guilty.

She crawled out of bed, wrapping the sheet around her. "All the stuff you said before, did you mean any of it? Was it all bullshit? Was it?"

"Sky, calm down."

"You fucking asshole."

"Babe, we had a good run. Let's not end it being ugly to each other."

"A good run?" She gaped at him. "Is that all this was to you?"

"Skylar, stop."

"There's someone else, isn't there?"

He shook his head. "No, babe. That's got nothing to do with this."

She stood there confused and watched him lean back

against the dresser.

"So, what was that, huh? What was that all about?" She flung her hand out toward the bed as she bit out the question."

He ran both his palms down his face, almost in frustration, and then folded his arms.

"Shades?" she pressed.

"That was me saying goodbye, Sky."

She actually pulled back, stunned by his answer. "You're serious? You're really saying goodbye to me?"

He stared at her a moment, and then responded softly, "Yeah."

She turned, gathering up her clothes, and moved into the bathroom, slamming the door. She hurriedly tugged on her jeans, bra, and shirt. When she went to button up her blouse she realized most of the buttons were missing from when he'd ripped it open. *Jerk*!

She stared at her reflection in the mirror over the sink, not believing this was happening. What had gone wrong? Last week everything was so good between them. She tried to think back to the exact moment everything had changed. He hadn't been distant the last time they were together. But after that, all week his texts had been short, and he'd never called. What they'd just shared had been so hot, and then so sweet. And then he *dumps* her?

The pain of every time she'd ever been moved from one foster home to another came back. The feelings of rejection and not being good enough flooded her. What was the point of ever letting herself get attached to anything or anyone, or of ever letting herself care? It always ended. It was always torn from her.

She thought she'd really found something with Shades. She'd thought she'd finally found someone she could trust and depend on and let her guard down with. She felt like such a fool.

She brushed the tears from her cheeks, refusing to let him see her cry, refusing to give him the satisfaction of seeing just how devastated she was. The only way she was going to be able to do that was to stop feeling hurt and start feeling angry. What an asshole dick move to fuck her one last time before he dumped her. *We had a good run, babe. Don't be ugly about it, babe.*

What a dick!

And then her eyes fell on the rosary hanging over the edge of the mirror. He'd obviously taken it off before he showered. Before she thought about what she was doing, she lifted it off the mirror and shoved it in her pocket.

She flung the door open, fully expecting to face Shades, but he was nowhere in sight. Obviously, he'd gone downstairs. She peered over the rail and saw him down in the garage, pacing, talking on his cell phone.

She moved to his dresser, opened a drawer, and snatched out one of his tees. There was no way in hell she was leaving in this torn shirt. She yanked it on over her destroyed blouse, and as she pulled it down, her eyes fell on a roll of bills that had been stashed underneath it.

Thinking of what an ass he was being to her, she had no problem grabbing up the money and stuffing it in her pocket.

Then she realized as soon as he saw her in this tee, he'd know she'd been in his drawer. *Fuck.* Glancing around, she spotted a flannel shirt hanging over one of the chairs. She tore off the tee, shoved it back in the drawer and grabbed up the flannel, putting it on.

Then she picked up her purse, stormed down the stairs and across the garage. Shades was still on the phone. He looked up as she headed toward the door, but she didn't stop.

"Sky, wait."

Not stopping. Not a chance. She stormed out the door and jogged across the lot to her car. She was backing up and speeding off the lot when she saw him shoving his phone in his pocket as he came out the door after her. Her last look at him was in her rearview mirror as she sped away.

That night, she packed her shit and left town.

And she never looked back again.

Present day—

Skylar stared up at the ceiling above the bed. Thinking of that last night still tore her heart out all these years later. And seeing him again today had been so hard. It had brought back all the feelings she'd had for him. The moment she'd looked into his eyes, it was like they hadn't been apart. It was like she was suddenly back in time ten years. He still had that power over her. He could still make her insides melt. She wasn't sure he felt the same way, though.

Shades had been so pissed at her today at the clubhouse. Yes, she'd taken his money and his rosary, but *he'd* been the one to end things. So why did he care where she'd been all these years? Why did he care if she was Crash's ol' lady?

She huffed out a laugh. Cole. God bless him. Making up that story about Crash being her ol' man. He must have sensed that was the only thing that was going to get a brother to back off a woman—if she already belonged to another brother. And since she'd ridden up with Crash, and Crash had been the one standing at the fire with his arm around her, it had only made sense for Cole to pretend she was Crash's and not his.

It'd worked. She had to hand it to Cole. Shades had immediately backed off and let her go. But before that, hell, they'd almost come to blows over her. And what was that stuff Shades had said about not being a prospect anymore? Had Cole done something to him when he'd been a prospect?

There definitely seemed to be some bad blood there.

Skylar closed her eyes, determined to put it out of her head, but all she could see were Shades' brown eyes staring into hers as he'd demanded to know where she'd been.

CHAPTER FIVE

Shades rode with his brothers in the procession behind the hearse that carried Bulldog's casket. The line of bikes, two wide, stretched back about a mile with hundreds showing up to escort the ol' man home. They rolled into the cemetery and circled around the drive to the far left section where a large, polished granite gravestone that read *Evil Dead MC* marked the area where all the Birmingham club members were laid to rest.

The hearse stopped near the marker. A green awning tent and a couple of rows of white chairs were set up where Bulldog's plot was to be. The line of bikes parked in formation and riders dismounted. Several cars carried immediate family members—Bulldog's ol' lady and two daughters.

The family made their way to the seating, while six brothers chosen from the Birmingham Chapter served as pallbearers bringing the casket from the hearse to the graveside.

Shades and his chapter brothers lined up in a row

opposite the grave from the chairs. Brothers from all over, that had shown up to pay their respects, encircled the gravesite. Shades noticed Cole and Crash standing among them.

When the service was over, as was the club's custom, the brothers themselves shoveled the dirt that filled in the plot. Man by man, each taking a turn with a shovelful, they lay to rest their brother-in-arms.

After the rituals of burying their dead were through, Shades searched the crowd, wondering if Skylar was there somewhere, if she'd accompanied Crash to the funeral. He never spotted her that day, and knowing the two men were headed back to California that night, he wondered if he'd ever see her again.

Had she'd slipped through his fingers once again?

***

Several days later, the brothers that had descended from all over the country had all left town, and the clubhouse was getting back to normal. Well, as normal as it could be without their beloved VP.

Shades rolled through the back gate and parked his bike. Noticing a couple of his brothers standing next to a dirt bike, he strolled over. "What's this?"

Ghost turned to look at him. "JJ souped-up this piece-of-shit dirt bike."

"Souped-up how?" Shades cocked his head, studying the bike.

Griz answered with a grin and a waggle of his eyebrows. "Nitro."

Shades looked over at the man who'd supplied the response, a man who got his name from his Grizzly Bear looks. That or his resemblance to the lead actor in the 1970's TV show, Grizzly Adams. Shades was never clear on that one. "You're shittin' me, right?"

"Nope. Stick around. This ought to be good."

JJ turned from his squatted position next to the bike where he was tightening a bolt. "That should do it."

"You're fucking insane. You know that, right?" Shades stared him dead in the eye. The skinny kid had just gotten his patch about a year ago. He was a bit of a daredevil and goofball but exceptional when it came to tense, stressful confrontations and situations. Shades was beginning to wonder if it was because he was too stupid to be afraid.

JJ grinned as he climbed on and fired it up. "Insane or *genius*?"

"No, seriously, JJ. This kind of shit didn't work out too well for the Coyote."

"Well, luckily this rocket wasn't made by Acme, and I ain't after a fuckin' Roadrunner," JJ replied.

"Let it rip, tater chip," Griz encouraged the insanity.

A moment later, JJ hit the throttle and nitro, and the bike shot forward like a rocket, slamming right into the side of the clubhouse.

The men doubled over with laughter.

Ghost observed, "Impressive. It goes from zero to pile-of-junk in 2.1 seconds."

Shades shook his head, chuckling. "Yeah, who coulda seen *that* coming?"

Ghost looked over at Shades. "You took off early last night. Missed a hell of a party."

Shades grunted.

"Yeah, I had a hell of a hangover this morning," Griz put in.

Ghost looked over at him. "Yeah? How's your headache now?"

"It's gone."

"Hi, Daddy!" came a sing-song voice.

"It's back."

The men turned to see Griz's sixteen-year-old daughter coming through the back gate. She had her father's long legs and his thick blond hair.

"Daddy, you know that car you said you'd buy me when I turned sixteen?"

"No."

"Daddy!"

"I don't remember saying anything like that."

Her hands landed on her hips. "Daddy! Yes, you did."

"Look out, Griz. She's doing the hands-on-hips ploy," Shades warned with a grin.

The men snickered.

"Anyway, I've decided I'd rather have a bike, like you."

"Like hell!" Griz replied. "You ain't gettin' no bike."

"Daddy! *You've* got one."

"Correct."

"But *I* can't have one?"

"You're two for two."

She stomped her foot. "That's not fair! Bobby got one

when he turned sixteen. Why can't I have one? You're being sexist."

"Watch your mouth."

"If you let me have a bike, I'll promise not to wear those cute little dresses you hate me wearing."

"You seem to have misinterpreted the matter as up for debate."

"Daddy!"

"And I better not catch you in those damn dresses!'

"Why can't I have a bike?"

"Jesus Christ, Mindy. You'll get a car. No bikes! We clear?"

She threw herself in his arms and kissed his face. "I knew you'd buy me a car!"

"Mindy, quit," Griz muttered in an embarrassed voice.

"You know you love me."

"Yeah, but you don't have to rub my nose in it."

After she'd skipped back out, Shades let out a laugh. "Thought you weren't buying her a car, Griz."

"I wasn't." Griz frowned and turned to Ghost. "What just happened?"

Ghost slapped him on the back with a laugh. "I think she just played you for a car, dude."

"Oh, man. Daughters. They ought to come with a handbook," Griz grumbled.

"Yeah, so you could smack 'em with it." Ghost laughed.

"Want a noose to hang yourself?" Shades offered.

"Nice parenting style, Griz. What's it called?" Heavy asked.

"It's kind of an existential philosophy. It involves a carrot and a stick."

"Yeah? How's that workin' for you?"

"It's not. I think she just got the carrot, and I just got the stick."

The men burst into laughter.

"Hey, JJ, isn't that your ex ol' lady at the gate?" Ghost turned to ask the man who was standing over by his mangled dirt bike, brushing himself off. JJ wandered over to the men and squinted toward the gate.

The men looked over to see a hot little redhead standing with her hands on her hips. The prospect at the gate wasn't stupid enough to let her in without permission.

"Damn, she was a fine piece of ass. Maybe she wants me back. How should I play this, cool and hard-to-get, friendly and laid back?" JJ had a crooked grin on his face.

"JJ, get your ass out here! I'm three months pregnant, you son-of-a-bitch!"

Griz and Shades turned from the woman just in time to watch JJ hightail it around the corner of the building. The two men exchanged a look. Griz pulled the cigarette from his mouth and observed, "Guess he decided to go with cowardly and terrified."

They chuckled.

"This place is gettin' to be like Grand Central Station. Let's go inside," Heavy suggested.

The men headed inside as the caterwauling at the gate continued. They walked into the darkened main room of the clubhouse and headed to the long bar at the back.

"Twisted. Manipulative. Devious," Tater was muttering, his shoulders slumped over the bar.

"What's that, your online dating profile?" Ghost asked with a smirk and a slap to his back.

"Shut the fuck up, smartass. My damn ol' lady just blew through all our fucking savings." He suddenly picked up the almost-empty bottle of whiskey sitting in front of him and threw it at the shelf of bar glasses mounted in front of the mirror on the wall behind the bar. All but one smashed into pieces. Tater was a big ol' teddy bear of a man. All the women in the club loved him and he almost always had a happy disposition. So this type of outburst was rare for him.

"You missed one," Griz pointed out helpfully.

Tater casually walked around the bar, picked the only remaining intact glass up off the shelf and promptly threw it at Griz's head.

"Something's wrong with you, Brother," Shades observed as Griz ducked.

Ghost clapped Shades on the back and corrected, "We don't say wrong, we say *special.*"

"Hey, Prospect!" Tater shouted toward the kid by the door. "Get over here and clean this fucking glass up!"

"He's gonna be a miserable prick to be around the next few days," Shades conceded in a low voice.

Griz grinned. "Yeah. Well, he's in the right place for that."

Shades nodded. The mood around the clubhouse had indeed been somber, each brother taking the loss of Bulldog in their own way. Some with anger and outbursts, some with humor and cutting up.

"So when's the meeting starting? Everyone here?" Shades asked, leaning back against the pool table.

Ghost moved around the bar, grabbed them each a bottle of beer, and passed them out as he slouched against the pool table next to Shades. "Waitin' on Spider. He's on his way."

Griz twisted the cap off his bottle and pitched it at Tater, who still stood behind the bar, his palms flat on the bar top, his shoulders slumped. When the bottle cap hit him in the side of the head, Tater looked up and flipped Griz off.

Shades shook his head with a grin.

***

Boot and Slick sat at the table, behind closed doors. Church was going to start soon, but before it did, Butcher had asked to speak with the two brothers privately.

Now he looked over at the two men, both brothers who had been with the club for a long fucking time. Both brothers he knew he could trust with his life. Either one he knew would make a good VP.

Slick was the club's Treasurer. In another life, he'd been an attorney. That was before he'd bought a bike, divorced his wife and, in her words, "*went off the deep end*".

Butcher remembered riding with him not long after that, down in Florida during Daytona Bike Week. The three of them, Butcher, Slick, and Boot had ended up hauled in for public intoxication.

When they'd been brought before the judge, the courtroom had been crowded. There was a line against the wall as defendants stood waiting for their turn to stand before the bench. When it had been Boot's turn, he took his place before the judge. Slick and Butcher waited in the line against the wall for their turn. The judge had asked Boot if he had an attorney present. The stupid fucker had looked back questioningly at Slick who was standing in the line in shackles with the rest of them. Slick had shaken his head furiously at him. Boot turned back to the judge and replied, "No, your honor."

Dumb motherfucker.

Butcher had looked at his feet as his shoulders shook with the laughter he'd tried to smoother in the quiet courtroom.

Even now, a lifetime later, it was still a funny story.

Butcher cleared his throat. Time to get down to business. "So, obviously we have a VP spot to fill. So let's cut to the chase. Either of you interested?"

He eyed the two men. Their eyes moved from him to each other. Slick was the first to respond, his chair creaking loudly in the room as he leaned forward.

"With all due respect—*fuck, no.*"

Butcher grinned. "Why's that?"

"I don't need the headache, for one. For another, I think it's time you bring up some younger blood. It'll do the club good. Especially, with recruiting. They see they got a shot at some kind of position without waiting for all us old guys to die off, it might make a difference."

Butcher nodded, considering his words. Then his gaze swung to Boot. "What about you?"

"Thanks, but no thanks. I'd rather stick with being

Sergeant at Arms. More fun." He waggled his eyebrows.

"You good with fillin' in until we can vote somebody else?"

"Yeah. I'm good with that. Just don't want the job permanent-like."

Butcher leaned back. "You two got any ideas who you want to see as VP, then?"

They both replied at the same time. "Shades."

Butcher nodded. "He's a good man. Got his shit together. No question about loyalty."

"But?" Slick prodded.

"You think he'd have the vote?"

Slick put his elbows on the table, his hand running over his chin. "Yeah, I do. Why, you don't?"

Butcher let out a long breath. "VP's only one shot away from being President."

"Come on, Butcher. Don't talk like that. *Who'd want to put a bullet in you*?" Slick asked sarcastically.

"*Besides* your ex-wife," Boot added with a chuckle.

A grin pulled at the corner of Butcher's mouth. "Right."

"So?" Slick quirked an eyebrow.

Butcher put his head down, studying the table and contemplated. "I think he needs to be given some more responsibility. See how he does with that before I hand over the VP patch."

Boot shrugged. "Give him the membership drive."

Slick leaned back in his chair and crossed his arms. "How about the shit goin' down on the Gulf Coast?"

"Think he can handle it?" Butcher asked with a frown,

looking up.

Slick grinned. “Only one way to find out.”

CHAPTER SIX

Three months later...

Shades sat at the table in the clubhouse meeting room. Church was just about to finish up. All their business had been discussed.

"Oh, one more thing before we adjourn. We're gonna be having some guests from out of town," Butcher said from his place at the head of the table.

"Yeah? Who's that?" Griz asked.

"Some of you may have heard in the news about that house fire the other day. Two people were killed."

Some of the brothers nodded.

"Y'all remember Crash from the San Jose Chapter? He and Cole were out here for Bulldog's funeral."

Heads around the table nodded. Shades sat up straighter at the mention of Crash, his mind immediately going to Skylar.

"They were his family. His grandmother..."

Shades looked over when Butcher hesitated.

"And his sister."

Oh my God, Shades thought, his eyes dropping down to the table. Not Letty. She'd been so full of life. Always laughing and cutting up with his brothers. And then his mind connected the dots.

Skylar. *My God,* she'd lost her best friend. This would rip her heart out. And then he couldn't stop the selfish thought from consuming his brain and pushing all the others out. She'll be returning. She'll come home for the funeral. He'll see her again.

"There'll be a group flying in from his chapter tomorrow," Butcher continued. He looked over at Boot. "They'll need someone to pick them up at the airport."

"I'm on it," Boot replied.

Butcher nodded and looked around the table. "Whatever they need, I want everyone to accommodate them. We're gonna make this as easy as possible on them."

The guys all nodded.

"Of course," Slick replied. "Damn. Little Letty. I can't believe it."

"Yeah. She sure was a sweetheart. A lot of us are going to miss her coming around."

"We putting 'em up at the clubhouse?" Heavy asked.

Butcher shook his head. "They've got motel rooms lined up. But we'll be supplying the guys with loaner bikes while they're out here, and they're gonna need a car as well."

"I'll take care of that," Slick offered.

Butcher looked around the table. "It's not mandatory,

but I'd like a good show of brothers from this chapter at the funeral."

"Yeah. Sure. Of course," Boot replied, speaking for the group. "I'm sure we'll all be there. Right, guys?"

They all nodded in agreement.

Three nights later...

Shades stood at the back of the viewing room in the funeral home where Crash's grandmother and sister were laid out. On one side of the room was his grandmother's casket. A spray of white roses lay across it. Cole and his wife, Angel, stood quietly paying their respects to her. On the far side was Letty's casket, hers covered in pink roses. In front of her casket stood a man he'd heard referred to as Ace. Someone had told Shades that Ace was Letty's man. Next to him stood Crash, his head bowed in grief. And next to Crash stood Skylar.

As Shades watched, her hand reached out and found Crash's. Shades saw Crash squeeze Skylar's hand in return, and then his head turned toward her. Skylar's shoulders began to shake, and Shades knew she must be crying. Crash's arm came up, his hand moving to her hair and pushing her head down to his shoulder. She rested both palms on the lapels of Crash's suit jacket and gave in to her tears. Crash enfolded her in his arms, his head coming down to rest on the top of hers.

Something inside Shades twisted. He wanted more than anything to be the one to comfort her. To be the one she turned to in her hour of grief. To be the one to get her through this. But he couldn't. She'd moved on from him, and he couldn't blame her. He'd fucked things up so badly, he wasn't sure she'd ever be able to forgive him. And now another man held her, and there wasn't jack-shit he could do about it.

***

The procession to the cemetery the next day was a long one. Shades was about seven bikes back. Crash followed immediately behind the two hearses, riding one of the bikes that had been provided. Behind him was his chapter brother, Cole, and his Chapter President, Mack, also on bikes. Then came Butcher and all their guys. Behind them was a car carrying Angel, Ace and his immediate family. And behind that was a long line of cars containing neighbors, church members, and friends.

The two women were buried beside the three grave stones already standing in a row. Crash's grandfather, his mother, and his brother, Shades learned. And now they would lay his grandmother and sister with them. Although there wasn't really any other family there other than a couple distant cousins, there were a lot of people who loved Crash's grandmother and sister. That was evident by the crowd standing around the graveside. Half the old lady's neighborhood and most of her congregation had turned out, along with many of Letty's and Ace's friends from the artist community.

Scanning the faces, Shades searched for Skylar.

Crash sat in the front row of metal folding chairs with

Cole, Angel, and Mack on one side, and Ace on the other side, whose family took up the second row. Crash's leg was jumping a mile a minute, his knee bouncing up and down. Shades knew this had to be one of the worst days in the man's life. He couldn't imagine the pain he must be in.

Shades eyes moved over the crowd, searching for Skylar, wondering why she wasn't seated beside her man. And then he spotted her, standing by herself at the back of the crowd. She looked lovely in a pretty little black dress, demure and to the knee, but sleeveless. Her dark hair was swept up in a bun that emphasized her slender neck. To Shades, she'd never looked lovelier, except for the sad expression on her face. Why the hell wasn't she up there with the family? Christ, Letty and Skylar were more than best friends, they were practically sisters. She should be up there in the front row with the rest of them.

Once the service started, Shades skirted around the edge of the crowd and made his way over to stand beside her. She looked up at him with surprise and maybe a trace of fear. He supposed he could understand her being afraid of him. Maybe she should be. After all, she'd stolen quite a sum of money from him. But not today. Today, the last thing he wanted was for her to be afraid.

"Sorry about Letty."

Skylar nodded. Her eyes flitted over him and returned to the minister. He watched as she sucked her lips in.

"Am I makin' you nervous, Sky?" He asked softly and watched her chin come up a fraction.

"Not at all," she whispered back.

He turned from her to look at the minister, but not really hearing a word the man said. Finally, he couldn't help remarking, "You should be up there. In the front row. You two were like sisters." When she didn't answer he turned his head to look at her, and he felt a fist tighten around his heart as he watched a tear slide down her cheek. Reaching up, he brushed at it with the back of his index finger. "Baby—"

"Don't, Shades. Please. Not here. Not now," she pleaded softly, her head moving back slightly.

He gritted his teeth and nodded. A moment later he walked away, returning to stand with his brothers.

***

After the minister said his final words over the gravesite, the mourners began to disperse, some stopping by to give Crash their personal condolences.

Cole, Angel, Mack, and Butcher hung back, waiting patiently until the mourners had all trickled off. Shades and several more of his brothers stood off by the paved drive, giving them space, but still within earshot of their Chapter President.

Shades bent his head to light a cigarette and looked over at where Crash and Ace stood alone, saying their own final goodbyes to the women they both loved. Shoving his lighter in his hip pocket, Shades blew a stream of smoke out and watched as Skylar walked up to the graves. She stood next to Crash, her hand sliding over to clutch his. He looked over at her and squeezed her hand in return, trying to offer her a smile, but his heart obviously wasn't in it.

Shades heard Butcher offer in a low voice, his eyes on

Crash, "Maybe it'd do him good to stay in town a while. We'd be glad to give him a spot at the table."

Damn, Shades hadn't seen that coming. His eyes moved from Butcher to Crash and Skylar, and he felt his heart catch. If Crash stayed, Skylar would stay. Before he had time to digest the ramifications, he heard Cole respond to the offer.

"To tell you the truth, I'm not sure what the right move is for him." He shrugged. "Might be too many memories lurking around every corner here."

Shades turned his attention to where Cole, Butcher, and Mack stood, knowing Crash's Chapter President was going to have to sign off on anything that big. Mack looked at Butcher.

"If you want to make him the offer, I'm good with it. Whatever he needs right now, whatever he wants, I'll back it."

Butcher nodded.

"Damn, Brother, you hear that?" Ghost whispered to Shades. "Butcher brings him to the table, you might have some competition for that VP spot you want so badly."

Shades took a hit off his cigarette. "*If* he stays, that is. He's been gone ten fucking years."

Griz nodded toward the fresh graves. "Yeah, and the last two reasons he had for coming back just got planted in the ground."

Ghost shrugged. "Just sayin'. Grief and guilt about being gone, who knows where his head's at."

"If he stays or goes. Don't mean shit to me," Shades growled. Ghost and Griz exchanged a look that told him they didn't buy his words for a second. He shoved one hand in his pocket, his eyes returning to Skylar, and he wondered if this was good news or bad. Part of him wanted nothing more than to have Skylar here, back home where she belonged. The way she'd run years ago, it never sat well with him. He wanted a chance to mend things between them.

On the other hand, he wasn't sure if he wanted another brother at the table who could possibly get in his way. And if he was being honest, he wasn't at all sure he could stand to watch Skylar with Crash. It had gutted him when he found out she was the ol' lady of a brother. She couldn't get any more off-limits than that. How the hell was he supposed to stomach seeing them together? Shades knew one thing about himself—he knew his limits. He hadn't been able to keep his distance from her when he was a prospect ordered to stay away from her. He didn't think for one fucking minute that he was going to be any better at keeping his distance now.

And one thing he knew for certain, if he ever *did* decide to make a play for her, he wouldn't care what or who stood in his way. Dropping his cigarette to the ground, he crushed it under his boot.

"I'll be at the bikes," he muttered to Ghost and Griz as he stalked away.

***

Skylar looked down at the freshly turned graves covered in flowers, and she felt her heart breaking. Letty had been the best friend she'd ever had, and Mama Rose had been like a grandmother to her. The grandmother she'd never had.

It was so unfair. *Life* was so unfair. Mama Rose was the

sweetest woman she'd ever known, and Letty had been in such a good place in her life. Her shop was taking off and doing so well. And she'd finally found a good man to love, one who loved her back.

Skylar glanced over at Ace. He seemed broken, lost, devastated, and her heart bled for him. But it was Crash who really concerned her. Through the entire service, she'd watched him sitting in that front row, his leg shaking a mile a minute, and she knew he was holding on by a thread. He'd had so much loss in his life. His mother, his grandfather, his brother. And now Mama Rose and Letty. No one should have to endure that much.

She knew how he felt though, to have another in a long line of people ripped from your life. She knew what it was like to have to lift your chin and get through it when your heart was breaking and it hurt to breathe. She'd had everyone in her life ripped from her. Her mother, whom she barely remembered, and then foster home after foster home.

Then along came Shades. And he'd made her believe again that she could have love—that she could open up to someone. That she could let them in. And then he, too, had turned out to be nothing but a lie.

So she'd packed her beat-up old car with her meager belongings, and she'd left town to build a life of her own. And she had, with a job she'd loved and co-workers who had loved her, and even a man. But that was all ripped from her, too. And now, to come back home and to lose Mama Rose and Letty, it was just too much.

It just never ended.

Every time she'd let someone in, every time she'd let herself care, they were torn from her. It all seemed so pointless and useless to get close to anyone.

She turned to Crash and took in his devastated face. He needed her. And she'd be there for him. It was the least she could do, after all the times he'd looked out for her when she was younger. Somehow, she'd get him through this.

She wrapped her arm around his shoulders and hugged him as she looked down at the graves.

Somehow, they'd get through this together.

***

As it turned out, Crash indeed ended up staying, and good to his word, Butcher gave him a spot at the table. Shades watched him closely at every church meeting they had. Crash would always give his input when asked and didn't hesitate to do any job Butcher threw his way, but Shades could see he was distracted.

His grief seemed to turn him into a man who didn't give a shit about anything or anybody, except maybe the club. Shades couldn't help but wonder where that left Skylar. Shades noticed that several nights a week Crash would bunk at the clubhouse, staying in the big room they kept for out-of-town brothers. It had four sets of bunk beds lined up around the wall, bare mattresses that brothers would unroll their sleeping bags on top of and not much more. Shades couldn't imagine choosing that over crawling into bed with a woman like Skylar. He supposed the magnitude of grief that Crash was dealing with could make any man pull away from others.

He often speculated on how that relationship was

holding up. If Shades knew one thing, it was that things like this had a way of either breaking a relationship or making it stronger. He couldn't help but wonder which way things would fall for this one.

He knew Skylar must be going through her own grief, which could only put more strain on the relationship. Shades could only speculate, because he hadn't seen them together since the funeral. He couldn't really ask why without arousing suspicion, but she hadn't attended any of the club parties they'd had. Crash had come, mostly out of obligation Shades figured, since he never seemed to actually party or have a good time. He mostly just sat off by himself and got quietly drunk.

Maybe the old man saw it, too, because Butcher was pushing Crash to bring Skylar to the club's annual shrimp boil which was this weekend. Maybe he sensed something needed to be done to snap Crash out of the funk he'd fallen into.

Shades wondered if Skylar would actually come.

He was dying to see her, even though he knew it was going to kill him to watch her with another man. She was starting to become all he could think about. She consumed his thoughts day and night. Maybe if he saw her again, maybe if they worked their shit out, rehashed the past, and he finally got some answers, then maybe he'd be able to get her out of his mind.

Then maybe he'd be able to let it all go.

And let *her* go.

Once and for all.

CHAPTER SEVEN

Skylar was in the kitchen. She'd just finished the breakfast dishes from earlier, and she was standing at the sink, looking out the window. Her mind had drifted back to that summer she'd first met Shades. That first time he pulled her to him and kissed her. At the memory, her hand lifted, her fingers absently touching her lips.

Boot steps behind her startled her from the daydream, and she turned to see Crash walk into the kitchen. When she found out he was planning to stay in town, she'd insisted he stay with her in one of the extra rooms in this big house. He'd taken her up on it, maybe because he'd sensed she was feeling just as lost and alone as he was. But he spent a lot of time at the clubhouse, even sleeping there some nights. She didn't think he truly felt comfortable in either place.

She smiled at him, her eyes moving over him as she noted that he seemed dressed to ride. A pair of sunglasses dangled from his mouth as he pulled his cut on. "Are you going out?"

He grabbed the sunglasses out of his mouth and slid them on top of his head. “Yeah. There’s this annual thing at the clubhouse today. They do a big shrimp boil, drink some beer. It’ll be a good time. Come with me.”

The smile faded from her face, and her stomach flipped at the thought of going back there and running into Shades. She couldn’t handle another confrontation. Besides, she wasn’t even sure she was welcome there. At least, not by him. She shook her head. “I don’t think so, Crash.”

“Skylar, you need to get out of the house. It’s a beautiful day. Come on, take a ride with me. It’ll be fun.” She shook her head again.

“No, you go ahead. I’m not feeling much like being around people today.” She watched him rub his hand over his face and realized he looked worried.

“I know how you feel,” he admitted softly.

She frowned, confused. “You don’t want to go either?” He shook his head, biting his lip. “Then why don’t you just stay here with me?”

“Skylar…” He paused, seeming to struggle with how to explain something.

“What is it? Crash? Tell me.”

“The thing is, I *have* to show, and I’m really not sure I can handle it without you. Most of the time I’m at the clubhouse, if I’m not tending to business, I’m off in the corner drinking alone. Drinking too much.”

She realized just how much it cost him to admit that to her. Still, going there wasn’t easy for her. Crossing her arms, she looked at the floor wondering if she could do it. She knew in her heart Crash would never make her face something like that by herself. She couldn't make him face it alone then, either. Turning back to the sink, she stared out the window, and then consented. "All right, then. If it's important to you, I'll go."

He approached her, his palm settling on her shoulder. "Does going to the clubhouse make you nervous?"

"A little."

"No one will bother you if you don't want them to, darlin'. I'll make sure of that."

"I know you will."

***

Shades sat on the top of one of the picnic tables, his boots on the bench seat, his elbows on his knees, a red plastic cup of beer between his hands. He surveyed the grounds of the clubhouse and the turnout for the annual shrimp boil.

Ghost took a hit off a joint and passed it to him. "You seen Tink?"

Shades' eyes scanned the crowd. Tink, a shortened version of her nickname, Tinker bell, was so named because she was a tiny little pixie of a girl with short spiked white-blonde hair. Her pointed chin, delicate features and big green eyes only added to her sprite-like appearance.

"Nope, why?"

Ghost blew out a stream of smoke and grinned. "She's got on a little leather skirt. It's drivin' Hammer crazy."

Hammer was young, like them. He was a muscular guy, built like a brick house. Tattoos covered most of his broad chest, shoulders, and arms. He had short dark hair and a heavy close-cut beard. The overall appearance gave him the look of a gladiator.

"Well, if he didn't nail everything in sight, maybe she'd give him the time of day," Shades replied.

"Yeah, but we both know a tiger don't change his stripes. He didn't get that name for nothin'."

The corner of Shades' mouth lifted at Ghost's remark. "He's never getting' in her pants, so he may as well hang that shit up."

"That ain't no lie."

Griz walked up and confiscated the joint out of Shades hands. Taking a long toke, he asked, "What are we talking about, boys?"

"When's the damn shrimp boil gonna be ready?" Ghost asked.

"Hell if I know," Griz replied, glancing over toward where a tall bald man stood over the big boiling pot. "Gator's in a mood today. I ain't askin' him."

"Gator's *always* in a mood." Ghost took the joint back from Griz.

"Yeah, but the man sure can cook." Griz looped an arm around the neck of one of the girls as she walked past and hauled her to him. "How's it shakin' Sherry-berry?"

Her strawberry blonde hair made her the perfect target for a million different nicknames which seemed to rotate daily. She was about five-foot-three and stacked. She put a hand on her hip and gave a little shimmy. "You tell me, big guy."

"Heard you got a story to tell," he teased with a knowing

grin.

She rolled her eyes. “You heard about last night?”

“I heard you went into thermo-nuclear meltdown with some guy.” Griz waggled his brows at her.

“It wasn’t just some guy.” Both hands landed on her hips.

“It wasn’t two guys was it?” Ghost teased.

“In my dreams.”

Griz grinned in response. “Hey, doll, go ask Gator if the shrimp are ready.”

Sherry made a face that said, no way in hell. “I’m not asking him. He’ll bite my head off.”

“Come on, Strawberry Shortcake, take one for the team,” Ghost put in with a wink.

She rolled her eyes and moved off toward Gator. Over her shoulder she said, “You’re all chicken-shits.”

The men laughed.

Shades eyes were drawn to the back gate as a single bike rode in.

Crash.

With Skylar ridin’ bitch.

Well, Goddamn, he actually brought her.

Ghost must have noticed as well, because he leaned closer. His eyes on the bike, he asked, “You ever gonna tell that tale, Brother?”

“Nothin’ to tell. It’s over. Ancient history now.”

Ghost let out a huff. “Bullshit.”

Shades turned his eyes on Ghost, his look deadly. “Drop it.”

Ghost grinned, but let it lay.

Shades' eyes returned to where Crash and Skylar were climbing off the bike. He took a drink from his beer, his eyes following the pair as they walked up to the blue canopy tent set up near the shrimp boil. There were several tables and chairs under it, and that's where Butcher, Slick, and Boot were sitting. Crash clasped their hands and sat down, pulling Skylar down to the chair next to his. Shades could see Crash reach over and take her hand in his, their clasped hands resting on her thigh. He couldn't stop the images of Crash running his hands over Skylar's body, and the thought had his jaw clenching.

Butcher snapped his fingers at one of the girls over by the food tables, and a moment later she brought over two cold beers, handing one to Crash and one to Skylar.

Shades took a sip of his beer and continued to keep an eye on them.

One of the new hang-around girls wandered by, giving him a look that read like an open invitation. She was young and blonde. His eyes ran down her body. He'd become a man always in the market for fresh pussy, and he'd been driving himself crazy the past few nights, lying awake with thoughts of Skylar filling his Goddamned head. At the reminder of her, his razor sharp gaze zeroed in on her across the compound, only to find her sitting in Crash's fucking lap now.

Goddamn that gutted him.

His attention turned back to the girl, and he lifted his chin at her. "Come here, darlin'." When she strutted over, he took a hit off his cigarette, blew the smoke out slowly and asked, "What's your name?"

"Ashley."

"Ashley? That's a real pretty name." He reached up to trace the side of her face with his index finger, a smile pulling at the corner of his mouth. Shades knew how to turn on the charm when he wanted. He knew how to work a girl, too. Show a little interest, then pretend to put them off, then reel 'em back in. Worked every fucking time. He nodded toward the prospect standing guard duty at the back gate. The one he'd sponsored about six months ago. "You see my prospect standin' over by the gate?"

She turned to look, and then nodded to him.

"Go bring him a sandwich and some water for me. Keep him company for a while." She looked confused, her bright smile faltering. There were a lot of girls that wanted his attention. They seemed to single him out as one of the prizes in this club. He knew he was younger than a lot of the members, but there were other young guys. Ghost, who was a little taller and broader in the shoulder. Hammer, who had the muscular build some girls swooned over.

Shades supposed it was his face that drew the attention he received, that and the hard look that stamped his expression most days. There were bigger brothers, but for some reason it was that cold hard look they all seemed to want to be the one to melt. Only one woman had ever done that. And she was across the compound, in the arms of another brother.

Ashley narrowed her eyes for a split second before

catching herself and pasting the smile back on her face. Shades watched her hand lift, her own index finger moving slowly down the leather of his cut, pausing to trace the 1% diamond. His eyes followed her movement and then lifted to hers. Maybe this one he wouldn't be so quick to toss back.

"Sure, darlin'," she mimicked him. "What's his name?"

A grin tugged at the corner of Shades mouth, and he reached up to grab her hand. He saw her eyes widen, probably wondering if she'd crossed a line in touching him without permission. He brought her hand to his mouth and brushed a soft kiss to the palm. His eyes moved over her shoulder and connected with Skylar's. He could see, even across the compound, her reaction. This was probably the first time—ever—that she'd actually seen him showing attention to another woman. His eyes returned to the cute little blonde, who, if he was being honest, didn't hold a candle to Skylar's beauty. But Skylar didn't know that. He knew women. They were a competitive breed when it came to the attention of men.

"His name's 12Gauge, darlin'."

She frowned. "12Gauge?"

He grinned. "He's good with a shotgun, babe. A 12 gauge shotgun."

"Oh." He watched her pretty pink mouth form a perfect circle and all kinds of thoughts crossed his mind. Lifting his chin toward his prospect, he raised a brow at her, his message clear. She'd yet to do as he'd bid her. He released her hand and grinned as she turned, moving off to do his bidding. Just like he knew she would.

Ghost shook his head as Shades lifted his beer to his mouth. "You're something else, Brother."

Shades eyes were on Skylar. "Why do you say that?"

"I've watched you pull this bit a hundred times. I'm just amazed it works for you."

"Can't let 'em think you want 'em too bad. Gotta let 'em think you could take it or leave it. Make 'em earn it."

"You're so full of shit. Especially when *I* know and *you* know that the girl you really want is standing right over there." He lifted his chin toward Skylar.

"You're full of shit."

"Am I? What's the problem? She ain't givin' you the time of day?"

"She's with a brother. She's not supposed to be giving me the time of day, now is she?"

"Point taken."

Shades eyes followed Ashley as she moved off toward the food, but they soon lost interest and returned to Skylar.

She'd taken his money. Stolen his mother's rosary. And now she was with one of his brothers, rubbing it in his damn face, and he had to stand here and take it.

Fucking hell.

Shades had tried satisfying the emptiness losing Skylar left with booze, pussy, and the club. He'd turned his frustration at having to give her up into a determination to climb the ranks of the club, but he hadn't counted on the fact that the pull he'd felt toward Skylar had only laid dormant in him all these years. Or that all it would take to reignite it was just one look at her. And he sure as hell hadn't counted on her showing up on the back of a brother's bike.

Since Skylar, he'd hardened. He'd tried replacing her, tried filling the emptiness he felt with a long line of pussy. Tried sating the need she'd left him with by leaving a string of broken hearts and devastation in his wake. He never looked back at any of those women. Not once in all these years. They knew the score. He was always upfront. He never made them any promises, but he always left them satisfied. He made sure of that.

Shades drained his cup, his eyes never leaving the couple across the yard.

Butcher must have asked Skylar to give them some privacy, because Shades saw him jerk his chin toward the food tent. Crash dipped his head to her ear, whispered something, and then she stood and walked off.

Shades tracked her as she walked up to one of the food tables and began chatting with Birdie and Cookie, two ol' ladies that were in their mid-forties. He saw the two women smile and greet her warmly, making her feel welcome, like they did with all out of town brothers and their ol' ladies.

From clear across the lot he could see the anything-but-welcoming glances that the younger women—Brandy, Desiree, and Darla—were giving her. Shades knew enough about women to know the look of them when they were sizing up their competition.

***

Skylar had moved to the food tent when Butcher had indicated he wanted to talk with the men alone. Crash had told her to stay close and within his sight before he'd squeezed her hand and let her go. She'd greeted the two older women, remembering them from the old days. But now she looked across the tables at the other three women standing nearby. They were younger and new. They'd probably still been in junior high when she'd used to come up to the club. The looks they were giving her told her they were sizing her up as competition, even though everyone knew she'd ridden in with Crash.

She took a drink of her beer and finished it off.

Birdie noticed and smiled. "If you're headed over for another one, doll, could you bring me back one?"

"Sure, Birdie." Skylar smiled at her and headed over to the keg with her empty red cup.

There were a couple full-patched members standing around it. Two of the big men who had their backs to her, moved off. When they stepped out of the way she stopped short seeing Shades standing with the nozzle in his hand, filling his own cup. His eyes lifted to hers, and they just stared at each other as his cup slowly filled.

Skylar broke eye contact, and to cover her nervousness she reached over to the stack of red plastic cups and pulled one off the top for Birdie. About that time, Shades finished filling up and held the nozzle aloft over her cup. With a nod from her, he began filling it.

"You a two-fisted drinker these days?" he asked, a quirk of a grin pulling at his mouth.

She gave him an answering timid smile. "One's for Birdie."

His eyes slid past her toward the food tent and then

move over to the blue canopy where Crash was sitting. She glanced back to see Crash's eyes on them. He gave her a chin lift.

Both her and Shades turned to each other simultaneously, and then his eyes dropped to the cup as the beer reached the top. He let off on the lever, and she held the other cup out. He began filling it.

The silence between them was awkward. It felt so wrong to be this close and not be in each other's arms. There were so many things she wanted to tell him. Explain. And yet this awful silence that gripped them like a vise said so much more.

She sucked her lips into her mouth almost as if she was trying to hold back the words that wanted to pour out of her. Words she could never say. Not here. Not with half the club watching.

He finished filling her second cup and hung the nozzle back on the tapper. "There you go."

She looked down at the two cups and murmured a thank you.

He took a sip of his beer, his eyes meeting hers over the rim. And then with a glance back at Crash, he turned without a word and walked off.

***

Shades could feel her eyes on him as he walked away. He headed toward the gate where his prospect was now happily munching on a hot dog and chatting up the lovely Ashley.

Walking up quietly with the prospect's back toward him,

Shades had the element of surprise on his side. He pounded his fist into 12Gauge's back and growled, "You lettin' this little girl distract you from your duties, Prospect?" At the same time 12Gauge spun around to look at him, Shades winked at Ashley.

"No, Sir." 12Gauge straightened up, coming instantly alert.

Shades hooked an arm around Ashley's neck and hauled her close, her back to his front. His face moved to her neck, his nose rubbing along her skin, inhaling her perfume. "She smells fucking amazing, Prospect. That could be real distracting."

At the devastated look on 12Gauge's face, Shades smiled.

"I wouldn't let my brothers down like that," 12Gauge vowed.

Shades, with one arm still around the girl, grabbed a fistful of 12Gauge's leather cut and got in his face. "Brothers? You don't have any brothers. Nobody here is your fucking brother until you've got that patch on your back, Prospect! You got that?"

"Sorry, man. Slip of the tongue. I swear." He swallowed, his eyes going to the girl, as he promised, "I won't let her distract me, Shades."

Shades made a disbelieving smirk and shoved him back, releasing him. "Not sure I'm believin' that, Prospect. No, I think I best take this little temptation away. Wouldn't want you to screw up a second time today. You better not make me sorry I sponsored you."

12Gauge swallowed and gave him a nod.

Shades led Ashley back to the picnic table he'd been sitting at. As he walked, he pulled her close, his eyes going over her head to find Skylar. She watched him from her place back at the food table with Birdie and the girls.

***

Skylar tried to make small talk with Birdie and Cookie for a while, but her heart wasn't in it. The sun was setting when she finally noticed Butcher, Slick, and Boot get up and move toward the clubhouse. Crash stood, but didn't follow them. She walked over, coming to a stop in front of him.

He looked down at her. "You get some food yet, squirt?"

She shook her head, looking up at him solemnly. "I was waiting for you. Aren't you hungry?"

"Not really. Maybe later."

"Everything okay?"

He wrapped an arm around her and pulled her to him, kissing her forehead. "I'm fine. You should eat."

"I'm not really hungry either."

"We're a pair, aren't we?"

She looked up at him sadly, and he drew her against his chest, his chin coming down on the top of her head. She wrapped her arms around him, knowing they'd get past this sadness that consumed them. Time would eventually heal them.

Skylar's face was turned to the side and straight in front of her, across the compound, Shades stared back at her. He sat on the top of the picnic table, the pretty blonde she'd seen him with earlier sitting between his legs on the bench below him. His hand was idly running through her hair, but his eyes remained on Skylar.

Crash bent his head to her ear. "You had enough?"

She nodded against his chest, her arms tight around him.

"Okay, baby girl. We'll leave."

She turned her head to look up at him. "You sure?"

"I made my appearance. Talked with who I needed to. Let's get out of here." And then he took her by the hand and walked her through the crowd toward his bike.

***

Later that night, Shades lay in his bed in the apartment above his auto body shop. He stared at the ceiling and smoked a cigarette, his thoughts once again consumed by Skylar. He looked over at the clock.

3 a.m.

He lay there. Wide awake. Wondering where Skylar was. In a bed somewhere with Crash no doubt, his arms wrapped around her sweet body. Why did he let these thoughts torture him? Twisting, he angrily jabbed out his cigarette on the rough wood floor, and then dropped the butt into an old beer can.

He leaned back, his arms folded behind his head and continued to study the ceiling. Fucking the blonde earlier tonight hadn't even worked Skylar out of his head. He knew better than to think it would. It never had before.

Skylar.

Would he ever be free of this longing?

Memories floated through his head of that summer they'd had together.

He went back in his mind to the place where it all went off track. The night he got the call-out that changed everything between them. When he'd still been a prospect, and she'd still believed in him…

Ten years ago—

Shades let off on the throttle and coasted into the darkened alley. At 2 a.m., it was empty.

He parked next to the only other bike there and climbed off. Dismounting, he pulled his helmet off and hung it over the handlebar.

The burning tip of a cigarette flared to life from the dark shadows against the brick wall, and then went sailing into the distance. A second later, a shadowy figure separated itself from the wall and stepped out into the dim starlight.

Cole.

The man who had called him out tonight.

He'd gotten used to these middle of the night call-outs, but they still sucked, especially when he had to leave Skylar in his bed, her skin all warm and soft. It made it hard for a man to get out of bed when he was leaving that behind.

"Cole." Shades greeted the man, and the hairs on the back of his neck immediately went up when Cole didn't return his greeting, but instead pulled a black glove on as he stared Shades down. "What's up?"

"You and me got some business."

Shades' eyes darted down the alley, wondering just what the fuck was about to go down. "What business is that?"

Cole approached him, flexing his gloved hand. *Opened, closed.* Shades resisted the urge to take a step back, and instead held his ground. A moment later he was blindsided by a powerful right hook to the head. He stumbled back a step, but stayed on his feet as pain exploded in his jaw. He tried to shake the stars from his vision as he wondered what new test this was. The back of his hand came up to wipe the blood that was trailing down from his split lip. "What the fuck, Cole?"

Another fist connected with his left cheek. And then Cole grabbed two fistfuls of his cut and drove him backward until he slammed into the side of a dumpster. Shades started to shove Cole back, but one word from the man stopped him.

"Skylar!" It came out in a snarl.

Shades eyes slid closed as he slumped back against the metal he was pinned to by one angry, pissed-off biker. "Shit."

Cole released him with a violent shove. "That prospect cut mean anything to you?"

Shades straightened. "You know it does."

"You were warned to stay away from her!"

Shades nodded, offering no excuse.

"You want that patch, you cut her loose. You hear me? You. Cut. Her. Loose."

"It's not what you think. She means something to me."

"I don't give a fuck, Prospect. I'm still your Goddamned sponsor. I can rip that fucking prospect patch off your back. At *my* fucking discretion."

"Cole, let me explain for Christ's sake."

"Fuck your bullshit explanations. Only two ways this is gonna go. You want that center patch, you cut her loose. You don't, you'll never fucking get my vote. You hear me?"

Shades spit a mouthful of blood on the ground and growled, "I hear you."

Present day—

Shades lay in his bed, staring at the ceiling and wondering if he could go back now, would he have made a different decision that night? Would he have had the guts to rip his cut off and toss it at his sponsor's feet? Would she have been his choice?

Cole had continued the beating that night, making sure his point was made. Shades hadn't even fought back, knowing he deserved it for breaking the man's trust. Hell, when Cole was done, Shades knew he couldn't go home. There was no way in hell he'd be able to hide his battered face from Skylar. So he'd texted her that he had business taking him out of town and to get her own ride home. He'd avoided her all that week, partially to give his face time to heal and partially to put off doing what he knew he had to do. Break up with her. And break her fucking heart in the process.

An empty ache cut through him, and he swore to God, he'd never felt so alone. And the shit of it was, she was so close again after all these years. So close and yet he knew, she was farther away than ever. In the arms of a Goddamned *brother*.

Just within his grasp and never to be in his grasp again.

Goddamn, it was like a fist squeezing his heart, squeezing the life out of him.

And he couldn't do shit about it.

CHAPTER EIGHT

Skylar wandered out onto the porch. The last few pink slashes of sunset were fading from the sky. She found Crash sitting on the front steps. He turned and glanced over his shoulder at her a moment before turning his quiet gaze back to the horizon. He looked so despondent and lonely sitting there.

It had been several days since the party at the clubhouse, and she could sense a restlessness about him, like he was ready to move on. Skylar settled on the step above him, and her arms encircled his neck from behind, her face close to his. "You okay?"

He responded softly, "Sure. Why?"

"You just seem sad."

"Do I?"

"Are you missing California?"

He shrugged, his eyes still on the horizon. Fireflies began to make their appearance and crickets were the only sound in the quiet peacefulness. "I thought staying here for a while would help. I just felt I needed to be close to them somehow. Like I couldn't just stick them in the ground and leave. But, there are just so many memories here. Everywhere I go, you know?"

She nodded, resting her chin on his shoulder. "I know. There are a million memories of Letty and I everywhere, too."

He reached up and ran his palm over one of her forearms looped around his neck. "You two were inseparable."

She smiled. "I suppose." They were quiet for a few minutes, each staring out over the pasture and hills in the distance. Remembering. Finally she asked what she'd been wondering, what she'd had a feeling about. "Are you thinking of going back?"

He was quiet a moment and then answered softly with a squeeze to her forearm. "Yeah."

She hugged his neck. "I'll miss you."

He grinned, his head turning to the side to kiss her cheek. "I'll miss you, too, squirt. You gonna be okay?"

"I'll be fine. We both will." She gave him a squeeze.

"Yeah, I hope so."

"There's a woman, isn't there?" she asked with a sly grin.

His smile faded, and he looked away.

"What happened?"

He pulled her arms free and stood, pacing a couple of steps off the stairs.

"Crash?"

"There was."

"Was?"

"It's over now."

"Tell me about her."

He shrugged and let out a huff of laughter. "I wouldn't know where to start."

"Hey." She caught his attention and dipped her head, grinning at him. "The beginning is usually a good place."

He laughed with a shake of his head. "It's complicated. We didn't even get along at first."

"But then you did?"

"Yeah. Then we did. Big time."

"Big time, huh?" She grinned. "Sounds interesting." When he didn't elaborate, she prodded, "So? What happened? What went wrong?"

Crash slid his hands in his hip pockets and took in a deep breath. "I tried to protect her. Did something I shouldn't have. She shut me out."

Skylar looked out over the hills. "Women are complicated."

He let out a huff. "No shit."

She grinned. "Sometimes when what we want most is right in front of us…"

"Yeah?" She had his attention now.

"We get scared and push it away."

"Why? Why do women do that?"

She shrugged. "We sabotage ourselves, I guess."

Crash folded his arms, leaned up against the post at the foot of the stair rail and shook his head. "Women."

"But then we usually rethink it and wish we could take it all back."

"I don't want someone who has to rethink being with me."

She nodded. "Guys are no easier to understand."

"Bullshit. Guys are simple. We want what we want and make no bones about what that is."

"Until you don't want it anymore."

That must have sent up red flags because he gave her a questioning look. "Sounds like you got your own tale to tell. So, spill. Who was he?"

She shook her head.

"Come on, I shared. Now it's your turn."

"It was a long time ago."

"When?"

"Before you left for California."

He frowned. "Babe, you were what, eighteen?"

She nodded.

"Someone you went to school with?"

She shook her head. "No. He was older."

"How much older?" He straightened, the frown still there, but now more intense.

"He was twenty-three." She watched his head tilt to the side, his eyes remaining locked with hers, and she could see the wheels turning.

"You were at the clubhouse a lot that summer." When she couldn't keep eye contact, he moved to stand over her. "Do I know him? Was it a brother?"

She kept her eyes averted and didn't reply.

"Skylar, answer me."

"You know him. But he wasn't a brother. Not then."

He sucked in a breath. "But he is now."

She nodded. "Yes." And then the pieces must have clicked into place because he snarled his name.

"Shades."

She looked up at him then. "What gave it away?"

"It explains why he's been drilling me with looks every time I see him. Every time he sees *us* together."

"I…hadn't noticed."

"Bullshit." He called her on it. "I've seen the looks pass between you. I just hadn't put it together till now."

"He looks at me like he hates me, and I suppose he does. But he was the one who broke it off."

"He was a prospect back then. He should have stayed clear of you. And you, babe, should have stayed clear of him."

"He knew what he was risking—sneaking around with me. We both did. I guess in the end, it was too much of a risk for him. I guess I wasn't worth it."

"Skylar, don't say that. You're worth it, and don't you ever let a guy make you think you're not. You hear me?"

She looked up at him, tears glistening in her eyes, and whispered, "I hear you."

"Babe, come here."

She was in his arms before he finished the sentence. Having his arms around her felt so good. She was filled with such emptiness. She felt like she had no one. No one in the world. No parents, no family, no man, no job, and now no Letty or Mama Rose. What did she have left?

And now Crash was leaving, too. She felt her heart

wrench.

"I'll miss you so much," she choked out. "I know it's selfish, but I don't want you to go." She felt him press his face to the top of her head, and he spoke softly into her hair.

"I know, squirt, but I can't stay."

Just hearing those words, had all those old feelings of abandonment sifting through her.

"Hey?" He pulled back, taking her face in his hands and brushing her hair back. "You know it's not me you want or need. It's Shades."

She shook her head in his hands. "That's over."

"I don't know what happened back then, maybe he came to his senses and realized you were way out of his league or that he was no good for you. But I know one thing. Whatever was between you two, it's *not* over. Not for him. Not by a long shot. Not judging by the way he looks at you."

"It doesn't matter now." She pushed out of his arms. "I'm tired. I'm going to bed."

"Skylar…"

"I'll see you in the morning." She dashed up the steps, determined to not let him see the tears that were spilling down her cheeks.

***

Crash watched her disappear inside, and then he pulled his phone out of his pocket and called Cole.

"Hey, Brother. How are you?" Cole's voice came on the line, and Crash realized he'd obviously read the caller ID.

"Okay, but I think I'm ready to head back out there."

"That's good to hear. You've been missed around here."

"I'll book a flight tomorrow."

"Okay. Let me know, and we'll pick you up at the airport. How's it been at the old chapter?"

"All right. Strange. Busy."

"Sounds like some stories for when you get back."

"Yeah. Hey, Cole?"

"Yeah, Brother?"

"You know anything about Skylar hooking up with Shades before we left for California years ago?" Crash could hear Cole take a deep breath before he answered.

"Yeah. I knew about that. Nipped it in the bud, too."

"What do you mean?"

"I saw them together. Cornered Shades on it and beat the shit out of him. Told him he needed to end it or I'd make sure he was never voted in. He could kiss that patch he wanted so badly goodbye."

"So that's why he broke it off with her."

"Yeah. Why do you care?"

"He's been giving me looks."

"What do you mean?"

"Like he wants to knock my teeth in." Crash could hear Cole laugh.

"Probably because when we were there for Bulldog's funeral, I led him to believe that Skylar's your ol' lady."

"You did *what?*"

Cole chuckled. "You could do worse."

"Why the hell would you do that?"

"Remember when we brought Skylar and Letty to the clubhouse?"

"Yeah."

"He was confronting her, had her up against the wall when I walked up. Anyway, he'd seen you two ride in together, and he just assumed you were together. I may have led him to believe that assumption was correct."

"Fuck. Think it might have occurred to you to let me in on this little scheme of yours?"

"He jumps your ass, I'm sure you can hold your own." Cole laughed.

"Thanks for your vote of confidence, bro."

Cole chuckled. "Call me tomorrow."

"Right." Crash disconnected and went inside. He strode up the stairs and straight to Skylar's room. Tapping lightly on the door, he called. "You up?"

"Come in," came her soft reply.

Swinging the door open, he saw she was sitting up in bed and reaching to switch the bedside lamp on.

"Sorry, were you asleep already?"

"No. Not yet. What is it?"

"I'm heading back. Tomorrow, if I can get a flight."

She looked down at her lap, plucking at the quilt. "Oh. That soon?"

"Yeah, babe. It's time." He moved toward the four-poster bed. He slid his palm high on the carved poster, his thumb brushing along it, his eyes on his hand. "I…ah…just talked with Cole. Found something out, and I wanted you to know."

"What is it?"

He leaned against the bedpost and met her eyes. The

confusion on her face was easy to read, so he just came right out with it. "It was Cole who forced Shades to break it off with you." He watched her reaction. Her mouth parted, and her brows drew together.

"What?" she asked softly. "Why would he care?"

Crash shrugged. "You know we've both treated you like a little sister. Him especially. Guess he thought he was looking out for you."

"Forced him how?"

"Beat the shit out of him, for one."

"For one?"

"Threatened to make sure he'd never get his patch. I'm sure that was the deciding factor."

"So the patch was more important to him than I was."

"Skylar, you have to understand, guys like us, that patch means everything. It's who we are. But that doesn't mean he didn't care about you."

"Right."

"Look, that's water under the bridge now. He's a full-patched member. Nobody can say shit about who he wants to make his ol' lady. That's not stopping either of you anymore."

"I don't think it's that simple, Crash. He looks at me like he hates me, now."

Crash looked down, rubbing his hand down his thigh. "Yeah, about that…"

"What?"

"Cole led him to believe you were my ol' lady. At Bulldog's funeral when we showed up together Shades assumed you were with me. Cole apparently reinforced that assumption." Her eyes looked everywhere but at him, almost as if she were embarrassed. When she stayed quiet, he crossed his arms and added, "You knew?"

"I…he…"

"Spill."

"Shades was talking to me, and Cole walked up and told me to get back to my ol' man." She looked up at him guiltily. "I knew he only said it to make Shades back off. And he did. Instantly."

Crash's brows rose, prompting her to continue. "And?"

"And I'm sure seeing us together since then has underlined it." Skylar looked up at him. "Not that I'm not honored to be your *pretend* ol' lady, but I don't think that's the only reason he hates me." She shrugged. "It doesn't matter now, anyway."

"Babe, that's a fuckin' flat-out lie. It's obvious there's still some unresolved shit there. If there wasn't, he wouldn't look at me like he wants to put his fist through my face."

"I doubt that."

Crash let out a laugh. "*I* don't."

"I'm sure you're exaggerating."

"You still stir up some feelings in him. That's no exaggeration. You should call him. Talk it out."

"I don't think so."

Crash blew out a breath. "Right. I'm gonna leave his number on the fridge. In case you change your mind." He bent and kissed her forehead. "Sleep tight."

He turned to go.

"Crash?"

Her soft voice stopped him at the door, and he looked back at her. "Yeah?"

"You should take your own advice."

A frown marred his forehead. "What do you mean?"

"I'm sure there's unresolved issues between you and that woman back in California."

A grin tugged at the corner of his mouth, and he winked at her. "Touché. Night, sweetheart."

CHAPTER NINE

Shades watched Crash walk out of the clubhouse. He'd just turned in the loaner bike he'd borrowed and said his goodbyes. He was heading back to his California Chapter. Shades followed him out the back door. He paused to light a smoke as he watched Crash walk toward the back gate, saying a few final goodbyes to a couple members in the yard.

Shades' eyes moved to the open gate and the alley beyond where a silver Miata idled, Skylar in the driver's seat. Crash climbed in, and Skylar gunned the engine, spraying gravel as she tore out of there like she couldn't wait to be rid of the place. Shades only hesitated a moment before crushing his cigarette beneath his boot and heading for his bike.

A few moments later, he was pulling out, following the Miata to the airport. He wasn't sure what he meant to accomplish. He probably wasn't thinking straight, but that was only because the thought of Skylar leaving again was twisting his gut. He just knew that he couldn't stand by and let her walk out of his life for the third time.

Yeah, he was wrong to do it. He knew there was a

brother standing between them, but he didn't think even that was going to stop him. Not now. Not this time.

Maybe she wouldn't want a damn thing to do with him. Maybe she'd tell him to go fuck himself. But he had to give it a shot.

They'd had something once. Something good. Something he'd never been able to find with any other woman. And he'd thrown it all away.

As they approached the airport, Shades expected them to pull into the parking garage, but instead, Skylar headed the Miata toward Departures. Shades followed after her, keeping a ways back and ducking behind some other vehicles dropping travelers off.

Shades watched as Crash got out of the car, grabbed his duffle out of the trunk, and then came around to the driver's side. He leaned over and gave her a quick kiss, and then headed into the terminal.

What the hell?

Why wasn't Skylar going back with him? He frowned as he watched Crash disappear through the revolving glass doors. And then his eyes moved back to the silver Miata still idling at the curb. Her head was turned toward the doors. She was watching him leave. And then her blinker came on, and she pulled away.

Shades stared after her. Skylar was still here.

She'd stayed.

Goddamn.

He only hesitated a moment, before letting out the clutch and taking off after her.

***

Shades followed the silver Miata back through downtown and over the mountain south of town. The whole time he trailed behind her, he couldn't help but wonder where in the hell she was going. And when he wasn't wondering that, his mind was consumed with the thought that she was still here, she hadn't left.

He still had a shot.

A shot at fixing everything with her. A shot at making things right again between them.

He was still pissed at her though. Pissed at her for taking that grand in cash. And even more pissed at her for taking his rosary. But mostly pissed at her for leaving town like she had. Yeah, they had a few things to talk about. A few things to get straight between them. And he was gonna need to maintain his cool and keep a lid on it if he was going to do that.

Finally, he was going to have a chance. Away from Crash. Away from her ol' man. Christ, it still made his jaw clench just thinking about her belonging to another man.

She exited off I-65 at Hwy119 and headed east. He followed her a couple of miles until she put on her blinker and slowed, making the turn off into a drive that led to a gate. Shades drove past, continued down the road over a rise and made a U-turn. He coasted back over the hill and glided to a stop, watching as the gate swung closed with a clank and two little taillights disappeared around a bend into the trees.

Shades pushed his bike behind some bushes in the tree-line, walked around the gate and crept up the drive, following it into the woods.

When he reached the house, he crept around to the corner and peered around it, hiding behind a bush.

Skylar was climbing out of the car, grabbing her purse, and heading toward the house. As Shades watched, she unlocked the door, stepped inside, and paused to deactivate an alarm. She snapped her fingers and cursed.

"Damn. I forgot to get milk."

Shades watched as she spun around and dashed back to her car. Then she fired it up, looped around the circle drive and headed back out toward the road. Shades ducked down behind the bush as she drove past. After her taillights disappeared down the road and he'd heard her shift through the gears as she pulled back out onto the highway, Shades turned to look up at the house.

Hell, is this where she and Crash had been staying?

***

Skylar grabbed the grocery bag from the passenger seat and climbed out of the car. She'd gone down the road to the combination quickie-mart/gas station and picked up a half gallon of milk, and then as an indulgence, she'd grabbed a box of Krispy Kreme doughnuts. They'd just been delivered, and the smell of them was too tempting to refuse.

She headed inside. Juggling her purse and the grocery bag, she went to deactivate the alarm, and then realized she hadn't activated it when she'd run out. Shrugging, she set it again, and then headed into the kitchen. There was a dim light burning over the sink, giving the room just enough light that she didn't bother with flipping on the overhead. Plopping her purse and the grocery bag down on the granite island, she dug the milk out and put it in the refrigerator. Turning back, she took the box of doughnuts out and tossed the bag in the trash can. As she crossed the kitchen to place the doughnuts on the counter next to the coffee maker something caught her attention out of the corner of her eye. She glanced toward the dining room.

A man was sitting in the shadows by the dining table, his chair angled toward her. It only took a split second for her eyes to flick over him. His face was completely in shadow, but a small amount of light spilled over his legs which were encased in jeans, one booted foot crossed over the opposite knee. He wore a black leather vest, a cut, covered in patches. In the dark, she couldn't make out what MC it was, but her panicked mind went straight to the Devil Kings. They'd found her. *A DK was sitting in her house waiting for her.*

Stumbling back, she whirled to make a dash for the back door. She didn't make it three steps before the man was on her, her body slamming up against the cabinet and countertop. One arm locked around her throat as he pulled her back against his chest, restraining her as easily as a child. Her hands grabbed his forearm, but she couldn't break his hold. As every worst possible scenario ran through her head, her eyes fell on the block of knives on the counter in the corner. She reached out, frantically grasping toward it and felt the smooth wooden handle in her palm as she closed around the cleaver and yanked it from the block. At the same time, the unmistakable cold metal of a gun barrel pressed against her cheek.

"Drop it." A man's voice. Deep and rumbling and somehow familiar. It triggered some part of her brain, a memory buried deep inside a vault she'd thought she'd locked away years ago. She froze, her hand still clenched tight around the handle of the cleaver.

"Sky, drop it. Now."

There was only one man that had ever called her that.

Shades.

The cleaver clattered to the granite counter as her body sagged back against him with relief. It was Shades. Not the Devil Kings. They hadn't found her. They weren't here to kill her.

The barrel of the gun was no longer pressed to her cheek. Shades stepped back long enough to spin her around, and then he was stepping right back in, crowding her against the edge of the counter again.

Something about the look in his eyes had her shoving him off of her. She managed to twist free of his hold, but didn't get two steps before his hand closed over her upper arm, and he was pulling her back. She fought his hold, slapping at him and yanking away. When he'd apparently had enough, he spun and pinned her to the wall, his right hand coming up to close over her throat, holding her there. He wasn't choking her, but there was enough pressure there to let her know he was serious.

"Calm the fuck down," he snapped.

"Let me go!" she tried to pull his hands away, but it was no use. He was too strong.

"I'm not gonna hurt you, Sky. Now settle down." He

stared at her, his eyes intent on hers. There were strong feelings reflected back at her, but hell if she could read them. Anger? Frustration? Desire? She couldn't be sure. And then she was distracted from figuring it out as the thumb of the hand on her throat started stroking, the sensation stirring something back to life within her. She suddenly remembered how gentle his touch could be when he wanted. Swallowing, she pushed the thought out of her head. Her voice trembled when she spoke. "You scared the shit out of me. What are you doing here?"

"You know why I'm here."

She shook her head, as much as his hand allowed. "There's nothing for you here."

He let out a huff of laughter. "You couldn't be further from the truth."

"I'm not yours anymore. Get your hands off me."

"Where's your ol' man?" he asked with a smirk because he already knew the answer. And that just pissed her off more.

"You know he left town. He was at the clubhouse saying his goodbyes not two hours ago."

"Then maybe the question ought to be… what are *you* still doing here? He leave you behind?"

"That's none of your business."

He shook her. "I'm makin' it my business."

"Why? Why do you care? You made your choice years ago and it wasn't me," she reminded him.

"Sky—"

"Let me go," she ground out.

He stepped closer, leaning down, his face just inches from hers. “Fuck no. Not until we’ve talked this shit out.”

“There’s nothing to talk about. It’s all ancient history now. You mean nothing to me.” She spit out the lie. That must have gotten to him, because she saw his head pull back as if her words had physically struck him.

“I went back for you.” His voice came out whisper soft, and his hold on her throat released, his palm gliding down to her collarbone where it stopped and rested warm against her skin.

She frowned, completely thrown by his words. She couldn’t have heard correctly.

“What?” she whispered back, barely audible.

“I went back for you. That night. I went back for you, Sky.”

She shook her head. “I don’t believe you.”

“I went to your house later that night. Your fuckin’ dick of a foster dad informed me you’d packed your shit and left without so much as a goodbye. Said you left without saying a word about where you were going. I wanted to punch him in his fucking smirking face.”

“Why? Why did you go there?”

“Because I realized I’d made the wrong fucking choice, Sky. I knew it the moment you drove away.”

“Bullshit. The club meant everything to you. I learned that the hard way.”

“It’s not bullshit.”

She let out a huff of laughter. “Right. Easy to say now, but I’m not stupid enough to believe that you would have given up the club for me." She watched his jaw work as he stared down at her. "You just want what you can't have. That's all this is. I was off limits before, and I am again. It's just the attraction of that. It's the challenge you crave, nothing more."

"Off limits? I don't see your man around. He left town. Left you."

"Let me go." She tried to pull away from him but he now had her wrists in a vise grip.

"I got somethin' to say to you, and I need you to hear it."

She settled down and bit out, "Fine. Say it and go."

He took in a frustrated deep breath, apparently not pleased with her attitude. *Tough shit*, she thought.

"Biggest mistake of my life was lettin' you go." He searched her eyes. "Sky, I'm sorry. For everything. For all of it. I've been sorry about everything since the moment you drove away. That's the God's honest truth. It's eaten at me all these years. Swear to God, not a day has gone by that I haven't thought of you or wished I hadn't done what I did. I fucked up. Big time."

She stared up at him, trying to maintain that cold shell that protected her heart, but with every word that fell out of his mouth she felt another brick of ice shattering.

"Forgive me, baby. Please." His hands released her wrists and they cupped her cheeks, tilting her face up to his as he stepped closer, mere inches between them. "I need you to forgive me."

His words were tearing her up inside. Part of her wanted to believe him, wanted to forgive him. But part of her was afraid she was just opening herself up to more hurt. If she let him in again, believed his words, it would break her this time, and she didn't think she'd ever recover from it. No, she couldn't afford to let herself believe his words, not when she had to protect herself. Protect her heart. So she let her face harden, her jaw tighten, and she looked away from him.

"See you're not gonna believe a word I fuckin' say," he ground out. "Guess I'm gonna have to show you."

Before she knew what he was about to do, she was up and over his shoulder like a sack of potatoes. She shrieked, "Shades! Put me down." He moved out of the kitchen and up the big staircase. When he got to the top, he only hesitated a moment before setting her down on her feet.

"Which room?" he demanded. His chest was heaving, and the look in his eyes told her he was a man determined to get his way.

Backing up a step, she whirled and dashed into the master suite, slamming the door in his face and quickly throwing the lock before he could react. A moment later, his voice was on the other side.

"Open the door, Sky."

She stared at the closed door, the words of his apology replaying in her mind. *He was sorry. He knew he'd fucked up. He'd thought of her every day. He'd gone back for her.* Was it true? Was any of it true? Oh God, he was going to break her. Her defenses kicked in.

"Go to hell."

"Baby, don't be like this. Let me in."

"Get out."

"That's not gonna happen. Come on, sweetheart, we have a lot of shit to talk about. I get that. I know you've got a reason to hate me, but I never wanted to hurt you. I never wanted to let you go."

Skylar closed her eyes, her forehead pressing against the door as he said the words she'd longed to hear once upon a time. A lifetime ago.

"Why are you here?" she whispered through the door.

She heard his voice close, as if he was bracing on his hands, leaning his face to the door. "Because I had no choice. Because I can't stay away. Because this confrontation was a done deal the moment I laid eyes on you again. You signed that deal the minute you rode back through the clubhouse gate, babe."

"I didn't come looking for you." She laid her palm on the wood.

"Maybe not. But now *I've* come looking for *you*."

"Shades, please, just go."

"Not happening, sweetheart, so open the door."

"No."

"Yes."

"Shades, what we had is over. You need to let go of the past."

"Have *you* let it go?" When she didn't reply, he continued, not giving up. "Sky, I'm not leaving until we work some shit out."

"There's nothing to work out." She pushed away from the door.

"The hell there's not," he growled.

"Go away, Shades. I'm not interested. Nothing about you interests me anymore. Get that through your head. I don't want you."

"Skylar, you want to play hard to get, I'm up for it, but don't go cutting my balls off sayin' shit like that."

"I'm not hard to get. I'm impossible to get."

"You're teasing me, baby. Wild crazy foreplay, that's all this is. You know it, and I know it."

"You're insane."

"You drive me crazy, woman, I'll give you that. Now be a good girl, and open the door."

She didn't reply.

"Sweetheart, do I need to point out that I could bust this door down at any time I want?"

"Go away, Shades. *Please*."

"Done playin' with you, babe. Nothing and no one is keepin' you from me. Not this time. No brother and no Goddamn locked door. You need to get that through your head and get it right fucking *now*." A moment later his deep, rough voice threatened, "I gotta break down this door, I will, Sky. Don't for a minute think I won't."

She blew out a breath. She didn't doubt him. She knew he wouldn't hesitate to do what he just threatened, and she couldn't allow him to damage the place. The man who'd been kind enough to allow her to stay here didn't deserve that. And she couldn't call the police. Not on a member of the Evil Dead. She knew better than that. That left her no choice but to let him in. Turning, she took a deep breath and threw the lock. Before she could even turn the knob, he was pushing his way in and just as quickly slamming it shut behind him.

Taking a step back, her eyes went to his face, studying his expression. It was dark. His head was tipped down, his eyes boring into her from under his brows. There was something about that look that had her backing up until she reached out behind her and found the bed post with her hand. Its solid carved wood smooth beneath her palm. A moment later, her back was pressed to it.

"Say what you need to say, and then please go." Her voice quavered, but she managed to lift her chin.

He stalked across the room toward her, slowly, intently. Saying nothing until he was standing in front of her, so close her rapidly rising and falling chest was just inches from brushing against him.

His hand came up and brushed a strand of her hair back and he breathed, "You were always beautiful, but damned if you aren't even more beautiful now."

Her breath left her, his words having the same effect they'd always had. She watched as his eyes swept over her body, her hair, her lips, before returning to her eyes.

"I should have never let you go, baby." His fingers sifted through her hair. "Biggest mistake of my life."

"But you did."

"I'm sorry, Skylar. For all of it."

She turned her head and tried to look away, but his hand came to her cheek and brought her eyes back to him.

"You don't believe me."

She shook her head slightly and watched his jaw tighten.

"I know I deserve that. That and more."

"Is that…is that all you came to say?" she whispered, her eyes dropping.

"No."

Her eyes came back to his, waiting for more. Whatever his more would be.

"I need to tell you about why I let you go. Why I ran you off."

It was on the tip of her tongue to tell him she already knew, but something inside her stopped her. She wanted to see what he would say, if it would match the story Crash had told her.

"So tell me."

"Do you remember that night we were in bed and I got that last call-out?"

She nodded. They'd been happy then, back when she'd foolishly been so sure of his love. Before it all went to hell.

"It was Cole. When I got to the meeting place, he was waiting for me. Told me he knew all about us. Laid it all out for me. I break it off with you or I could kiss my patch goodbye."

She looked away, swallowing, her throat suddenly tight. She already knew he'd chosen that patch over her, but it still hurt to hear the words come out of his mouth.

"Sky."

She didn't respond.

"Look at me, please, baby."

Taking in a deep breath, she lifted her eyes to his.

"Ain't tellin' you this shit to hurt you. I just want you to know the truth. You deserve to hear the truth."

"So tell me."

"He thought I was just playing with you."

The words tore through her, and her eyes shifted away.

"I tried to tell him it wasn't like that. That you meant something to me. That what we had was real."

At that, her eyes came back to his. His searched hers, filled with regret and maybe looking for understanding.

"He didn't buy it, or if he did, he didn't care. Didn't give a damn what I said. There was only one outcome that he was going to settle for, and that was him ending us."

"*You* ended us, Shades. Not him."

She watched his jaw clench, and his head dropped. Then it came back up. "Yeah. I ended us."

She looked away again. "Was that all he did? Threaten you with keeping you from getting your patch?"

"No. He beat the shit outta me that night. *That* make you feel better about it?"

Her eyes came up at that.

"I didn't put up much of a fight. I knew he was right. I'd lied to my brothers. I'd lied to my sponsor. And maybe a part of me thought he was right about the rest, too."

"The rest?"

"That I didn't deserve you. That you deserved a lot better than me."

"That night, you didn't come back."

He huffed out a breath. "Hell, my face was busted up. I didn't want you to see. It's why I stayed away so long. I waited until I was mostly healed before I finally called you."

He shrugged. “That and I was puttin’ it off as long as I could. But, Cole, he wasn’t having any of it. So I called you. And I did what he’d ordered me to do. I broke it off.”

“Why didn’t you just tell me the truth? Why did you make me think you were just tired of me?”

“Because if I had, I knew you would have fought it. You wouldn’t have let me end it.”

She looked away, knowing he was right.

“I know you, babe.” He swallowed then, as if he didn’t want to admit his next words. “You’re stronger than me. You would have broken me down.”

“And you didn’t want that,” she snapped.

“The club meant everything to me. That patch meant everything to me.”

“Yes, Shades. I found that out.”

“Until you walked out. And I realized what I’d done.”

“Right.”

“I went back for you. I did, Sky. Maybe it would have still been the end of us, but I wanted to apologize, to let you know it wasn’t your fault. I couldn’t handle how destroyed you looked. I’d done that to you. *Me*. And it tore me up.”

She didn’t say anything. She wasn’t sure what to believe.

“Where did you go?” he asked.

She shrugged. “It’s not important anymore.”

“Yeah, it is. It is to me. Tell me. Where have you been all these years?”

She looked up at him then. “Atlanta, Shades. I’ve been in Atlanta.”

His head pulled back an inch. “Atlanta?”

She nodded.

His brows rose in shock. "All this time…you've been just a couple hours ride from here?"

"Yes."

"Fuck."

She looked away and could feel her eyes filling. How she'd wanted him to come for her back then.

"Fuck. All these years. All these wasted years." His head was bent, his eyes on the floor. And then he lifted his head, his eyes soft, filled with what looked like regret. He shook his head. "I should have tracked you down. I should have come for you, Sky."

"But you didn't."

"No, I didn't. I can't change that. But, you and me, Skylar, we're not over."

"We are."

He shook his head. "Not by a long shot, honey. Now that I've got you back—"

"What makes you think you've got me back?"

His head pulled back, and he studied her face for a long moment. "Crash? You're with him still? He left town. For good, the way I heard. And you're here. I thought that was over."

She swallowed, considering for a moment letting him continue thinking what he'd been led to believe. But in the end, she couldn't do it. "No. I'm not with him, Shades. I never was."

His eyes narrowed. "What do you mean *you never were*?"

"Crash and I, it's not what you thought. We're just friends."

"So you and him…"

"No."

"He never fucked you?"

"God, Shades!"

"Need to hear you say it. Need to hear those words come outta your mouth, Sky."

"No, he never *fucked me,* Shades. Happy?"

He studied her a long time, and then a slow grin pulled at his mouth. "Yeah. Ecstatic"

She rolled her eyes.

His smile faded. "All this time you let me think you were with him. Why?"

"It was the only thing I knew would keep you away. A brother doesn't mess with another brother's ol' lady."

He took a step away and ran an aggravated hand through his hair. "Christ, Skylar, you've been lying to me since the minute you rolled through those gates."

She watched him pace back and forth in front of her. "I never lied to you."

He spun around back to her. "Okay then, half-truths and bullshit. You withheld the whole story, and that's just as bad."

"And what about you? You've done the same. You never told me the truth about why you sent me away. You told me you didn't want me anymore."

He stalked toward her. "I never said that. Never."

"You let me believe it."

His eyes searched hers, something powerful flaring to life in them. And then the words that came out of his mouth shocked her.

"Just get naked, and show me how sorry you are."

"Sorry? For what?"

"For letting me think all this time you were with Crash. For all this time we've wasted."

"Any wasted time we've had is your fault," she argued right back.

A moment later, she found herself on her back. He'd bent, wrapped his arms around her thighs and lifted, heaving her onto the bed, his big muscular body coming down on top of her, pinning her down. Her breath huffed out with her surprise, and she pushed on his shoulders. "Wait, Shades. What are you doing?"

"Done talkin', babe."

She looked up into his eyes. They were hungry. A hunger she remembered from so long ago. And suddenly it was like no time had passed since they'd last been together like this. In each other's arms. She paused only a moment before she found her arms winding around his neck, pulling him closer, her eyes falling to his mouth, wondering why he was hesitating when she wanted that mouth on hers so badly.

He was up on his elbows, his hands cupping her face. He must have seen the questioning look in her eyes, because he explained, "I've waited forever to have you under me again. Let me take it in."

She watched as his eyes roamed over her face, his thumbs stroking her cheeks gently. And then his eyes returned to hers.

"I've missed you, baby. God, how I've missed you."

"I've missed you, too, Shades. So much."

And then, finally, his head lowered, and his mouth touched hers. A soft tender kiss, just a brush of his lips. She felt his soft, close beard brush against her skin, and she moaned, remembering the erotic feeling of it touching her throat, her belly, her thighs. Her hands slid up into his hair, scratching his scalp, clutching handfuls, and she felt his body respond, his hips arching into the cradle between her thighs. He brushed the hair from her face, and his tongue licked along her lips seeking entry. She opened and he didn't hesitate to sweep inside, twisting his head to deepen the kiss. It wasn't long before he was breaking free, his mouth skating along her cheek to her throat, the soft underside of her jaw, and then finally, to her ear.

She heard him growl, "I'm gonna make it all up to you, Sky. I swear. You let me in, I'll never hurt you again. I'll never let you down again."

Her legs locked around him, giving him his answer.

He drew back to look down at her, an almost stunned expression in his eyes, and she had to smile and nod, letting him know that yes, he'd read that response right. And then she saw an answering smile form on his mouth. And then that beautiful mouth descended to hers again. This time his kiss was more urgent, filled with all the pent up desire she was feeling as well. *Need. Hunger. Want.* It was all rolled up in that kiss.

His hand moved to the hem of her shirt and began

tugging it up. He broke the kiss long enough to pull the shirt over her head and toss it to the floor. And then his mouth was moving down her throat, to her collarbone, to the cleavage pushed up by her bra. His fingers curled around her strap and he pulled it slowly down her arm until it caught on her elbow. Then, with his mouth still on her skin, he slid his arms under her, his hands going to the clasp. She arched her back to help him. A flick of his fingers and he was pulling the bra free, lifting up to yank it from her arms and toss it aside.

She watched his eyes take her in, moving over every inch of her. And then his head was dipping, his mouth latching onto a nipple, his arms tightening around her ribs.

Her hands stroked over his biceps, his shoulders, up his neck to slide into his hair. Her head fell back as he sucked hard, a jolt zinging through her straight to between her legs. Her mouth fell open, a shuddering gasp escaping.

He moved to the other one. Another hard pull and tug of his mouth sent a second jolt through her. Her hips lifted, instinctively rubbing against him, urgently seeking some relief.

He responded by sliding down, his mouth moving over her exposed belly. He stopped to play with her navel, his tongue dipping inside, and then his hands were on the fastening of her jeans, and he rose to yank them down, pulling them free and tossing them on the floor.

He tore his cut off and swept his t-shirt over his head, tossing it aside. One hand went to the base of his spine, yanking his pistol free from his waistband. He planted one hand in the bed, his chest looming over her as he stretched across her to lay the gun on the nightstand. Then he was back on his knees, staring down at her, as his hands moved to his belt, unbuckling it.

She stared up at him, taking in his chest, his abs, the muscles in his arms flexing as he worked the belt free. He slid off the edge of the bed, jerked his boots off, and then his jeans hit the floor. And her eyes took him all in.

He crawled up over her, one hand planted in the sheets near her head, one warm palm settling low on her soft belly, the heat of his touch melting into her skin.

And then his hand slid up, and he picked up the rosary that hung from her neck and lay between her breasts. His thumb brushed over the cross.

"This brought you back to me," he murmured softly, reverently. Then as she watched, he lifted the cross to his lips and kissed it before setting it back down on her.

Her eyes moved from his hand up his chest to his eyes. His heated gaze bore into her. Her chest rose and fell in anticipation as he hesitated, drawing the moment out. Her tongue slipped out to wet her lips, and his eyes dropped to her mouth. The arm holding him suspended over her flexed, lowering him an inch at a time in a slow one-handed pushup until his mouth dipped to brush hers. Her palms moved up his chest, gliding over his skin, and she felt him tremble. He whispered against her mouth.

"I want to take my time. I don't want to rush this."

Then he was back up on his knees, his hands going to her hips, his fingers curling in the fabric of her panties, and he glided them down her thighs.

Her mind flashed back, and the words tumbled out of her mouth in a soft whisper. "I remember the last time you took off my panties. You kept them."

He pulled them free and tossed them aside. His hands sliding slowly up her thighs, and his eyes connected with hers.

"I still have them."

As their eyes held, he dipped his head, his mouth brushing a soft kiss to her belly. And then one large hand slid to the inside of her thigh, down to just above her knee, and he nudged her open.

She tried to reach for him.

"Lay back, baby."

She did as he asked, her hands dropping away. He slid down, his broad shoulders pushing her thighs open and up. His mouth came down on her, softly at first, teasing, gentle licks designed to arouse and torment until she was undulating beneath him. When she couldn't take it anymore, he got more aggressive with the attention his mouth lashed over her.

Her hips lifted, seeking more, *needing* more. He didn't deny her. He slid two fingers inside her, seeking her sweet spot with one hand, while the thumb of his other took up its own stroking rhythm, bringing her closer and closer with every perfectly-timed caress. Over and over and over and over. He wouldn't let up until she was thrashing on the bed, her hips lifting to meet each of his strokes in a craving need driven by a rhythm as old as time.

"Shades," she panted, her breath nothing but short huffs now.

"So wet, baby. So wet. Do you know how bad I want you, baby? How bad I want to sink my dick inside your sweet pussy?" His voice was deep, rumbling, and so very sexy.

His words brought her closer as his hands kept working her.

"Then do it. Please," she begged, no shame left. "Please."

"Not yet. Not till you've come. Not till I've satisfied you, baby." His mouth came down on her, and her head arched back as she sucked in a shuddering breath and held it. She soared higher until she was teetering on the edge for a moment, and then he pressed his palm down on her lower belly, his fingers pushing up against that sweet spot inside her, and she tumbled over the edge in an explosive orgasm that had her groaning out loud.

She could feel her arousal coat his hand in a fresh drenching of release. She sunk back, melting into the pillow, her breathing heavy as she floated back down to earth. Shades withdrew his fingers and ministered to her with soft licks and nuzzles.

He kept at it until his stimulations had her desires awakening again. Urging her on, provoking her senses, drawing out her need and arousal once more.

Her hands grabbed at his biceps, urging him up, wanting his weight on her once more, wanting him inside her, wanting him to take her.

"Please, Shades. Take me. Now."

"You on the pill, Sky?"

She nodded.

"I always use a condom, baby. Always. With every woman but you. I'm clean, Sky, and I don't want anything between us. You ready for me, Sky?"

"Yes. So ready. Please."

"Good, baby. Because I can't wait another second." He slid up her body and surged inside her with one forceful thrust, sinking all the way to the hilt. She gasped at his entry. She'd forgotten how large he was, how he filled her so deep. She felt pinned, immobilized, claimed, owned.

He stared down at her, eyes searching hers with awe.

"Hello, love," he whispered.

"Hello, love," she responded, remembering—as he must have—that those were the words they'd murmured to each other the first time they'd made love.

Her hand came up, her thumb brushing over his lower lip. Once. Twice. And then her arms slid around his neck, clutching tightly as he began to glide in and out of her, gently at first, and then with each repeated stroke he grew more rough and urgent until he was pounding into her, his hands planted in the bed, his arms locked, holding his weight off her. He stared down at her, their eyes connecting as his chest grew slick with sweat from his exertions. Her eyes couldn't help but trail over his beautiful body, his sculpted muscles flexing, his hair growing damp, his breathing labored, his pulse pounding in a vein in his throat.

She watched his jaw clench, and she tightened her legs around him, her pussy clamping down on him, and he thrust one final time, letting out a roar as he climaxed inside her, his body going rock solid above her for a long moment before collapsing on top of her.

She stroked his back, holding him close, loving the feel of his weight pinning her down. His breathing sawed in and out. Her mouth moved to his throat, pressing soft loving kisses from his collarbone, to his jaw, to his ear. She nuzzled and nipped at his earlobe.

She heard him groan and felt the vibration rumble through his chest. Her hands slid from his back, down his spine, to the dimples at the base, to his buttocks.

At her stroking touch, she felt him growing hard again inside her, and he arched his hips against her. She moaned as the insides of her tender thighs protested. He rose up to search her eyes.

"Was I too rough? Did I hurt you, baby?"

Her foot moved over the back of his leg, stroking his calf.

"I'm good."

He grinned. "You're very good. But that's not what I asked."

She smiled at his compliment. "No, you didn't hurt me."

She felt so contented, so at peace, so truly happy for the first time in so long, maybe even for the first time since she'd last been in his arms. Sex was not only an expression of how they felt about each other deep down, it was also a bridge back to each other. It was a powerful way to reconnect. It cut through all the bullshit, straight to the feelings. Straight to the soul. Straight to the heart.

Still buried inside her, he lifted up enough to again take

the cross in his hand. She watched as his eyes studied it.

"I made a deal with God. If he opened your heart to me again, I promised him I'd be a better man, the kind you deserve."

She took his face in her hands, cupping it gently, bringing his eyes to hers. "I don't need you to be a better man, Shades. I fell in love with the man you are, faults and all."

He grinned at her. "I've got a few of those."

"I don't need anything but your love."

"You have it, Sky." He pressed a soft kiss to her mouth, and then lifted back up to look at her again. "I do love you, baby."

"I love you, too."

Then he pulled out and fell to his back on the bed beside her. Wrapping his arms around her he gathered her close. They lay that way for a long time, her head tucked under his chin, her cheek on his chest. His fingers stroked lightly up and down her back, and her fingers moved over his chest, tracing idle patterns.

"Babe, how'd you end up in such a big house like this?"

She smiled remembering how Shades always liked pillow talk. When she'd stay at his place and they'd make love, afterward he always liked to talk, about his day, about hers, about something funny one of the guys did. It really didn't matter what the topic was, but they'd murmur back and forth for a long time before one or both of them would drift off to sleep. She'd always loved that about him. And she'd missed it.

"A friend is letting me stay here," she replied.

"Huh. A friend, eh?" She felt him tense under her.

"A friend of my boss."

"Your boss?"

"I needed a place to stay when I came back to town. Eric made a call for me. His friend had this place, and it was standing empty, so he told Eric I could use it for the summer."

"Eric, huh?"

"Jealous?"

"Maybe. Do I need to be?"

"Hardly. He's gay."

"Thank you, Lord."

She giggled.

"It's a nice place. I like this big bed."

She grinned. "I'm sure you do."

They were quiet for a minute.

"Shades?" she whispered.

"Hmm?"

"I'm scared." She felt the hand stroking her back go still.

"Of what?"

"I'm afraid this is all going to be taken away again."

He pressed a kiss to her forehead. "I'm not going anywhere, baby."

"You don't understand. My whole life has been about letting go. I've had to let go of so many people, Shades. Every time I got attached, allowed someone to become important in my life, I've had to learn to let them go. It's hard to allow anyone to become important after that. But I let you become important. And you tore my heart out. And I'm afraid it's going to happen again."

Shades was quiet for a long moment, and then he started talking.

"That summer we met…I'd almost reached the end of my prospecting. At the time, I couldn't imagine having gone through everything I'd already gone through only to have that patch yanked away from me.

"I was young, Sky. Young and selfish. Too young to realize that losing you would be the bigger loss. I made a mistake, Skylar. I never should have fucking let you go the first time.

"If I hadn't, maybe you wouldn't have had to go through all the pain you did. All I thought about was what *I* was going to lose. I didn't think about you. How it would affect you. I see that now. I was an alpha dog, and you were a sweet, innocent shy girl. I thought Cole was right to protect you, run me off.

"And these words are gonna hurt, and that sucks, but I gotta say 'em. You need to hear 'em. Maybe a part of me knew you'd be a commitment, and it was a commitment I wasn't ready to make at that time in my life.

"Gotta say, babe. Truth? Back then, part of the appeal of the club was the women. I wasn't ready for an ol' lady or locking myself down like that. You deserved better. Even then, I knew that. I knew if I was sweet about it, you'd convince me to stay, so I was a dick. It was the only way I could run you off. I had to turn it around and make it your fault. It never was, Sky. It was never you. I was angry with myself, and I took it out on you. I convinced myself you were trying to ruin everything I'd worked so hard for. You weren't. You never would have. You would have stayed and taken any shit I shoveled your way."

Skylar took in his words. It hurt to hear them, but he was right, she *needed* to hear them. They had to talk this all out if they were going to come out on the other side. And there were things she'd needed to get out, too. "What you did? It broke me. I felt worthless. Like I didn't deserve to be loved." A tear slid down her cheek and dropped to his chest.

"You're not worthless. You know it deep inside. You don't dress like you think nothing of yourself, you don't do drugs. You never did. Sky, you were always meant for better. It's in you. You can't be broken. Please don't tell me you're broken."

"What does it matter? Things never worked out. You. Letty. My life."

He rose up over her, his hand lifting to her face, his thumb brushing the wetness from her cheek.

"All that's fuckin' over, Sky. You hear me? It's long fucking done."

CHAPTER TEN

Skylar woke, her hand sliding across the sheets. Empty. Lifting up from her stomach, she looked toward the open French doors to see Shades leaning against the frame, his eyes on the horizon as dawn was breaking. He was bare chested, his jeans left undone, hanging loose on his hips and showing that sexy V. At her movement he turned to look at her, a grin pulling at his mouth.

"Mornin', babe."

She returned his smile. "Morning."

"Great view."

"I know, you can see for miles from that window."

"Not talkin' about the window," he corrected with a lazy grin, letting his eyes sweep over her naked back down to where the sheet laid draped low across her ass.

She smiled. "Come back to bed."

She watched as he pushed off the doorframe and sauntered toward her, his shoulders rolling as he moved. Her eyes skated over his muscular arms, chest, and cut abs. He stopped at the end of the bed, leaning against one of the four posters.

She looked back at him over her shoulder, a coquettish smile on her face.

"Roll over, babe."

She took in the hungry look in his hooded, dilated eyes. She rolled and pressed back against the pillows, one foot coming up to rub seductively, temptingly back and forth over the sheet

His eyes ran over her.

"Grab the headboard."

She did as he asked, her hands closing over the polished wooden spindles. He continued to stand there, his eyes sweeping over her, and she grew impatient for his touch. She couldn't stop herself from writhing on the sheets, beckoning him with her body.

"Shades, please."

"You want something, pretty girl?"

"You know I do."

"What do you want?"

"You."

He shook his head. "Nuh-uh. More specific. Ask for it."

"I want you to climb on this bed, climb on top of me."

"And?"

"I want to feel your weight on me. Feel your hands sliding over my skin."

His hand reached inside his jeans and pulled his cock out. He stroked it and her eyes widened with fascination.

"Keep goin'," he ordered.

"I want to touch you like that. I want to put my hands on

you, my mouth on you. Please, Shades."

"I like hearing you talk like that. Sexy as fuck, babe." His eyes skimmed over her body. "Like watchin' you writhe like that, too. Fuck, yeah." His hand kept stroking slow and sure.

Her chest rose and fell. She loved foreplay, but this was torture. She let go of the spindle with one hand and ran it down her body to between her legs.

"That's mine. You don't touch it unless I say you can."

She pouted.

"Put your hand back on the headboard, babe."

"Shades," she pleaded.

"Is that mine or not?" he pressed.

"It's yours."

His brow lifted, waiting for her to comply.

She huffed out a breath, but returned her hand to the headboard.

He made a tsk-tsk sound. "That'll cost you, babe."

"Cost me what? Don't you want me, Shades?" She writhed again and watched as his control practically snapped in front of her eyes. He kicked his jeans off and crawled up between her legs. His mouth trailed gentle kisses up the inside of her thigh, and she felt the soft brush of his beard. He had a hand planted in the bed on either side of her hips. She ran her eyes up his muscled forearms to his biceps to his strong shoulders. His head came down to press a kiss to her smooth belly, again his soft beard brushing erotically against her skin. She sucked in a breath, her stomach jerking, and his eyes lifted to hers. His mouth was still just an inch off her skin. She watched a smile pull at the corners.

"Still ticklish, I see."

"I want to touch you," she half begged, her hands still on the spindles.

"Looked more like you wanted to touch *you.*" He grinned.

"Maybe I was just trying to stir you up."

"You tryin' to rattle my cage? You got me." He dipped his head and gave her another brush of his lips. Then he rose up. "Still gonna cost you, baby."

He slid down, and his mouth found her. Just barely a touch at first, just enough to have her writhing on the bed as he kept at her. One big warm palm came down on her belly, holding her still while he continued to work her with his mouth and his tongue. Her thighs were pinned wide under his biceps, holding her just where he wanted her, open to him as he tortured her with his mouth until she didn't think she could take anymore. Then he added his hand, his thumb brushing over her, making her arch under him.

"Yes. Yes, more."

"Gonna make you squirm and beg for it now, pretty girl."

And true to his word, he kept at her for a long time until she couldn't take anymore.

"Please, Shades. *Please.*"

And then he gave it to her, and her head fell back, her neck arching and she came all over him.

Only then did he slide above her, moving so quickly she gasped as his strong chest came down on top of her, and he thrust inside hard, deep, and fast.

She rode her orgasm out on his cock as he thrust over and over.

He rose up on his arms, his head dropping, and his eyes locked on where they were joined. He watched himself pump in and out of her, watched her take him. And she watched him watch, and it was erotic as hell.

"Fuck yeah," he growled. "Love watchin' you take me." One hand dropped from the bed to grab her leg and pull it up high, pushing back into the bed, opening her wider to him. He grunted as he pounded into her roughly. "You like it like this?"

"God, yes. Don't stop. Don't stop."

His mouth came down on her breast and latched onto her nipple. He tugged hard and she arched under him. Yes. *Oh God, yes*. He rolled his hips and ground himself against her with each thrust, and he soon had her climbing toward another orgasm.

"Oh, Shades."

"That's it, Sky. Find it. Let go." His breathing sawed in and out of him, his chest slick with sweat as he pumped and thrust and worked her.

A minute later, she shuddered under him and let out a soft, low moan as another orgasm rolled over her.

He pumped hard and glided once, twice, and then he went solid above her, and she watched as it broke across his face, and his release shattered through him, his body shivering with the aftershocks.

He sank down, and her arms wrapped around him tight,

her hands stroking his back, her fingers gliding into the hair at his nape. She pressed soft kisses along his jaw, his throat, his ear.

It took a few moments for him to rouse enough to raise his head and look down at her. His hand came up to brush the hair away from her forehead, and then his head dropped, his mouth touching hers in a soft kiss.

"Hmm. Missed that," he groaned.

"Fucking?" she asked with a smile.

"You touching me like that. Soft kisses, hands gliding on me."

"Oh," she breathed, letting the sweetness of his words melt through her.

"And the fucking, too." He grinned.

She giggled. "Of course, the fucking, too." She watched the crinkles at the corners of his eyes as he laughed, and she stroked along his back again.

"I have to go into the shop today."

His change in topic threw her, and her smile faded. "Oh. Okay."

"I want you to come with me."

She frowned, not understanding.

"Come with me to the shop. I have to go, and I want you near me." He grabbed her hand and brought it to his mouth, pressing a kiss to her palm. "I just found you again. I don't want to be away from you today."

"I have a better idea. Stay here in bed with me all day."

He grinned, his eyes sweeping down over her breasts. "As tempting as that sounds, I got work to do today.

Promised a guy his car would be ready by one."

"And what would I do while you're working on a car?" she asked, stalling, not sure she wanted to go back to his body shop when all she could think of was the last time she was there and the awful memories of that day.

"Sit your pretty ass in a chair and watch me work." He grinned.

Her hand fiddled with the hair at his nape. "Shades, that place kind of has bad memories for me."

He studied her, his eyes moving from hers to his hand stroking through her hair. Then they returned. "Oh, but sweetheart, there are a lot of good memories there, too."

Her hand came to his jaw, cupping his cheek, her thumb sliding over his lips, and she let those good memories float through her mind. She watched his mouth open and capture her thumb. Her eyes lifted, connecting with his. They were filled with warmth and heat.

"Okay," she breathed.

He released her thumb and grinned, repeating her word back at her. "Okay."

***

An hour later, after a taking a shower together and getting dressed, they rode toward his shop on his bike. Shades felt Skylar tuck in behind him, her breasts pressed against his back. It felt right, natural, like it was where she'd always belonged—on the back of his bike, her arms wrapped around his waist.

Before they'd left her place, while she was getting ready he'd stepped out on her balcony and called his sister, begging her to make a quick run to his shop to change his sheets. He owed her big time now. Oil change, tune up, and a new paint job.

Damned if she didn't drive a hard bargain, but she'd finally given in, like he knew she would. And he'd made her promise to get the good shit. 600 thread count or Egyptian cotton or whatever it was chicks liked.

She'd laughed at him, but she'd done as he'd bid.

When they'd gotten to his shop, he'd worked faster than usual and had the car ready by eleven. After a call, the car was picked up early.

Now he watched through the glass door as the car drove off the lot, and then he reached up and flipped the open sign over to the closed side.

Then he turned to her.

***

Skylar watched a grin form on Shades' face. A grin she knew so well. She watched him move toward her with purpose, and then he was taking her hand and leading her toward the stairs.

The stairs to the loft.

The loft where his bed was.

She pulled back, digging in her heels.

That had him stopping and turning to look back at her.

"What's wrong, baby?"

She shook her head, her eyes lifting to the loft. "No, Shades. I can't. Not here."

He took both her hands in his and searched her face. "Sweetheart, we had one bad hour there. And a lot of good ones. *A lot.* The bad? It's over. It's done. And I'm as sorry as I can be, and I think I told you that. But now I need you to let it go. 'Cause, babe, you pull that out and throw it up between us over and over, we *are never* gonna get past it."

Shades was direct, he always had been. It's one of the things she'd loved about him.

Still.

"Shades, I can't," she whispered, her eyes again going to the loft.

"Do you forgive me?"

"Shades—"

"Do. You. Forgive. Me?"

She nodded.

"Say it."

He waited.

"Say it, Sky. I need to hear you say it. Out loud."

"I forgive you, Shades."

"Part of forgivin' me, Sky, is lettin' this shit go. You gonna let this shit go?"

She studied him, knowing he was right, but still unsure if she was capable of it. Then again, if she didn't at least try, they'd never have a start—a real start—at a second chance. "I'll try. That's all I can give you."

"I can work with that." He kissed her softly on the lips. Then he took her hand and led her upstairs.

CHAPTER ELEVEN

Skylar stared at the ceiling, Shades' warmth pressed against her, both their bodies sweaty from the bout of sex they'd just had. They were lying on the sheets she'd totally noticed were new, the square folds in the fabric giving it away. He confessed the whole story. She thought it was sweet, him wanting to do that. For her. For them. Then her eyes dropped, and she frowned at the item nailed into the opposite wall. Were those her…?

Oh. My. God.

She sat straight up in the bed and turned to look at him, her mouth hanging open.

His arms were folded behind his head, and he too was staring at the object nailed to the wall. Then his eyes came to hers.

"What?" he asked, all innocent.

"Are those *my panties*?" she practically shrieked.

He grinned. "Yup."

"Yup? Is that all you have to say? *Yup*?"

He shrugged, his hand coming up to catch the chain of his rosary that still hung around her neck, and he gave it a little tug. "*You* kept a souvenir. Only fair I got one, too. And before you get all pissed, take note, babe, they're the only pair up there."

"Why are they *nailed to your wall?*"

"They're up there so I can look at them every night when I hit this pillow and every morning when I open my eyes. So I can remember what a sweet, pretty girl I once had and how big I fucked that all up. They're up there to remind me of everything I lost."

Not exactly flowery words, but they were deep, heartfelt even, because he meant them. Every word. And that was as sweet as she could hope for. She was still going to make him take them down, but for now, she settled back beside him.

He pulled her tight against his side. She felt him press a kiss to the top of her head, and then his head dipped, his mouth coming to her ear.

"Ain't gonna fuck up again, pretty girl. Those days are fucking done."

Her arm came across his gut and she squeezed. "Okay, Shades."

He squeezed her back. "Okay, sweetheart."

They both must have drifted off, because the next thing Skylar knew, Shades was shaking her awake, the rumbling sound of pipes shaking the windows in the building as a pack of bikes rolled onto the lot.

"Fuck. We got company," Shades growled, his voice deep and gravelly from sleep. Then he added, "Lift up, babe, my arm's asleep."

She moved, and he pulled his arm free and swung his legs over the side of the bed. He stood and yanked his jeans on.

"Were you expecting them?" Skylar asked, clutching the sheet to her chest as she sat up.

He turned, doing up his pants, and his eyes dropped to where her hand was fisted. He shook his head. "Stay here."

"Shades—"

"I wanna know you're up here naked in my bed, waiting for me to come back."

"How long will you be gone?"

"Long as it takes to get rid of 'em, babe." He leaned over, his fists in the bed, and dropped a soft kiss on her lips.

As he pulled back, she reached up with both hands to cup his face and bring him back down for a deeper kiss. When she released him, his eyes dropped to her breasts, and she realized she let the sheet fall in order to grab his face.

"Naked, babe. In my bed," he repeated the instruction.

She smiled and nodded. "Whatever you want, baby."

At that, his brows rose and a sexy-as-hell smile spread across his face. "I'm holdin' you to that when I get back up here."

She gave him a saucy smile, tossing her hair over her shoulder. "Are you, now? Then you'd better hurry or I might just get tired of waiting."

With that he cupped the back of her neck, kissed her forehead, and then dipped to whisper in her ear. "You'll wait. 'Cause you want it just as bad."

Then he was gone.

Skylar fell back in the bed and listened to the rattling of the glass door, as if they were trying to get in. Then a pounding on the glass, followed by someone bellowing his name, calling him to "open the fuck up."

***

Shades made his way down the stairs and across the shop, for once in a long fucking time, *not* pleased to see his brothers. Excuses were already forming in his head to try to get rid of them.

He reached the door, flipped the lock, and strode outside.

Whoever had been banging on the door, had walked off. The guys were now gathered around Ghost, who sat sideways on his parked bike, one boot on the ground, one propped on his foot peg, one wrist slung over his hand grip, a cigarette in his other hand. Griz stood next to him lighting up his own smoke.

Gator, Heavy, and Spider were all there, too.

Ghost blew a stream of smoke into the air, and then grinned as Shades approached, taking in Shades' shirtless chest and bare feet. "We get you out of bed, Brother?"

Shades glared. "Sorta."

Ghost took another drag off his smoke and eyed him closely. Too closely. Shades knew he needed to change the subject before his too-perceptive brother was onto him.

"So, what's up?" he asked.

"What the fuck do you mean 'what's up'?" Ghost asked back.

"Got that benefit for Bulldog's widow today. You

forget?" Griz reminded him.

"Shit. That's today?" Shades ran a hand through his hair in exasperation.

"It's Saturday, ain't it?" Gator growled.

"Fuck. I forgot."

"How the hell did you forget?" Heavy snapped.

"Got other shit on my mind, Brother."

Ghost blew another stream of smoke in the air, his eyes narrowing, and replied with a suspicious look, "Apparently."

Shades' eyes narrowed back at him for a moment, and then he asked Griz, "What time's it start again?"

"In like an hour. Stopped by the clubhouse earlier. Your prospect's already over there helpin' the girls set up."

"Let me bum a cigarette," Shades said to Ghost who dug his pack out of his shirt pocket and held it out to him. He took it and shook one out, thinking how he'd neglected to call his prospect that morning to make sure he was on it. Thankfully, 12Gauge was an awesome prospect and knew what he was supposed to be doin' without bein' told all the time. Thank fuck for that small saving grace today.

He couldn't believe he'd forgotten the benefit for Bulldog. Fuck. That really put a kink in his plans with Skylar today. Dipping his head, he lit up, and then blew a stream of smoke into the air.

"Where's Hammer?" he asked.

"He was supposed to meet up with us this morning, but he didn't show," Griz replied, flicking his ashes off his cigarette. "Hope nothin' happened to him."

Ghost grinned. "Oh, I think little Ashley was *lookin' to*

happen to him in a big way last night."

Griz chuckled. "No doubt." Then he looked over at Shades. "Heard you took a taste of that a couple a nights ago."

"I think everybody's had a taste of that by now," Shades replied.

"She's only been comin' round for a couple weeks."

"Well, it doesn't take long for some."

"I disagree," Ghost cut in with a teasing look at Shades. "I think she's been real particular with who she's lettin' in her pants."

"Your point?" Shades asked.

"Brother, she's had her sights on you since she walked on the property."

Shades let out a huff. "That's the case, she needs to get over it, 'cause I ain't goin' back for seconds." Those days were fuckin' done now that Skylar was back in his life. He took another drag of his cigarette with a quick glance over his shoulder back at his shop. Thank Christ this conversation was taking place out in the lot and not inside where she would have overheard every word of this crap.

"Why, bro? She a piss-poor lay?" Spider asked.

No, she was actually quite good, but he'd be damned if those words would ever come out of his mouth. Instead he replied, "You climb on that, you're boarding a fucking crazy train to Loopsville. But hey, you wanna take that ride, have at it. But *I'm* not interested, and I sure as hell don't need her following me around thinkin' that's gonna fuckin' change."

Ghost's eyes narrowed on him again. And Goddamn, he

wished Ghost wasn't so fucking quick to pick up on shit.

"Well, maybe I'll get the down-low from Hammer when he shows up," Spider added.

"Maybe you will."

"Where *you* goin'?" Heavy shouted after Gator as he wandered off.

"I got a board of director's meeting over here. Ya mind?" Gator yelled back over his shoulder, then he ambled to the side of the dumpster and took a piss.

"Fuck, Gator. We don't want to see that shit," Ghost complained.

"Then don't fuckin' look, asshole," Gator yelled back. A minute later he was zipping up and heading back across the lot when Hammer roared in off the street. Hammer turned his handlebars and hit the throttle, aiming right for Gator, who had to jump out of the way to avoid being run over.

"You son-of-a-bitch!" Gator yelled after him as Hammer rode to the back of the lot and made a circle turn, coming back and parking next to the guys.

He dropped his kickstand and climbed off.

"I can't believe you tried to run him over." Ghost laughed.

"Oh, like *you've* never thought about it," Hammer replied, pulling his helmet off and running his fingers over his short hair.

Ghost chuckled.

"Gotta talk to you 'bout something," Spider mumbled, grabbing a fistful of Hammer's t-shirt and pulling him off to the side.

Probably to ask him if he nailed Ashley last night, Shades thought, shaking his head.

Gator walked up. "Did you fuckin' see that? The motherfucker tried to run me over. Why the hell would Hammer want to kill me?"

Griz turned to him with a straight face and said, "Why would *I* want to kill you? Why does your *ex* want to kill you?"

The guys tried to hide their grins.

Gator's eyes narrowed in Hammer's direction.

"Heard you had a minor mishap on the job last week?" Shades asked Gator, hoping to distract him before he decided to retaliate against Hammer for that stunt.

"Yeah," he grunted out.

"Minor mishap? Is that what they call it when you dig through an underground power-line and cut power to half the fuckin' grid?" Griz taunted.

The guys all snickered openly this time.

"Weren't you up for supervisor, Gator?" Heavy asked, pulling a beer out of his saddlebag and popping the top.

"My career path may have taken a minor detour," Gator admitted.

"Yeah, *off a cliff*," Griz added with a snort.

Gator shoved his arm. "Shut the fuck up."

Hammer and Spider walked back over, and Hammer leaned an elbow on Ghost's handlebar. "My bike's makin' that damn noise again. You got a socket wrench I can borrow?" he asked Shades.

Before he could answer, they all heard the roar of

another bike approaching and turned to look as JJ pulled into the lot and parked next to them. He sat astride his bike and took his helmet off, revealing a newly shaved head.

Ghost blew out a stream of smoke, trying not to grin, and asked, “You listenin’ to that little voice in your head again, JJ?”

They chuckled.

JJ ran a hand over his smooth head. “You don’t like it? Tink told me I looked sexy.” He grinned at Hammer, knowing the dig would eat at him.

“You little shit,” Hammer growled and made a move toward him, but Heavy pushed him back.

“Take it easy, bro. Tink wouldn’t waste her time.”

Hammer relaxed back, but pointed a finger at JJ. “Steer clear of her. She’s mine.”

“Oh, really?” Shades asked, turning to Hammer with brows raised.

“Yeah…she…uh…just doesn’t know it yet.”

“Right.” Shades drew out the word with a grin. “Come on, I’ll get that socket wrench. Pull your scooter in.”

Shades moved toward the door, walked in, and hit a button on the wall. An overhead garage door began to slowly roll up. Hammer rolled his bike inside, and Shades walked over to a big red tool chest and opened the top drawer.

The rest of the guys wandered into the shop to get out of the sun.

Shades handed the socket wrench to Hammer. “So, you and Ashley?”

Hammer ran a hand down his face. “Yeah. Me and

Ashley."

"What made you want to fuck that crazy bitch?"

"Well, somebody had to do it. And you know me. Work, work, work."

Heavy almost spit his beer out laughing at Hammer's response.

Shades stifled a grin. "Come on, seriously, Hammer."

"Hell, I don't know. She was looking to hook up with a brother, and I was the only fool in sight."

"You got that right," Heavy snickered. "The fool part I mean."

Shades shook his head. "You've been tryin' to get into Tink's pants forever. You really think rubbin' Ashley in her face is gonna help your chance there, Brother?"

"After three long mutha-fuckin' months of tryin', yeah. Thought maybe it'd make her jealous. Or at least I'd get some kind of reaction out of her."

Shades shook his head. "One of these days I'm gonna have to sit you down and explain women to you."

Hammer bent down and started working on his bike. "Shit, last I heard, you weren't doin' much better."

He couldn't be more wrong, Shades thought. Which reminded him, Skylar was still upstairs waiting for him. In his bed. Naked.

Shit. He needed to get rid of these yahoos. Quick.

"Just fix your damn bike, already," he snapped.

The next bay over, JJ was goofing off with the air ratchet, hitting the trigger and sticking it in Griz's face. *Whir, whir, whir.*

"Get that thing out of my face," Griz growled, grabbing JJ's arm and shoving him.

"Yeah, I hear that's what your ol' lady says," JJ teased back.

"I'm gonna shove that up your ass, you little shit."

"You couldn't catch me, Griz. You're too slow."

Just then a sneeze came from upstairs.

Ghost, who was kicked back in an old metal chair, let it fall to all fours with a bang. He looked over at Shades. "Well, well, well. What have you got stashed up there, Brother? You been keepin' secrets?"

Shades gave him a look that said, *shut your damn mouth.*

Ghost only grinned, then yelled up, "Come on down, darlin'. We know you're up there."

Shades glared at Ghost. "I don't think I've ever been as pissed at you as I am right now, Brother."

Ghost chuckled. "Oh, sure you have."

"You need to keep your mouth shut."

Ghost looked at Shades and grinned. "And you need to perfect your poker face. I knew you were up to something."

A couple of minutes later, a dressed Skylar appeared at the top of the stairs. The guys all turned their eyes to her as she started down.

"Hot damn."

"Holy shit."

"Um, um, um."

"Shut up boys. Show some respect," Shades snapped as he walked over to meet Skylar. He took her hand and helped her down the last couple of steps, then pulled her close, leaned down, and kissed her. Might as well lay it out for the boys right now—she was *his*, off-limits to them all.

"We gonna be here all night?" one of his brothers grumbled, rolling his eyes. Shades glared at him over Skylar's shoulder, not breaking the kiss.

There was a round of laughter.

Shades finally let Skylar up for air. He winked at her, and she turned to face his brothers, and they got a good look at her face. There was silence for about a split second before the shit hit the fan.

"You lucky son-of-a-bitch." This from Gator.

"You *stupid* son-of-a-bitch," Ghost corrected, realizing his brother had just broken a major fucking rule.

"Wait a minute. Ain't she Crash's ol' lady?" Gator asked with a frown.

"Brother, what the fuck are you doin'?" Hammer whispered.

"You messin' around with a brother's ol' lady?" Heavy asked.

"She's not his ol' lady," Shades protested.

"You sure about that, bro?" Spider asked.

"Tell 'em," Shades told Skylar.

"It's true."

"Need more than *her* word on it, Shades. You talk to Crash about this?" Griz asked.

"No."

"Then a call needs to be made."

"He went back to California."

"Don't care if he went to fuckin' California. Don't

matter if he's eatin' chop suey in China. You need to get this straight from him. Not her. You know that, Brother," Griz insisted emphatically.

"Wait. What? You two are together now?" JJ asked, putting the air ratchet down, finally catching up with the conversation.

"Now we know the speed of stupid." Hammer shook his head.

Ghost's phone chirped, and he dug it out and looked at it. Then he looked up at the guys. "Butcher wants to know where the fuck we all are. Let's head out, boys."

Griz pointed at Shades. "Clear this shit up."

With that they all headed out to their bikes.

Ghost hung back. His fingers moved over the keys of his cell as he sent back a reply to Butcher. Then he shoved it in his pocket. His eyes moved from Shades to Skylar and back again, and he shook his head.

"You got something to say?" Shades bit out.

"You know that moment when you give someone advice, they don't fuckin' take it, and then you sit back and watch everything you predicted actually happen? I'm havin' one of those."

"Just shut the fuck up."

"I fuckin' warned you, didn't I?"

"She's nobody's ol' lady, Ghost. I'm not repeating it again."

"Yeah? Well the verdict's still out on that one."

Shades blew out a frustrated breath. "Drop it."

Ghost nodded toward the bikes in the parking lot. "You

comin'?"

"Yeah. You go on."

"You bringin' her?"

"Yeah, we're both coming."

"Better make that call first," Ghost warned.

Shades huffed out a breath. "Okay, Ghost. I got it."

"Later." Ghost turned to leave.

"Tell Butcher I'm on my way," Shades called after him.

"Yup."

When the last bike rolled off the lot, Shades walked over and slammed his palm over the button to lower the garage door. Then he dug his phone out of his hip pocket and scrolled through the contacts until he found Crash. Then he made the call, putting the phone to his ear, his eyes meeting and holding Skylar's.

"Crash, this is Shades. Just got one question. All I need is a one word answer, yes or no, Brother, then I'm hanging up 'cause I'm not in the best mood right now. I don't want to say shit I'll regret. So I'm asking, is Skylar yours?"

His eyes stayed on her as he listened to the response. Then he disconnected the call and shoved his phone back in his pocket. His eyes still on Skylar, he said, "Guess we'll have to save that naked 'anything you want' fun we had planned for later. Go get ready. We got a party to get to."

She smiled, and then ran back upstairs.

CHAPTER TWELVE

Shades was standing in the yard of the clubhouse next to the keg and barely half a beer down before Griz approached.

"You make that call yet?" he asked, his eyes taking in Shades' arm hanging loosely around Skylar as he picked up the nozzle of the tap and began filling his red cup with beer.

"Yeah. It's all good, Brother," Shades replied.

A big grin formed on Griz's face. "So, you claimin' her?"

"Yup."

Then Griz met Skylar's eyes. "Welcome to the family, darlin'."

She smiled. "Thank you, Griz. That's sweet of you."

He turned pink with embarrassment at her words. "Hell, I ain't sweet." Then he turned to Shades. "She better learn how to bitch and moan like the rest of 'em or she ain't gonna make it in this group."

Gator and Hammer walked up.

Gator's baldhead gleamed in the bright sunlight, his eyes

covered by black wraparound shades, and he aimed them toward the gate. "Place sure is packed. Bulldog got one hell of a turnout, huh?"

"Yeah," Hammer agreed, his eyes searching the crowd.

Gator looked over at him. "Let me guess who you're lookin' for."

"Nobody. And mind your own damn business, fuckface."

"Touchy. Touchy. What's eatin' your ass?"

Just then Tink walked up to the keg.

"Nothing now." Hammer snatched a cup off the stack and began filling it. "Here, darlin', I'll pour you one."

Her eyes flicked up to him. "Thanks."

"My pleasure, Tink." He gave her a smile. "And might I add your hair looks particularly lovely today."

"Shouldn't you be sweet talking Ashley? She's the one you fucked last night."

Hammer looked ashamed. "Who'd you hear that from?"

"Her. Are you denying it?"

He looked away. "No. Just saying it was a mistake, Tink."

"You tryin' to get back on her good side?" Gator asked.

"He'd have to suck up at the speed of light," Griz put in with a snicker.

Tink attempted to ignore them as JJ and Heavy walked up.

"Hey, Tink, tell Hammer how much you like my new look," JJ teased, rubbing his shaved head.

Tink rolled her eyes.

"What's the matter, Tink? You on the rag? You ever heard the saying, 'don't trust anything that bleeds for five days and doesn't die'?" Gator smirked.

Everyone hissed in a breath; even his brothers knew not to joke about that shit. At least not right to a woman's face.

"Say the word and I'll kill him for you," Hammer offered.

"I can handle him." She pushed past Hammer and got in Gator's face. "Well, I don't trust anything with two heads and only one brain."

There were a round of "ooowws" among his brothers.

Tink stalked off.

"Boy, you're screwed. She's gonna poison your next draft," Griz advised Gator.

"I mouth off to everybody. People love that about me," Gator insisted.

"Guess again." JJ grinned.

"This shit cracks me up," Heavy added.

Griz looked over at Hammer. "So what exactly *is* your plan to get Tink? 'Cause if that was it, I don't think it's workin'."

"I thought I'd stand next to you."

"Huh? What for?"

"Cause next to you, I look like a catch."

"Seriously, shithead, what's your plan?"

"I'm gonna flirt shamelessly with her, tell her how pretty she is, and then stand back and let her fall at my feet."

"You had me till that last part." Griz grinned.

The guys all burst out laughing.

"Why do you think she's so fucking hard to get?" Hammer grumbled. "You know what? I don't care."

"*You* don't care," Gator mumbled under his breath sarcastically.

"Go on, Hammer. Take a shot. What have you got to lose?" Griz encouraged.

"You're right. Enough of this game playing." Hammer nodded and headed in the direction Tink had gone.

Griz grinned. "I should take up motivational speaking."

Shades shook his head.

"Y'all get a shot glass yet?" Ashley asked as she approached Shades and Skylar. She had a bottle of Jack Daniels in one hand and a stack of little throwaway plastic shot glasses in her other hand. "We're going to do a toast to Bulldog in a minute."

Shades took two off the top of the stack and passed one to Skylar. "Thanks."

Ashley held the bottle up and poured them each a shot. "Now remember to save it for the toast," she reminded them with a wink at Shades.

Shades made no reply, just gave her a cold look.

She moved off through the crowd, making sure everyone had one.

Shades kept Skylar pretty much glued to his side throughout the event. He knew he needed to have a conversation with her about the women here—women he'd been with. There were some good girls who wouldn't cause him a lick of trouble. But some were like Ashley, who most probably would.

He hadn't had time for that with his brothers showing up today. Hell, he'd never intended to bring her by the clubhouse this soon. Things were moving really quickly between them, not that he was complaining.

***

Skylar stood, Shades arms wrapped around her from behind, and watched Butcher bring Bulldog's widow and his two teenage daughters on stage. He approached the microphone that had been set up for the event.

"If I could get everyone's attention…" He waited a moment for the crowd to quiet down. "I want to thank everyone for showing up today. I see a lot of club supporters and friends of the club in the crowd today. The Evil Dead want to give a warm welcome to everyone. We appreciate you coming out today. As you all know, today's event was organized to help out a fallen brother's family. Bulldog was with this club for over thirty years. What some of you outside of the MC may not know is today is also Bulldog's birthday. Before we talk about the money we raised, we got a tradition here on the birthday of fallen brothers. Everybody got a glass?"

The crowd replied with a roar of assurance that they did.

"Then raise 'em up." Butcher held his glass in the air and a hundred others went up as well. "Happy birthday, Bulldog. We miss you, Brother." Then Butcher knocked his back and everyone in the crowd followed suit.

Butcher cleared his throat, took in the crowd, and then he turned to look at Bulldog's widow.

"Darlin', we were hoping to come up with enough to

cover all those medical bills and make the last two payments on your mortgage. We fell a little short on that…"

Suddenly, Shades was dipping his head to Skylar's ear.

"Something I gotta do real quick, babe. Be right back."

And then he kissed her cheek, and he was gone. She watched him make his way through the crowd to the stage. And with two bounds, he was up and on it.

"Hold up, Butcher. Got one more." Then she watched him turn to Bulldog's widow and smile softly at her. His hand went in and under his cut and came out with a long white envelope. He held it in his hands as he explained. "Had a kid bring his car in for repairs about four months ago. Needed a lot of work. Bill ended up bein' about close to two grand. Long and short of it was, he couldn't pay. I gave him time. Then I gave him more time. Kid never came back for it. So, a couple of weeks ago I sold it. Got five grand for it." Then he held the envelope out to her. "There's a cashier's check in here for that amount. I want you and the girls to have it."

Skylar watched as Bulldog's widow broke down in tears and shook her head.

"Shades, I can't take that," she whispered.

"Please, honey. Let me do this for you."

Shades heard one of his brothers' yell out, teasing, "God, is that what you sound like on a date, Shades?"

The crowd chuckled.

"Shut up, asshole," Shades yelled into the crowd. He turned back to Bulldog's widow and held the envelope out to her again. "Take it."

"But you'd be out all that money on the repairs."

"Don't worry about that, honey. It's a done deal. I want you and the girls to have it. That and in the future…any repairs your cars need, I'll do 'em for free. Oil changes, tune-ups, whatever. From now on, you bring 'em to me. That's all taken care of."

She reached out and took the envelope with shaking hands. "Oh, Shades."

"We take care of our own, darlin'."

She broke down and Shades hugged her.

Then Butcher hugged him, pounding him on the back. Then Boot and Slick, who seemed especially choked up, each clutched him in a man-hug, pounding his back as well.

Butcher returned to the mic, but his eyes were on Shades. He grinned big and joked, "You're one fish and a loaf from being a fuckin' saint, Brother."

The crowd roared with laughter.

Butcher turned to the crowd and yelled, "Guess that puts us over our goal!"

A huge cheer went up.

Then he turned his head toward Bulldog's widow, his mouth still at the mike. "You're family, darlin'. Always will be. Guess I can't say it any better than Shades just did. We take care of our own."

She nodded to him, tears in her eyes. Then he turned back to the crowd.

"Thanks to everyone who donated today. Not just members, but we got a lot of club supporters. Many of you participated in the poker run we had last week for Bulldog's family. A lot of you donated today. You know who you are and I want to thank each and every one of you."

He paused as a round of applause burst out.

"And to all the ol' ladies and the women who helped put on this shin-dig."

Another round of applause.

"So enough talkin'. Let's get to celebrating. There are tables of food laid out and the kegs are tapped. Thanks, everyone."

With that another cheer went up, and the party began.

Skylar watched Shades get swamped by his brothers and other people who had shown up for the event. There must have been over a hundred people crowded into the compound.

She felt a presence at her side and looked over to see the girl that had passed out the shots. The pretty blonde they'd called Ashley.

Ashley took a sip from her red plastic cup, observing the melee over the rim, and then her eyes came to Skylar and she smiled… but not a friendly smile, a fake smile.

"I know right now you think you're with Shades," she said, "but I just wanted to set you straight on that. Shades and I are really close. And yeah, when a pretty girl walks by she'll catch his eye. He may even give her like, fifteen minutes. But then he comes back. To me. Because he and I have a connection. Now, whatever you think you have going on with him won't last, and then it'll be time for you to leave. If you don't, you will be sorry."

Before Skylar could even come up with a response, she

was gone, disappearing into the crowd.

What the *hell?*

When Shades returned to her a few minutes later, she straight out asked him about it.

He stared at her for a moment, frowning, his expression saying *what the fuck?* But that's not what came out of his mouth.

Instead he said, "Right. We need to talk. Come on."

He took her hand and pulled her inside the clubhouse, past the bar, up a flight of stairs and into a room that faced the back of the property. It was an office of sorts, but it didn't looked like it was ever used. There was a window that looked out over the back, and that's where Skylar moved after she yanked free of Shades hold. Tossing her purse on the dusty desk, she folded her arms and stared out the window. Noise from the party below drifted up to them.

"Been meanin' to have this conversation with you. Thought I'd have more time. Didn't think we'd be back at the clubhouse this quick. With the boys showin' up like they did today, I didn't get a chance. Should have made time. Should have taken the time."

"Just say what you have to say," she said impatiently.

"Skylar, there've been women since you left. Not gonna deny that. Some of 'em are even here today. But none of 'em have ever meant anything to me. We have some fun, and they go on their way. They know the deal, and they don't expect more. Because I don't *let* 'em expect more. But those times are in the past. You're mine now. And I'm not gonna fuck that up again. Told you that."

"What does that mean?" she asked, still staring out the window at the crowd below.

"Means those women are a thing of the fuckin' past. Means I won't be with anyone but you from now on."

"That's not what Ashley just told me."

"And what *exactly* did Ashley tell you?"

"She said you and her have a connection. She said you may stray, but you always come back to her. She said I wouldn't last fifteen minutes."

"Skylar."

She remained at the window.

"Sky, look at me."

When she wouldn't turn, he took her by the arm and pulled her around.

"First, Ashley's half crazy. Serious, babe, she's delusional. You can believe about one-tenth of what comes outta her mouth. Second, I was with her once. *Once.* You hear me? And I'm not goin' back for seconds. Ever."

Skylar's eyes searched his, wanting to believe him, but not sure she could trust him.

"Baby, we both have pasts. We've been apart ten years. I haven't been a monk. Women come around the club, and, yeah, I partook in that and all that entails. But it's done. I'm tellin' you it's done, and my word needs to be enough for you.

"And although I'm tryin' hard not to think about it, I'm sure you've been with other men. We both need to set that aside if we're gonna be together from now on. And honey, I know with me, you'll be setting aside a hell of a lot more than I will ever have to with you. I get that. And I know the gift you're givin' me in setting that all aside. And the gift you're giving me just in giving me another chance. But bottom line, you giving me another chance has got to mean letting go of all that shit."

He took her head in his hands and pulled her close, staring down at her.

"Do you understand me?"

"You promise me there won't be anyone else?" she asked softly.

"I promise you." He searched her eyes. "That being said, doesn't mean some bitch isn't gonna blindside you like Ashley just did. But you ignore it. You have questions, you come to me. If there are explanations I gotta make, I'll make 'em. But I will never be explainin' that I just fucked someone else. 'Cause that ain't ever gonna happen."

He stared down at her.

"You clear on that?"

She nodded and smiled. "Yes, baby."

He pulled her to him and pressed a tender kiss to her mouth.

A knock sounded at the door. They both turned as the door opened, and Ghost poked his head inside.

"DKs are at the gate."

Skylar felt her stomach drop, and her hands tightened at Shades waist.

"What the fuck for?" Shades growled back at Ghost.

He shrugged. "You better get down here." And then he ducked back out the door and was gone.

Shades looked back at Skylar, kissed her quickly on the mouth and ordered, "I gotta go deal with some stuff. Stay here. Don't leave this room till I get back. We got more shit to talk about. Hear me?"

She nodded, too dazed to say anything, her mind reeling from the terror that pulsed through her veins.

Shades moved through the door, closing it behind him.

Skylar turned as if in a trance and made her way woodenly back to the window. With shaking hands, she jerked the curtains shut, afraid they might spot her. Then she peeked through the side.

She had a perfect vantage point—she could see the crowded yard, and at the big gate in the back of the six-foot wooden privacy fence that enclosed the property sat four bikes.

DKs. The Devil Kings. They were here. Why in God's name were they here? Had they found her? Had they tracked her down? Would the MC give her away? Would they turn her over to them?

Or was she overreacting? Were they here for some other reason? Were they here to join the party? Were the Evil Dead and the DKs friendly? Would they come inside?

If they came inside, if they saw her, then what? Her mind immediately went to an escape plan. She had to run. She had to get out of here.

But she couldn't move.

She stood there like a statue and watched.

She saw a number of club members standing at the gate now, Butcher and some of the older members among them.

Their broad shoulders and leather cuts formed an imposing line, an impressive show of strength and force.

She saw Shades and Ghost make their way through the crowd toward them. Shades pushed his way to the front. There was an exchange between Butcher and one of the DKs—they talked for a few minutes

And then her mind started going to all those dark, suspicious places. What were they doing here? Why were they even in town? This wasn't their territory, she knew that much. It was one of the main reasons she'd come here.

She saw Shades and Ghost heading back toward the house.

Shades eyes flicked up toward the window momentarily. She wasn't sure, with the curtain drawn, if he could even see her. He continued stalking toward the house, a man with a purpose. And he didn't look too happy.

A moment later, the door opened and she turned.

Shades and Ghost strode in.

Shades looked furious as he slammed the door shut and stalked to her.

"You want to tell me why the fucking DKs are at the gate looking for you?"

She tried to play dumb, too afraid to admit the truth. "Me? Why would they be looking for me? That's crazy." She turned away, fiddling with the curtain.

Shades grabbed her arm, spun her around, and bit out, "If I were you, I'd get serious real fast, Skylar."

***

Shades studied Skylar's reaction. She was hiding

something. Apparently something huge if the Devil Kings MC was searching for her.

What the hell had she gotten herself into?

When he'd heard the words come out of that DK's mouth as he talked to Butcher, when he heard the purpose of their visit today, he was stunned speechless. He'd frozen in his boots.

Butcher, thank God, had played it cool, acting nonchalant, pretending he didn't have a clue who this chick was that they were hunting. His brothers, like he knew they would, kept their mouths shut and followed Butcher's lead. But Shades hadn't missed the looks both Boot and Slick had given him or the subtle nod of Slick's head that told him without words to get the fuck inside and talk to Skylar. Which is what he was doing now.

"You heard me," he bit out. She looked panicked and Shades' anxiety went through the roof. What the hell was she involved in? "You want to tell me where you've been the last ten years?"

"I've been in Atlanta, I told you that."

"In Atlanta doing what?"

"Working in a law office."

"Working in a law office?"

"Yes."

"And how does that put you anywhere near the Devil Kings? How would you even cross paths?"

"Six months ago I…" She paused, swallowing.

"Six months ago you what?"

"I delivered papers to a client one day and ran into one."

"And? What happened?" He watched her. Silence. Fidgeting. "Skylar, why do they want you?"

"They think I stole from them."

Holy fuck. He took a deep breath and blew it out. "What *exactly* do they think you stole?"

"Money. Drugs." She shrugged.

He gave her a look that said that answer wasn't enough. "Goddamn, Skylar. Does everything have to be like pulling teeth with you? Just fucking tell me."

"One of them…Rusty is his name…it was his money…and…"

"So this Rusty thinks you stole drugs and money from him?"

"I'm sure Rusty doesn't think anything. He's dead."

"He's dead?" Shades brows shot up, and his mouth went dry. The thought of where this story was headed scared the hell out of him.

"And I'm sure his brothers think *I'm* the one who killed him."

"Why would they think that?" he asked with sick dread filling his stomach.

"Because they found the dagger they knew he gave me for my birthday sticking out of his chest."

"*What?*" Jesus Christ, what had she done?

"I didn't do it. I swear."

"How the hell do you even *know* a DK? Why the hell would he give you a birthday present?" At her silence, the pieces tumbled together in his mind. "You were his fucking *ol' lady?*" he roared the question in disbelief.

She swallowed. “Shades—”

“Christ, that makes you property of the Devil Kings, babe.”

There was stunned silence in the room for a moment before Ghost cleared his throat and waded in.

“The Dead and the DKs are rivals, darlin’,” he clarified for her as well as tried to calm the situation down with a little humor. “So that kind of makes you two like Romeo and Juliet.”

“More like Hatfields and McCoys,” Shades growled.

“Yeah, and *that* ended well,” Ghost added.

“Holy shit.” Shades collapsed in a chair, running his hands through his hair.

***

Skylar studied Shades. He looked infuriated and maybe even devastated. Reading his body language, it was as if she couldn’t have fucked up any bigger than this. But he had to understand. She had to make him understand.

“Please, Shades. It wasn’t like that. I’m not sure you’d say I was an old lady, really,” Skylar tried to explain, really terrified now. They thought she was property of the DKs? Did that mean they’d have to turn her over?

“What *would* you say?” Shades looked at her intently, and she had the feeling her next words were very important. She tried to choose them carefully.

“We were seeing each other. But it was casual. We weren’t living together or anything. I…”

“He give you a property patch?” At her confused frown, he clarified. “You wear a vest?”

"What?"

"A vest. He give you a leather vest? One that said 'Property of Rusty' on the back?

"No. Of course not." He looked at her like he didn't know her. "I'm telling the truth, Shades."

"And the rest? The money and killing him?"

"I didn't do it, Shades. I swear it. How can you even ask me that?"

"How can *I* ask you that? Are you seriously standin' there asking that shit, knowing you took a grand from me on your way out?"

She bowed her head at the reminder. "I did that. I admit it. But I didn't do this. I didn't steal from them. And I didn't kill a man. I could never do that."

"Not even in self-defense?"

"What?"

"He hit you? He hurt you?"

"What? No. He was good to me. It wasn't like that."

"Then how was it exactly?"

"I woke up that morning. He was still asleep. He'd partied the night before and passed out when he came in. I went out to get us coffee at Starbucks. He was fine when I left. When I came back, I found him stabbed on the bed. The bag was gone."

"The bag?"

"He kept it with him all the time. I never looked inside, but I'm sure, the way he kept it close, that it always had something of value in it. I'm not stupid. He was in an MC. Had to be either drugs or money. Payments, extortion, something."

Shades and Ghost exchanged a look.

"Then what happened?" Shades pressed.

"I felt for a pulse. I couldn't find one, and he was so cold, but I called 911 anyway. Before they could arrive, his brothers showed up, and I panicked. It was my dagger sticking out of their brother's chest. If they'd walked in and found me standing there with his blood on me…they'd have killed me. Pulled out a gun and shot me dead on the spot. No questions asked. I knew that. So I ran out the back."

"They see you?"

She nodded. "Yes. One of them saw me driving off. He fired off a couple of shots at me, but I got away."

"So Rusty's dead—by *your* dagger—the money's gone and they see *you* fleeing the scene. Could this situation be more fucked?"

"We need to talk to Butcher," Ghost said, informing Shades of something he already knew.

"We finally found each other again, and it has just brought a shit storm down on my club," Shades growled.

"I'm sorry, Shades. I never meant to cause any trouble for you."

"Fuck."

She paced to the window, peering through the one inch gap in the curtain. She could see the group of men in their leather cuts standing at the back gate, their bikes parked in a line in the alley beyond.

"Get away from the window, Skylar."

She stepped away and turned to study Shades,

wondering what he was thinking, what he would do now.

His eyes bore into hers, as if he was trying to read her as well.

"Are you going to turn me over to them?" she asked in a whisper, fearing his response. If he or his President thought the Devil Kings had some claim on her, they'd feel obligated to give her up to them. She was sure their President wanted no part of this mess. Would they just drag her down there and hand her over? Would Shades allow it? Would he have any choice or say in the matter? What if it was out of his hands?

At his continued silence, she pressed, "Shades?"

He ran a frustrated hand through his hair. "Hell, no. Butcher's getting rid of them."

"They knew I was here? How?"

"They don't know shit. They don't have a clue where you are. They just wanted the Evil Dead's help in tracking you down. Guess you must have told Rusty you were from Birmingham."

"I didn't. I didn't tell any of them about Birmingham."

"Well, they figured it out somehow."

"And if they find out you're harboring me?"

"It could start an all-out war."

"Don't sugarcoat it or anything." Ghost leaned back against the wall, his arms folded.

Shades jumped to his feet and spun on him. "She needs to know what she's done, what she's dragged this club into."

"Oh my God." Skylar grabbed up her purse. "I should go. I..."

Shades grabbed her by the bicep as she made to move

past him. "You're not going anywhere, Sky."

"I don't want to bring trouble down on you. I never meant to do that."

"Too late. Trouble just showed up at the gate. So now you're going to do what you're told."

"And what's that?"

"For starters, you're staying right here while the club meets to talk about this. I'm not letting you run again, babe. Get that through your head."

Not letting you run again. Skylar let his words sink in as their eyes held. He meant them. She'd run once, and he had no intention of letting her do it again.

She heard the bikes fire up in the distance, and they roared off down the street. Skylar exhaled, not realizing she'd been holding her breath. Her whole body sagged with relief and a sob escaped her lips. Shades hauled her close, her face pressed into the leather of his cut. One arm locked around her waist and the other pulled her head tight against him. Being held so close, feeling the strength of his arms around her, she melted into him and felt his protection enfold her. She needed him so. Not just his physical protection, not just his club's protection. She needed the man. *This* man. She needed the emotional support he gave her. When she was weak and scared and tired, he was strong and sure. She felt like she could give it all over to him and he'd take care of it, take care of her.

As if he'd read her thoughts, his voice whispered in her ear, "I'll handle it. I'll take care of it, Sky."

Then his hands were on her upper arms, and he was

pulling back to look down at her, his jaw tight, his face firm. His grip tightened, giving her another shake. "You do what you're told, Skylar. You hear me?"

She had no choice but to nod.

"Let's go." Shades looked at Ghost and jerked his head toward the door.

They left her alone in the room. When the door closed, she hadn't heard it lock. It being an office, she'd noticed it had a deadbolt that opened with a key from the other side, and she'd feared they would lock her in. Moving to the door, she tried it and sighed with relief when the knob turned. Opening it a crack, she could hear them stomping down the stairs, boots pounding on the steps and then down the hall.

She waited, giving them a few minutes, then she crept down the stairs, determined to sneak out and disappear while Shades was meeting with his President. No matter what Shades said, she couldn't cause him trouble. She couldn't involve him in this or put him in any danger.

Reaching the bottom, she dashed down the hall through the clubhouse, past the bar and almost made it to the door. Looking over her shoulder to make sure Shades hadn't seen her, she slammed right into a hard, male body.

CHAPTER THIRTEEN

Slick was jolted by the beautiful woman who'd just slammed into him, but he made a grab to catch her before she fell flat. Unfortunately, her purse fell to the ground, the contents scattering across the floor.

She looked up at him, and he realized it was Skylar.

"Whoa, there, darlin'. You okay?" he asked, his arms reaching out to steady her.

"Yes. I'm fine. I'm so sorry." She bent to gather her things, and he crouched to help her. She frantically grabbed up her wallet which had flipped open, a rolling tube of lipstick, a set of keys, breath mints, and a multitude of other items, and began cramming them back into her purse.

Slick picked up a piece of paper that had obviously fallen out of her wallet. He held it out to Skylar. "I think this is yours." His eyes studied the paper. It was one of those photo strips you get at a photo booth. There were four shots. He could tell they were from a long time ago, maybe twenty plus years ago. They were of a man and a woman. The woman was beautiful and could almost be a dead ringer for Skylar, except for the hairstyle, makeup, and clothes that dated the photo. The man stood behind the woman. He had dark hair that hung to his shoulders, a headband tied around his head, a dark goatee, and light eyes. In one photo he was making bunny ears over the woman's head and she was smiling bright at the camera. In another, he was grabbing her tit, and she was laughing. In another she was kissing the side of his cheek, and he was making a goofy face at the camera.

There was something familiar about the man. Slick could swear he'd seen him somewhere before. And then his eyes tracked back to the middle photo. And he saw it. The ring on the man's hand. The big, silver Evil Dead ring.

Holy shit!

His eyes studied the face again and it clicked.

That was Undertaker.

Skylar tried to snatch the strip from his hand, but he held it just out of her reach.

"Can I have my picture back, please?"

"Who are they?"

"That's my mother. It's the only picture I have of her."

"Your mother?" That explained the resemblance. "And the guy?"

She shrugged. "I always figured he might be my father, but I don't know. Maybe just a guy she knew."

Boot came up and looked over Slick's shoulder at the photo strip. "What are we lookin' at?"

Slick held the pictures up for him to see. "Skylar's mom. And maybe her dad." He nonchalantly pointed with his thumb to the ring on Undertaker's finger.

"Fuck, is that—?"

Slick cut him off with an elbow to the solar plexus. Then he handed the photo back to Skylar. "Your mom's real pretty, darlin', just like you."

She shoved it into her purse. "Thanks," she said distractedly.

"Where you goin' in such a hurry?"

Just then Shades grabbed her by the arm, twisting her around. "She's not goin' anywhere. Are you Skylar?"

She looked up at him with a stricken face, and then he was pulling her along behind him.

Slick watched them go.

Then he turned to Boot. "Come on. We need to talk to Butcher."

They made their way through the clubhouse, down the hall past the bar to the back office that sat next to their meeting room. They found Butcher sitting behind his big desk, one hand running over his beard, appearing lost in thought.

Ghost sat in one of the chairs in front of the desk, his elbows on his knees, his hands clasped loosely between them.

They both looked up as Slick and Boot appeared in the open doorway.

"Come on in, boys. We've got some shit to talk about," Butcher said.

They both stepped into the room, Slick closing the door quietly behind him. "Yeah, the DKs, I know, but there's something else I just got wind of. You need to know."

Butcher's hand dropped. "What's that?"

Slick leaned his palms on the side of the desk and dropped the bomb with no hesitation, as was his style. "Pretty sure Undertaker is Skylar's father."

Butcher, who had begun tapping a pencil on the desk, suddenly stopped and boomed, *"What?"*

"Pretty sure it's true, boss." Boot gave Slick his backing.

"She tell you that?" And then without giving a moment's pause to let Slick give an answer, Butcher's gaze immediately swung to Ghost who was looking up from his chair, stunned. "You know about this shit? You and Shades know about this shit when you not ten minutes ago traipsed in here and dumped that nightmare in my lap about her and the DKs?"

"Fuck, no," Ghost insisted loudly. "Undertaker? The New Orleans *fucking* Chapter President? *That* Undertaker?"

"Yup," Slick replied.

Butcher's eyes swung back to Slick. "What the fuck are you talking about? How the hell did you come up with this bullshit?"

"It ain't bullshit, Butcher," Boot defended.

"She dropped her purse," Slick explained. "Shit went everywhere. One of those little photo strips fell out. I picked it up and looked at it. The girl in the shot was Skylar's mother, back when she was maybe her age. The guy in the picture is Undertaker. Twenty-five years ago, maybe. But it's him. He looked familiar. At first I couldn't place him. Then I saw the ring on his hand. It was an Evil Dead ring. Then I knew where I'd seen him. Knew who he was."

"She tell you that was her dad?"

"Said that was the only picture she had of her mom. Wasn't sure who the guy was. Thought it might be her dad, but she didn't know."

Butcher shook his head. "Skylar was in foster care. Why would she be in fuckin' foster care if—" And then he paused as if putting it all together.

"Exactly," Slick cut in. "That was back when Undertaker was in prison."

"Fuck. That's right. Undertaker did time. I heard he got sent up to Angola. Did eleven years." Butcher ran a hand down his face.

Slick looked Butcher in the eyes. "I heard there was a kid. I also heard when he got out, he lost his shit when he couldn't find this chick or his kid."

"You think Skylar's that kid?" Ghost asked Butcher.

Butcher's eyes narrowed. "I don't know. But I aim to find out."

Ghost stood. "I'll go get Shades."

Butcher looked up at him with menace. "You don't say shit to him about this. Not until I make a call. You hear me?"

Ghost stared at him a moment before nodding slowly. "Yeah. I hear you."

"Christ, if this is true, there goes any option of turning her over," Butcher grumbled.

"That wasn't *ever* an option, was it, Butcher?" Ghost asked, knowing the answer. "She was pretty upset. Scared to death, actually. Shades isn't gonna turn his back on her."

Butcher ran a frustrated hand down his face. "Nothing he can do about it now but hole up for the night and get her calmed down." Then his eyes connected with Ghost. "Go tell him to get her out of here and lay low until we figure this shit all out. Then you come back here."

Ghost nodded and left.

CHAPTER FOURTEEN

Skylar was on the back of Shades' bike.

They'd left the clubhouse and were headed south of town. At first she thought he was taking her back to her place, but he didn't get off the interstate at that exit. Then she thought he must be taking her to his shop, but he didn't take that exit either.

He'd been terse with her when he'd pulled her out to his bike, threw his leg over it, and told her, "Climb the fuck on." She knew he was angry with her, and he had a right to be. She'd really dropped a bomb on him today.

Still, she couldn't help worrying her lip, wondering where he was taking her as they rode on for another fifteen minutes past the exit for his shop.

Finally, he exited the interstate. Skylar frowned when they passed the signage indicating this was one of the exits for Lay Lake.

She'd been out here a time or two with Letty during high school. God, that seemed like a million years ago now.

They drove a few miles before Shades slowed to make a

left turn onto a gravel road. They passed a row of about a dozen mailboxes out by the paved road, and he headed down the gravel at a much slower speed.

It was dusk now. The sun had set, but there was still a vibrant blue light in the sky. They rolled on past several homes—some of them cabins, some of them doublewide trailers. All were neatly kept with pink azalea bushes or camellias. She could see glimpses of the lake between the dark shadows of the towering southern pines, still as glass and reflecting the vibrant blue of the sky. She also could see a dock out in front of each place with pontoon and bass boats tied up to them.

Skylar looked over Shades' shoulder and down the road, and she couldn't imagine where in the world he was taking her.

Finally, as they reached a curve in the shoreline, he turned off onto a dirt drive that led to a small A-frame cabin. It was set up on a slight rise that gave it a magnificent view of the lake and the mountain ridges in the far distance. It was a spectacular vista.

He stopped the bike and shut it off. She stared, stunned.

"Babe, climb off." His words shook her from her daze. She scrambled off, and he dropped the kickstand.

"Where are we?" she asked, glancing around. The place appeared to be quiet, as if it was deserted.

"My place," he informed her as he headed toward the entrance.

"Your place?" she asked, and she was sure her voice couldn't have come out more stunned.

He looked back at her as he jammed a key in the door. "Yeah, my place."

She followed him inside. The interior of the cabin was beautiful, honey-golden wood—the floors, the walls, the ceilings. And beyond, facing the lake, was a stunning wall of windows. It really was breathtaking.

In front of the windows was the living area, a small stone fireplace off to the right. Next to the back entry was a small kitchen with an open bar that faced the lake.

Shades threw his keys on the bar, shrugged out of his cut and tossed it over the back of one of the several barstools, and then stalked into the small kitchen.

Skylar took a few steps into the living room. The view was amazing. There was a deck out front and a dock beyond that, but no boat. Skylar's eyes lifted to the high vaulted ceilings, and she saw the loft above with the kitchen area tucked in under it. There was a staircase leading up off to the left.

"You want something to drink?" Shades asked, and Skylar's eyes dropped from the loft to see that he was standing in front of the refrigerator, one arm propped on the open door.

"I'll take a cola if you have one."

He reached inside and grabbed a couple cans and held one out for her.

"Thanks."

He popped the top on his and guzzled some down.

That he owned this place was just so shocking. Her eyes scanned the room, looking for clues to just who this new

Shades was. There was a plaid couch, but it wasn't old or ratty. It actually seemed like good quality. An old wooden chest served as a coffee table, motorcycle magazines scattered over it. She glanced to the fireplace. A few knickknacks on the mantle, a candle, a small clock, and what looked like a bike part. Her eyes lifted to the large, framed black and white photo. A line of guys on bikes sat facing the camera, some western mountain range in the background.

He came to stand behind her, and she felt his heat against her back.

"Trip to Sturgis couple years back," he enlightened her. "Black Hills. Way in the background, that's Mount Rushmore."

"It's a great shot." She leaned closer. "Which one are you?"

"Third from the right."

"Oh, yeah."

"We still got some shit to talk about. You want to do it in here or out on the deck?"

She turned back to him. His expression was unreadable, but there was tension around his mouth and eyes. He wasn't as pissed off as he'd seemed when they'd left the clubhouse. Perhaps the ride had calmed him down. She looked toward the windows. "The deck."

He opened the door, and she followed him out. It smelled fresh and clean, like pine trees, water, and flowers. She could hear frogs croaking and crickets chirping.

"Have a seat."

She glanced around. The deck wasn't overly large, but it

was V shaped, thrusting out to a point toward the water. Instead of your standard wooden railing with spindles, the deck was enclosed with clear glass panels, so as not to obscure the view. Skylar couldn't help but think that was worth every penny of added cost.

There was a small table and chairs. Shades sat in one, and she took a spot next to him. She sipped her drink and looked out over the lake, suddenly nervous around him, no longer sure he wanted her around. And the last thing she wanted was to be some place she wasn't welcome. She'd had enough of that while growing up to last her a lifetime. Instead of ignoring it, she decided to face it head on. She turned to him and asked, "Do you want me here?"

He looked over at her and frowned. "Of course I want you here."

"Doesn't seem like it."

He let out an aggravated breath. Great. Now she was an aggravation.

"Sky, it's just a lot to take in. You and the DKs and all the rest of it."

"I told you I don't want to cause you trouble, I can go…"

"Skylar, would you shut up about that? It's not about you causing me trouble, and I don't ever want to hear you say anymore shit about leaving."

"Then what is it about?"

"Things just got way more complicated."

"Complicated as in no longer worth the trouble?"

"I didn't say that. Don't go putting words in my mouth."

She shut up and brought the can to her lips, taking a pissed-off drink.

"Babe…" He broke off, took a second to collect his thoughts, and then continued. "We already had some stuff to work through. The list just got longer is all." He shook his head. "Still tryin' to wrap my head around you bein' with a DK."

"Shades, earlier at the party, before they showed up, you went to great lengths to explain to me that we both were going to have to set our pasts aside if we were going to make this work. I think the problem is you only thought it was going to be me having to put your shit aside, not the other way around."

He ran his hand through his hair, his eyes on the horizon. "Maybe. Maybe it's just that if there were any guys in your past…"

"What?"

"In my head, I guess I figured it'd be a pencil-pushing, geeky accountant or some piss-ant sales manager." He lifted his can and shook his head. "Not a member of the fuckin' Devil Kings."

She watched him take a drink, his eyes still on the horizon. "So where do we go from here?"

"I don't know."

Her stomach dropped. That sounded like he wasn't sure their relationship could go *any*where. "Tell me we can work through this, Shades. Please. I don't want to lose you again."

He turned his head then, his eyes coming to hers, and his hand reached for hers. "You're not going to lose me again,

Sky. I'm in this. You understand? For the long haul."

She nodded and felt the pressure around her heart ease.

His eyes went back to the view. "Just gotta figure some shit out."

"Can we…figure it out in bed?" she asked softly.

His head swiveled, and he studied her a long moment. He set his can down and took hers and set it down as well. "First smart thing you've said all day."

She rolled her eyes.

He stood up and pulled her from her chair, and then he strode through the door and up the stairs. And she was hurrying to keep up with him.

When they got to the loft, she realized it was much bigger than it'd looked from below. There was plenty of headroom where she'd thought the ceiling would have been closing in on them. There was room enough for the large king that sat front and center. How he'd gotten a bed that size up here, she couldn't imagine. Behind it was a large window. He moved to it and pushed it open, letting in a cool breeze. When they slept, their heads would be right next to it. She liked that. She'd be able to lie and listen to the night sounds.

Shades moved toward the bed, pulling his t-shirt over his head as he went. Her eyes drifted over his powerful shoulders to his narrow hips and the two dimples at the small of his back. Then he turned, catching her checking out his ass.

He grinned.

As he tossed his shirt to the floor, she took in his chest and abs. And then his hands were unbuckling his belt. He jerked it free and it hit the floor with a bang and a clatter, and their restraint seemed to fall with it, as if the sound triggered the release of their self-control. They both moved simultaneously toward each other, coming together with grasping arms and clutching hands.

Shades grabbed her head, and his mouth plundered hers. It was almost as if he had something to prove, as if he was claiming her, as if all the talk of her with a Devil King member had driven something in him.

She was just as urgent to prove to Shades that it was him she wanted; it was him she'd *always* wanted.

He broke the kiss long enough to pull her shirt over her head. His hands immediately went to the waist of her jeans, but even in his hurry, his eyes took the time to travel over every inch of her exposed cleavage. He opened her jeans, and then squatted to yank them to her feet. She stepped out and kicked them aside. The pretty, matching lace bra and panties had him pausing a moment to take in the sexy vision she presented to him.

He hit his knees, and his big hands closed over her waist, then slid up to the edge of her bra and back down to the top of her panties. He pressed a soft kiss to her belly, and then his hands slid up her back to the closure of her bra. The hooks popped free with a flick of his fingers, and then he drew the straps slowly down her arms and tossed the bra aside.

On his knees, he was the perfect height to capture a nipple with his hot mouth. Skylar's head fell back as her eyes closed, and she felt the pull and tug shoot through her as his mouth drew deeply. Her fingers threaded through his hair, clutching him to her.

His hands ran over her bottom, his fists kneading her cheeks as his mouth moved to her other nipple. She felt her knees weaken, and then his arms were locking around her thighs, holding her upright during his unrelenting ministrations.

Then his mouth broke free as he trailed a line of soft open-mouthed kisses down her belly. His hands hooked in the lace at her hips and drew them down her hips.

Before she could draw a breath, he was on his feet and tossing her on the bed, his body coming down on top of her. She wrapped her arms around him, loving the feel of his weight on her as his muscular chest pinned her to the bed.

His hands held her head still as his mouth plundered hers.

The rough material of his jeans stroked over her skin as he moved on top of her, his knee forcing her legs apart. He settled his hips in the cradle of her thighs, the course fabric rasping over her sex, and she moaned. He rocked his hips, dragging against her again as he held himself above her. Studying her reactions as they played across her face, he smiled, repeating the motion again and again until she was writhing underneath him.

“I want you wild and needy and hungry for it, baby.”

“I am. I am.”

He shook his head, stroking again. “More.”

Her hands slid down his back, scratching lightly, and she grabbed his ass, pulling him even harder against her. She could feel his erection, hard and long pressed against the placket of his jeans, pressing against *her*.

And then it wasn't enough anymore—she reached her hands between them, frantically working the opening of his jeans. He lifted his weight to give her better access, dipping his head to watch as she yanked his jeans down and pulled him out.

"Hurry, honey," she whispered.

As soon as his loose fitting jeans fell to his knees, he dropped down, his weight coming between her thighs and he thrust his hips, driving into her as her legs wrapped around him, urging him on.

He rolled them over, letting Skylar straddle him. His warm big hands clasped her hips, and he moved her up and down.

"Ride me, Sky."

She put her hands on his rock solid chest, and leaning forward, began to undulate on him, rocking her hips slowly against him, rubbing against him over and over.

"Oh God, that feels good," she whispered brokenly.

He grinned, his hands squeezing tighter, and he ground her against him. "Let me see you come. I want to see you come, pretty girl."

She threw her head back and rocked against him again and again until a sheen of sweat broke across her skin. As she got close her gaze dropped and took in his sexy half-closed eyes that were locked on her jiggling breasts. His hands broke their tight hold on her hips to glide up her waist and close over her breasts as he thrust up into her.

She collapsed on top of him with a groan as an orgasm

broke over her.

His arms wrapped around her, and a moment later he was rolling them, putting her back on bottom, taking control.

She could feel him still rock hard within her.

He brushed the hair back from her face.

"I want to take you hard, baby. You gonna let me?"

"Yes. I want you to."

He went up on his knees, his hands clutching her hips as he began thrusting hard, pounding into her in a frenzy of need. His breathing became ragged, his body a mass of raging need as his control broke. He hammered into her, and she'd never seen anything so erotic, except maybe a few minutes later when he crashed over the edge in a wave of ecstasy. He slammed home, and his chest heaved as he floated down. All the strength and energy drained right out of him, and he lowered on top of her.

And it was beautiful.

Her arms went around him, holding him close, her fingers threading in his hair, her lips trailing soft kisses up his neck to his ear. She felt him smile against her cheek.

"I love that," he murmured.

"Sex?"

"No, you touching me like that." And then he chuckled into her neck. "The sex too."

She continued touching him softly, stroking his back and neck.

"I can't move." His voice was muffled against her.

"I don't want you to."

"Good."

To prove her point, she wrapped her legs around him, moaning lightly when the tenderness in her thighs made itself known.

"You're gonna be sore tomorrow." Was that pride in his voice she heard?

"Yes." She couldn't help the smile on her face.

"Good."

"Good?"

"I want you to think about me being between your legs, deep in your pussy, every time you feel that tenderness." He arched into her to underline his words, and she moaned again.

His mouth moved to her neck, and he began sucking.

"What are you doing?" she squealed.

He released her with a pop, and then lifted up to grin down at her. "Marking you, baby."

"Did you give me a hickey?"

He grinned, his eyes dropping to her neck. "Maybe."

"What are we, sixteen?"

He brushed a thumb over the mark. "It's kind of turning me on."

Since he had yet to pull out of her, she could tell.

He dipped his head, and his eyes skated down her body. "Maybe I'll put some more in other places."

"You'd better be teasing."

He waggled his brows without answering.

***

Shades pulled out slowly, moved to his back and drew Skylar against his chest. He stroked his fingers absently through her hair. Now that they'd both gotten off, thoughts crowded his mind again. Life never seemed to give them a break or cut them any slack; it was like the fates were plotting against them. Fuck that. They'd make their own fate. He wasn't letting anything get between them again.

"I'm scared, Shades," she whispered. Obviously reality was crowding her head also.

"Of the DKs?" he murmured against the top of her head into her silky hair.

She nodded against his chest.

"I'll take care of it, honey. Don't you worry about it. I'm not going to let anyone hurt you."

"I messed up big time."

"No you didn't." He grinned. "Except maybe your choice in men."

She lifted her head to look at him.

His eyes studied hers. "You deserve better, you deserve that good life.

"But babe, gotta say, you seem to have one fatal flaw." He shook his head. "You always seem to choose the worst men for you. Men who do nothing but bring you down."

"Not always. Not you."

"Babe."

"Maybe after you pushed me away I didn't think I *deserved* good, deserved what I wanted. You get pushed away enough, you stop expecting anything good. All my life I've been passed from home to home. Do you know how that makes a person feel? Unwanted. Unloved. Why should I expect that pattern to change? It's been engrained in me my whole life. Don't get attached. Don't let yourself care, because the moment you do, whatever it is you care about will be ripped from you. That's life. That's *my* life."

He took her face in his hands. "Not anymore, Skylar. Not anymore."

Her arms tightened around his gut.

He kissed her forehead and murmured with a smile pulling at the corner of his mouth, "You're not off the hook for this, though."

"I'm not?"

"I'm gonna think up some ways you can pay me back for all the trouble you're causing, woman," he teased.

"Payback, huh?"

"Um hmm. And you can start with this." He slid his hands in her hair and pushed her head slowly toward his crotch.

She lifted up and looked at him with a smile. "Oh, for starters, huh?"

"Yup. I'll come up with some other stuff while you're down there getting busy."

She slid lower. And she got busy.

***

Shades looked down at Skylar.

His fingers threaded through her hair as she worked him. She looked so beautiful, her mouth worshipping him, taking him. He thought back to the events of the day, the DKs showing up at the gate. He knew she wanted to run. It was always her first response, her mode of operation. She got scared or nervous and *bam*, she took off. But not this time.

This time he wouldn't give her a chance to get skittish. This time he'd make sure she didn't run.

His eyes closed as she worked her magic, and he relaxed, letting go of all the problems weighing down on both of them. He rode the high, stroke after stroke, until his jaw clenched, he growled and exploded into ecstasy.

When he fell back to earth, she slid up on his chest and his arms wrapped around her, rough palms stroking her satin skin. He murmured in her ear, "It's all gonna be all right, Sky."

"You don't know that," came her soft response.

One hand threaded into her silken hair, fisting gently at the back of her head. His arms tightened. "Baby, you gotta have some faith in me."

"I'm scared I'm going to lose you," she murmured into his chest.

He tugged her head back to search her eyes. "No one and nothing is going to get in our way or pull us apart again. Do you understand me?"

She nodded.

"I love you, Sky."

"I love you, too, Shades. I always have."

He guided her mouth down to his, his tongue delving inside for a long tender kiss. Then he gathered her close, her head tucking under his chin.

"Sleep, my baby. I've got you."

And she did, at least she tried, for a few minutes.

"Shades, you awake?" she whispered.

"Hmm?"

"You awake?"

"I am now."

She propped up on one elbow and looked down at him, running her fingers absently across his abs and over his chest. "Can I ask you something?"

He cocked one eye open to look at her questioningly.

"Do you bring women here?"

A smile pulled at his mouth. "Nope."

"I'm the first?"

"You're the first."

She smiled.

"I see you like that."

"I do like that."

"Go to sleep," he ordered, his eyes already closed.

A moment later, "Hey, honey?"

"Yeah, babe."

"Where's the bathroom?"

"Gotta pee?"

"Uh, yeah."

He grinned, his eyes still closed. "Sucks for you, then, babe, 'cause it's downstairs, behind the kitchen."

"Damn."

He chuckled.

CHAPTER FIFTEEN

Skylar laid awake in Shades big king size bed. The window was open and she could hear the early morning sounds coming through it—a bird call echoing across the water, the quiet trolling motor of an early rising fisherman setting out at dawn.

She sat up and gazed out the wall of windows that faced the lake. In the early morning mist, with just the pale gray light of dawn before sunrise, she could see a small boat moving slowly across the glass-like stillness of the water, broken only by the small trail of ripples left in the boat's wake.

She felt a strong arm lock around her waist as Shades pulled her back down. He was on his stomach, facing away from her, the sheet riding low on his ass. His head turned on the pillow, and he cracked one eye to look at her.

"Goin' somewhere?"

She smiled, twisting in the bed, and ran her palm lightly over the smooth bronze skin of his back, her eyes moving over him, following the trail of her hand.

"Just looking at the water," she replied lazily and watched his eyes slide closed again.

"It still there?" he asked, his sleepy voice muffled by the pillow, and she saw a small smile pull at the corner of his mouth.

She grinned. "Yeah, it's still there."

"Funny how that works."

Her fingers trailed up his spine to his neck and over to his ear to toy with the curls there.

"My baby want to play?" he asked in a deep, gravelly voice, his eyes still closed.

"Maybe." She leaned down to press a line of kisses down his temple, his cheekbone, his jaw, his neck.

"Mmm. Feels good," he murmured with a moan. "Keep goin'."

She trailed soft brushes of her mouth across his shoulder to between his shoulder blades, and then her lips began a descent down his spine, one slow soft kiss at a time. She didn't miss a single vertebrae.

"You get low enough I'm gonna roll over," he warned.

She rose up and smiled down at him, her hand running over his ass, pushing the sheet down with it. "Sounds like a workable plan."

Her palm stroked over his firm buttocks, her eyes taking it in. He had the best looking ass she'd ever seen.

"You likin' what you see, pretty girl?"

"You have a beautiful backside."

He rolled over with a grin. "And how do you like the flip

side?"

She grinned back, her hand stroking over him. "Impressive."

"Damn straight," he insisted, his brows raised and his teeth flashing.

Her mouth came down on his nipple, and she drew hard on it. His hand fisted in her hair, and his dick bobbed in reaction. "Babe."

She trailed a line of kisses down his abs, pausing to dip in his bellybutton with her tongue and then lower, following the sexy trail of hair down, down. She kissed his erection from root to tip. She pushed his hands down on the bed, and he fisted them in the sheets.

"You gonna tease and torment me, babe?"

She grinned up at him. "Maybe I'll give you a hickey?" she teased with a wink.

"Ouch." He grinned.

"Payback's a bitch, honey."

"Baby, have mercy."

Her mouth moved to his inner thigh and she clamped down, sucking hard.

"Ummm," he groaned. Then he sat up, grabbed her legs, and clamped his mouth on her inner thigh, giving her one right back.

"Hey, no fair. You already gave me one."

"Then you better find a better use for that mouth of yours," he warned with a brow raised and a smile.

So she did.

***

Several hours later, the midmorning sun had risen in the sky, its heat having burned off any lingering morning mist.

Skylar could feel the warmth of the sun coming in through the window, heating her skin. It was such a delicious feeling that she didn't want to open her eyes. Apparently, neither did Shades, as he hadn't moved an inch from where he'd collapsed after their last bout of amazing morning sex.

She smiled, recalling it.

The distant rumble of a set of motorcycle pipes broke through her quiet meditations. She tilted her head up, the crown of her head burying into the pillow as she looked out the window behind the bed. She paused and listened.

Yep. A motorcycle. Coming this way.

"Fuck. Not again," she heard Shades growl into the pillow. He was flat on his stomach, his head in the pillow, facing away from her.

She laughed. "You realize the only place this doesn't happen is at my house."

"Yeah, babe, cause they don't know where you live yet. Give it time. It'll happen."

"Oh no, it won't. I'm never telling them where I live. Besides, the entrance is gated."

"Did that stop me?"

"No. I guess not. Damn."

The motorcycle sound got closer, and she went up on an elbow, twisting to peer out the window to the drive below and the gravel road beyond.

"Just one bike," she announced.

"Yeah, babe. I know. That was obvious by the sound of

only one set of pipes."

"Oh."

"I'm guessing it's Ghost."

"Yep," she confirmed as the bike pulled right up to the cabin, and she got a good look at the rider. When Shades just continued to lie there, she asked, "Does he do this often?"

"No, not this early."

"Does that mean there's trouble?"

He rolled over and looked at her, chuckling. "Yeah, and I'm lookin' at it. You're the only trouble around here, baby."

She whacked him with her pillow.

He grabbed it out of her hands, threw it on the floor, and hooked his hand to the back of her neck to pull her down for a kiss. One kiss turned into two, then three, until she finally pushed against his chest and rose up to look down at him.

"Go greet your guest."

"You gonna wait for me naked in my bed till I run him off and come back up here?"

"Yeah, that worked out so well the last time."

He laughed as he swung out of bed and yanked his jeans on.

"One of these days, babe." He leaned down and kissed her. "That's what I want. To come home and find you naked in my bed, waiting for me." He kissed her again, then drew back an inch to look down into her eyes. His crinkled at the corners with his smile. "Fucking heaven, all laid out and waiting for me."

"Baby," she murmured softly, touched by his words.

He cupped her face and pulled her up to her knees. He

gave her another long kiss, her naked body flush against his jeans. When he broke the kiss, he reached down with one hand, and his palm cracked against her ass as he grinned, "Better get dressed, pretty girl."

"Oww," she whined with a grin.

The back door opened, and Ghost's voice could be heard.

"Who wants coffee?"

"Me!" Skylar shouted back down.

"Then get your sweet butt down here and make us some, Sugar."

She laughed and rolled her eyes.

"I got it, babe," Shades said, kissing her again and then bounding down the stairs.

How did that man have so much energy this early, especially after all the sex they had last night, and then again this morning?

And then she smiled. Maybe that's what gave him all that energy.

***

When Skylar came downstairs, Shades was in the kitchen making coffee. She wandered up behind him and gave him a kiss on the neck. "Need any help?"

"I got this. It'll be ready in a minute. Why don't you go keep our visitor company?" He nodded toward the deck.

Skylar followed his eyes and spotted Ghost out on the deck leaning his elbows on the railing, taking in the lake, and smoking a cigarette. She wandered outside.

Ghost looked over his shoulder when he heard the sound

of the sliding glass door opening and closing.

"Hey, Hotrod," he greeted her.

"Hotrod?" She frowned questioningly. "Why Hotrod?"

Ghost grinned. "Saw you do that burnout in that cute little sports car of yours the other day. Spinnin' tires and throwin' gravel, girl."

"Right." Skylar grinned as she came to stand next to him, her eyes taking in the lake.

"Mind if I smoke?" he asked, turning the hand that held his cigarette, showing it to her.

"Go right ahead." She leaned on her elbows, like he was.

He took a drag, blew the smoke up, and then looked at her. "You doing okay today?"

"I'm fine."

"You weren't yesterday. You were a borderline basket-case."

"Yes, I suppose I was." She looked out at the lake, and then met his eyes again. "Every time I think everything is going along fine, life always finds a way to knock me back down."

"Well, darlin' you know what I always say? When life gives you lemons, squeeze them in people's eyes."

He made her laugh. "Are you *ever* serious?"

"Try not to be."

She grinned. Then her face sobered. "You don't have anything to say? I mean, about yesterday and well, everything?"

He grinned and shook his head. "Oh darlin', I have a lot to say, but I'll keep my mouth shut because I've learned that anything that starts with the phrase, 'don't take this the wrong way' has a zero percent success rate."

She tried to hold back a grin. "I appreciate that."

"I will say this, though—you mean something to him. I don't know the story of whatever went on between you years ago. He won't talk about it. But I do know he's happy you're givin' him another chance."

"Thanks for telling me that."

Then Ghost leaned closer, bumping shoulders with her and teased, "So, when he did you last night, I hope he showed you just how really, *really* grateful he was."

She blushed, and he turned back to the lake, taking another hit off his smoke.

"I should be the one who's grateful. I've caused him so much trouble. I never meant to bring my problems to him. He was so angry yesterday."

Ghost turned to look at her. "Maybe Shades isn't the most subtle guy, maybe he can be a little demanding…"

"A little?" She laughed.

"And maybe he doesn't have my awesome sense of humor…" He paused to smile at her, but then he got serious, his eyes capturing hers. "But if your life's in danger…he's your guy."

Skylar thought about his words as Ghost went back to quietly smoking and studying the lake. Her life *was* in danger, and there was no one she trusted to protect her more than Shades. *My guy*. That's what she wanted more than anything.

"Ghost?"

"Yeah, darlin'?" He turned back to her.

"What do you know about Ashley?"

He let out a huff. "Ashley, what a waste of boobs."

Skylar couldn't hold back the giggle this time. "That so?"

He looked over at her. "Just sayin', she's not just crazy, she's bat-shit crazy. She's *beyond* bat-shit crazy. Something's not right in that girl's head."

"What do you mean?"

"I mean, if she were a guy, I'd be wondering if there wasn't someone locked in her basement. *That* kind of crazy."

"Ew." Skylar made a face.

"Exactly."

"So why do you guys let her come around?"

"She's got a rockin' body. It's not any more complicated than that, darlin'. Guys take a taste and throw her back. Eventually that'll get old, and we'll run her ass off."

"God, that sounds cold."

He shrugged. "Way of the world."

She huffed out a laugh. "No, it's *not*."

He grinned. "Correction. Way of the MC world."

"That's pretty jaded. Don't you ever think about these girls' feelings?"

"Nope."

"Nope?"

"They know what they're signin' up for. Nobody's forcing 'em. They come of their own free will. They party. They have some fun with a brother. No harm in that."

"How did you manage to get this far in life without some

woman driving a stake through your head?"

He grinned big. "Never said they haven't tried."

Shades walked out with three mugs of coffee and set them on the glass table. They all sat down.

"You're out early," Shades said to Ghost over the rim of his mug. "Know this ain't no social call, so spill."

"Butcher sent me out. Wants you to come in and talk to him."

Shades stared at Ghost. "What, a phone call couldn't have done that?"

Ghost shrugged. "No clue. I do what I'm told."

"Something you're not tellin' me, Brother?"

Ghost's eyes moved from Shades to Skylar and back, and she suddenly felt like they needed privacy. She started to push her chair back. "I'll leave you two to your business."

"Not necessary, darlin'," Ghost insisted. Then he looked at Shades. "I've got nothing I can tell you, Brother. I just need to make sure you show up. Maybe he thought you and Skylar might slip town."

Shades stared at Ghost, and then took a sip of his coffee. He looked calm, but Skylar noticed his jaw tighten. Something was up, and he knew it. But apparently, he was letting it slide.

"What time's he expecting us?"

Ghost lifted his chin toward the mug in Shades' hand and grinned. "You got time to drink your coffee."

"Gee, thanks."

"You're welcome," Ghost replied, still grinning.

CHAPTER SIXTEEN

Shades walked into Butcher's office.

Butcher looked up. "Sit down."

Shades frowned at his gruff tone. He closed the door and took a seat.

"This about the DKs?"

"This is about a lot of shit." Butcher paused to light up a cigarette, and then he tossed his silver Zippo lighter on the desk with a clatter. His eyes met Shades' through the smoke. "You plan on makin' Skylar your ol' lady?"

Shades didn't hesitate. "Absolutely."

Butcher took a deep irritated breath. "I get it, Brother. I do. She's beautiful. Fuckin' gorgeous, and we all love her. But she's comin' with a shit ton of baggage. You sure you want to sign on for that?"

Shades ran a frustrated hand down his face and blew out a breath. "I know what kind of shit storm this is bringing down on the club. The DKs showin' at the gate yesterday and—"

"This ain't about that. The fuckin' DKs I can deal with."

"Then what's this about?" Shades frowned in confusion.

Butcher hollered out, "Ghost, get in here!"

The door opened immediately, as if Ghost had been waiting right outside. What the fuck was going on?

"You get it?" Butcher snapped.

Shades watched Ghost's eyes flick to him, and then he reached inside his vest. He pulled out a small rectangular paper and slid it across the desk to Butcher. Then he looked at Shades and said, "Sorry, Brother. Boss's orders."

Shades eyes dropped to the paper. It was a photo strip. Butcher snatched it up and held it out.

"She look familiar?" he asked cryptically.

Shades eyes moved from Butcher to Ghost, and then finally to the photo strip. He took it from Butcher's hand and examined it. *Fuck.* The chick was a dead ringer for Skylar.

"What the hell? Where did you get this?" His question was for Ghost, his eyes boring into him.

"Skylar's purse."

"You took it out of her purse?"

"I told him to," Butcher barked.

"What the fuck for?"

"Slick saw that yesterday. She dropped her purse on the floor, and it fell out. She says that's her mother."

Shades looked back down at the photo, and then back at Butcher. "Okay. That's her mother. What of it?"

"It's the man in the photo who's important," Butcher clarified.

"Yeah, what about him?"

"Take a closer look. See his ring?"

Shades studied the series of photos again until he found the only shot that showed the man's hand. And then his stomach dropped. *A fucking Evil Dead ring*. His eyes snapped up to Butcher. "Who is he?"

"I'm thinking that's Skylar's father."

"Who the fuck is he?"

"Undertaker," Butcher paused, and then he dropped the bomb. "The New Orleans Chapter President."

Shades slumped back in his chair, his eyes sliding closed as the implications of what this all meant washed over him. Christ, could this girl get any more complicated? Could this situation get any more fucked?

"I made a call down there yesterday and had a chat with him."

Shades eyes came open. Butcher had his full attention now. "What did he say? He claim her? Where the hell has he been all these years? Fuck, he just abandoned her to the system when she was barely three years old. Do you know what hell her life has been because of it?"

"Whoa. Pull the reins in, Son. You don't know the whole fuckin' story."

"Do you?"

"I know some of it. I know what Undertaker told me."

"And what the fuck was that?"

Butcher yanked open the bottom drawer of his desk and brought out a bottle and a short tumbler. Then he poured a double shot of Jack and slid it across the desk toward Shades. "Knock it back, and we'll talk."

Shades tipped it back then slammed the glass down.

"Need another?"

"No. Just tell me."

"Undertaker was seeing some girl when he got sent up to Angola. There was a baby. He ended up doing eleven years. When he got out and couldn't find them, he lost his shit. Way he tells it, he searched. I'm not sure how hard or how long. All the pieces fit. It's possible Skylar's mom is the girl he was seeing, and Skylar was that baby."

"So, he's on his way here?"

Butcher shook his head. "He can't leave right now. Too much shit goin' down with the Death Heads MC. He's dealin' with the same problems we got. They're trying to push into their territory in Louisiana from Texas, just like they're trying to push into the Alabama Gulf Coast from Florida."

"And he can't take time to figure this out? A lead on his long lost kid comes up, and he can't be bothered?"

"Settle down, Shades. He was torn up when I told him. I'm the one who offered a solution to make it easier on him."

"And what's that?"

"You're taking her down there to meet him."

"I'm *what*?" Shades roared.

"You and Ghost are going to take her down there."

Shades' eyes darted to Ghost who appeared to want no part of this, but he was a good soldier, and he would do what he was ordered. Shades' eyes returned to Butcher.

"Take her down there? You're joking, right?"

Butcher shook his head. "No, I'm not joking, Shades.

You're taking her down there to him. But you aren't telling her why. If we're wrong, if he doesn't recognize her or this photo, then she never has to know."

"And what reason would I have for taking her down there? What the fuck you want me to tell her?"

Butcher shrugged. "You gotta make a run, and you want her with you. It makes sense. You'd want to be protecting her from the Devil Kings, right? You wouldn't leave her here alone, unprotected. It's a short run. A road trip. You'll have fun. Convince her. You two just got together. I wouldn't think you takin' off for a few days would be such a hardship."

Shades listened to all of Butcher's reasons.

Ghost looked down at Shades. "I'll meet you and Skylar by the bikes, Brother."

Then he walked out the door.

Shades ran a frustrated hand through his hair, scratched his scalp in aggravation, and then looked back up at Butcher. "You expect us to leave now? Right now?"

"Sooner the better, Son. Get it over with. Plus it keeps her well away from the DKs' reach."

"For now."

"Right. We'll sort that fuckin' mess when you get back."

"If I get back."

Butcher grinned. "Afraid Undertaker won't accept you as a son-in-law?"

"One of us may kill the other before this is through."

Butcher's brows rose, and in all seriousness he growled, "I trust you to not let that happen. Either one."

***

Shades stalked out into the main room of the clubhouse and approached the bar where Griz, who'd been tasked with keeping an eye on Skylar for him, sat drinking a beer. Only she wasn't sitting next him where Shades had left her.

"Where's Skylar?" he snapped.

"She's upstairs in the witness protection program. Her new name's Bambi." Griz grinned. When Shades didn't crack a smile, he continued, "What, too soon?"

"There's something seriously wrong with you."

"What? I kid. I joke. People love that about me. I'm a fun guy."

"Where is she?"

"Chill out, she's throwing darts with Hammer." Griz nodded toward the dartboard across the room.

Shades stalked across the room. With a chin lift to Hammer, he grabbed Skylar by the arm. "Let's go."

As he hustled her out the door, she asked, "Where are we going?"

"To your place, then to the shop. I'll explain later."

Without another word, she dutifully followed him out to the bikes, took the helmet he handed her, and climbed on behind him. If she kept this blind obedience up throughout the trip, maybe things wouldn't go so bad after all, he thought. Though, chances were, it'd all go to hell.

Ghost revved his throttle and looked over at him. "I'll pack a bag and meet you at your shop."

Shades nodded and Ghost took off. Shades gunned his own throttle and pulled out before he gave Skylar time to ask about what Ghost meant. They rolled through the side streets, got up on I-59, and headed for I-65. He took it south of town, over the mountain, exiting on 119. A few minutes later he was pulling down her drive and parking in front of her door.

They both climbed off. He trailed her up the stairs and waited by the door while she unlocked it, and then deactivated the alarm. He followed her inside, where she turned to him.

"So, are you dropping me off here or…?"

"No. Go upstairs and pack a bag. Something small that can fit on the bike."

She frowned up at him. "Why? Am I staying at your place?"

He shook his head. "I'm getting you out of town. Away from the DKs."

She swallowed and her voice got soft. "Oh. How long will we be gone?"

"Four days. Maybe longer. Until this blows over."

"Shades, I don't think this is going to just blow over."

"It's being taken care of," he lied.

"How?"

"Sky, just go upstairs and do what I told you."

"Four days?"

"Yeah."

"And you think I can pack all that in a backpack? Baby, you don't know women."

"One pair of jeans. A handful of tank-tops. Some panties." Then he grinned. "No, scratch that last item. And a jacket. That's all you need. Anything else, we can pick up along the way."

"Where are we going?"

"You'll find out when we get there. Now move."

"Okay, okay." She headed up the stairs.

He shouted after her, watching her ascend in the cute pair of sandals she'd been wearing. "And wear boots. We'll be riding."

***

Twenty minutes later they were pulling up at his shop. Ghost was already sitting in the lot waiting for them.

Shades went inside, grabbed a couple of things, and came back out. He knelt and shoved them in one of his saddlebags. When he stood, he looked at Ghost. "Sorry you got dragged into this shit."

Ghost grinned. "That's okay, I totally wanted to drop everything I was doing today to take care of your bullshit."

The corner of his mouth turned up in a half-smile. "Wasn't my choice, Brother."

"I know it."

Shades turned to Skylar and asked, "You need to hit the john, do it now. I ain't stoppin' a million times."

With that, she nodded and headed inside.

Ghost leaned sideways back against his bike, his ass in the seat, his legs crossed at the ankles. His head turned as he watched Skylar leave, then his eyes swung back to Shades and he asked, "She ever ridden long distance?"

"Not that I know of."

"You do realize this ride is over three hundred miles."

"Know how far it is, Ghost."

"Just sayin'."

"She'll be fine."

"Right. We won't make it past Tuscaloosa before her ass is sore."

"Probably not."

"You're not stoppin'?"

"Not sayin' that. We'll have to stop for gas."

"These tanks, we got two hundred miles. Maybe. My bet? She'll give out long before we have to stop for gas, Brother."

"Yeah, probably," Shades conceded with a huffed out breath. "Meridian's about halfway. We may end up there."

"Two days down. Two days back. And how many you figure in Louisiana once Undertaker gets a look at her?"

"One, if I have my way."

Ghost grinned. "Fifty bucks says we're gone a week."

Shades scowled at him.

***

Skylar came out of the shop, and Shades walked over and locked the door.

"So, where are we going exactly?" she asked.

"Told you. Getting you out of town," Shades replied.

"I know, but where?"

"New Orleans."

He watched a slow smile form on her face.

Shit.

"We're going to New Orleans? I've always wanted to see the French Quarter. Bourbon Street. Jackson Square. Oh, and that place with the coffee and beignets that's been there since, like, before the Civil War."

"Café Du Monde," Ghost clarified.

"That's the place." She looked up into Shades' eyes, her arms sliding around his neck. "Can we go there? Will you take me?"

He tried to pull her arms from around his neck. "Babe, this isn't a fucking vacation. You're supposed to be laying low."

"I thought Louisiana wasn't their territory."

"She's got ya there, Brother," Ghost added helpfully with a grin.

"Yeah, well they could be looking anywhere for you." He knew it was unlikely that there'd be any DKs near New Orleans, but he didn't want to spend any more time around Undertaker than necessary. He sure didn't want to go fuckin' sightseeing.

"Oh," she said despondently, and he felt her arms sliding away from him.

Shit. He hated to see the joy sucked right out of her face. And it was such a little thing she'd asked for, really. "Okay. *Maybe*. We'll see how it goes."

"Oh, thank you, Shades." She kissed his cheek.

He brushed her cheek with his thumb. "You ready to roll?"

She nodded and moved toward his bike.

Ghost threw a leg over his and lifted it off the kickstand. He grinned at Shades as he moved past him. "Shit, she's already got you wrapped."

Shades shook his head and rolled his eyes. "Shut up."

Ghost let out a low chuckle and fired his bike up, the thunderous pipes drowning out any further conversation.

"So, are we going to be staying close to the Quarter?"

"We're not actually going to be staying in New Orleans. We're gonna be staying across Lake Pontchartrain in Slidell."

"Slidell? In a motel?"

"Not exactly."

"What's not exactly mean?"

"We're gonna be staying with some friends."

"By friends you mean the MC?"

"Yeah."

"Oh."

"Don't look so scared. You'll be fine."

CHAPTER SEVENTEEN

When they reached Meridian they exited the interstate and pulled into a diner. Skylar climbed off the back of Shades' bike and rubbed her sore ass. She eyed the motel across the street longingly and asked, "How much farther is it?"

"We're about halfway, Hotrod," Ghost informed her with a grin.

"Only halfway?" Her hopeful expression fell in devastation.

"Yep. Come on," Shades took her hand and pulled her along behind him into the diner.

They were immediately seated in a booth, and a waitress came over with a coffee pot.

"Coffee?" she asked. When they all nodded, she began turning the cups right-side-up in the saucers that sat on the table and filled them while Ghost grabbed the plastic coated menus from behind the napkin dispenser and passed them around.

Shades barely glanced at his before he slid it back in its holder and looked up at the waitress.

"I'll have the pulled-pork barbeque plate."

"Sides?" the waitress asked.

"Baked beans and coleslaw."

"And to drink?"

"Sweet tea."

Ghost shoved his menu behind the holder. "I'll have the same."

The waitress scribbled on her pad, and then her eyes fell on Skylar. "And you, Miss?"

"Um…" She studied the menu. "I'm thinking maybe a salad."

Shades yanked the menu out of her hand and told the waitress. "She'll have the same."

"Hey!"

The waitress scribbled on her pad and made a hasty retreat.

"Why did you do that?" Skylar asked him.

"You don't need a salad, Sky. You didn't eat breakfast. You have to be hungry."

Skylar looked over at Ghost, her brows raised, and popped her lips. "Guess I'm having pulled-pork."

Ghost chuckled. "That's what the man said."

"He always like this?"

"Oh, no, no, no. Don't be putting me in the middle of whatever fight y'all are about to have."

"We're not about to have a fight," Shades insisted.

"Right," Ghost agreed sarcastically.

"I'm just making sure my woman is well fed."

She looked back at Shades. "Maybe I don't like pork. Ever think of that?"

"Do you like pork, Skylar?" he asked.

"Well, yes, but that's beside the point."

"No, it's *not*."

She rolled her eyes and gave up.

"Good decision." Ghost grinned at her.

Skylar fidgeted in her seat.

"What's wrong with you?" Shades asked.

"You know exactly what's wrong with her, bro. Her ass is sore."

"Ghost!" Skylar hissed, turning to see if anyone in the diner heard him.

"What? It's true, isn't it?"

"Yes, but you don't have to bring it up."

Skylar again looked longingly out the plate-glass window at the motel sign across the street. Shades eyes followed, and he huffed out a breath, taking a sip of his coffee.

"What was that for?" Skylar asked, turning to him.

"What was what for?" he replied.

"That huff."

"You want to check into that motel."

"I didn't say that."

"No, but it's what you're thinkin', isn't it?"

She looked away.

"Isn't it?" he repeated, nudging her shoulder.

"Maybe." Her eyes came back to him. "Okay, yes, it is."

"Christ," he muttered.

Ghost just grinned at him from across the table. "Did we bet on this?"

"No," Shades growled. "We bet on four days versus seven."

"What does that mean?" Skylar asked, frowning.

"It means we're getting a room."

Ghost tapped her with his foot. "Just shut up and tell him thank you."

She smiled at Shades . "Thank you, honey."

He just looked away, shaking his head, but she could see the grin he tried to hide behind his coffee cup.

Half an hour later, they rolled across the street to the motel. Shades went in, and Skylar waited outside with Ghost.

Skylar kept her eyes on Shades as he walked away, watching the sexy way his hips rolled with his gait. He'd grown even better looking in the years they'd been apart. He seemed broader in the shoulders, and his arms and chest were more muscular. He'd really filled out as a man in his prime. And as she watched him walk away, she realized she'd never be able to watch him walk away *for real* again. It terrified her that it may still happen. No matter what he'd said, she knew things could change his feelings. But she wanted him more than she'd ever wanted anything. She only wished everything could work out for them.

She caught Ghost's eyes on her and turned to look at him.

He watched her, his arms folded, his feet wide apart.

"What?" she asked, frowning at the way he studied her.

And then, as if he'd read her mind, he said cryptically, "Be careful what you wish for darlin'."

"What do you mean?"

"Let me tell you something about our boy in there." He nodded toward the motel office. "When he's bound and determined to do something, he's gonna do it.

"I understand that."

"I don't think you do, Skylar. He's on the road to be VP. It's all he's wanted for a long fuckin' time. You on board for that? Because let me tell you, ain't nothing gonna knock him off that road."

"I—"

"If you're gonna be the old lady of the club's VP, you're gonna have to toughen up. You're gonna have to be strong for him when he needs you. There'll be times—behind closed doors—when he's gonna need to lay some heavy shit on you, when he's gonna need to let the shield down. You're gonna have to be able to take that weight off his shoulders even if it's just for a few hours. Things can be stressful with the club; he doesn't need stress at home, too. Home—that's gotta be solid. You understand where I'm coming from?"

"I think so."

"Shit may even go down this weekend. He's gonna be watchin' to see how you handle it. See if you're the woman who can stand by his side through all the shit this club can bring. Make no mistake, good times are gonna outweigh the bad. Wouldn't be a single member if they didn't. But it's how a person handles the bad times that speaks volumes. He's got to know you believe in him. Gotta feel it to his bones. That goes for when he tells you to do something; he's doin' it for your own good. He's got to know you trust in him enough to do what he says without questions, backtalk, or arguments. And it's more than just that. It's knowin' he can count on you to be there for him. Knowin' you'll always be there for him when he needs you. That's what it's all about."

"And what about me? What *I* need?"

"Darlin', you prove yourself, he'll be there for you, too. In all the ways you need him to be."

"I have to prove myself to him?"

"Don't we all have to prove ourselves in some way? Aren't you waiting for him to prove himself to you? That he won't ever let you down again the way he did before?"

"I thought you didn't know anything about that."

"I don't, but I'm betting he's the one who fucked up. Am I right?"

The way she looked away must have given him all the answer he needed, because he continued, "If you think he's not watching to see how you handle the shit this life, *the MC life,* can throw at you, you're wrong."

"Shit this life can throw at me?" She repeated his words back at him.

He let out an aggravated breath. "You know what I'm talkin' about, Hotrod. Shit like Ashley. Shit like the DKs at the gate yesterday."

She dipped her head, studying the blacktop under her feet.

"Shit like that happens, you can't run and hide or bury your head in the sand."

"All right, Ghost. I get the message."

"For what it's worth, I think you've got it in you. You could be a damn good ol' lady to him if you just step up, girl."

She smiled at him then. "Thanks."

"I know it's none of my business, and I should stay out of it, but maybe I just want you two to work out. I'm givin' you a piece of advice because I don't want *either* of you to fuck this up. So take it in the way it was intended. You want to make this work, I'm givin' you a little guidance to ease your way into this life."

"I appreciate that, Ghost. I do."

"Yeah, well, nobody wants unsolicited advice, but you took it pretty well, darlin'."

She chuckled and repeated his words from earlier that morning. "Don't take this the wrong way but…"

"Yeah, yeah. From now on just tell me to shut the fuck up."

When Shades came back out, he didn't look happy.

"They're full up."

"You're kidding? In this Podunk town?"

"Some family reunion. Clerk said there are hundreds of 'em in town."

"So, we riding on to Slidell?"

"Guy at the desk called around. Place two blocks down on the left has one room left."

"One?" Skylar asked.

"Yup. Just one."

Ghost grinned over at her. "Don't worry, Hotrod, I don't

snore."

They headed over there and checked in. After unloading their bags and storing them in the room, Ghost headed for the door.

"I'm going to that bar across the street." He winked. "Give you two a little alone time."

"You don't have to do that, Ghost," Skylar offered, hating to run him off.

"Oh, yeah he does," Shades said with more force.

Ghost grinned. "I turn into a pumpkin at midnight, so that gives you a couple hours, Romeo."

"Thanks, man."

Ghost winked at Skylar before he left.

***

Skylar was still awake when the door opened quietly and Ghost moved into the room. She glanced at the clock radio on the nightstand. One a.m. She was on her side, facing the door across the empty second bed in the room. Shades was pressed up against her with his chest to her back, his arm tight around her waist.

"The bikes okay?" Shades murmured sleepily without moving a muscle.

"Yeah, man, they're fine," Ghost replied, pulling his shirt over his head.

Skylar couldn't help but let her eyes run over him admiringly.

"Close your eyes, Skylar," Shades murmured, again without moving.

Ghost's eyes dropped to hers, and he grinned as he

reached for his belt buckle. “She can watch; I ain’t shy.”

Shades hand came down over her eyes. She reached up, managing to peek through his fingers while giggling.

Ghost dropped his pants and crawled into bed.

“Oh my,” Skylar whispered in awe of all that was Ghost.

Shades flipped her over to face him. “Okay, babe. Enough of checking out a brother.”

She giggled again.

“Guess there’s only one way to shut you up,” he grumbled, and his mouth descended on hers.

“Oh, good. The shows about to start,” Skylar heard Ghost tease and broke the kiss long enough to peek over her shoulder and see Ghost turned on his side facing them, his head propped in his hand.

She shoved against Shades chest in a panic. “No show. Just sleeping. Goodnight, Ghost.”

He fell back onto his back and folded his arms under his head. “Damn. Night, Hotrod.”

***

The next morning, Shades awoke to feel Skylar crawl out of bed and go in the bathroom. He remembered from before that she was an early riser. The sound of the shower turning on carried through the bathroom door. A minute later, the sound of her humming in the shower drifted out.

“She always this cheerful in the morning?” Ghost grumbled, his eyes still shut.

“Yeah, usually.”

“Christ,” Ghost muttered sleepily. “How do you handle it?”

"I usually fuck her, and she goes back to sleep," Shades replied with a yawn.

"During or after?"

"Smartass."

The singing continued, a little off-key.

"Well, don't let me stop you," Ghost grumbled and put a pillow over his head.

"Fuckface."

Fifteen minutes later, the door opened, and Skylar walked out wrapped in a towel, followed by a cloud of steam.

Ghost whistled, and Shades lifted his head turning to look at her.

"Hey, baby. Come over here a second," Shades said in a sexy rumble.

She grinned at him, shaking her head. "I'm on to you."

"Come on, baby. Don't be like that. At least come over here, and give me a shot of what's under that towel."

"You know what's under this towel."

"Yeah… that don't mean I don't want to see it every chance I get."

She blew him a kiss as she moved toward her pack, dug through it for a change of clothes, and returned to the bathroom, closing the door.

***

Ten minutes later, Skylar came back out and moved toward the in-room coffee maker. She was dying for a cup of coffee. After fiddling with it for a minute, she had a pot brewing.

Ghost lifted his head off the pillow as the rich aroma

filled the room. "Make me a cup, darlin'?"

Skylar turned to him and smiled. She glanced over at Shades, but he appeared dead to the world. It didn't take long for that man to fall back asleep.

When the coffee was ready, Skylar poured two cups and carried one in each hand. She held one out to Ghost. He sat up, swinging his legs over the side of the bed, grabbing a handful of sheet to keep his crotch covered. Her eyes skated over all the exposed skin.

"Thanks. You're an angel." He took the cup from her hand and took a sip.

"You have a girl, Ghost?"

His eyes met hers over the rim of his cup, and he almost choked. Pulling the cup away and swallowing, he replied, "What?"

"A girl. An ol' lady. Do you have one?"

"Nope. Why?"

She shrugged. "You're a good-looking guy. I figured with your looks and your humor, there had to be someone."

"Thanks, darlin'." He took her hand and lifted it to his mouth, pressing a kiss to the back.

Shades twisted in the bed, turning to look, his hair rumpled from sleep, he grumbled, "Quit tryin' to steal my woman."

"Wouldn't be hard, cranky ass," Ghost replied, smiling at Skylar.

"And where's *my* coffee?" Skylar and Ghost both chuckled at his pouting, and then she moved to get Shades coffee. When she handed it to him, he asked, "Isn't it your man you're supposed to bring coffee to first?"

She rolled her eyes. "I was just being nice."

"You don't have to be nice to Ghost. He's used to women being mean to him."

"Hey, speak for yourself, whiny ass. Women *love me*."

"Yeah, right."

CHAPTER EIGHTEEN

They arrived in Slidell, and Shades and Ghost rolled the bikes into the parking lot of a bar and grill.

Skylar followed Shades inside, her hand gripped firmly in his. He pulled a stool out for her while he and Ghost took the stools on either side of her. Shades ordered them a couple of beers, and then he took his cell out of his pocket.

It was a short phone call—Shades just telling whoever was on the other end that they were here and to meet them down at Boudreaux's.

When he disconnected, she asked, "Who was that?"

He looked over at her. "Brothers are gonna come and lead us into the clubhouse. We've never been there, and apparently it's hard to find."

"Oh."

"You hungry?" he asked, looking down at her beer.

She shrugged. "I could eat."

"Ghost?"

"Yeah, I'm starved, Brother."

Shades motioned the bartender over and ordered them all shrimp po'boys. When the food came, Skylar tore into it.

"Mmm, this is awesome. I can't believe I've never had one of these," she exclaimed enthusiastically around a mouthful of food.

Shades grinned and wiped a glob of sauce off her mouth. "Glad you like it, babe."

They were just finishing their food when the door opened, and in strolled two guys in Evil Dead cuts, except the bottom rocker on theirs read Louisiana. Shades and Ghost both got up off their stools and did the whole back-slap thing men do. Skylar stayed seated, her eyes running over the two men.

After Shades took care of the bill, they headed outside and mounted up. Shades and Ghost followed the two men out of the parking lot. They rode out of town and down several back roads. They passed some old fish camps and houses up on stilts over the water of the many inlets. Spanish moss hung from the trees draping over the road and creating an eerily beautiful canopy for them to pass under. At several points the narrow road they were on ran adjacent to the bayou, no more than ten yards from the pavement. Skylar couldn't help but gaze around, wondering about alligators.

Eventually they rode into what reminded Skylar of a stockade. There was a tall wooden privacy fence surrounding the entire compound. The gates swung open as they approached, and Skylar realized there were a couple of guys up on a walkway behind the wall next to the gate. Once they passed through, two men scrambled to push the heavy gates closed again.

There was a large dirt and gravel parking lot with a big metal building that sat to the back of the property. The front section of the v-shaped roof extended out over a cement slab creating a large, covered patio. On it were four picnic tables scattered around, and about two-dozen bikes were parked out front.

They parked the bikes in an open space and climbed off. Shades grabbed Skylar's hand and pulled her along behind him until they were out of the line of bikes.

Skylar's eyes darted everywhere, taking it all in—the clubhouse, the number of bikes, the brothers smoking by the corner, and the guy at the door. She pulled back.

That must have gotten his attention because Shades turned to her, tightening his grip on her hand. "Skylar, eyes on me."

Her wide eyes came to him immediately.

"I'm not gonna let anything happen to you, understand?"

She nodded.

"Just stay close."

"Okay."

They walked through the door, following the two men that led them there. The inside of the building was cavernous. Skylar had expected the ceiling to go all the way to the roof with exposed metal beams and such, but the ceiling was low, indicating there must be a second story above them. There was a large half-circle bar on the right with about a dozen bar stools. Recessed lighting cast the room in a soft amber shade.

The floor was polished concrete stained to a rich caramel color. Some tables sat off to the left, then there were a couple of pool tables next to those. Back in the far right corner, Skylar could see a small workout area set up with weights and punching bags.

The building also appeared to be empty except for a couple of prospects behind the bar.

"Grouch, get them whatever they want," the bald man ordered one of the prospects. Then he turned to Shades and Ghost and ordered, "Wait here. I'll tell Undertaker you're here."

The two men moved off toward a large staircase in the back of the room.

Once they'd disappeared, the prospect came over and asked, "What'll you have?"

Shades turned to Skylar. She looked at the prospect and said, "Cola if you have one."

"Sure thing." He nodded and reached into a cooler, pulled a can out, and set it in front of her.

Shades and Ghost both opted for a beer, and two long necks were set in front of them.

Ghost turned to Shades. "You got about two minutes before they come back, Brother. You might want to give her a head's up." He nodded in Skylar's direction, and she frowned, wondering what he was referring to.

"Not exactly the way Butcher wanted it."

"Don't be an ass. No matter what Butcher said, you can't let her walk in blind."

Shades set his bottle down, and Skylar could see his jaw

clench. What on earth was going on?

Before she could form the words to ask, Shades was off his stool and pulling her across the room, out of earshot of the two prospects who were trying to look busy wiping down the spotless bar.

Shades came to a stop on the other side of one of the pool tables and turned to face her. He took her other hand in his, holding both of them, and he looked down at her.

"I've got to come clean with you about this trip, sweetheart."

"What are you talking about?"

"Gotta tell you something. I need you to keep your cool and hear me out."

"Okay." He was really starting to scare her.

"There was a reason we came down here. A reason I brought *you* down here."

"To lay low from the DKs, right?"

"No."

"No?"

"Butcher wanted Undertaker to meet you."

"Who's Undertaker?"

"New Orleans Chapter President."

"Why in the world would he want me to meet him?"

"Because, he thinks…" Shades blew out a breath. "He may be your father."

"*What?*"

"Just listen to me a minute before you freak out. That photo strip you have of your mother? Slick recognized the man in the photo. It was Undertaker."

Skylar tried to pull free of his grasp, feeling completely betrayed, but Shades held on tight. “Let me go. Why would you do this to me?”

“Listen to me, Skylar. This wasn’t my idea. I didn’t want to bring you here. I had no choice.”

“I want to go home. I don’t want any part of this. Let me go.”

“I can’t, baby. He wants to meet you.”

“Well, I don’t want to meet him!” She was suddenly filled with an uncontrollable rage. She didn’t know this man they claimed may be her father. He was a complete stranger to her. And where had he been all this time? How could he have left her to be put in foster care? All those years she’d felt alone and abandoned. *He’d* done that to her. *He’d* put her through all that. Why?

Shades’ grip on her held tight. “It’s happening, Skylar. You have to accept it.”

“Because you’ve given me no choice!” she shrieked. She felt like she’d been backed into a corner, which never failed to make her want to come out swinging. She began to really fight him, twisting and kicking and trying to run. He spun her and got her in a tight hold from behind, his arms wrapped like steel bands around her upper arms and chest.

“Settle down and behave yourself!” When she finally settled, he growled, “Goddamn it, woman, you’re always so fuckin’ quick to run.”

“I don’t want to see him,” she whispered brokenly. He turned her in his arms to face him.

“Swear to God, Sky, no lie, you meet him and we’re out

of here. I promise." He paused to study her face, and she knew he could read how unconvinced she was. "Don't you want to know? Isn't there some part of you that's longed for this day? Don't you have anything you want to say to the man?"

His words sifted through her brain and suddenly her mind did an about face. She did want to see him, if only just to tell him off, if only just to tell him what a lowlife she thought he was for abandoning her and her mother.

She heard boots stomping down the stairs at the back of the room and looked over Shades' shoulder to see the two men returning. They stopped between Ghost at the bar and Shades by the pool table, but their eyes were on her and Shades.

"He's waiting. Door at the end of the hall." The man nodded toward the stairs.

Shades nodded, and with one hand locked firm around hers, he moved out from behind the table pulling her behind him.

As they passed Ghost, he grabbed her free arm, stopping them. Shades looked back at him questioningly, but Ghost's eyes were locked with Skylar's.

"Remember what we talked about yesterday. Show me that backbone, girl."

She nodded and straightened, her chin coming up.

He winked at her and released her arm. His eyes moved to Shades' for a moment, and he nodded.

Shades continued on, leading her toward the stairs. She glanced back to see Ghost watching them. The long hallway at the top of the stair had numerous doors off it on both sides. *And one door at the end.*

Skylar stared at it and felt like she was being led to the slaughter. Ghost's words returned to her, and it strengthened her resolve to get through this farce as Shades led her down the long hall. They passed a set of double doors on the left and Skylar could hear a jumble of voices coming from behind it like there was some kind of meeting going on. They continued on past it.

Ten feet from the door at the end of the hall, Shades suddenly stopped, pulled her to him and grabbed her face in his hands. "I promise you, it's all gonna be all right, Skylar."

"You don't know that." Her voice came out in barely a whisper.

"Baby, you gotta have some faith in me."

She looked into his eyes a long moment and then nodded. "I do, Shades. I do. I'm just so angry."

"With me?"

"No, with him. So angry and…so scared."

"Listen to me. If he is your father, we'll deal with it. And if he does something to upset you, I'll deal with him. Okay?"

"Okay."

"I'll be right here waiting for you."

Her eyes got big. "You're not going in with me?"

He shook his head. "You gotta do this on your own, Sky." Then he led her the last few steps and tapped on the door.

"Come in," she heard a man's deep voice growl.

Shades reached for the knob and swung the door open,

stepping back to let her pass him. She walked three steps into the room, noticing that Shades stayed in the doorway, his hand on the knob.

It was a very big office. There was a large desk with a couple of empty chairs facing it. Behind it sat a man. He was the only person in the room. He had his head down at first, and he was rubbing his palms together in a nervous way and suddenly she realized he must be as nervous about this meeting as she was. But that didn't reduce her anger. Finally, his eyes lifted, hesitantly, reluctantly, almost as if he was afraid to look up and get his first look at her. Was he afraid he would recognize something in her or afraid he wouldn't?

"Skylar?" he asked, standing.

She nodded and hearing a click behind her, she looked back to see that Shades had left her alone. Her eyes came back to the man who claimed to be her father. He walked around the desk and took a few steps toward her, his eyes running over her face.

"My God. I can't believe it. You look just like her." He stopped, a stunned expression on his face, it was almost as if he was looking at a ghost. "My Angie."

At that, Skylar's eyes flared. "I'm not my mother. I'm not your Angie. I'm not your anything!"

He visibly flushed at her outburst.

"I knew your mother."

She looked at him, really looked at him. He was in his early fifties, maybe. His dark hair was peppered with gray, as was his goatee, but there was no denying that he was the man in the picture. She'd stared at it enough over the years to know that much.

“So, what of it?” she snapped, not about to make this easy for him.

“Angie and I had a baby together. A little girl. *You*. I loved Angie, and I loved you. But I got sent to prison shortly after that. After about a year, she stopped coming to visit, she stopped writing. I spent eleven years in prison. When I got out, I couldn’t find her. She’d moved and—”

“She didn’t *move*. She *died*,” Skylar snapped.

“I didn’t know. They never fuckin’ told me.”

“I was put in the system. Five different foster homes. One after another.”

“I’m so sorry, kid.”

“I’m not your kid.”

“You are. I know you’re pissed, but you *are* my kid.”

“You’re nothing but a sperm donor to me. That’s all you’ll *ever* be to me.”

“Baby girl don’t say that. I’m sorry. For all of it. But I swear to God, no one ever told me she died. I tried to find you both when I got out.”

“Apparently not very hard. Not hard enough.”

“Baby, you have to understand. We didn’t have computers back then. I couldn’t just do an Internet search for her.”

“You could have found me. You didn’t try hard enough.”

“I’m sorry. I thought she left me. I thought she wanted nothing to do with a loser like me. I guess a part of me figured you’d be better off without me fucking your life up.

Better off without me."

"Well, you were wrong. I wasn't better off."

"I'm so sorry, Skylar. Forgive me, please."

He stood there, looking truly hurt and devastated and yes…sorry. But her anger went deep. Suddenly she found herself flying at him, her arms swinging to hit him. He grabbed her forearms and held tight while she wailed and ranted and let out twenty-five years of hurt and anger and resentment.

He just held on tight, until finally, she collapsed against him, and he wrapped his arms around her, hugging her tight, and they both sobbed, their heads bent together. They cried out all the years of pain and loss.

His hand rubbed her back and stroked her hair. "Forgive me, my baby. I'm so sorry."

***

Shades leaned against the wall outside the door. He'd heard Skylar's raised voice and some of the things she'd said to Undertaker, and his heart broke for her. He wanted to burst inside, take her in his arms, and comfort her. But deep down, he knew they had to work this out between them, as father and daughter.

But swear to God, if she was broken by this, he'd tear Undertaker apart, even if it meant his crew would jump him for it. And then he'd spend the entire night holding Skylar and getting her through this, preferably somewhere far from here.

They were in there a long time. Shades didn't move from his place by the door. He'd promised her he'd be waiting right there, and that's what he would do. He'd be right there when she needed him. And she would need him; that much he was certain of.

He watched as whatever meeting had been going on in the room down the hall broke up, and a couple dozen brothers strolled out. Some turned and gave him a curious look, their eyes taking in his cut, but they either knew what was going down, or they knew better than to stick their nose in.

They all turned and wandered downstairs. Shades only recognized a couple of faces. He'd been to numerous chapters around the country, but for some reason he'd never been down here before. The two he *did* recognize he recalled having met at a rally in Gulfport a couple of summers back. The rest were all strangers, but brothers just the same.

Finally, after almost an hour, the door opened, and Shades straightened from the wall, turning to see Undertaker standing in the door and motioning him inside. As Shades moved through the door, his eyes immediately sought out Skylar's. Her eyes looked red from crying, but she managed to give him a tremulous smile.

"You okay?" he asked, his concern for her grabbing him by the heart as he moved toward her and took her face in his hands.

"I'm okay," she replied, her hands coming to his waist, her fists closing on his tee like she didn't want to let go.

Shades turned to Undertaker, a man he'd yet to be introduced to, and asked, "We done here?"

Undertaker nodded toward his desk. "No, we're not *done*

here. Sit down. Both of you."

Shades eyes returned to Skylar's, searching for any indication that she wanted him to get her out of there. Because he'd do it, and to hell with what Undertaker wanted.

"It's okay," she murmured and pushed out of his arms to turn toward the desk. He drew one of the chairs out for her and she sat. Then he sat next to her. Undertaker sat behind the desk.

"My daughter told me about the Devil Kings."

That surprised Shades, and his eyes flicked to Skylar. "Did she?"

"Yeah. You got a plan on that?" Undertaker's eyes bore into him.

Shades' eyes locked with Skylar's as he answered. "Keep her out of their reach. They don't fuckin' touch her."

"Exactly. So I'm thinking the best place for her is right here. I can keep her safe better than you can."

Both Shades and Skylar exclaimed at the same time, *"What?"*

"You heard me, Son." Undertaker glared at him as he picked up a two-way radio and barked, "Mooch, get in here."

"Yeah, boss," broke through the static and Undertaker tossed it back down on the desk.

Skylar looked at Shades with a panicked expression. Her hand reached out to clutch his. "Don't leave me here."

Hell, no, he wasn't leaving her here. "I won't, baby. I promise."

Undertaker ran an aggravated hand over his beard and glared at Shades. "Maybe it's time you and I have a talk."

Shades nodded and turned to Skylar, bringing her hand to his mouth for a kiss. "Go wait downstairs with Ghost, baby. Your father and I have some things to work out."

"No, I'm staying right here. The two of you aren't deciding my future. Don't even think it."

"Sky, I need you to do what I say." Shades dipped his head, staring into her eyes. Something must have clicked, because she swallowed, looked between him and her father, and then surprised him as she rose to her feet, actually obeying his request.

"All right. But don't be long. I want to go home."

"Darlin', you are home," Undertaker clarified with a look that told her she'd better not argue.

Shades watched her move toward the door, and then it slammed shut behind her. A moment later, the brother Undertaker had summoned came through the door, shaking his head as he looked back down the hall. "She slammed right into me. Didn't say a fuckin' word."

"Feisty little thing, ain't she?" Undertaker commented, his eyes falling to his desktop. "Come on in, Mooch."

"She's not staying here." Shades wasted no time laying that out as Mooch walked across the room, folded his arms, and leaned against the credenza against the wall to the right.

Undertaker leaned back in his chair and studied Shades. "Butcher told me about you."

"Yeah, what did he say?"

"He said you want to make her your ol' lady."

"That's a done deal. She's mine."

"Maybe she is, maybe she's not."

Shades surged to his feet. "You think you can stop me from seeing Skylar, think again!"

Undertaker stood just as fast, planted his palms on the desk, and shouted back in his face, "I think I can stop you from seeing next week."

The two stared each other down, neither willing to back down. Finally, Undertaker straightened and snapped, "Sit down! We got more to discuss."

"We've got nothing to discuss until you understand she's mine."

"We'll see," was all Undertaker would concede as he sat back down. "I don't like this shit with the DKs. That's gotta be dealt with. And I mean fuckin' now."

"Agreed."

"This is the safest place for her."

"I'm not leaving her. Just fuckin' get that out of your head. She may be your daughter, but she's my woman."

***

Ghost sat at the bar. A couple dozen brothers had clomped down the stairs and were now busy drinking at the bar or playing pool. Skylar's boot heels clicked angrily across the floor as she headed toward where Ghost sat.

"You okay, sweetheart?"

She stopped, crossed her arms over her chest, and threw her hip out. "No! They think they can just boss me around? Decide *my* life? Screw that. Argh! Men!"

Ghost's brows rose. "Yeah, so men suck. Guess there's nothing left to do but pull up a stool and pick a liquor." He nodded toward the shelf of assorted bottles on the wall behind the bar.

She plopped her butt on the stool next to him.

"So? What happened?" he pressed.

"He's my father."

Ghost nodded and bumped her shoulder with his, grinning down at her. "Tough break, kid."

"Don't make me laugh, Ghost. Not now."

"I think now's the perfect time for you to laugh."

She tried to hold back a grin.

"What did he say?"

"Said he was in prison and didn't know my mom had died. They never told him. He told me he figured she didn't want anything more to do with him after he was sent up for so long. He said he tried to find her when he got out."

"Do you believe him?"

She shrugged. "Maybe. I just wished he'd tried harder, you know?"

Ghost wrapped his arm around her and pulled her up against him. "It's too late for him to have a relationship with that little girl that you *were*, but it doesn't mean you can't have some kind of relationship with him now."

She nodded. "I suppose. It's just…"

"What?"

"It's hard to let go of that little girl…for so long she wanted her dad. Waited for him to come for her."

"That little girl is gone, sweetheart. She grew up into a strong, beautiful woman. A woman who finally found the father she wanted for so long."

She nodded.

"Give him a chance. He might surprise you."

"He's already trying to control me."

Ghost huffed out a breath. "Come on, darlin', now *that's* gotta come as no surprise."

***

Undertaker stared at the door that Shades had just left through. Then he leaned back in his chair. "He doesn't back down. I'll give him that."

Mooch looked over at Undertaker and grinned. "He's every bit the stubborn, hard-headed brother you ever were."

Undertaker let out a grunt. "Yeah, and where'd that get me? Doin' ten to fifteen with no parole. That's not the life I want for my daughter."

"What that *got you* was Chapter President," Mooch corrected.

Undertaker looked down at his desk, his eyes taking on that vacant quality of a man lost in his past. "And look at all I lost along the way."

"Past is done and buried. Future's what counts."

Undertaker looked up at his VP and nodded. "That's what I'm worried about. Her future."

Mooch straightened. "That's a worry for another night. Come on, old man. You've got a daughter to introduce to the club."

A smile pulled at Undertaker's mouth. "I do, don't I?"

***

Shades came down the stairs and moved straight to Skylar's side. He stood behind her barstool, one hand coming down on her hip, the other resting on the bar, caging her in.

He signaled the prospect behind the bar for a beer and kissed the side of her neck, whispering in her ear, "You all right, baby?"

She nodded. "You?"

"Will be when we get out of here."

"Um, Shades, about that…"

"Yeah?"

"My father wants to show me New Orleans."

"What?"

"New Orleans. When I told him I'd never been here before, he insisted."

Before Shades could respond, Undertaker came down the stairs, Mooch on his heels. He stopped at the end of the bar and called to the one woman—a short blonde—who was bartending with the two prospects.

"Marla, do that thing that calms me down with the glass and the alcohol."

Grinning at his joke, she set a short glass in front of him and filled it with a shot of whiskey. He slammed it back and set it back on the bar. Then he turned, cleared his throat and called everyone's attention.

"Got an announcement to make. Listen up, y'all."

Shades twisted to look back at him as he closed a hand over Skylar's nape. She had also twisted on her stool to look at her father.

"This pretty gal is my daughter," he announced, nodding toward her. "Her name is Skylar."

There was a murmur among the crowd, and Shades realized that this came as a shock to most of them.

"Come here, Skylar," her father ordered.

Skylar's eyes came to Shades, and he nodded. She slid off the stool and slowly approached her father. When she got within reach he hauled her close, looping his arm around her shoulders. "We lost track of each other, but that's done now. She's family, and you'll all treat her with the respect she's due. Understood?"

There were murmurings of agreement and approval.

"This is a happy day for me. A real happy day. And my daughter wants to see the Quarter, so that's what we're gonna do. We're all going down to the Quarter to celebrate her homecoming."

To that there was a roar of approval.

Skylar's eyes connected with Shades, and he motioned with his head for her to come back to him. She moved to comply but Undertaker's hand closed over the back of her neck, holding her in place and turning her to face him. As he looked down into her eyes, he said loud enough for all to hear, "You end up with a brother, I'd be happy with that. You end up with the right brother, all the better."

Shades felt the eyes of every brother in the club bore into him before Undertaker released her. His meaning was clear—maybe the "right" brother wasn't him.

CHAPTER NINETEEN

A couple hours later, they were roaring through the streets of the French Quarter. The sound of the pipes of two dozen bikes made a hell of a noise reverberating off the close-set eighteenth century buildings in the narrow brick paved streets. They rolled down St. Peter Street and stopped in front of a bar on the right. They backed their bikes to the curb in a long line that stretched from the middle of the block all the way to the corner of Bourbon Street, chrome gleaming in the night lights.

The brothers all dismounted, stepping onto the curb of the narrow sidewalk. Tall green shutters folded open to the street, revealing white French doors, giving the bar an open air quality—a feature Skylar noticed that many establishments in the Quarter had.

Undertaker led the way inside, taking up a spot at the corner of the bar near the street. Skylar took a spot between him and Shades. The bar was long and narrow with a bar running the length on the left and tables along the right wall. The almost-empty bar soon filled shoulder-to-shoulder with tall, leather-clad bikers. The bartenders quickly filled drink orders. Many of the brothers wandered out to stand with their drinks on the sidewalk, taking in the scene. Crowds moved down Bourbon and an occasional horse drawn carriage—horse complete with plumed headdress—made its way up St. Peter. The music from the Jazz Preservation Hall half a block down bled through the streets.

After a couple of drinks, Ghost, Shades, and Skylar all wandered down Bourbon Street. Skylar dragged them into several souvenir shops, but didn't buy anything. Shades told her if she wanted something he'd get it for her, but she was content to just window shop. She noticed many of the female tourists strolling down Bourbon Street had souvenir feather boas around their necks. When they passed a store that had a large display of them on the wall, she tugged Shades inside and pointed up at them.

"I want one."

A sexy grin pulled at his mouth and he nodded. "Sure, baby."

A few minutes later, they continued down the street, a feather boa now draped around Skylar's neck.

When they passed a club playing some good rockin' music, Ghost dragged them inside for a drink. They found one available stool at the bar, and Shades planted Skylar on it while he and Ghost took a spot standing on either side of her. They soon had drinks in hand and were leaning back against the bar, surveying the crowd. The place was packed with a mostly young crowd. There were several tables and a tiny dance floor in front of the band.

Something at the end of the bar caught Ghost's eye. A moment later he turned back to Shades and said, "Go tell that pretty blonde what a catch I am."

Shades leaned back to check her out. "I would but I don't like to lie, Brother."

"Come on, bro. Why you gotta be like that?"

Skylar couldn't help but giggle. "Tell her yourself."

"Don't encourage him," Shades warned, taking a sip of his drink and watching as Ghost turned and winked at the blonde.

"Why not?" Skylar asked.

"Just watch and see. They'll be all over him in a moment."

"Oh, and not you?"

He leaned down and laid a hot kiss on her. When he let her up for air he said, "Nope. Not with you all over me."

"I'm not all over you."

He grinned and guided her hands up, settling them on his shoulders. "Then maybe you should change that."

She smiled and wrapped her arms around his neck. His eyes flicked over her shoulder.

"Told you."

Skylar turned to see the pretty blonde standing before Ghost. They heard her ask in a tinkling voice, "Are you single?"

Ghost grinned down at her. "I prefer the term 'independently owned and operated'."

The girl giggled—a high-pitched irritating sound that had Skylar giving Shades a look that had him struggling to keep a straight face. A moment later, the girl was pulling Ghost toward the dance floor.

"This ought to be good." A smile tugged at the corner of Shades' mouth.

"Why?" Skylar frowned.

"Ghost can't dance for shit."

Skylar laughed, and a moment later his mouth was on hers.

When the song ended, Ghost returned to the bar, the blonde in tow.

Shades shook his head at him. "Don't ever make me watch you dance again. That shit was traumatizing."

"Shut up, fuckface."

Shades downed the rest of his beer. "You ready to relocate?"

"Sure." Ghost finished off his beer while Skylar slid from her barstool. She watched as Ghost turned back to the blonde. "You comin', Blondie?"

"Where are you going? Why don't you stay and party with me and my girlfriends?" She nodded back to a table full of hot women.

"Hell, darlin' bring 'em along. I've got some friends who'd love to meet 'em."

"They bikers, too?"

"Damn straight."

A few minutes later, Shades and Skylar were being followed down the street by Ghost and five hot babes. Shades looked back and grunted, "Christ, he's like the damn Pied Piper."

Skylar giggled. "He *is* pretty amazing. Does this happen a lot?"

"Yup."

"And I'm sure it's not just him. I bet you've had your share of women falling all over themselves around you."

Shades grinned and pulled her against his side. "Maybe."

"Um hmm."

"Babe, I'm all about you now."

"You better be."

He leaned down and kissed her as they rounded the corner and strolled toward the bar where they'd left the MC.

The brothers were happy to see Ghost's little trail of women following behind him and soon surrounded them with offers to buy them drinks.

***

Several drinks later, Shades rose from his barstool, his torso brushing against Skylar's side. His hand slid to her nape, his fingers threading through her hair, bringing her face up to his.

"Goin' outside to smoke. Be back in a minute. You good here?"

She nodded. "I'll be fine."

Her father spoke from where he was sitting on the other side of Skylar. "She's fucking fine, for Christ's sake. I'm sitting right here."

Shades' eyes connected with Undertaker's quickly before returning to hers. "I won't be long."

Then his head dipped, his lips capturing hers. With a squeeze of her neck, he turned and walked out onto the sidewalk by the bikes. He bent his head and lit up a cigarette. Ghost walked out behind him.

Shades flicked his lighter closed and took a long drag, blowing it out. He looked over at Ghost. “Where’s Blondie?”

“Bathroom.” Ghost took a sip of his beer. “Do you ever just wanna grab someone by the shoulders, look them deep in the eyes, and whisper, “No one gives a fuck.”

Shades let out a huff of laughter. “She gettin’ on your nerves already?”

“Yammer, yammer, yammer, on and on. Christ, I wish women came with a mute button. That way you wouldn’t have to listen to all the bullshit before you got to the good stuff.”

Shades grinned and took a hit off his smoke, looking away.

“You doin’ okay, Bro?”

“Yeah.”

Ghost looked behind him. “Where’s Skylar?”

“With her father.”

Ghost looked at Shades, one brow raised. “Interesting.”

“Hardly. Do you ever have the urge to tell someone to shut the fuck up even when they aren’t talking?”

Ghost chuckled. “You can’t wait to get out of here, can you?”

“You said it.”

Ghost looked back. “She’s havin’ fun, though.”

“Yeah.” Shades took in the crowd moving up Bourbon

Street before looking back at Ghost. A pair of punks dressed in full Goth attire passed by.

"The dregs of sin city."

"I look at people sometimes and think, 'For real? That's the sperm that won?'"

Shades snorted. "No shit."

A pair of arms slid around Ghost's waist from behind, and he twisted his head.

"I wondered where you'd run off to," Blondie said.

"Apparently not far enough," Ghost muttered under his breath.

"What was that?" she asked.

"Nothing, babe." Ghost tossed his cigarette into the street and pulled her around to his front, wrapping his arms around her. "Been right here, darlin', waitin' on your ass. And one sexy ass it is." One big hand snaked down to squeeze one of her cheeks and she squealed, letting out a high-pitched giggle.

Shades looked at him over her head, his fingers going to his ears to block out the annoying titter as he rolled his eyes.

***

Skylar took a sip of her drink and looked over at her father. There was a lot she wanted to ask him—the man was practically a stranger to her, after all. "So… do you… um, have any other children?"

His head turned toward her, familiar blue eyes staring back at her. She'd often wondered where she'd gotten the vibrant shade of blue since her mother had had green eyes. She watched them crinkle at the corners with his smile.

"You askin' if you've got any brothers or sisters?"

"Yes."

He shook his head.

"No? Or none that you know of?"

He grinned. "Okay, none that I know of."

"Is there a woman?"

"Not at the moment. Not for a while actually."

"Why's that?"

He shrugged. "Guess I'm not the easiest son-of-a-bitch to get along with."

She grinned and took a sip of her drink.

"I suppose that doesn't surprise you."

"Nope."

"You don't seem to have inherited your ol' man's temperament. You seem just like your mother."

"I don't remember much about her."

He looked down at his drink clutched between his hands. "She was a good woman. Real sweet. Never gave me a lick of trouble. I didn't appreciate what I had until I'd lost it all." He tossed his drink back.

Skylar studied him. There was so much she didn't know about either of her parents. "Where did you meet her?"

A wistful smile tugged at the corner of his mouth, and his eyes studied the bar top. "I was on my bike, sitting parked at a stoplight. She pulled up behind me in this old VW Bug. The thing had a manual transmission, and apparently she was just learning how to drive a stick-shift. Anyway, when the light turned green, she dropped the clutch, and her car lurched forward right into my back tire. Bam! Knocked me on my ass."

Skylar couldn't help the giggle that escaped her. "I'm sorry I shouldn't laugh. Were you hurt?"

"No. I was pissed. I lifted the bike up off my leg and climbed to my feet ready to tear some guy a new asshole. By that time, she'd climbed out of her car and had run up to see if I was okay. I took one look at her, and I was a goner." He looked over at Skylar and smiled.

"Love at first sight?"

"Lust anyway."

She laughed.

He shrugged. "The love followed pretty quickly."

They were quiet for a few moments, and then he looked back at her.

"I'm sorry, Skylar."

"About what?"

"About what happened to your mom. And to you. About everything."

She nodded.

He put his hand to the back of her neck and hauled her close, pressing a kiss to her forehead. When he pulled back, he said, "I'm glad we finally found each other."

She looked into his eyes, noting the sincerity there. "Me, too."

He gave her neck a little shake, and then his hand slid away.

She turned back to her drink. A moment later, she felt heat at her shoulder and twisted to see a solid chest wedged between her and Shades' empty stool, and a hand sliding an empty glass across the bar. Her eyes followed up the leather-clad torso to see a man looking down at her. He was dark-headed, with a dark beard to match. His eyes, a dark brown under slashing brows, were giving her a penetrating look and as he stared, her lips parted and his eyes dropped to her mouth.

Suddenly, Undertaker was making introductions… sort of.

"Skylar, this is Blood."

Blood did little more than make an almost imperceptible nod, his eyes dropping to the neckline of her dark slate tank with its silver beaded trim.

The bartender came over, and Blood nodded toward his glass.

"Set her up, too," he told the bartender who quickly pulled a short rock glass out from under the bar and set it in front of her. He tipped up a bottle of Crown filling Blood's glass. Before he could move it to the glass set in front of her, Skylar held her hand up.

"None for me, thanks."

The bartender looked from Skylar to Blood, the bottle poised in the air, obviously unsure what to do.

"Fill it," Blood told him.

The bartender filled the glass and made a hasty retreat.

Coward, Skylar thought.

Blood slid the glass toward her.

"Gotta toast the new club Princess." He held his glass up waiting for her to clink glasses with him. Skylar blew out an exasperated breath and picked hers up, clinking his. He waited, his eyes on her until she brought the glass to her mouth and took a sip. She watched as his eyes fell on her mouth and stayed there, even as he tossed his back in one gulp. He set his glass on the bar, and then leaned forward, his arms folded, his head turned toward her.

"Say my name."

She frowned, confused by his bizarre demand. He repeated it.

"Say my name."

"Blood."

"Remember it, Princess."

"I'm not your Princess, *Blood*," she spit out.

What could maybe pass as a smile pulled at one corner of his mouth, and then his eyes lifted over her head to Undertaker.

"She's gonna be a handful."

"I'm not going to be *anything to you*," she informed him.

"We'll see, Angel."

"Aren't there some other women in the bar you could go bother? More your speed?"

His eyes narrowed, and then he straightened.

"Whatever you say. But know this—you and me, we're not through."

"Enough, Blood." Undertaker's voice was tight.

Blood moved off without another word.

She turned back to her father. "What's his problem?"

"That's just Blood being Blood."

"Whatever."

Undertaker gave her a knowing grin.

"What's that grin supposed to mean?"

He smiled even wider, shaking his head. "Nothing, darlin'. Not a thing."

Skylar took a sip of her new drink. Movement in the reflection of the mirror behind the bar caught her eye. Three of the women that had followed Ghost back to the bar were heading to the restroom down the hall in the back. Skylar's head swiveled to watch them.

Blood, who had taken up a spot in the doorway to the hall, suddenly put his arm out, his hand bracing on the opposite wall. He cut off the redhead at the end of the line, separating her from the herd. Skylar could see, even from her seat at the bar, when his eyes strayed down the girl's body. And then he stepped closer, backing her against the wall, his mouth coming down on hers.

A moment later, she shoved him back. A loud crack resounded through the bar, turning everyone's head as the girl slapped his face.

"Aw, Sugar. You've just done the dumbest thing in your whole life," Mooch muttered to the girl from his place near Blood.

A scary grin pulled at Blood's mouth as he looked down at her. "Don't worry, Mooch, I love that in a woman."

"Morals?" Mooch asked with a quirk of his brow.

"*Violence*." His palm landed on the center of her chest, just over her breast bone, and he pressed her back against the wall, pinning her there.

"Blood!" A voice boomed from the bar.

His head turned.

Undertaker snapped, "Let her go."

Blood's head came back to the scared girl looking up at him, and Skylar watched his eyes running over the girl's face as if he were considering whether or not to comply.

"Blood!" Undertaker snapped again. "She's just a tourist. She didn't ask to play your kind of games. Let her be."

Blood released her.

She scrambled out from between him and the wall and shoved past several laughing brothers as she made for the door.

"You're all fucking crazy!" she spat as she ran out, followed by the men's laughter.

Skylar's eyes followed the girl's retreat and then returned to Blood. He was staring right at her and grinning that cocky grin as if he'd done that just to get to her. She ran her hand over her throat as a chill went up her spine, her eyes still locked with his, and then she watched his eyes drop to the hand at her throat, and then farther down to her chest.

Spinning on the barstool, she turned toward her father. "His kind of games? What does that mean?"

"Let's just say, a man like Blood doesn't ask nicely; he just takes what he wants. Some girls are down with that. Some aren't. She obviously fell into the latter category."

"And if you hadn't stopped him?"

"Oh, I think we both know that little show was all about you."

"Me?"

"Don't play coy with me, honey. I was sitting right

here."

Skylar swallowed and looked away.

"Thought so." Undertaker leaned closer to her. "Fair warning, you give him an opening, he's gonna walk right in, darlin'."

"I'm not…giving him an opening."

Undertaker nodded. "That's your call. Just so you know who you're dealing with. He's not a man to be trifled with."

"I'm with Shades."

"Maybe you are."

"No, not maybe. I *am*."

He gave her a condescending grin. "We'll see, won't we?"

"I don't like you very much."

He sobered immediately. "I just want what's best for you. Whichever man that turns out to be."

"That's for *me* to decide."

He just grinned that insufferable grin back at her.

"Wipe that smile off your face," she snapped.

Then he burst out laughing.

"What's so funny?"

"I smile because you're my daughter. I laugh because there's nothing you can do about it."

She rolled her eyes as he continued to laugh.

Shades, Ghost, and "Blondie" came back into the bar. Blondie headed off to the restroom when Skylar told her that's where her friends had gone. After she left, Ghost turned to Skylar.

"Do you have anything sharp I can stick in my eye?"

Skylar laughed. "She that bad?"

He rolled his eyes. "Let's just say I won't be tattooing her name on my arm any time soon."

Skylar almost spit her drink out. "Ghost, *do* you have someone's name tattooed on you?"

Ghost groaned and looked over at Shades. "I don't know when to shut up, do I?"

Shades chuckled. "Apparently not."

"Let me see!" Skylar insisted with a grin.

Ghost shoved his short sleeve up to his shoulder and tapped his fingers on a large skull shaped design. "Used to be a name. I had it covered up."

Skylar's fingers reached out to touch the intricate art with awe. Then her eyes lifted to his.

"Do tattoos hurt?"

Ghost looked at her and said with a straight face, "Not at all. They feel like a million kittens licking your skin."

Skylar turned to Shades. "I want to get a tattoo."

He about choked on his beer before managing to bite out with brows raised, "Oh, hell no, you don't."

"Just how many drinks have you had, Hotrod?" Ghost asked with a grin, dropping his sleeve.

She grinned. "I don't know. I lost count."

***

Shades sipped his drink, waiting for Skylar to return from the restroom. The bar was now crowded with not only the club, but with other tourists. He finally spotted her making her way through the packed bar. As she passed a group of several guys, one of them stepped in to block her way and then he leaned down to whisper something in her ear. She gave him a pissed off look and tried to push past him, but he grabbed her arm, yanking her back.

Shades was off his barstool in a flash, coming between the punk and Skylar, pushing her behind him.

"You don't touch her, motherfucker," Shades snapped.

"Who the fuck are you?"

"Her ol' man. What the fuck did you just say to her?"

"I asked her what the hell she was doing with a bunch of losers like you."

Shades' fist came out and connected with the man's jaw, dropping him to the floor.

Skylar gasped and Ghost snatched her out of the way.

"Sometimes people don't know when to shut up," Shades said, standing over the body of the guy he'd just knocked out.

"You got a short temper tonight, Brother?" Ghost asked, peering over Shades' shoulder at the guy out cold on the floor.

Shades shook his hand out and flexed it. "I don't have a short temper, I just have a low tolerance for bullshit."

The guy groaned.

Shades kicked him in the gut. "Talk shit, get hit, motherfucker."

"Why did he do that?" Skylar murmured from next to her father, where Ghost had shoved her.

"It was your honor he was fighting for, baby girl," Undertaker said in a low voice. "Here, finish your drink."

She turned away from the scene, a little shaken. She'd

never seen Shades like that before.

Ghost came up behind her and whispered in her ear, "Sometimes your knight in shining armor turns out to be a badass biker in dirty boots."

Undertaker got up off his stool and pulled Skylar off hers. Then he hooked an arm around her shoulders and the other around Shades'.

"Let's take a walk."

He led them out of the bar. Over his shoulder he ordered, "Somebody take out the garbage." About half the brothers followed them, the other half dragged the man outside, dumped him in the street, and continued drinking.

CHAPTER TWENTY

Blood stood on the street outside the bar and dipped his head to light up a smoke. His eyes locked on the little group as they walked down the street. One of his brothers came to stand by his side.

"I've got a bad feelin' about this, Blood," Sandman murmured.

"What? We're having a nice night out, and Undertaker's in a good mood."

"So you feel it, too?"

Blood rolled his eyes and chuckled. "You've had too many beers."

Sandman started silently counting on his fingers and then grinned. "In dog beers, I've only had one."

Blood suppressed a grin as he took a hit off his cigarette, his eyes following Skylar as she walked away in the distance. "What do you think of her?"

Sandman shrugged. "Don't know. Why?"

"She's hot, isn't she?"

"Yeah. She's also Undertaker's daughter."

Blood looked back at him and grinned.

Sandman shook his head. "You always did like a challenge."

***

Undertaker, Mooch, Shades, Skylar, Ghost, his harem of women, and a few other brothers prowled the streets of the Quarter. They walked down St. Peter to Royal and cut over to Pirate's Alley, coming out at Jackson Square and skirting it on Chartres and St. Ann. They took in the Cathedral as well as all the street artists selling paintings, the tables of fortune tellers, and the painted artists doing impressions of statues. There was a man dressed as a cowboy, painted up in solid silver. Skylar stopped to pose next to him, and Shades took her picture with his cell phone, her bright, laughing smile lighting up the shot. They moved on, crossing Decatur and ending at Café Du Monde. They got a table and ordered café au lait and beignets. Skylar couldn't hold back her laughter seeing half a dozen leather-clad bikers, their scruffy beards covered in powder sugar as they wolfed down the sugary treats, leaning forward so as not to let it snow sugar onto their cuts.

They eventually headed back to the bar to hook up with the rest of the club. Undertaker had taken a seat next to Skylar again, but he went back outside to talk to some of his guys and smoke a cigarette.

While he was gone, Blood moved onto his vacant stool.

Shades was turned the other way, talking to Ghost, and hadn't noticed.

Skylar looked over at Blood, admittedly a little nervous that he'd approached her. He smiled, his eyes dropping to the feather boa she had wrapped around her neck. He lifted his hand and stroked the feathers with his knuckles.

"I could think of some uses for that boa," he purred in a deep voice.

Skylar looked back at her drink, trying to ignore him, which only encouraged him. She felt his fingers brushing the hair from her face.

"Don't go all shy on me, Princess."

"Don't call me that," Skylar bit out, pulling away from his touch. Spinning on the barstool, she turned toward Shades who was leaning the other way, his head dipped as Ghost said something in his ear and nodded toward Blood. She'd never seen Shades' head swivel so fast, his eyes narrowing on Blood, and then he was up and off his barstool, moving around her to get to Blood.

Skylar reached out, trying to grab him, but he shook off her hold. Blood stood, ready for the confrontation. As she slid off her stool to try to come between them, Skylar felt a solid arm wrap around her waist, and she was hauled back against a hard chest. She twisted to see her captor.

Ghost dipped his head and whispered in her ear. "Let your man handle this."

"But…" She turned back to see that Shades and Blood were toe to toe, eye to eye in some kind of standoff. And then both Shades' fists slammed into Blood's chest, shoving him back a foot.

"Get her out of here," she heard Undertaker growl as he

moved back into the bar.

And then a split second before all hell broke loose, Ghost's arm hooked around Skylar's ribcage, and he practically lifted her off her feet as he yanked her out of the way, spinning her toward the entrance, her arms and legs flaying to get free. She could hear a scuffle behind her, chairs scraping and brothers running to break up the fight. When Skylar finally twisted free of Ghost's hold, she turned to witness a sea of leather cuts shoving the two men apart.

"Stay the fuck away from her!" Shades jabbed a finger toward Blood as two men held him back, and Mooch stood in front of him, shoving him back.

"Calm the fuck down!" Mooch yelled at Shades.

Skylar's eyes moved to Blood to see him smirking at Shades, and then Ghost was hauling her out the door.

***

Shades glared at Blood. Motherfucker better get out of his sight.

"Blood!" Undertaker shouted. "Sit back down." He pointed toward the back end of the bar by the hallway to the restrooms. He stood there, eyeing him down until Blood finally shrugged off his brother's hold and moved to the far end of the bar. Then Undertaker turned to Shades. He grabbed a fistful of his vest and hauled him close. In a threateningly low voice he growled, "Calm the fuck down."

Shades' fist clamped around Undertaker's thick wrist and wrenched his hold loose. "Get your hands off me."

Undertaker's eyes narrowed on him for a moment, and then he backed off. He nodded toward the front of the bar.

"We need to talk."

"Done talking."

"Humor me. I got something to say to you."

Shades stalked to the other end of the bar, and Undertaker followed. They sat, and Undertaker waved the bartender over, getting them both another drink. After the bartender served them and withdrew, Undertaker turned to Shades. He was quiet a moment, and then he announced, "I don't fucking know you. I don't know what kind of a man you are except for what those colors you wear say about you. So let me be clear. You hurt my girl, I'll see those colors ripped off your back. You got that?"

"Told you, old man, she's mine. I take care of what's mine. No one is going to hurt her. Especially me."

"When you leave here, I'm trusting you to keep her safe."

Shades nodded.

"But just to be sure, I'm sending a couple boys back with you."

"Thanks, but no thanks."

"I'm not asking you. I'm telling you."

Shades glared at him.

"Consider it an escort. You don't have a problem with me puttin' more men on her, do you?"

Shades took in an aggravated breath, riled at the thought that Undertaker didn't really trust him to keep her safe. "You think I ain't up to the task?"

"There are two of you." He lifted his chin toward Ghost standing outside with Skylar. "You run into a pack of DKs, get into a situation where you're outnumbered, it won't matter how tough you are."

Shades glared at him.

"Son, put yourself in my shoes. I'm her father. I haven't been there for her whole life. I need to do this."

Shades clenched his jaw, and then nodded once.

Undertaker stalked off to the other end of the bar. Ghost walked back in with Skylar and with a grin, he observed sarcastically, "And everything seemed to be going so well."

Shades turned and slugged him in the chest, and then grabbed Skylar's hand and stalked back outside, Ghost's laughter following him.

"You okay?" he asked her as soon as they stepped out the doors.

She nodded. "I don't like when you fight."

He dipped his head to light a cigarette, and then looked at her as he blew a pissed-off stream of smoke out. "And I don't like when guys overstep their bounds with you."

Skylar swallowed and looked back into the bar. "Maybe we should just leave."

He nodded, taking another drag off his cigarette, his eyes moving to the crowd on Bourbon Street. "So, you get enough time with your father?"

She searched his face. "It wasn't my idea to come down here, Shades."

His eyes came back to her. "It wasn't mine either. And it sure as hell wasn't my idea to see the Quarter."

"Fine. Then let's go." She whirled toward his bike, and he tossed his cigarette into the street and grabbed her arm, stopping her.

"I'm sorry. I'm pissed and I'm taking it out on you." He dragged her into his arms. She was stiff at first, but then she melted into him.

"I don't want to fight with you," she whispered against his chest.

He kissed the top of her head. "I don't want to fight either. It's just been a hell of a day."

"Imagine how I feel."

He tightened his hold. "I know. You've had a lot thrown at you today."

"Shades?"

"Yeah?"

"I have to pee."

He grinned and let her go. "Okay, babe. You go pee and I'll see if Undertaker's ready to leave."

"And if he's not?"

"Then we're leaving anyway."

CHAPTER TWENTY-ONE

"You ready?" Shades asked Skylar when she returned from the restroom. She looked around. Most of the guys were already outside, mounting their bikes.

"Yes."

Shades held her jacket out and she turned, slipping her arms in. He took her hand and led her out to his bike. Skylar strapped on her helmet as Shades threw his leg over and lifted off the kickstand, firing it up. He looked over at her, and she climbed on the back.

The line of bikes pulled away from the curb one by one and headed out of the Quarter, across the city and finally taking the old Pontchartrain Drive Bridge across Lake Pontchartrain. They got halfway across and were stopped as the drawbridge rose for an approaching sailboat to pass underneath.

The boys shut off their bikes and dismounted, going to the side to watch. A full moon was reflected on the water, the running lights of the sailboat glowed, and the lights from the bridge lit the water below. A couple of the guys waved down to the captain, shouting hellos. The captain waved back as he motored his way to the bridge, his sails furled. With the bikes shut down, the only sounds were the quiet motor of the sailboat and the clanking of the bridge.

***

Raising the bridge was a slow process, and Undertaker lit a cigarette while they waited. Skylar, Shades, and Ghost stood not far away. Blood moved in next to Undertaker. He bent, leaning his palms on the rail, watching the sailboat, and then he turned his head toward the Chapter President.

"So, what do you make of this guy?"

Undertaker blew out a stream of smoke. "Too soon to tell."

"What makes him worthy of her?"

"You takin' an interest?"

"Maybe."

"Well, let me tell you"—he nodded toward Shades—"*he's* a hell of a lot more sure about her than just a 'maybe'."

"Hell, Undertaker, I just met her. *You* just met her."

"You're a good man, Blood, but—"

"And you just met *him*."

"That cut on his back tells me a hell of a lot."

"Yeah, okay, I'll give him that, but she's your daughter. You need to be sure." Blood's eyes bore into him.

"Don't need you tellin' me what I need to do, Blood."

"Right." Blood looked off over the water.

"There is something you can do for me, and it might

work in your interest."

"What's that?" His head swiveled back.

"He wants to take her back to Alabama."

Blood straightened. "What the fuck? You lettin' him?"

"I can't force her to stay here."

"Oh hell yeah, you can."

Undertaker smiled. "Right. But our relationship's on shaky enough ground right now. I push her too far, I'll lose her completely."

Blood shook his head and looked away. "She's your daughter; she does what she's told."

"Relax, Blood."

"So, what's this 'chore' you got for me?" He crossed his arms, leaning back against the rail.

"I want to send a couple boys back with them. Escort 'em."

"Escort 'em? What the fuck for?"

"They've got some trouble with the DKs. I'd feel better with more men on her."

Blood frowned. "DKs? What kind of trouble?"

"They're looking for her. Think she stole from them. Stabbed one of them to death."

Blood's arms came unfolded. "What the hell? You serious?"

He shrugged. "It's one hell of a story."

Blood looked over in Skylar's direction, and a half grin pulled on his mouth. "Maybe she's more like her old man than I thought."

Undertaker chuckled. "Yeah, if she did it, but she says

she didn't."

"You don't see her for all these years, then as soon as she gets herself neck deep in shit with the DKs she shows up here. And this is all just a coincidence?"

"She didn't just show up here. I sent for her."

Blood looked back at Undertaker with a frown. "Sent for her?"

"It's a long story. I'll fill you in when we get back."

Blood folded his arms again and stared back toward Skylar and Shades. "Seems like there's a lot of shit you need to fill me in on. Like why the hell I shouldn't run his ass off."

Undertaker slapped him on the shoulder. "Relax. You take that trip back with them, you may have a shot yourself."

Blood gave Undertaker a deadly look. "Don't think for a minute I won't take it."

Undertaker grinned and blew out another stream of smoke. "One thing I've learned about you, Blood, I never doubt you."

"What kind of game are you playing this time?"

Undertaker shrugged. "No game. He falls down on the job, I'd like to see her with you."

"Old man, what are you trying to do?"

"Keep you motivated."

Blood looked over at Skylar, his eyes running over her body. He lit up a cigarette and blew a pissed off stream of smoke into the air. "You *do* know how to keep a man motivated."

Undertaker chuckled.

***

When they got back to the clubhouse, Undertaker informed them that he had rooms made ready for them. He had one of the girls show them upstairs. She led them down the hall to the last two rooms on the right.

"The sheets are clean," the girl said, and then walked away.

"Great," Ghost commented and walked into the first room.

Shades and Skylar took the next. Walking in, Skylar took in the double bed. There were a couple nightstands on either side and a chair in the corner. Shades tossed their bag on the chair, eyeing a highboy dresser on the other side of the room that held an ancient television.

There was a tiny adjacent bathroom and Skylar headed into it as Shades collapsed back on the bed.

Once inside the bathroom, Skylar looked at herself in the mirror. She slipped her jacket off and her hand brushed down the feather boa she still had wrapped around her neck. Blood's words from earlier came back to her. *I could think of some uses for that boa.*

She looked toward the bathroom door, thinking of Shades, and a sly smile pulled at her mouth.

***

Shades lay on the bed, the remote aimed at the television as he flipped through the channels. Nothing but infomercials about everything from acne cleanser to kitchen mops. The door to the bathroom opened, and his head swiveled to see Skylar step out. And then he did a double take. *Holy shit.*

She was standing there in nothing but that feather boa

hanging from her neck and covering the front of her breasts. The side curves of each breast were in view as were the curves of her hips. His eyes slid down the center of her, down her cleavage, to her smooth flat belly, to her pretty little bellybutton, to the juncture of her thighs where she held one end of the boa, hiding it from his view.

He clicked the TV off and tossed the remote, swinging his legs over the edge of the bed.

"Come here, pretty girl," he growled.

She gave him a flirty smile, and then twirled the other end of the boa.

He grinned. "My baby wants to play. You gonna give me a little show?"

"Maybe." She shimmied the boa around her neck as she approached him. "*You're* a little overdressed."

He didn't hesitate in standing and stripping for her. First the vest was tossed to the floor, then the shirt went up and over his head. Then he unbuckled his belt.

He watched her eyes trail down his body as she slowly twirled the end of that feather boa. He grinned and dropped his pants, kicking them out of the way.

"Keep goin'," he encouraged, nodding to the boa. "Show a little more."

And she did, playing a little peek-a-boo show with him, pulling the boa to the side to give him a flash of nipple before covering it back up. And then, as if she'd realized she'd pushed him far enough, she swept both ends of the boa to the outside of her breasts and his eyes skated down as her body was completely revealed to him.

She stepped forward and took the end of the boa and tickled it over his skin, sliding it slowly from his chin, down his chest, his abs, and finally to his dick that was standing at attention, practically reaching out for her. She circled it, teasing him.

He stood it for about two seconds before his hands landed on her waist and he lifted her, twisting to toss her on the bed. Then he came down on top of her.

She gasped at his sudden aggressiveness, and he grinned.

"My turn. Hold real still now." He drew the end of the boa from her grip and began to torment her with it, tickling it over her cleavage, and then the underside of her breasts, and then her nipples with a barely-there touch.

She shivered.

His mouth dipped down to brush his lips in a trail following the feathers, pausing to suck on her nipples. Then he trailed the feathers down her belly, tickling her bellybutton. He grinned as she squirmed, and he couldn't resist brushing her parted mouth with a soft kiss.

He lifted his head and watched her eyes as he dragged the feathers between her legs. "Open for me, sweetheart."

She did as he bid, and he pushed his knee between her legs, holding them open as he drew the length between her folds. She moaned.

"You like that, pretty girl?"

"Yes," she gasped, her voice stuttering as he teased and tormented her with a whisper-soft touch.

He bent and pressed a kiss to her trembling belly, and then he threw his leg over her and sat up, straddling her thighs. Slowly, his hands drew up the boa, watching it gradually slide from around her neck, the feathers slithering over her soft skin. When it pulled free, he tossed it to the floor with a growl. "Enough playing."

Then he came down on top of her, his hot body pressing against her soft-as-silk skin. He kissed her, his mouth delving deep, tongue sweeping inside to rub against hers over and over as he devoured her intoxicating taste.

When finally he broke off to suck some air in, his breathing sawing in and out, he grinned. "I love that mouth of yours."

She tried to lift her head to reach his mouth again, but he retreated just out of her reach. She looked up at him questioningly, and his eyes dropped to her mouth as he brought his hand up and ran his thumb across her lips, the pad brushing lightly over the softness.

And then he gave her a sly grin. "Got a better use for that pretty mouth."

Her pretty little arched brows drew together as he lifted off her to slide his arm under the small of her back. His strong biceps locked around her as he hauled her up to the headboard in one powerful move.

She gasped at his quick forceful movement.

He straddled her chest, and her eyes dropped to his erection, before looking up at him with a smile. He grinned down at her as he took her head in his hands and plunged into her soft mouth that opened for him, eagerly taking him in.

It never got old, the feel of the sweet heat of her mouth surrounding him. He sucked in a breath and felt her hands on his ass pulling him closer, deeper as she moaned.

His hips moved, taking up the age-old rhythm, thrusting in and out as she clutched at him. It didn't take long before he knew he wouldn't last much longer. He pulled out and slid down her body, his knees spreading her legs. Locking his arms around her thighs, he yanked her down, her back sliding across the sheet. When he had her where he wanted her, he hooked his arms under her knees and pushed her legs back, pinning her open as he plunged into her in one powerful thrust.

She cried out as he drove into her over and over, pounding for all he was worth. His chest grew slick with sweat from his exertions, his muscles flexing with every surge. Looking down into her face, flushed with desire as she writhed beneath him, he growled, "Who do you belong to, Sky? Whose baby are you?"

"Yours, Shades. Only yours."

He slammed into her again. "Mine. Remember it. Don't ever forget it."

She reached up and dragged his head down to hers, locking her lips to his. He let her have the hungry kiss, but had to break off after only a moment to bury his head in her shoulder. He shuddered as an overpowering orgasm tore through him.

When his breathing returned to normal, he lifted off her and felt her arms tighten around him as if she didn't want to lose his weight. Brushing the hair back from her face, he kissed her.

"Sorry, I know that was all for me."

"You needed it. I want to be what you need."

"You are, baby. You are."

CHAPTER TWENTY-TWO

The next morning, Skylar was sitting at the bar with Shades and Ghost, eating scrambled eggs and bacon off a paper plate. A couple of the old ladies had come in and made breakfast. There were several other club members up and eating breakfast as well—Blood and Sandman, Undertaker and Mooch.

She looked over at her father. She knew Shades was anxious to get back on the road, but in a strange way she was going to miss Undertaker, and she was dragging her feet over breakfast.

Most of the men were done, even with their second helpings, and were now sipping on coffee. She appeared to be the only one still eating.

Movement at the end of the bar caught her eye, and she saw her father get up off his barstool and head over, his eyes on her. She turned her head as he stopped behind her.

"I want to talk to you, Skylar."

She looked at Shades and then nodded, slipping off her stool to follow her father. He led her upstairs and to his office. She stood in the middle of the room as he moved behind his desk, opened a drawer, and retrieved an item. Then he came around the desk to stand before her.

"I've got something for you. Something your mother would want you to have." He looked down at his hand, and her eyes followed his. A silver chain was looped over the fingers of one hand, and a pendant rested in the palm of his other.

He handed it to her. It was a marcasite diamond shaped pendant with four small pear shaped onyx stones in each corner. It was beautiful.

"I got that for her on a trip we took together to Sturgis. She always loved it." He swallowed and then continued. "One day while I was inside…"

"You mean prison?"

He nodded. "A letter came. It was her handwriting on the envelope." He nodded toward the necklace. "That was all that was inside. No note. No letter. Just that. I figured that was her way of telling me she was through." He shrugged.

Skylar looked from his sad face down to the pendent. She'd always wanted something of her mother's. Her eyes started to pool as she looked up at her father. "Thank you."

He took in her teary eyes. Then he swallowed and moved behind her. "Here. Let me put it on you."

She lifted her hair aside and stood still while he fastened the latch at the back of her neck. Then he stepped back, and she turned to him, fingering the pendant. "How does it look?"

He smiled. "Beautiful. Like you. Like your momma."

"Thank you."

He hugged her tight, and then just as suddenly, released her as if he was uncomfortable with the emotions he was feeling. "Okay. Good talk."

They walked downstairs, and as they approached the bar, Shades slid off his stool, his eyes searching hers.

"Butcher called. Wants us to swing by the Gulf Coast Chapter on our way back."

"For what?"

"I just need to check on some things. We'll probably stay overnight there."

Skylar groaned internally at the thought of staying at another clubhouse, but she didn't say anything.

"You ready?" he asked.

She nodded, noticing Blood and Sandman slinging packs over their shoulders.

"Let's get this show on the road already," Blood growled as he headed toward the door.

Skylar frowned and looked at Shades questioningly. "They're coming with us?"

Shades' eyes moved to Undertaker, and then back to her. "Daddy's orders."

She whirled on him. "What? Why?"

"Because you're my daughter. I'm makin' sure you're safe."

"You don't need to do this."

"Don't give me any mouth about this, baby girl. You don't get a say. It's a done deal."

Shades bent to grab his pack, apparently already reconciled to this change in plans.

"But—"

"Done. Deal."

Ghost came up behind her and whispered in her ear, "This world you're in now, it's a man's world, Hotrod. Better get used to it."

She rolled her eyes at him.

Shades turned with his pack over his shoulder and looked at Skylar. "Come on."

Undertaker stepped in front of her. He took her in his arms and hugged her gruffly. When he released her and looked down at her, he appeared choked up, his jaw tight.

"Skylar?"

"Yes?"

"See ya." Then he ambled off toward the stairs to his office.

Mooch watched him leave, and then turned to Skylar as she watched her father disappear upstairs.

"I hope you know how hard that was for him," Mooch informed her with a grin.

Her eyes came to him and she nodded, the corner of her mouth pulling up at his joking words. Then Shades had her elbow in his gentle hold, and he led her toward the door.

CHAPTER TWENTY-THREE

They blasted down I-10 and exited onto the beach expressway. Two and a half hours after they'd roared out of Slidell, Louisiana, they were rolling into Gulf Shores. Skylar could smell the ocean several blocks before she saw the blue water. The sun was setting as they pulled up at a light behind several cars. They had ridden two by two all the way from New Orleans, and they stopped in the same formation. Shades and Ghost with Blood and Sandman behind them.

Shades looked over at Ghost and shouted over the rumbling engines. "You guys go on, I'm gonna make a stop, pick up some shit. I'll meet you out there."

Ghost nodded. "We'll stop and pick up some beer and ice."

Shades nodded back.

"This Gulf Coast Chapter you talked about, are we staying at their clubhouse tonight?" Skylar asked Shades over his shoulder.

"No, babe."

"Then where are we staying?"

"Ghost has an aunt with a beach house out in Fort Morgan." He nodded toward the road to the right and the road sign above that indicated the turn. "She lets him use it once in a while when she's out of town. Lucky for us she's at a reunion in Charleston and won't be back until mid-week."

When the light changed, Shades went straight, and Ghost and the others made a right turn onto Hwy 180, the road that led out to Fort Morgan. Shades drove down a couple blocks and turned into the parking lot of a huge souvenir store.

They both climbed off the bike. Skylar looked up at the huge, two-story building with the glass front and huge shark hanging in the atrium visible through the glass. "What are we doing here?"

Shades just grinned at her. "You'll see."

He took her hand and led her inside. Then he led her through the store, past displays of cups, mugs, key-chains, refrigerator magnets, and an assortment of things made from seashells. They wended their way through racks and racks of t-shirts and sweatshirts. Skylar tried to look at things as Shades tugged her along, moving with purpose through the store, until he stopped suddenly and she plowed into his back. They'd arrived at the swimsuit section. Her eyes traveled over the racks of bikinis. She looked up at him questioningly.

He grinned back. "Pick one out, darlin'."

Her brows rose. "Seriously?"

"You got five minutes. I'll meet you in front. Make it

sexy." Then he winked and walked off. She watched him grab a pair of men's trunks as he headed toward the register.

She turned back to the racks and quickly began flipping through the hangers.

***

Twenty minutes later, they were heading down Fort Morgan Road. Civilization fell away and they passed under a canopy of trees, Spanish moss swaying in the breeze. There was sand on either side of the road. After several minutes, the trees opened up, and the bay appeared on the right. Several miles down, they made a left turn and rode a couple blocks to the shore. They made a right and rode along the beachfront homes. Shades pulled down a drive that was barely visible in the sand and rolled up to a bright pink house. It was up on stilts, beachfront facing the Gulf, the blue water visible underneath. The place didn't look like much from the outside. In fact, it looked kind of rundown with its peeling paint. A line of bikes was parked under the house. The guys having stopped to load up on beer, ice and booze, judging by the bottles and bags they were carting in, had arrived just ahead of them. Ghost was heading up the stairs to unlock the door.

Skylar and Shades dismounted and climbed up after him, following the men as they trooped inside. There was an open floor plan with a kitchen on the right, a long bar between it, and the living area. On the left was a small dining table. Straight ahead in the living area was a couch facing the windows that revealed the partially covered deck beyond. On one side sat a loveseat, and a chair and ottoman on the other.

A flat screen sat on a stand at an angle in the corner. There was an open doorway on the right and another on the left.

"There are two bedrooms and a bath on each side of the house," Ghost explained, pointing toward both doorways. "So pick a room, guys."

Skylar walked over to one side and checked out one of the bedrooms. It faced the Gulf with its own wall of windows. A large queen bed, with a nightstand on either side, faced the gorgeous view.

Shades walked in behind her and tossed their bags on the bed. Then he approached her from behind and wrapped his arms around her as she admired the view. The sand was sugar white, and the ocean was deep blue.

"It's so beautiful."

"We can open a window tonight and listen to the surf roll in with the tide all night."

"I love this place."

"You've been here two minutes."

"I don't care. I love it. I never want to leave."

Shades kissed her neck. "Come on, babe."

He took her hand and led her back to the main living area. The door to the deck stood open, and the ocean breeze beckoned them outside to join the others.

"My God, I could throw a rock and hit the surf, the water is so close," Skylar exclaimed.

Shades smiled at her.

Ghost pulled a cooler out and loaded it with beer. Then he broke a bag of ice open and dumped it over the bottles.

"You guys hit the quick-rip?" Shades asked, watching

Ghost.

"Nah, I wanted to get a few pounds of shrimp to boil so we stopped at the grocery store."

"The three of you in a grocery store? I can only imagine." Shades chuckled.

"It was all going fine till Blood almost got us kicked out of there," Ghost replied with a grin aimed at Blood.

Blood gave his best "what are you looking at me for" look and replied, "What, her kid was running all over the store like a little terror and *I'm* the bad guy for tripping him?"

Sandman snorted.

Ghost hit him with a look. "You were no better. 'Lady, can't you count to ten?'"

Sandman grinned. "Hey, we were in the express lane, and she had thirty-seven items. It was a fair question."

Shades shook his head with a smile and moved behind Skylar, wrapping his arms around her. He whispered in her ear, "Go get that bikini on."

She twisted her head to look up at him. "Are you going in with me?"

He winked at her. "Gotta talk to the guys a minute."

She moved off to do as he'd asked.

***

Shades watched her go as Ghost handed him a cold one.

"Did I hear she's puttin' a bikini on? Is that what that detour was about?" Ghost asked with a grin.

Shades twisted the bottle top off and leaned back against the railing as Ghost did the same. "Hell, yeah. I'm not gonna pass up a chance to see her in a bikini, am I? Do I look like a stupid man to you?"

Ghost grinned. "Guess not."

Shades looked over at the men seated at the glass patio table. They looked out of place at a beach house, sitting on the deck in their boots and leather, kicked back smoking cigarettes and drinking beer.

"I made a call earlier. Boys from the Gulf Chapter are gonna meet up with us later tonight."

"Where?" Blood asked.

"Place on the Florida-Alabama state line."

Blood nodded and looked down at his smoke. "Heard you've had some trouble down here."

Shades stared at him until Blood's eyes lifted to meet his, then he nodded. "That's what I'm here to find out."

"What exactly are you lookin' for?"

Shades shrugged. "Whatever seems off. Shit's not right with this chapter. I'm gonna get to the bottom of it. Tonight."

"You leavin' Skylar here at the house?"

"Yeah."

"What time's this meet?"

"Ten."

Just then Skylar appeared in the doorway and caught Shades' eye. His gaze moved over her. Hot damn, she was gorgeous. She was in a hot-pink string bikini, her long dark hair cascading over her shoulders to fall at her waist.

The guys turned to look.

"Come here, gorgeous." Shades held his hand out to her, and she moved toward him. His hand went to the bare curve of her waist and he pulled her close. His head dipped in for a kiss. He looked down at her and grinned, his hand sliding to her hip, his thumb brushing up and down along her skin. Then he hauled her into his arms and glanced up at his brothers.

"She's fuckin' mine, boys. All mine."

"Show off!" Ghost said.

Shades grinned.

"You coming?" she asked, looking up at him.

He looked over her head at his brothers, who were all smart enough to keep silent at her double entendre, even though he knew there were a lot of catcalls on the tip of their tongues. He noticed their eyes moving over her bare back, down to her ass and long legs.

"Eyes on your own paper."

"What? You're the one that paraded her out here in that," Ghost replied.

He looked down at her smiling face. "You go on in. I'll be there in a minute."

"Promise?"

"Promise."

She looked toward the water. "You think there are any sharks around?"

"Baby, the only sharks you need to worry about are up on this deck."

She smiled and slugged him in the gut.

"Just stay close to shore." He kissed her, and she skipped down the stairs and into the sand. He turned to watch her walk across the beach toward the surf. There were beach houses to the right and left as far as the eye could see, but the beach wasn't crowded. Almost deserted, actually.

He turned back and moved to go inside to change.

"You are one lucky son-of-a-bitch," Blood said, tilting his beer up.

Shades grinned at him. "Luck had nothing to do with it."

***

Hours later they sat around the table out on the deck eating shrimp that Ghost had boiled, peeling the shells off and tossing them onto a platter in the center of the table, the pile rising higher and higher.

"We need more cocktail sauce," Blood announced.

"I'll get it," Skylar replied, standing up. She was still in her bikini, but she had the matching pareo she'd bought tied around her hips.

"Shake what your momma gave ya, sugar," Sandman teased.

She did a little shimmy and giggled. Then she moved into the house and found Ghost in the kitchen draining another pot of boiled shrimp. He smiled up at her.

"Another batch coming right up."

Skylar smiled back at him. "Good thing. They're almost through the last bowl you carried out."

"Well, this is the last of them. You need something, Hotrod?"

"More cocktail sauce."

Ghost nodded toward the refrigerator. "I think there's another bottle in the door."

She opened the fridge and found one. As she took it out, she noticed some bottles on one of the shelves. "Corona!"

Ghost looked over. "Those are my aunt's. I'm sure she won't mind. Go ahead and have one. There are probably limes in there somewhere, too."

"Awesome." She set the sauce and beer down and dug out a lime. Ghost slid her a small cutting board and knife. She sliced up the lime and put a wedge in her beer.

"Make me one, too, will you?" Ghost asked.

She smiled at him. "Sure."

They carried out the shrimp and sauce and their beers and sat down with the others.

Skylar took a sip of her beer, and it caught the eye of Sandman.

"Beer with fruit. I never got that," he commented.

"You ever tried it?" Ghost asked.

"Nope."

Ghost passed him his beer, and he took a slug.

"Damn, that's good."

"Beats the hell out of that Clydesdale piss *you* drink," Ghost advised with a smirk.

Sandman looked down at the bottle in his hand. "Beer with fruit, who knew."

They all chuckled.

"Get your own." Ghost grabbed his beer back.

CHAPTER TWENTY-FOUR

At nine o'clock they headed toward the state-line. They pulled into the crushed-seashell and gravel lot of the bar that stood on the beachfront location for more than fifty years. They parked their bikes in a line near the side of the building.

A cool breeze blew in off the Gulf, and the sound of the surf crashing on the beach carried to them as they headed inside. Shades led them to the far end of the bar where they all took a barstool.

The brothers they were to meet up with had yet to arrive, but they were half an hour early, as was Shades' plan.

The bartender dropped coasters in front of each of them as he eyed their vests, then their faces. The colors they wore may look familiar, but Shades knew their faces were all new to him.

"What'll you boys have?" he asked.

As Ghost, Blood, and Sandman surveyed the room, Shades ordered for all of them. The bartender began pulling bottles of beer from a tub of ice and popping the tops off as he set them down in front of each man.

"We don't want any trouble in here," he said.

Shades looked at him. "We don't want any trouble either."

The bartender gave him a nod and walked away.

Ghost leaned into Sandman and nodded toward a skanky blonde. "There's one for ya. She's not the best lookin' girl here, but beauty's only a light switch away, bro."

Blood almost choked on a mouthful of beer.

***

At ten to 10:00, they heard the roar of pipes and watched through a window as a pack of bikes rolled up, their chrome gleaming in the moonlight. A few moments later, seven of their brothers trooped in.

Shades straightened and moved forward to greet them.

He embraced one after another, as did Ghost, Blood, and Sandman.

Shades knew Case, Coop, and Deez, but he'd had to be introduced to the other five. There was Moon, the Chapter President. Rocker, their VP, and Brick and Pipe.

He could see by looking at Moon and Rocker that they were both hopped up on something. Coke, maybe. Methamphetamines, more likely.

They moved off to a table, and Shades' eyes connected with Case. Case joined the five of them at the bar.

"How ya been you furry bastard?" Ghost asked him.

Case stroked his three-inch long beard. "It's purty, ain't it?"

"A thing of beauty. What have you been up to?"

"Got my Dyna up and running finally."

Ghost grinned. "It's about time you put that moped back together. Come the fuck home for a weekend. We need a night out."

Case chuckled. "Hey maybe we can grab Griz and drive 50 miles to the nearest Thai spot that's closed."

Ghost started laughing. "That was some night. I wanted to kill him."

Case pulled a cigarette from his pack, put it in his mouth, and then talked around it. "Remember we were so hungry by then that we ended up eating five dollar pizza?"

"It was fucking good, too."

"By then gas station hotdogs would have tasted good."

Sandman looked over. "Hey, I like gas station hotdogs."

Blood swiveled his head toward him. "You would. Don't you have a blonde to go bother?"

Sandman looked over at her. "I'm lettin' her ferment a while."

"Yeah, that'll help."

"Your Shovelhead still leaking oil everywhere you park it?" Case asked Ghost.

"It's not leaking oil. It's marking its territory."

Case chuckled. "Right."

The bartender took his order and brought him a beer. Case's cell went off, and he looked down at the screen. "Mutha-fucking hell. Twelve missed calls. Women. If I don't answer the fucking phone she immediately thinks I'm cheating. It's like, *Bitch, I'm riding!*"

"No shit," Sandman agreed with a laugh. "Testify."

"Am I right?" Case asked him.

"You're right."

"Thank you."

"But you do manage to keep her happy and around."

Case shrugged. "I got a sweet ass."

Shades looked over his shoulder at the table in the corner where the other Gulf Chapter members had taken up residence, and then back at Case. "This the usual with them?"

"Yup. Been binging for two days now."

"You?"

"Me? Shit no. I steer clear of that crap. I'm high enough on life, can't you tell?"

A grin pulled at the corner of Shades' mouth, but he nodded toward the table. "It becoming a problem?"

"Hey, he's my Prez. What do you want me to say?"

"We're here to help, Case. I'm gonna be straight with you. This is between you and me, understood?" Shades said in a low hushed voice.

Case nodded.

"Future of your whole chapter is on the line."

"Fuck."

"Exactly. You don't want the Nomads showin' up to clean house do you? So just give it to me straight. How bad is this shit?"

"Bad. And getting worse. The binges are starting to become more frequent and lasting longer every time."

"That where the profits are going? Cause I know your business isn't down."

Case nodded. “Yeah, most likely.”

“So you’ve got a President and VP strung out half the time. How the hell does anything get done down here?”

“The rest of us are all trying to hold it together. It’s been rough.”

“Case, get your ass over here,” Rocker yelled across the room.

Case moved off to join the brothers from his chapter.

Ghost and Shades exchanged a look.

“It’s fucked up worse than Butcher thought,” Ghost observed, leaning on the bar.

“Yeah, I don’t think he had any idea things were this bad,” Shades replied.

Blood and Sandman kept silent, quietly smoking and staring at a sign above the bar that read, *Alabama: where the weak are killed and eaten.*

Blood grinned. So prophetic.

***

Shades nursed his beer, his elbows on the bar, and thought about his options. He couldn’t really give Moon any orders, not that it would help. If this drug problem was as bad as he suspected, nothing short of pulling his patch would fix the problems in this chapter. That wasn’t something he had the authority to do. The state authority fell to Butcher, so that was a call *he* was going to have to make.

A few minutes later an older gray-haired man went behind the bar and to the register. He ran a tally report of the day’s business so far. His eyes strayed to Shades and the rest of his crew, his gaze flicking over all of them, taking note of their colors.

"You Jerry, the owner?" Shades caught his attention. Butcher had filled him in with some information.

"Yeah." His look said, *what of it?* He strolled over to him.

"I was sent down here to take a…shall we say, closer look at our Gulf Chapter. Clean up any problems we may have."

"And?"

"And I want to know how this *relationship* is working out for you."

"It's not."

Well, that was abrupt, Shades thought. "Tell me why."

"Look, most of your boys mind their own business and don't cause trouble."

"Most?"

Jerry nodded, his eyes going to the group at the table.

Shades turned his head, following his gaze. Then he turned back. "Let me guess. The two in the corner?"

Jerry nodded again. "Mostly when those two are high on something."

Shades nodded, taking it in.

"Death Heads are worse."

Shades frowned. "The Death Heads MC has been coming round?"

"Yeah. Stick around. They'll probably be in here tonight. There was a time they wouldn't dare. Now they're running off all my business. I was led to believe that being in with the Evil Dead was going to keep those assholes off my back."

Shades reached his hand under his cut, pulled out the envelope Butcher had given him, and slid it across the bar. "For your troubles." Then he lifted his chin toward the table. "That will be taken care of. You got my word."

"Thanks. Appreciate it." Jerry slid the envelope in his pocket and walked off.

"That was diplomatic," Blood commented, sipping on his beer.

"We alienate the locals, we become persona non grata around here. That's not happening."

"Makes sense."

"We need to move the bikes to the back."

"What for?"

"The Death Heads have been showing up here." Shades shrugged. "They do tonight, we'll have the element of surprise. They'll walk in here blind."

"Doesn't hardly seem like a fair fight, does it?" Sandman asked.

Blood grinned. "If you find yourself in a fair fight your tactics suck."

CHAPTER TWENTY-FIVE

The rumble of pipes could be heard from outside. Brick, who'd been posted at the window, turned his head and announced, "Six Death Heads rollin' in."

Shades, Ghost, Blood, and Sandman all knocked back their drinks and rose from their barstools.

"Show time, boys," Shades announced. The other seven Gulf Chapter members joined them in heading toward the entrance, slowly pulling on black leather gloves as they went.

Shades put his arm out, holding them back from going out the door. "Let 'em dismount first. We don't want to give 'em a chance to pull back out."

Blood dipped his head, peering through the blinds and past the neon sign in the front window. "Least not until we beat their asses first."

The men all watched through the window as the Death Heads dismounted. Five headed toward the door. One hung back making a call on his cell.

"Now," Moon ordered.

The six members of the Death Heads froze as twelve members of the Evil Dead MC poured out the front door.

"Oh shit!" one of them hissed.

Taking advantage of the surprise, the Evil Dead jumped them in a fight that was two on one. Even though they were outnumbered, the Death Heads MC had no intention of going down easily. They fought back viciously. Fists connected with jaws. Bodies charged each other. When one of them went to ground, he was stomped and kicked. The fight was a violent and brutal confrontation with no holds barred.

It wasn't long before a dozen squad cars barreled into the lot, lights flashing.

Soon the fight was broken up, and the two MCs were separated. The Death Heads were cuffed face down in the gravel, and the Evil Dead were cuffed to the metal railing that ran along the front of the building.

***

"Christ, Blood, I thought you were gonna kill that guy," Shades grumbled, shaking his head.

Sandman spit some blood on the ground. "He probably would have if the cops didn't show up."

Blood shrugged. "I may have some unresolved childhood issues."

"No shit," Shades agreed with a chuckle.

Ghost looked over at Blood. "How does a man with your obvious people skills end up like *this*?" He rattled his cuffs against the rail.

"Shut the fuck up," Blood growled back with a half grin.

Sandman, who was cuffed to a support post with Blood, looked over and remarked, "I can't think of anyone I'd rather be cuffed to a pole with than you, Peaches."

Blood glared back at him. "Yeah, well I can think of a few people I'd rather *you* be cuffed to a pole with."

"I fuckin hate handcuffs. This sucks," Ghost grumbled.

Sandman mumbled, "Life should be more like hockey. When someone pisses you off, you just beat the shit out of them, then sit in the penalty box for five minutes."

Ghost rattled the metal cuffs against the pole again. "Clue in, Sandman. This is the MC version of the penalty box."

"Yeah well, we've been here a fuck-of-a-lot longer than five Goddamned minutes."

***

It took the officers a while to get everyone's story, including that of the owner, who nodded toward Shades.

Shades could only wonder what he'd said as the County Sheriff ambled his way over. Since both the owner and the sheriff were on the Evil Dead payroll, he had an inkling how this little chat was gonna go. The sheriff stopped in front of him and put his hands on his hips.

"The owner says the Death Heads started this. Said you all were quietly drinking inside and not causing any trouble. That true?"

"Of course, Sheriff," Shades agreed with a smug smile.

Sandman went to lean back against the horizontal railing that attached to the vertical post he and Blood were cuffed to. He stumbled and landed flat on his ass.

Ghost looked down at him. "You missed."

"You are so disappointing," Blood muttered down at Sandman who lay on the ground at his feet.

"I'm okay," Sandman replied and tried to stand, but banged his head on the connecting horizontal railing with a loud crack. "Less okay."

Ghost chuckled.

The Sheriff peered down at Sandman, then asked Shades, "Your friend here party a little too hard?"

"Don't worry, Officer, I'm the designated driver," Blood put in.

The sheriff, who apparently had a pinch of chewing tobacco between his cheek and gums, turned his head and spit on the ground. "Smart ass is what you are."

Blood looked over at the man's chew. "That's just gross."

The men all snickered.

Even though the two MCs were separated, the Death Heads began yelling shit to the Evil Dead across the parking lot.

"You're all dead, motherfuckers!"

Without missing a beat, Case yelled back, "Yeah. *Evil* Dead, and don't you fucking forget it!"

Ghost shouted, "Go back to Gatorville, dickhead! We claim this bar. This coast. This state. It all belongs to the Evil Dead, and the fucking Death Heads aren't welcome in this state."

"Not for long, asshole!" came the response back from across the parking lot.

Shades looked over at the sheriff and quirked a brow. "You hear that? Is that what you want? The Death Heads MC getting a foothold in this town? In this state? Because let me tell you that's only the start. You allow them to cross that inter-coastal, and you are opening hell's gates."

"And your boys are a bunch of boy scouts, huh?"

"Have we caused any trouble in this town?"

"Not yet."

"No, we haven't, and you got my word, we won't."

"Your word? That supposed to mean something to me?"

One of the Death Heads shouted, "We'll be back tomorrow with the entire chapter at our back!"

"We'll be waiting for you, motherfuckers!" Blood shouted back.

Shades' brows rose, giving the cop an I-told-you-so look. "You hear that? They're gonna be coming enforce tomorrow. Right across that state line, and then right across the inter-coastal bridge. And then they're gonna roll right through your pretty town. Makin' a statement."

The sheriff smiled back at Shades. "Maybe we'll be makin' a statement of our own tomorrow."

Shades grinned back. "I'm all for that."

***

Twenty minutes later, the Evil Dead members were all being released.

As Blood threw his leg over his bike and lifted it off its kickstand, he looked over at Shades.

"How the hell did we get released, free to go, and the Death Heads are all still face down in the gravel?"

Shades grinned back at him. “It’s good to have the local boys in your pocket.”

Blood grinned back and shook his head. “That and the owner who’s pressing the charges.”

CHAPTER TWENTY-SIX

Skylar awoke to the sound of four motorcycles approaching. She could hear their engines rumbling as the men rolled up under the stilts of the house to park their bikes underneath.

An impish smile pulled at her mouth. She'd crawled into bed naked, remembering what Shades had told her about his wish to someday come home and find her waiting for him like this. It was going to be his lucky night.

As she lay in bed waiting, she heard the sounds of the men as they trooped in the door.

"Fuck, where's the ice? My eye is swelling up like a motherfucker," one of them grumbled, his voice carrying to her in the bedroom.

"Freezer, dumbass. Where else would the ice be?" she heard Ghost reply.

"Fuck, my knuckles are so fucked up I can't straighten my fingers. I could barely hold the throttle on the way back," she heard Blood mutter.

"You beat the crap out of that big guy though." Shades laughed.

"You weren't so bad yourself."

Skylar frowned. They'd been in a fight? She threw the covers back and quickly threw on jeans and a tank top. Then she walked out of the bedroom and into the common room. Blood and Sandman were sitting at the table. Ghost stood in the kitchen area, dumping ice into a bowl, and Shades was sitting at the bar.

Ghost was the first to notice her. His head came up, and his eyes connected with hers. *Oh my God.* The side of his face was bruised, and his lip was split.

"Hey, Hotrod," he said quietly.

At his words, Shades' head came around, and Blood twisted in his chair to look at her.

Holy crap. They were *all* battered. Her fingers came to her lips as she gasped in a soft breath.

Shades arm lifted toward her. "Come here, babe."

When she reached him, her hand went to his face, her fingers gently brushing his hair back. The side of his jaw and cheekbone were bruised, one eye starting to swell.

"Baby," she whispered softly.

His hand slid over hers as she cupped his cheek, and he tried to smile. "It's not as bad as it looks. We're all fine."

"Yeah, the other guys look worse," Ghost put in.

She turned her head to look at him. He stood at the sink running water over the bowl of ice he'd been filling. His face looked just as bad, one eye swollen.

"Ghost," she whispered.

He attempted to smile at her, but winced when his split lip started bleeding. He walked over to the table and set the bowl down between Blood and Sandman, tossing some dishcloths down next to it.

The two men each grabbed up a towel and quickly wrapped some ice, bringing it to their jaws. Then Blood dunked his whole hand in the ice water.

Her eyes moved back to Shades. "What happened?"

"Just a bar fight."

She made up a towel of ice and brought it back to Shades. She pressed it against his face, and he groaned.

"Why were you fighting?" she asked.

"Had a run-in with another club," Sandman mumbled.

"Sandman," Blood warned.

"What? She's knee-deep in this club, she don't get to know?"

Skylar turned back to Shades. "The DKs?"

"No, Death Heads, babe."

"You ran into the Death Heads? I thought they were only in Florida."

"Seems they want to expand their horizons."

"How many were there?"

"Half dozen."

Skylar turned to the other guys. She moved around the room, studying their injuries. She took Ghost by the chin and turned his face to the side, taking in the bruising.

He smiled down at her. "I'm good, Hotrod. Just a little swelling."

She moved to the table and lifted Blood's hand out of the ice water. "You need to put something on those cuts."

"You wanna play nurse, darlin', I'll be your willing patient." He jerked his head toward the hallway. "We could go in the other room, and I'll let you take real good care of me."

"Blood," Shades growled in a warning voice.

Blood's eyes remained riveted on her, but a smile spread across his mouth, and he winked. "What? I'm just playin' with her."

"Well play nice."

"Do you have an old lady, Blood?" Skylar found herself asking.

"Nope."

"I can see why."

"Ooow. The claws are coming out."

"Someone needs to take you down a notch."

"And you want to be the one to do it." It was a statement, not a question. "Babe, you couldn't handle me even if I came with instructions."

"Oh really? You know what that sounds like? Not my problem."

"I could make it your problem, if you want me to."

She shook her head. "You're unbelievable. Your arrogance knows no bounds. Is there any situation you won't take advantage of, twisting it for your own benefit?"

"Look who's talking about taking advantage."

Shades started to come off his stool, but Ghost held him back with a palm to his chest, murmuring, "Give her a chance. See how she handles him, bro."

Shades eased back onto his barstool.

"You have something to say, say it," Skylar snapped at Blood, her hands on her hips.

"You got yourself into trouble, where'd you run?"

"What's that supposed to mean?"

"You need it laid out for you? I got no problem with that. You're taking advantage of your man, your father, *and* this club."

"Is that what you think I'm doing?"

"You *bet* I do."

"It's not true."

Blood let out a huff of laughter. "Right."

Her chin lifted. "I know what your problem is. You just don't like that fact that because he's my father, you got stuck with this shit detail. Go back to New Orleans. I don't need you."

"That's not an option."

"What's your problem with me, Blood? Is it the fact that I stand up to you, tell you what I think?"

"No, darlin', I admire your backbone *and* your smart mouth."

"Up to a point."

"Damn right. *Up to a point!*"

"I know we're brothers, Blood, but if you don't lay off her, we're gonna have a problem," Shades warned.

Blood stood and stalked toward the deck. "I need some fucking air anyway."

Skylar glared after him. "Coward."

That brought him to a stop. He turned and glared back at her.

Shades stepped in front of her. “Babe, enough.”

“You better get her in hand, Brother, or I will,” Blood growled.

“Just go the fuck outside,” Shades snapped over his shoulder at the man.

Blood turned and moved through the sliding door.

Shades turned back to Skylar. “What’s got into you, woman? Talking to Blood that way.”

“Blood can kiss my ass.” God that man was so infuriating.

“Ok, he’s a bastard. But calling him a coward? Those are fighting words.”

“I thought she was awesome.” Ghost winked at her.

Shades glanced at Ghost with a look that said, “Stay out of this” and then his eyes returned to Skylar. “Babe, never seen you like this before. Never seen you go off on someone like that before. What happened to my quiet little Skylar?”

Skylar’s eyes connected with Ghost’s, remembering what he’d told her about being the tough woman Shades would need her to be. That she needed to step up. Had she just *overstepped*? Damn, this MC life was confusing as hell.

“Don’t let Blood get to you, Hotrod. He was an abused child,” Ghost teased with a grin.

“I’m sorry. I shouldn’t have done that,” Skylar apologized.

“Hey, never water yourself down just because someone can’t handle you at a hundred proof, darlin’,” Ghost assured her.

Sandman looked up, blinking as if he were trying to focus after dozing off. "Blood bein' an ass again?"

Ghost looked at Sandman and shook his head. "Buy a clue, Brother."

"What? What'd I miss?"

"Skylar just put Blood in his place."

"Did she now? Fuck. That calls for a drink. Let's do a shot."

"Jesus Christ."

"Ghost, a woman ever put you in your place?" Sandman asked.

"Okay, what response on my part would bring this conversation to a close?" Ghost muttered.

"We're goin' to bed," Shades informed the room, taking Skylar by the hand and heading toward the hallway.

"Thanks, Brother. Leave me here with Mr. Shitfaced."

"Hey," Sandman muttered. "I'm not shitfaced. Okay, maybe I am. Actually, I may be more high than drunk." He slumped back in his chair, eyes closing.

"Crap. Can you even move?" Ghost asked.

Sandman cracked one eye open. "Why, am I in the way?"

Ghost shook his head and moved outside to join Blood on the balcony.

***

Blood stood at the railing, watching the lights flickering in the distance from the oil rigs out in the Gulf. Off to the left was a slow moving shrimp trawler, its riggings illuminated by spotlights high up on the mast. Its towing booms extended out on each side of the boat, the nets trailing below.

He turned at the sound of the sliding glass door. Taking in the look on Ghost's face, he said, "Yeah, yeah. I'm on your 'who's been naughty' list."

"Wound up a little tight, are we?"

"Okay, okay, I sounded off more than I should have. I'm a little on edge."

"More like over the edge. The only thing missing was gunfire."

A half grin pulled at Blood's mouth, and he turned back to the Gulf.

"Nice night out here," Ghost observed, moving to stand next to him.

"Yup. Thanks for letting us stay here."

"No problem."

"It's real soothing, listening to the waves. It calms my shit down."

"Right. Damn, that short fucker tonight had a wicked hook." Blood turned to see Ghost touching his sore jaw.

"I've got just the cure for that." Blood held out the joint he'd been smoking. Ghost reached for it, took a toke, and passed it back. Blood took his own long drag, and then slowly exhaled the smoke, his eyes taking in the moon shining down on the water, the waves reflected in its silvery light.

"Skylar's always been quiet, reserved. You know what I mean?" Ghost said quietly beside him.

Blood looked over at him, cocking a brow.

"I sorta told her she needs to toughen up if she's going to be with Shades."

"Why's that?"

"He's gonna be our next VP."

That was news to Blood. "Oh, really. How do you know that?"

Ghost shrugged. "Position's vacant. It's gonna be him."

Blood turned back to the Gulf, his eyes on the surf. "Huh. So he gets VP, she's gotta be a bitch?"

"That's not what she's doing."

He let out a huff of disbelief. "Isn't she?"

"Don't be an ass, Blood. You've both rubbed each other the wrong way since you met. Why is that?"

He shrugged, not willing to admit too much. "She's my president's daughter. That makes her our new little chapter princess," he said with a sneer.

"It's more than that. So what gives?"

Admitting the truth—that maybe he was interested in her for himself, and it irked him every time he saw her with Shades, and that he baited her just to get a rise out of her—that wasn't gonna happen. So he threw up a distraction. "Maybe this whole setup rubs me the wrong way."

"How so?"

"You don't think it's odd? She shows up suddenly when the DKs are after her?"

Ghost shrugged. "Don't know. I just know her and Shades go back a long way."

"Yeah, so?"

"I'm talking like ten years. Like when she was about

eighteen. He knows her. He trusts her. And so do I."

Blood looked away wondering if he'd misjudged the whole thing. Maybe Skylar and Shades *were* meant to be together. If Shades was her first love, he'd never be able to compete with that. And that sucked for him, but it wasn't the first time he'd taken an interest in a woman only to have it dangled in front of him and then yanked away.

***

Shades shrugged out of his cut, tossing it on the bed. Next came his t-shirt, which he tossed toward the floor of the closet.

Skylar couldn't help but gaze upon all that beautiful exposed muscle, the cut abs, that sexy V that disappeared into the low waist of his jeans.

There was a low stuffed arm chair in the corner by the picture windows that overlooked the beach. He sat down in it and bent to pull his boots and socks off, tossing them into the closet. Then he leaned back into the chair, and she could see the exhaustion rolling off him.

Coming to stand behind him, she started rubbing his shoulders, his skin smooth and warm beneath her hands. His head fell back, and his eyes slid closed as her fingers dug into the knotted muscles.

"Hmm, that feels good."

She worked his muscles harder.

She thought about the fight he'd been in tonight. This was a whole new side of Shades—a side of him that was being revealed to her on this trip. First the violence in New Orleans when he'd decked that creep in the bar, then his confrontation with Blood that same night, and now this fight tonight. This was a side of Shades she hadn't seen when they'd been together years ago. Maybe it had always been there, maybe he'd just kept it hidden from her. But she'd never been confronted with it before. She'd never been actual witness to it. Witness to its fallout.

She took in Shades' face, still unbelievably attractive despite being all bruised up. She'd been taken with his good looks from the moment she'd met him, but it had always been about more than that. It was his overwhelming masculinity, his intensity, his strength, his dominant personality. It was the rousing sex and the sweet kisses. The way he brought out the wild side in her, and the way he drew out her most guarded fears, secrets, hopes, and dreams.

She'd fallen in love with his gruff voice and his dirty words, the gentleness of his touch and his growly commands. The way he could be rough and playful with her one minute and sweet and tender with her the next. She never knew what to expect. He was anything but predictable. And she loved that about him. Skylar's lips touched the skin of his neck and she felt Shades relax into the caress.

"You should sleep." She slid her arms around him. "You've been going non-stop for days. You barely slept when we were in New Orleans."

"If you wanted me to sleep, you shouldn't have started touching me like that, sweetheart. When I walked in the room, sleep was all I had on my mind. Now you've got me thinking about something else."

His hand came up to cup her neck, pulling her head

down as he tipped back and claimed her mouth with his. The kiss was gentle, sweet, but she felt him holding back. When he released her, she looked down into his eyes.

"Come here, pretty girl." He pulled her around in front of him and onto his lap, his arms encircling her hips. "We need to have an actual honest conversation."

CHAPTER TWENTY-SEVEN

Shades studied Skylar. He knew what was going through her mind. Skylar might try to act the part of the tough biker chick, but she'd never fully pull it off, not when everything she felt played across her face.

"You're upset." He watched a frown form, but she wasn't fooling him. She knew exactly what he was talking about. "The fighting. You don't like it."

She did that cute thing she always did when she sucked in her lips as if she was trying to literally hold back the words. His eyes dropped to her mouth. "Say it. Tell me."

When still she stayed quiet, he squeezed her. "We have to be able to talk about shit, Skylar. We always could before."

"It scares me. I've never seen this side of you. Maybe it was always there, but—"

"I did my best to keep that all away from you."

"So, it was always there?"

He shrugged. "It's been a stressful week, Sky. I won't always be coming home with bruises."

"But, the life you lead—"

"Is the same one I've always led. You're just in it now, in a way you weren't before."

"Is this the norm for you? First New Orleans and now here? Are you going to get in fist fights everywhere we go?"

"Sky, I don't go looking for fights, but if someone's insulting you or some Goddamn club is trying to invade our turf, then hell yeah, I'll make the motherfuckers bleed."

She turned her uncertain eyes toward him.

"That look tells me you're questioning what the hell you've signed up for," Shades said in a low voice.

She looked down and he knew that was exactly what she was doing.

He lifted her chin. "Babe, look at me." When her eyes connected with his, he searched them. "You don't get to pick which parts of me you accept. You don't have to agree with me or like all the decisions I make, but if you accept me, you've got to take all of me."

"So this will always be a part of our lives? The violence?" There was a bite to her words, and it wasn't lost on Shades. He took a deep breath and nodded.

"Yeah. I can't sit here and lie to you. More than anything, I want us to be honest with each other, about everything. I want to be able to talk to you about things without fear of upsetting you or that you won't support me. If you take me on, you're taking the bad with the good. I don't want to have to hide shit from you. If I'm going through a rough time, there are going to be nights when I'll need to be able to come home and talk to you about it. I need to know I can do that. I need to know that I don't have to make up stories about why my face is bruised or whatever. Bottom line is I need you, Sky. I need your support, your encouragement…" He paused to smile. "Sometimes I'll need you to tell me when I fuck up. And lastly, I'll always need your love."

"I don't know if I can be that person, Shades."

He frowned, fearing she was having second thoughts about being with him. Real honest-to-God second thoughts. "What do you mean?"

"I don't know if I can be all those things. I don't know if I'll ever be the kind of woman you need."

"You're exactly the kind of woman I need, Skylar. I've never found another woman who's fit me better, who's suited me better."

"Shades—"

"Do you love me? Because that's all it comes down to, Skylar."

"You know I do."

"That's all I need, baby. Just give us a chance. Can you do that?"

He was right. A life with Shades had to be all or nothing, and nothing wasn't an option. She nodded. "All right. I'll take the bad with the good, Shades. Because without you I'm lost, I'm only half alive."

Shades pressed his lips gently to hers. He felt her arms slide around him and he deepened the kiss, his hand cupping the nape of her neck. The kiss turned hot and heavy until suddenly she pulled back. He looked up questioningly, and then caught her sly smile. A moment later, she was slipping off his lap to drop to her knees between his spread thighs. Her hands began working his belt buckle as a half grin formed on his mouth.

"Baby, you gonna take my mind off my injuries?" He brushed a lock of hair back from her face, enjoying the desire he saw in her eyes.

"I'm going to make you feel all better. I know what my man likes," she whispered as she undid his pants and pulled his erection out.

His hands threaded into her silky hair as she wasted no time teasing him, but instead settled her mouth over him, taking him all the way to the back of her throat.

He hissed in a breath and his hips involuntarily thrust forward as he clutched her head. "Christ, Sky. That feels fucking good. Yeah, my baby knows what her man likes."

His head dropped back against the chair as she made him forget every bruised part of his body.

CHAPTER TWENTY-EIGHT

The next morning, a shirtless Blood shuffled out of his room to find Ghost wailing on the toaster oven with a wooden spoon. He took a seat at the dining table with Shades and Skylar.

"What did that toaster oven ever do to you?" Blood squinted at Ghost.

"Die, toaster. Die," Ghost growled.

"It burnt his fucking Pop-Tart," Shades explained, sipping his coffee.

"Jesus Christ," Blood grumbled. "Where's the aspirin?"

Ghost stopped banging on the toaster and pointed the wooden spoon toward the bathroom between Blood and Sandman's bedrooms. "In the cabinet."

Before he got up, Blood reached over and tugged on a lock of Skylar's hair. "Sorry about last night. I can be an ass. We good, darlin'?"

Her expression softened at his apology. “We’re good.”

“No hard feelings?”

She shook her head.

Blood got up and moved to the bathroom, rummaged through the cabinet, and pulled out a bottle. As he carried it back to the main room, he glanced into the partially open door of Sandman’s room. There was a woman passed out in the bed with him. Blood did a double take at the door and asked as he returned to the table, “Is that the blonde skank from last night?

Ghost grinned and turned to Shades. “Am I a matchmaker or what?”

Shades gave him a tired thumb’s up.

“How the hell did she get here?” Blood asked, knowing they’d all ridden back, and Sandman hadn’t had any blonde ridin’ bitch last night.

“Apparently she followed us in her car. It’s stuck in the sand out there,” Shades informed the group.

Ghost peered out the window over the kitchen sink. “Son-of-a-bitch. She’s sunk up to the wheel wells. We’ll have to push her out.”

“I ain’t pushin’ shit,” Blood growled. “He tapped her, let him cart his ass out there.”

A moment later, Sandman stumbled out of the bedroom scratching his chest. “Did I hear my name?”

“Take a look out the window, bro,” Blood advised.

“Yeah, your date’s car is stuck.”

“Christ it’s bright as fuck in here,” Sandman grumbled.

“That’s called daylight, Brother,” Ghost put in.

Sandman's squinting eyes searched around for his black, wraparound sunglasses. He grabbed them up off the bar, slid them on, and then moved to the window. He groaned when he saw the car sunk in the sand.

"Kill me now."

"Oh, oh, I'll do it!" Ghost had his hand in the air.

Shades and Blood burst out laughing.

Sandman collapsed into a chair at the dining table, joining the rest of them.

"My head hurts."

"Everybody's head hurts. Get over it," Blood barked and threw the bottle of aspirin at him.

"Why does my face hurt?" Sandman tenderly touched his cheek below the dark sunglasses.

"Because you let some douchebag Death Head blindside you, dumbass."

"Oh, yeah. I forgot about that. We beat the crap out of 'em, though, didn't we?"

"Yup."

He suddenly turned to Blood. "Was I cuffed to a pole with you or did I just dream that?"

"You dreamt that," Blood replied with no hesitation.

The rest of them snickered.

Shades looked over at Blood. "Thanks for the help last night."

"A chance to pound some Death Head faces to a pulp? Wouldn't have missed it."

Shades grinned.

Out of the blue, Sandman, who was now fingering a

ceramic pumpkin that sat as part of the silk-floral centerpiece, mumbled, "We don't carve pumpkins at my house…I don't trust my children with knives. They may turn on me."

Shades almost snorted his coffee out his nose.

Turning to Blood, Skylar frowned and whispered, "Is he on drugs?"

Blood took a sip of his coffee. "No, but he should be."

Sandman stood up and moved toward the coffee maker mumbling, "I need coffee." He took down a mug and turned to Ghost. "You want some?"

"Yeah, black, with two heaping spoonful's of whatever you're on."

The table chuckled.

"Why do you all think I'm on drugs? This is me stone-cold sober."

"God help us," Ghost muttered.

"I need a smoke. Let's take this out on the deck," Shades muttered.

They all moved outside, and Shades lit up.

A couple of brown pelicans flew overhead.

"You know what would be good right now? A Bloody Mary," Sandman said, going to stand by the railing, looking out over the Gulf.

"Go make you one," Ghost offered, taking a seat and leaning back in his chair. "I'm pretty sure my aunt has some mix and vodka in there."

"That does sound good," Blood agreed, lighting up a smoke.

An hour later, they were on their second pitcher, and Skylar was munching on a celery stalk. Blood shook his head, grinning at her.

Shades looked down at the time on his phone. "It's time we head back to the state line and see what kind of statement the county boys have planned."

Blood tipped his glass up and finished the last of his drink. "It's a beautiful day; now watch some asshole fuck it up."

CHAPTER TWENTY-NINE

Shades and the boys rolled up to the state-line bar. There were squad cars everywhere. The county sheriff strolled over to Shades as he sat astride his parked bike, dipping his head to light up a smoke. Shades flicked his lighter closed, shoved it in his pocket, and blew out a stream of smoke.

"You ready for 'em?" he asked, looking up at the sheriff.

"Yep."

"What's your plan?"

The man grinned. "You just keep your boys out of our way."

"I'd like to stick around and watch the fun."

"Fair enough. But stay out of it."

"If you handle it, we will. But if you fall down on the job, we're stepping in."

The sheriff's radio crackled. *"They just crossed the canal bridge."*

The sheriff responded back. "How many?"

"About thirty."

"Ten-four."

Shades grinned at him. "Showtime."

The sheriff walked off.

Shades climbed off his bike and stood with his arms crossed, watching with Ghost, Blood, and Sandman at his back.

With only minutes to spare, the Gulf Chapter rolled in the parking lot with a roar. Shades watched as they parked. Case wandered over.

"Any word?" he asked, his eyes on all the squad cars and uniforms.

Shades nodded. "Should be rollin' up any minute. They just crossed the canal bridge onto Perdido Key."

They all stood and watched as law enforcement brought out barricades and set up a check point. A line of officers moved into position, blocking the road and forming a line, each holding a shotgun across their chest.

Shades grinned over at Case. "Guess that's makin' a statement all right."

Case grinned back. "That would definitely make me think twice about rollin' up on 'em."

The line of bikes stopped in the distance, pulling to the side of the road.

The men watched closely, waiting to see what the Death Heads would do.

"How many you count?" Case asked.

Shades squinted into the distance studying the men and the line of motorcycles, heat rising up from the pavement distorted the image with shimmering waves. "A shit load. Twenty-eight if I counted right."

Shades could see the men in front squinting back in their direction and knew that not only did the Death Heads see the major statement law enforcement was making, they also saw the sixteen members of the Evil Dead MC standing, their arms folded across their chests, in a line in the parking lot of the bar, making their own statement.

The line of bikes sat in the heat of the sun for a long time and tensions grew as everyone waited to see what the Death Heads would do. After about twenty long, tense minutes, they finally turned around and rode off.

Shades and Case turned to each other, and Shades informed him, "Hopefully, they'll rethink their plan to make a move into this state. But I doubt this is the end of it. More likely, it's just round one. Your chapter's gonna have to continue to hold 'em off. You're gonna have to be vigilant about that, Brother."

Case nodded, but grinned. "True, but gotta say, it was fun watching them turn tail and run."

Shades put his palm in the air, and Case grinned back, slapping his hand in a high-five. Shades turned to the other men. "Let's get a drink, boys."

Blood stopped him, asking, "You gonna be good to go? Make it back to Birmingham okay?"

"Yeah, man. We're good."

"All right, then we're leaving." Blood jerked his chin to Sandman.

Ghost, who was standing behind Shades, looked at

Blood and grinned. "Don't toy with us, Blood."

Blood shook his head. "You're a hoot."

"I try." Ghost shrugged.

They bumped fists. "Later."

"Later, Blood," Shades gave him a chin lift. "Thanks for your help."

Blood headed off toward his bike with Sandman in tow. He lifted his hand and gave a thumb's up without looking back.

CHAPTER THIRTY

Shades pulled out of Skylar and slid off her. Turning her and spooning up to her back, he wrapped his arms around her. He nuzzled her neck, and then he gave her earlobe a nip before his voice was in her ear.

"You good, baby?"

She grinned. "I'm great."

"How's your new job going?"

They'd been back for a couple weeks now. Shades had put the word out in the club as soon as they got to Birmingham that Skylar was looking for a job. Tink had told him her uncle, who was a partner in a realty company, had a training program for people interested in becoming realtors. She'd gotten Skylar an interview, which had gone great, and she was now in the program.

"I really like it."

"That's great, baby."

"Everybody is really nice. I really like the idea of finding people homes."

“Happy for you, sweetheart.”

“One thing worries me, though.”

“What’s that?”

“Well, they had this photographer there today. He was taking professional head shots of all the realtors. They told me they use them for business cards, yard signs and such.”

“Yeah, so?”

“They went ahead and took my picture, too. Put me in this gold jacket and everything. Shades, I’m worried about those pictures.”

He frowned. “What do you mean?”

“I really don’t want my picture on yard signs. Of course, it’ll be a while before I actually have any clients of my own. The training program lasts a long time. It’ll probably take me six months before I’m licensed.”

“Let’s not worry about that now. I’m sure the DK problem will be taken care of by then.”

She snuggled back against him, her arms covering his. “How?”

He kissed the top of her head. “Let me worry about that, baby. That’s my job now. Takin’ care of you. Keepin’ you safe and happy.”

She sucked her lips into her mouth, and he could tell he hadn’t eased all her fears. He rolled her to face him. Taking her face in both his hands he brought her eyes to his as he demanded, “Hey, look at me. You’re everything to me, Sky. I’m not gonna let anything happen to you. No one’s taking you away from me again. Not your dad, not my club, and sure as fuck not the DKs. You hear me?”

She nodded, her throat closing.

"Okay, then. Get some sleep, my baby." He pressed his lips to her forehead and then pulled her to him, tucking her head in his neck.

***

Frank Bowman and his partner Gary Jenkins had owned Progressive Realty for about ten years now. It was a damned competitive business, and they were always looking for any edge they could. Frank leaned back in his executive chair and said, "So we need to decide who to put up on the billboard."

Gary stood on the other side of Frank's desk staring down at their options. He shuffled through the photos, his hand pushing them around on the desktop until he stopped on one.

"I think we have a winner." He twirled it around and slid it towards Frank.

Frank looked down.

"The others on the team are going to have a jealous fit if you put this newbie up on the sign. Hell, Janice has the highest sales. She's going to expect—"

"Janice has a horse face. Who'd want to look at that billboard? *This* is the face that will bring in business. She's gorgeous. Look at that smile. Hell, *I* want to buy a house from her."

"All right. Fine. We'll go with her."

"How soon will the billboards go up?"

"Should be able to get them up right away."

CHAPTER THIRTY-ONE

Butcher sat at the head of the table, leaning forward on his elbows. His eyes traveled around the room. “We’ve got a problem with the Gulf Coast Chapter. Some of you may already be aware. They’re getting out of hand—they’re reckless, unnecessarily violent. Drawing attention of local Law Enforcement and probably the Feds. Not to mention the accounting problems.”

“Accounting problems?” one of them asked.

Butcher looked at him, and then swung his gaze to Shades who was leaned back in his chair, arms folded across his chest. “You were down there. What’s your impression?”

Shades met his stare. “My impression is that a couple of specific members are using more product than is hitting the streets.”

There was a general grumbling around the table.

“Fuck.”

“That’s fucked up.”

"Anything else?" Butcher snapped.

"Yeah. That's what's fueling the violence. But you've got to understand the position we put them in. They've got the Death Heads pushing in from Florida, breathin' down their necks, knockin' on their fuckin' door. Had a run-in with 'em on the Florida-Bama line when I was down there. Those boys are the only thing holding 'em back. And we're the ones who hung 'em out there in the wind."

"And what do you think we need to do to fix it?"

"Look, there are some bad apples in the barrel, but not all of 'em. There are some good brothers down there, too. Ones I was fuckin' glad to have at my back when I was down there. I say we clean house, get rid of the few, and then reinforce the rest. Major membership drive down there."

Butcher's eyes dropped to the table. "Nomads usually do clean up."

"Fuck that," Shades spit out, causing Butcher's eyes to snap back to him. "Alabama handles its own problems. We go down there and do it ourselves."

Butcher grinned. "I was hoping you'd say that."

Shades' eyes narrowed.

Butcher returned the look, instructing him, "Take who you need, and go handle it."

Shades couldn't believe he'd heard right, but he wasn't about to back down from the challenge he'd been handed. He'd prove his mettle, which he was sure was what this was all about. He nodded. "Done."

Butcher slammed the gavel down. "Meeting adjourned."

***

Skylar lay in bed that night, nestled against Shades. His hand stroked up and down her arm, his fingers brushing gently along her soft skin.

"I have to make a run tomorrow," he announced.

She lifted her head off his chest, the moonlight from the window behind the bed shining down on them, lighting his features in a soft blue-gray color.

"To the Gulf Coast?" she asked.

"Yeah."

"Will you be gone overnight?"

"Probably."

"Will there be more trouble with the Death Heads?"

A smile pulled at his mouth. "You worried about me, babe?"

"Yes."

His hand cupped her cheek, his thumb stroking. "I'll be fine."

She dipped her head, her lips pressing soft kisses to his chest. Then she lifted her head and looked at him with an impish grin. "Are you too tired for sex tonight?"

His eyes connected with hers. "Kind of, babe. That okay with you?"

She rolled her eyes. "I suppose I'll live."

A grin tugged at the corner of his mouth, and he dipped his head to give her a quick kiss on her lips. "I'll make it up to you later. Promise."

She lay her head down on his chest, her hand caressing his abs, and she felt his hand sink into her hair. Her thoughts drifted to her new job. The photos they took of her last week bothered her. She couldn't get them out of her mind. They'd said they would only be used on her business cards and on those yard signs realtors used.

She worried about having her picture up in yards around town. Thankfully, she was still just learning the ropes. It would be a while before she had actual clients and any signs of her own. But when she did, she worried the DKs might see them.

Shades' breathing settled into a steady rhythm, his chest rising and falling under her ear. She smiled, knowing he'd drifted off to sleep, something she knew she needed to do as well.

Sunday she was assisting one of the girls with an open house. Learning the ropes, so to speak. Soon she'd be hosting open houses on her own. She smiled. She really loved this job. Showing people houses, helping them to find their own home—it was fun. Hard work for sure, especially when dealing with picky or demanding clients, but rewarding just the same. Her mind drifted over the home showings she'd already accompanied other realtor's on. She remembered the expensive home from a couple of days ago that actually had surveillance cams hidden in the…

She gasped, jerking straight up in bed as a memory clicked into place.

Oh my God.

Shades bolted upright in the bed beside her, reaching for his gun. He glanced around the room seeing no one, and his gaze returned to Skylar, his breathing heavy. "Babe, what the fuck?"

"Sorry."

"You scared the shit outta me."

"Sorry, I just remembered something."

"Remembered what?"

She bit her lip, not knowing how Shades was going to take what she was about to tell him.

"Sky?"

"It's, um, about Rusty."

Shades' eyes narrowed. "What about him?"

She took in a breath and let it out, murmuring, "God, how do I tell you this?"

"Babe, just spit it out."

"Before I left, Rusty's birthday had been coming up, and after he'd given me that dagger, I'd been racking my brain to come up with something that would mean something to him, that would be something I knew *he* wanted…"

"Sky, cut to the chase."

She blew out another breath. "There was only one thing I knew he wanted." She fiddled nervously with the covers. "He'd talked about it, you see, and so I thought…" Her voice trailed off softly, embarrassed.

"Skylar."

She looked up at him

"Spit it out."

"He wanted to film us."

Shades head came back an inch, and he frowned. "You talkin' about…in bed?"

She nodded.

"And?"

She shrugged. "I bought one of those little spy-cams and stashed it on a shelf in a bookcase in his bedroom. I thought if what it captured wasn't too vulgar, I'd give it to him for his birthday."

Shades ran a hand down his jaw. "Well, shit."

She frowned. "What? What are you thinking?"

He cracked half a smile. "Hadn't realized you were into that, babe."

She hit him in the head with her pillow. "I'm not." Then she pulled the pillow back and covered her face with it, mortified.

His hand reached up, and he yanked it free. She looked up to find him staring at her, trying to hold back his grin. "So, as enjoyable and enlightening as this conversation has been, what was your point in telling me all this? You wanting me to up my game, babe?"

"No! The *camera*, Shades…"

"What about it?"

"I set it up that night. The night we went out. The night before he was murdered. It's motion-activated. And it's still there."

He frowned. "So, it would have captured whoever it was that came in that morning, stabbed him, and took the bag."

She nodded. "I think so. At least, it should have."

"Does it transmit to something?"

"No, it records onto an SD card."

"You think someone might have found it by now?"

She shook her head. "I doubt it. It's small and I wedged it between two books.

Shades studied the floor, absorbing what she was telling him. "It could be the proof they need to back off."

"We have to go get it, Shades."

His eyes flashed to hers. "Whoa, whoa, whoa. First, *you're* not going anywhere near them. Second, I've got shit to deal with tomorrow. I've got that run to make, and you've got that open house the day after tomorrow. We'll figure it out when I get back, and *I'll* go take care of it."

"But, Shades—"

His brow rose. "Enough, babe. I'll handle it. Okay?"

Skylar knew arguing with him would be pointless. He'd never give in. Not on this. "Okay. All right."

He leaned back against the pillow, pulling her down with him. "Now, I want my woman. So shut up and kiss me."

"I thought you were too tired?"

"I was. Now you woke me up. Got me all stirred up with that talk of cameras and sex. Now I want your body."

She grinned up at him.

CHAPTER THIRTY-TWO

"So, what's wrong with it?" Reload asked, glancing from the road to his passenger, one wrist resting on the top of the steering wheel of his pickup.

Quick slumped against the door of the pickup, chewing on a toothpick. He looked over at his Devil King brother. Thank God he'd been close enough to come to his rescue when Quick's bike had broken down on the side of I65 just south of Birmingham.

"Bent pushrod on the rear cylinder intake. Luckily there was no damage to my new top end. But I'm gonna go ahead and replace the lifters when we get back. It could be a lot worse."

Reload shook his head. "You do know 'drive it like you stole it' is just a saying, right?"

Quick snatched the toothpick from his mouth and growled, "Hell, I was being gentle with her. Just trying to get all the new stuff broken in good and proper. Fuckin' glad you were close."

"How the hell did you bend a pushrod?"

"Just shit luck. They were perfect. Heat cycled the motor three times and everything was good to go before I left Atlanta."

Reload aimed his wraparound shades at him and grinned. "Well, I guess the asphalt is safe for at least one more day."

Quick sat up straight. "You hear that?"

A clanking noise could be heard coming from the bed of the truck. He turned to look through the rear window to where his bike was loaded up in the back. "Damn it. A tie down came loose. Pull over."

Reload shook his head in disgust. "Shit, Quick, can't you even manage to strap the fucking thing down right?"

"Just shut up and pull over."

Reload pulled to the side of the road, and they both climbed out. Quick hopped up in the bed. It only took him a moment to re-secure the hook and tighten the ratchet down pulling the strap taught. He stood, examining the other tie-down straps and making sure it was all secure. A big rig tractor-trailer passed by, horn blaring, the gust of wind rocking the truck. It drew Quick's attention, and he looked up.

"Motherfucker. He almost sideswiped us!" Reload shouted above the interstate noise.

Quick's eyes followed the semi-trailer as it rode off. Then something caught his eyes. He looked up to see a giant billboard.

And the face of the woman they'd been in this

Goddamned state searching for all these months.

Fucking hell. She was here.

"Reload!" he shouted back over the noise.

"Yeah?"

Quick pointed up at the billboard with Skylar in her gold blazer, arms folded and a big smile on her face.

Reload looked up. "Progressive Realty. So what? You buyin' a house?"

"No, moron. The chick in the picture! That's our girl."

Reload looked again, his eyes squinting. "Well, hell, how about that."

Quick pulled his phone out of his back pocket and dialed up Rat.

CHAPTER THIRTY-THREE

Saturday—

Shades and Ghost rolled up to a stop sign in some bumfuck town in the middle of nowhere. Griz, Hammer, JJ, Gator, Spider, and Heavy pulled up behind them.

"It's a nice town," JJ commented.

Heavy gave him a strange look. "Yeah, right. Have you looked around?"

Shades studied the navigation on his cell phone.

"You lose service, and we're screwed." Ghost chuckled.

Shades pointed to the road on the right. "This way."

Ten minutes later, they headed down a gravel road in a wooded area, finally pulling up to the Gulf Coast Chapter clubhouse. It consisted of a doublewide trailer on a large wooded lot. The yard, if you could call it that, was dirt. Any grass having long ago been trampled under the tires of dozens of motorcycles.

"Jesus Christ," Gator grumbled, looking at the

doublewide as he took off his helmet. The siding was green with mold and mildew. The wood of the deck and stairs that led to the door looked like it was rotted.

"What's the matter, ain't you happy to be here?" Hammer asked, dismounting.

"Oh, yeah. Just the other night I woke up sobbing, wishing I was here."

"Where the fuck are we?" Griz asked, dropping his kickstand.

Ghost grinned at him. "We're in hell."

"I got a bad feeling about this," Spider said, his eyes moving around the quiet clubhouse.

"That your spidey-sense?" Ghost asked Spider with a grin.

Case and Brick stepped out the door. Case lifted an arm in greeting.

"Hey, guys. What's up?" He frowned.

Shades came up the creaky stairs onto the small deck that led into the trailer. His face showed no emotion, and Case's smile faded.

"The whole crew here?" Shades asked.

"Yeah," Case responded, his entire body taking on a defensive stance.

"Relax, Brother," Shades reassured him. "You, Brick, Pipe, Coop, and Deez back me up on this, and everything's gonna be fine."

Case's eyes moved to the crew Shades had at his back, and then nodded once uncomfortably. "You're putting me in a spot here, Shades."

"I'm saving your fucking chapter, Case," Shades bit back. "Stay smart. Stay cool. Time to prove to your brothers that you're worth a damn."

Case sucked in a breath and then nodded, resolving himself to the inevitable. "Okay."

"Glad we got that cleared up." Shades opened the door, and they walked inside. There was a pool table set up in the middle of what he assumed was supposed to be a living room. Ratty sofas and chairs lined the walls. Coop, Deez, and Pipe were playing a game of pool. Rocker and Moon were lounging in easy chairs, smoking a joint and looking stoned out of their heads. A trashy little blonde sat on Moon's lap.

Coop turned when they walked in. "Hey man," he said to Shades. "What are you doing here?"

Shades nodded to him, but didn't stop to explain. As he moved around the pool table, he noticed Case lean in and whisper something low in Coop's ear. Shades could only hope that Case and his guys backed him on this. If not, there was gonna be one hell of a fight. Shades was determined to take advantage of the surprise and the doped up look on the President and VP's face. He took control. This was either going to work or not. No sense hesitating.

"Troops, make yourselves at home," he told his guys who spread out around the room. Then turning back to Moon and Rocker, whose eyes were now narrowing in confusion, Shades pointed a finger at them. "You and you. Meeting room. The rest of you, outside."

Everyone froze for a moment at Shades' sharply given orders. They looked to their President and VP, not sure what to do.

Shades spun. "This is state business. Outside, fucking now!"

"Come on, guys," Case backed up Shades, nodding toward the door. "Let's give them a minute."

Thankfully, Coop elbowed Deez, and they began herding the men out.

Shades swung back to Moon, and he jerked his head toward the door, his eyes piercing the blonde's. "Outside, darlin'."

Moon stared at Shades with a cold look, and then blinked slowly. His hand squeezed the girl's waist. "Go on, baby doll. Give us a minute."

Shades waited while the girl scrambled off Moon's lap and headed outside.

Moon and Rocker rose to their feet, and then led the way into a back room. Shades eyed the place. It had apparently been a bedroom at one time, but now contained a conference table and half a dozen chairs. Moon sat down at the head of the table, Rocker taking the chair next to him. Shades stood at the other end and leaned his palms on the table, his men crowded around him, lining the walls and blocking the entrance.

Moon's eyes suddenly changed as he sensed the mood in the room and knew something was about to go down. Shades could see that much in his drugged out eyes, the man just couldn't comprehend much else.

"Chain's only as strong as its weakest links. That'd be you two." Shades looked them both in the eye.

"What the hell did you just say?" Rocker growled half coming out of his chair. Ghost pulled a gun and aimed it at his chest so fast the man flinched.

"Sit down, asshole."

The blood drained from Rocker's face as he eyed the barrel pointed right at his heart. He swallowed and sat back down, his eyes going to his President.

"What the fuck is this?" Moon growled. "You think you can come in here and—"

"I can come in here and do what I was Goddamn sent here to do."

"And what the hell was that?"

"Pull your fuckin' patch."

"Pull my patch?"

"Both of you."

"What the fuck for?"

"Don't play me for a stupid son-of-a-bitch, Moon. You've been stealin' from the club. Drugs, profits. You think that's the kind of thing we let slide? We're taking your cuts, your bikes and anything else that belongs to this club."

"You're not taking our bikes," Rocker protested.

"Your bike is club property."

"This is bullshit," Moon snarled. "I'm gonna talk to Butcher about this."

"Who the fuck you think sent us?" Shades asked.

That made Moon pause.

"You take this cut from me, it'll be off my cold dead body," Rocker insisted.

Shades' eyes cut to him. "That can be arranged. There's

a limestone quarry nearby, isn't there, Gator?"

"Yeah, not too far from here."

Shades stood, folded his arms and grinned down at Moon. "Perfect place to dump 'em."

Ghost gave their big bodies a once over and gave Shades a cockeyed grin, shrugging. "Not sure they're gonna fit in the trunk."

Shades gave him half a grin, and then looked over at Griz, who with the signal from Shades, stepped forward and hefted the ax he'd held tucked behind his leg.

Shades looked back at the two men who'd just turned white as a sheet. "Not like this they won't."

Griz hefted the ax to underline their meaning.

Moon's hands lifted. "Okay. Okay."

Hammer moved behind him and yanked his cut off, tossing it on the table. Spider did the same with Rocker's.

"Take their rings, anything with Evil Dead on it. Claim everything…It's all Dead property," Shades growled to Hammer and Spider.

"You're seriously taking our bikes?" Moon protested.

"As much product as you've stolen from the club, you're lucky that's all we're taking.

A few minutes later they exited the trailer, Hammer and Griz had a hold of Moon, and Gator and Spider had a hold of Rocker. They dragged them outside and tossed them in the gravel, and then began boot stomping them, kicking as they rolled farther and farther toward the street. The rest of the chapter brothers all stood quietly in shock, but stayed out of it. Obviously Case had spoken to all of them.

When the men had been kicked—literally— to the curb, Shades gave the two men a wicked grin. “Get your asses off club property, and don’t ever show your fucking faces again.”

The two stumbled to their feet, spitting blood.

“You motherfuckers, I’ll get you for this!” Moon swore.

Ghost pulled his piece and aimed it at his head. “Get out of here, before I change my mind and blow your brains out.”

The two men stumbled off down the wooded road.

Shades turned and motioned for JJ who held the two cuts in his hands. JJ tossed them to Shades. Shades turned and looked at Case, tossing the president’s cut to him. “Pull the president patch off that cut.”

Case looked down at the cut in his hands.

“And sew it on yours,” Shades finished.

“Holy shit.” Case’s eyes went wide.

“Got a problem with that?” Shades asked him.

Case grinned. “Fuck no.”

Shades looked around the men standing in the clubhouse yard and asked, “Anybody got a problem with that?”

He was met with shaking heads all around.

“Good.” Shades grinned. “Now break open the whiskey, we got a membership drive to organize.”

As the men all headed inside, Shades hung back and pulled out his cell. He dialed up Skylar.

A moment later, her soft voice came through the receiver.

“Hi, honey.”

“Hey, sweetheart.”

"Are you coming home tonight?"

"Afraid not. Gonna be here till tomorrow."

"I miss you."

"I miss you, too, baby."

"I don't like being apart. Sleeping in an empty bed."

Shades grinned. "You in bed?"

"Yes," came her soft reply.

"Naked?"

"Yes. You sure you can't make it home tonight?"

"Damn, woman, you're making me rethink that."

"I know you have to take care of business. And it is a long ride back."

"Four or five hours, babe."

"I'll see you tomorrow, then?"

"Yeah. I'll be here most of the day, but I'll call you when we're headed back."

"Okay, honey. I love you."

"Love you, too, Sky."

"Shades?"

"Yeah, babe?"

"Be careful."

"Always."

"Goodnight."

"Night, babe."

CHAPTER THIRTY-FOUR

Sunday—

"Thank you so much for coming." Skylar smiled at the young couple who had just toured the open house. Closing the door behind them, she lifted the cuff of her cream silk blouse to look at her wrist watch. Then her eyes lifted to Betty, the realtor she was training with today. "Three-fifteen."

"Well, forty-five more minutes, and we can wrap it up," Betty replied.

Skylar peered out the window at the sky. "There are some really dark clouds; it looks like it may start raining."

A crack of thunder boomed, as if to underline her words, and she jumped.

"Great, that'll probably be the end of our foot traffic. People never come when it's storming out." Betty turned and headed back toward the kitchen. "You want coffee and cookies? We have plenty leftover."

"Sure. Pour me a cup," Skylar replied as she began straightening the sales flyers on the table in the foyer. The house they were showing was a beautiful four bedroom brick home in Vestavia Hills in a pretty little subdivision called Stone Ridge. It was the kind of home Skylar had longed for as a child.

As she turned to again glance out the window, she wondered if Shades was headed back yet. Late last night when he'd called her and woken her up, he'd said that everything had gone as expected, but that he still had some details that had to be worked out today before he came home.

Another rumble of thunder shook the house. Skylar was glad she'd put the top up on her Miata as she heard the patter of rain begin to fall against the windows. Biting her lip she wondered if Shades would run into the storm on his ride home.

"Hey, Betty, have you heard the weather reports lately?" she asked as she walked through the living room to the dining room, which led to the kitchen. She froze in the doorway, the scene before her eyes shocking her almost as much as when she'd found Rusty's body.

Before her, lying on the floor next to the kitchen island, was Betty's motionless body, partially face down. But the truly terrifying thing was the man squatting down beside her. Skylar had just a split second to take in the long-handled silver flashlight he held in his hand like a weapon, and the black leather vest he wore with the Devil Kings top rocker, the devil's head center patch and the bottom rocker that read, *Georgia*.

They'd found her.

She felt her heart drop, a sick feeling forming in her stomach, and her breath caught in her throat as the man looked over his shoulder and grinned. Before she could think to run, even though she knew in her high heels and skirt she wouldn't get far, an arm clamped around her waist, and a hand clamped over her mouth.

A voice whispered in her ear. "Remember us, Skylar?"

The man squatting rose to his feet and turned toward her fully.

Her eyes took in his face. She remembered him.

Quick.

Not one of the nicest of Rusty's brothers.

He gave her a cold look, then looked over her shoulder to the man holding her. "Get her in the truck. I'll deal with this one." He jerked his head toward where Betty lay.

The man holding her yanked her arms behind her, and a moment later she felt the cold plastic of a zip-tie being tightened around her wrists.

"No, wait. Please. Don't hurt her. It's me you want. You don't have to hurt her," she pleaded.

Quick walked over to Skylar and took her jaw in his hand, tilting her face up roughly. "You get in that truck quietly like a good little girl, and you don't give Reload any trouble, and maybe I'll think about letting her live."

She nodded. "I swear I'll do whatever you say. Please, just don't hurt her."

Quick released her jaw and stepped back. Then he lifted his chin toward the back door. She walked slowly toward it,

Reload's hand clamped over her arm. He yanked the door open and shoved her through. The last sight she had of Betty was that of her legs sticking out from around the side of the island, one shoe askew, and all she could think of was that Betty had two small children, three and five years old. Skylar prayed that Quick would let her co-worker live.

Oh God. If anything happened to Betty because of her, she wouldn't be able to live with herself. All of this was her fault.

Reload steered her to a dark pickup truck parked in the driveway, and she went along quietly. He opened the passenger door and shoved her in.

"Scoot over to the middle," he ordered.

She did as she was told.

He leaned in the open door and bent over her to zip-tie her ankles together.

"Sexy shoes." He grinned as his hand ran over her black high-heeled pumps before trailing up her leg. When he got to her knee, his fingers slid under the hem of her tight black skirt, and he grinned at her. He was halfway up the inside of her thigh when the driver-side door was yanked open, and Quick jumped in.

"Get in the fucking truck," he yelled at Reload. "We don't have time for that shit now."

Reload yanked his hand out of her skirt with a curse and jumped in next to her, slamming the truck door behind him. Quick hit the gas, and they sped out of the driveway and down the street.

The rain was coming down pretty heavily now, and

Skylar could barely see the street through the downpour, even with the wipers slapping back and forth a mile a minute. There was no traffic on the residential street, no one out in this weather, no one to witness the dark pickup pulling away. Quick made several lefts and rights, maneuvering his way out of the subdivision.

Skylar finally found the courage to look over at him and ask the question she feared the answer to. “You didn’t hurt her, did you?”

Quick glanced from the road to her, but didn’t say anything.

“Quick, please. Tell me you didn’t hurt her.”

Reload suddenly grabbed her jaw and turned her face to him. “Maybe you should be busy worrying about yourself, sweetie-pie.” Then he leaned over and licked the side of her face. Skylar stiffened and tried to pull away, which made his grip on her jaw only tighten all the more.

“Reload,” Quick barked. “Leave her be.”

Reload looked over the top of her head toward Quick. “What the fuck for? Might as well have a little fun on the trip back.”

“Cause I fuckin’ said so,” Quick snapped.

Reload released her with a shove, and her left shoulder and breast slammed up against Quick’s arm.

“Fuckin’ fine,” Reload snapped. “You suck the fun right out of everything, you know that, Brother?”

“Just fucking shut up and make the call,” Quick growled.

Skylar straightened, twisting to try to regain her upright position. She also tried to nonchalantly inch her way closer to

Quick and farther away from Reload without being obvious about it. Reload didn't seem to notice. He was too busy digging his cell out of his pocket and dialing. But Quick must have noticed, for he looked over at her, and their eyes connected for a moment.

"Where are you taking me?" she couldn't stop herself from asking.

Quick ignored her question.

"We've got her. We're on our way back," Reload said into his phone.

"Did you hurt Betty?" she asked again.

Quick gave her a stony look. "Baby-doll, I've had me one hell of a bad day, so I suggest you just sit there and keep your mouth shut the rest of the trip."

"Or what?"

"Or I'll pull over, and let Reload have his fun with you."

Skylar turned her face forward and swallowed. He'd do it, too. He absolutely would. Her eyes watched the road, trying to memorize the route they were taking. She couldn't help but wonder if there were more DKs holed up somewhere in town and if they would be taking her somewhere close. But then as minutes went by and she watched the roads, she noticed they took the ramp onto I-20 east toward Atlanta.

A cold chill ran through her as she realized they were taking her out of state and back to their chapter. Skylar swallowed, wondering what fate awaited her. Did they want information? Did they just want to make her suffer? Or did they just want to kill her?

***

A couple of hours later they were reaching the outskirts of Atlanta. Quick took an exit and pulled into a gas station. It was still raining heavily as he opened his door, pausing to look back at Reload. “Watch her.”

Reload smiled and put his arm around Skylar, pulling her close. “Take your time.”

Quick slammed the door and dashed through the rain into the store.

Reload’s hand immediately drifted down from her shoulder to her breast, giving it several squeezes. With her wrists still zip-tied behind her there was nothing she could do to stop him. His hot breath was in her ear.

“When we get where we’re goin’ I’m gonna get a taste of you, and Quick ain’t gonna get in my way. Maybe you and me will spend a good long time together.”

Skylar wanted to spit curses at him and tell him how disgusting she thought he was, but she held her tongue. There was no sense pissing him off; it wouldn’t do her any good. So she stayed mute, looking straight ahead.

That only encouraged him to try to get some reaction from her.

His other hand went to the buttons of her blouse and he began to work them free. “You’re a classy broad. Always were.” He pulled the sheer blouse apart, revealing the lacy camisole underneath. He ran his finger along the lacy edge. “I’ve never been with a chick who wore shit like this.”

Skylar sank back into the seat, trying to avoid his touch.

The driver’s door was yanked open and the truck rocked with Quick’s weight as he slid into the seat. He had a fountain cup in his hand, complete with lid and straw. He glanced over at her, taking in Reload's hands.

"What the fuck are you doing?"

"I was just tellin' the pretty little girl what we're gonna do and how we're gonna do it." He ran his finger down her cheek. She tried to pull away.

"We're in a public fucking parking lot, dumbass. Do up her shirt before you attract someone's attention."

"Party pooper," Reload grumbled, but buttoned up her shirt. At least a couple of the buttons.

Quick held the cup toward her and guided the straw to her mouth. "Drink."

He gave her little choice, so she sucked on the straw. Cold cola swirled into her mouth. After a couple sips, she released it.

"More," he insisted. "I ain't got all day. Drink it."

She thought about arguing with him, but didn't see the point, so she did as she was told. After a minute, Quick passed the cup to Reload.

"That's hers, not yours."

"You didn't get me one?"

"No, I didn't fucking get you one." Quick threw the truck into reverse and backed out.

They were soon back on the interstate.

Reload kept holding the straw to her mouth, so she drank, until it was just ice remaining.

A few minutes later she started to feel woozy.

"I don't feel so good," she murmured. The last thing she remembered was Quick looking over her head at Reload and smiling. And then Reload's response.

"You roofie her drink?" he asked with a chuckle, his voice sounding thick and distorted to her spinning head.

***

Reno sat at the bar in the DK clubhouse. He was nursing a whisky and ignoring everyone else when the door banged against the wall as it was flung open. Reno watched the reflection in the mirror behind the bar as Quick and Reload trooped in. Quick had a woman thrown over his shoulder. Reno's gaze moved over the perfectly rounded ass, so well outlined by the tight fitting black skirt. Judging by the way her head lolled from side to side, Reno assumed she was unconscious. He took in her long dark hair and wondered if this could be the elusive Skylar they'd all been trying to track down for months. She sure had been one hell of a bitch to find. Being able to elude them for all this time, he'd have to give her credit. She'd turned out to be one smart cookie.

Reno continued to watch the show in the mirror, not wanting to turn around and get involved. Quick stopped in front of Growler, their President, and Rat, their Vice President, who were sitting at a table talking and enjoying a bottle of tequila.

Quick tossed the girl to the carpet at their feet. "I brought you a present."

The two men dropped their eyes to the woman crumpled on the floor.

"Well, my, my, you certainly did," Growler replied, taking in the sight of the woman unconscious at his feet. He nodded toward the table. "Sit down and have a well-deserved drink."

After they sat, Growler tipped up the bottle over two more glasses that a prospect hurried over to provide, carefully stepping around the woman passed out on the floor. Growler's eyes strayed to her again, and then he let out a sharp whistle.

"Reno, get over here and take care of this."

Reno tossed back his drink and stood. As usual, they always left the dirty work to him.

CHAPTER THIRTY-FIVE

Shades pulled the phone away from his ear and squatted down in the gravel yard of the Gulf Coast Chapter, feeling like the ground had just shifted under his feet.

They had Skylar.

The fucking DKs had Skylar.

Holy fucking shit.

He'd fucked up. Christ, had he fucked up. He'd promised her he'd take care of it, that he'd keep her safe. But he'd done nothing to end the DK threat to her. Instead he'd handled his own club's problems first, always putting his club first, always putting her problem to the back burner. *When we get back from New Orleans, babe. When we get home, babe. After I make this last run, babe. I'll take care of it, I promise.* All bullshit. It didn't matter that he'd meant to take care of it. He hadn't. And now she was in the hands of his enemy, and it was all his fault.

He felt his chest tighten and thought for a moment he

was going to be sick.

***

Ghost looked down at his brother, wondering what the hell that call was about. Shades looked shell-shocked. Reaching down, he took the cell phone from Shades hand and put it to his ear.

"Who is this?" he barked into the phone.

Boot's voice came across. "Ghost. He okay?"

"No, he's not fuckin' okay. What the hell is going on?"

"Christ, Ghost. Shit. It's bad. We got a call from the DKs. They told us to forget about looking for that chick anymore. Said they had her."

"Skylar?"

"Yeah."

"You sure?"

"Tink checked with her uncle. Skylar was at some open house with some other broad. When the homeowners returned, they found the other lady collapsed on the floor. She'd taken a bad blow to the head."

"And Skylar?"

"Skylar's gone."

Ghost looked over as Shades suddenly lunged to his feet and headed toward his bike. Ghost growled into the phone, "I gotta go."

Shades threw his leg over his bike as Ghost got to him, grabbing his arm.

"Whoa, Brother. Take a minute. Think it through. Let's get a plan."

"I have to get that spy-cam, Ghost."

"What the fuck are you talking about?" Ghost frowned.

Shades tried to shake him off.

"Shades, Brother, we'll do whatever we gotta do to get her back, but I need to know the plan."

Shades took a breath, obviously trying to regain his concentration, and then he explained about the spy-cam.

Ghost ran a hand down his face. "Christ."

"We're wasting time, Ghost."

Ghost nodded. "Yeah. Let me tell the guys."

"Just you and me, Ghost. We have to move now."

"Yeah, okay. Just give me a minute."

"I can't lose her."

"You won't."

Shades nodded, but it wasn't with conviction.

Ghost stepped away and quickly dialed up Blood. He glanced over at Shades, who was firing up his bike and a moment later tore out of the lot.

"Yeah?" came Blood's voice through his phone.

"Blood, it's Ghost," he yelled over the thundering pipes. "They got Skylar. They took her."

"Who took her?" he barked. "What the hell are you talking about?"

"DKs. We need you, Brother."

"I'm on my way."

"You gotta tell her father."

"Shit," Blood cursed, and Ghost knew he was thinking about how this was going to destroy Undertaker.

Without waiting for an answer, Ghost disconnected. Griz walked up and heard what Ghost had said to Blood. Ghost snapped at him, “Wrap it up here, and you and the guys get to Atlanta. I’ll call you.”

Griz nodded somberly.

Ghost started up his bike and roared down the road after Shades.

CHAPTER THIRTY-SIX

Skylar's mind was still so fuzzy from whatever drug she'd been given, she had a hard time focusing. She tried to lift her arm to rub her face and stiff neck, but she couldn't move. She writhed and yanked, only to realize her arms were pulled behind her and zip-tied to the metal chair she found herself sitting in.

Panic flooded her system, and the adrenaline boost helped to clear her mind. And then it all came flooding back.

The Devil Kings had her.

She looked around, noting the empty room, except for the chair that appeared to be bolted into the cement floor. What looked like old, dried blood stained the ground directly underneath the chair and appeared to be splattered around the walls.

Oh, God. What was this place? Some kind of torture or interrogation room where they beat whatever they wanted out of someone? A house of horrors couldn't be more terrifying.

She began to whimper, knowing there was no way out.

No escaping for her. She was totally at their mercy. She wasn't even sure where she was. She'd never been to Rusty's clubhouse, but then, she wasn't even sure if this was it. She could be in some abandoned warehouse for all she knew.

The door opened, and one of Rusty's brothers walked in, closing the door behind him. Reno was his name, she remembered. He wasn't the kind of man that was easy to forget. He was a big man, six three at least, and muscled. But it wasn't just his size that made him stand out, it was also his demeanor. He took badass to a whole different level and to Skylar, he had always been one of the scarier members.

Although he'd been at the nightclub on the night of her birthday, he'd hadn't come to the table. Instead, he'd stayed off to himself at the end of the bar. But she'd seen his eyes watching her that night. Almost as if, even then, he hadn't trusted her.

He never laughed. Hell, she'd never seen him so much as crack a smile. And it would have been a beautiful smile, too, because aside from the fact he was a terrifyingly scary dude, he was also very good looking. He had dark hair that hung past his jaw and brows that slashed low, giving him a stern look. But it was his piercing light eyes that caught one's attention. They practically burned a hole when he turned them on you.

He had a bottle of water in his hand, and he unscrewed the cap as he approached her. Then, without a word, he fisted a handful of her hair and yanked her head back. The bottle was pressed to her dry lips and he tilted it up, pouring it down her throat. She gulped, trying to keep up with the flow of water streaming from the upturned bottle, but she soon couldn't. As she began to choke, his grip relaxed, and she managed to twist her head to the side. Ice cold water spilled down her chin and over her chest before he let her go and pulled the bottle away.

She sucked in a lungful of air, gasping and coughing.

Reno stepped back and looked down at her while he nonchalantly screwed the cap back on the bottle like he hadn't just tried to drown her.

She glared up at him.

He took a step toward her again, threatening, "You still thirsty, I got more."

She took the comment for what it was—a veiled threat. He'd seen the way she'd glared at him, and he didn't like it.

Skylar dropped her eyes, ready to play the obedient, submissive prisoner. She didn't want to make this any worse for herself than it already was.

"No. Thank you for the water." She tried to say the soft words with sincerity. Glancing up at him, she saw that his eyes had dropped to her chest. She looked down at herself. Oh, God. With the water all down her front, she was practically a contestant in a wet t-shirt contest. And with her arms manacled behind her, she could do nothing to cover herself from his lustful gaze. She looked at his face. "You meant to do that, didn't you?"

His eyes lifted to hers, and he smiled. The first smile she'd ever seen from him. It revealed even, white teeth. But it wasn't a pleasant smile. It was absolutely terrifying.

"You ready to talk? The drugs wear off enough?"

She nodded her head. "Yes."

"You better tell Rat what he wants to hear. You don't, it's gonna go bad for you," he warned.

"I can only tell the truth."

"Truth better include where our damn money is."

She watched as he moved to the door, opened it, and yelled for someone to get Rat and let him know she was awake.

A few minutes later, Rat stalked in.

Reno moved to lean against the wall, his arms folded across his broad chest, obviously turning over the reins to his VP who moved to stand over her.

She looked up at him. He was almost as terrifying as Reno. His face was just as hard and spoke of years of callous violence and disregard for anything that threatened his club. But where Reno was probably only in his thirties, this man was much older. Fifties if she had to guess.

His long scraggly hair was solid gray, as was his scruffy beard. He wore glasses on his long thin nose and when he smiled down at her with his evil smile, his teeth were yellow with age.

"Well, girly, did you really think you could run from us? You think we couldn't find you? There's no place on this earth DKs can't find you."

"I'm sorry I ran, but I didn't kill him. I swear."

Rat and Reno exchanged a look that seemed to read to her as half surprise and half confusion. What was that about? What weren't they telling her?

"Please, you have to believe me."

“I ain’t gotta do shit, little girl,” Rat snarled.

“If you didn’t do it, why’d you run?” Reno asked, his eyes narrowing on her. There was just enough of a thread of something in the way he asked the question that had her clutching to a shred of hope that maybe, *just maybe,* some part of him was giving her just the shadow of a doubt that what she said might be true.

“I went out to get us coffee. When I came back I found him with that dagger sticking out of his chest.”

Rat leaned down in her face. “Yeah, the dagger he bought *you.*”

She trembled at the look in his eyes. “Yes, I know it was my dagger, but I didn’t stab him. I swear it’s the truth.”

“Then why’d you run?” Reno asked again. She could hear it in his voice. He was cutting through all the other bullshit side issues. He didn’t give a fuck whose dagger it was. He knew the important, pivotal issue was why she ran. She’d bet that whether he believed her or not all hinged on that one answer.

“Because I knew you wouldn’t believe me. It was my dagger, like you just pointed out. I was standing there with not just the proverbial, but *actual* blood on my hands. I knew you’d think I did it. It’s obvious you still do.”

Reno’s brows rose. “*Because you ran.* You and the bag were *both* gone.”

Rat must have had enough, because he grabbed a handful of her hair and yanked her head back. Then he growled down at her, “You think you can steal from the club? Stab a brother?”

She was so scared she could barely find the voice to whisper, "I'm the one who called 911. I swear I didn't kill him."

Rat released his grip on her hair, shoving her head violently. "Yammer. Yammer. Yammer. She sounds like a broken record." He looked over at Reno. "See if you can get anything out of her."

Reno met his look and nodded once.

The door slammed behind Rat, and then Skylar was alone with Reno. She stared up at him, and her heart dropped to her stomach. Oh, God. What was he going to do?

He straightened from the wall and moved to stand over her. She had to tilt her head up a long way to meet his cold eyes. She knew he was trying to intimidate her, and it was working. God, was it working.

"I don't like doin' this. So I'm gonna go easy on you at first 'cause hurtin' women ain't my thing. But make no mistake, Cupcake, I will get answers from you."

"Reno, please…" Her eyes fell to his hands as he pulled his rings off. He flexed his fingers once, and fear shot through her as her brain scrambled for any words that would make him believe her.

"Please, Reno, I'm telling the truth. Rusty had a lot to drink that night. When he came home, he practically passed out the minute he hit the bed. He was still out like a light when I woke up. So I went out to get us coffee. Starbucks. His favorite. I was trying to do something nice for him. When I came back, he'd already been stabbed, and the bag was already gone."

"So, you want to stick with that story?"

"It's not a story. The club has enemies don't they? Someone must have known about that bag and whatever was in it."

"Like you don't know."

"I don't know."

"Right."

"It's true."

"I think more likely it's true that, yeah, he passed out, and then you went lookin' in that bag and decided to take the money and run."

"Reno, do I look stupid to you?"

He didn't say anything, just narrowed his eyes.

"I'd have to be not just stupid, but an idiot to steal from the club. I'd have to be *out of my mind.*"

"Well you bitches all got a little crazy in you."

Skylar shook her head, trying to think how she could convince him.

"Or maybe you were just desperate," Reno added.

"I wasn't desperate. I had a good job that I loved. I made decent money. I had no reason to steal from the DKs. And I would never have done that to Rusty. He was good to me."

"Yeah, he was. Always good to the broads. Always believing every motherfucking word that comes out of their mouths. *His* flaw, not *mine*."

He leaned forward and grabbed a handful of her hair and jerked her head back. He got right in her face and said, "So don't go makin' the mistake of thinkin' I give a shit about you. I don't trust you as far as I can throw you."

Skylar's breath was coming rapidly now. "Please, Reno. I know you don't give a shit about me. I know that, but that doesn't mean what I'm telling you isn't the truth. Someone else knew about the money. They had to have, because someone else did this. You have to stop focusing on me and think of who else it could have been, because right now, they're getting away with it and probably laughing about how *easy* it was. Laughing their asses off at the whole lot of you." She snarled the last part, trying to shake some sense into him. It got to him, but not the way she intended.

He moved so abruptly, it took Skylar by surprise. He straightened, drew his arm back and backhanded her across the cheek. Her face exploded in pain. God, if that was him going gentle, she was in real trouble.

"Watch the way you fuckin' talk to me, woman."

She knew she'd pushed too far, but she had to get through to him. "As long as you keep focusing on me and not the real killers, they'll keep laughing… all the way to the bank."

Crack. He backhanded her again.

"You want, I can keep this up all day. You're nothing to me but a murderous, thieving bitch who turned on one of my brothers, you understand?" he roared.

The door opened, banging against the wall.

"Where is she?" someone thundered.

Skylar's head was bowed, her hair hanging in her face, blood running down her chin from her busted lip.

"Didn't know you were back," she heard Reno growl. She peered up as Reno stepped aside, revealing her to the man that had just burst into the room.

Her eyes blinked.

It couldn't be. Perhaps that blow had knocked her brains loose, because she swore the man looked like Rusty. But that couldn't be. Rusty was dead.

Wasn't he?

The man grabbed a fistful of Reno's cut and shoved him back against the wall. "You don't fucking touch her."

Reno's hands lifted. "She's all yours, Brother."

The man released him with a shove, and then dropped to his knees in front of her.

Her mouth fell open in shock, but she managed to whisper in a confused voice, "Rusty?"

"Surprised to see me, babe?" He pulled a bandana from around his neck and wiped the blood gently from her mouth and chin.

"Y-you're alive. Oh, m-my God, you're alive. Thank God. Thank God." She stared at him, stunned, and then her eyes filled as she broke down in tears, her shoulders shaking.

He rose to his feet to stare down at her. He just stood there, his expression cold.

Skylar tried to pull herself together. She studied his expression. He thought she did it. He may not want Reno to beat her, but that didn't mean he thought she was innocent. She could see it in his face. Oh God, no.

"Rusty, I didn't stab you. I swear I didn't. I went out for coffee, and when I came back I found you like that. I felt for a pulse. I couldn't find one. You were so cold, and there was so much blood."

"Yeah, I was in critical condition for a long time."

"Do you remember what happened?"

"Remember goin' to sleep with you. Remember waking up in the hospital days later."

"Rusty, please, you have to know I didn't do it. Why would I do that?"

"You tell me? You needed money, all you had to do was ask, babe."

She shook her head. "I didn't take it. Your bag. It was gone when I came back with the coffee. I swear, Rusty."

"So you just ran. Left me there."

"I called 911. I was on the phone with them when the club rode up."

"Why'd you run?"

"Because it was the dagger you'd given me sticking out of your chest. I panicked. Do you really think they wouldn't have thought I did it?" She nodded toward Reno. "I was standing there with your blood on my hands."

"My blood."

"Yes. I felt for a pulse. I shook you, calling your name. Your blood was on me. I knew what they'd think, what it would look like to them. I panicked. I was afraid they'd kill me." She paused to study his eyes, searching for any shred of understanding. "Rusty, I'd die before I'd hurt you."

Rusty's eyes flicked to Reno, and then back to her. "Well that was being arranged."

The door opened, and a head poked in.

"Rusty, there's a call for you."

"Not now," he snapped, not bothering to turn away from

Skylar, his eyes still boring into her.

"You're gonna want to take it."

Rusty blew out a breath and stormed out the door, slamming it behind him.

Skylar frowned, looking at the floor as she tried to process the fact that Rusty was still alive. All this time she'd thought…

And then her eyes lifted to Reno. "You let me think he was dead. You knew all this time he was alive, and you didn't tell me. Why?"

"It was entertaining to see how far you'd go with this bullshit story of yours. It'll be more entertaining to see how Rusty deals with a double-crossing bitch like you. Have to admit, you had me goin' there for a half a second." He let out a huff of cruel laughter. "Look on your face when he walked in. Priceless, babe."

***

A few minutes later, Rusty returned. He stood over her and jammed his hands in his hip pockets, almost as if he didn't trust himself not to touch her. And then he shocked her by saying, "Well, babe, seems you've got friends in the Evil Dead."

Skylar swallowed. Oh, God. *Shades*. What had he done?

"That where you ran? To the Dead?"

"N-not exactly."

"You want to explain that? Explain why they give a shit about you?"

"I…I used to know one of them. Well, more than one of them. My best friend's brother was a member."

"Really? That so? Seems you neglected to ever mention that to me."

"Rusty, it was years ago."

"And now? Did you hook up with one of 'em?"

She looked away. Apparently that was all the answer he needed.

"I see. Guess you didn't grieve long over me."

"Rusty, please, it wasn't like that. I swear. I was terrified. I was sure the DKs would hunt me down and kill me. I didn't know where to go, I—"

"Save it."

"You don't understand—"

"Says he's got proof you didn't do it."

"What?"

"Only one explanation for him to be comin' for you. You must mean something to him."

Skylar's chest rose and fell. "I used to mean something to *you*."

"Yeah, you did."

Past tense.

His eyes moved over her face and then returned to her eyes. "You love this guy?"

"Rusty—"

"Do. You. Love. This. Guy?"

She was terrified of what he'd do if she spoke the truth, but she couldn't deny it. Her mouth wouldn't let her form the word. And besides, he deserved her honesty. "Yes."

He sucked in a breath and studied her long moments. Then surprised her by asking, "He good to you?"

She frowned, not sure if this was some game he was playing with her or if he was seriously wanting to know. Apparently she hesitated too long.

"Skylar. Asked you a question."

"Yes. He's a good man."

He huffed out a breath. "Guess I'll be the judge of what kind of man he is when he gets here."

"What?" Her face filled with shock. Shades was coming here? For her? She looked up at Rusty. Oh God, they would kill him. "Rusty, please, it's me you're mad at, not him."

"Evil Dead lied to us. Hid you out. Got in our business. That's not something we let slide."

"And if he has proof I didn't do it?"

"You better pray he does," Reno bit out with a curl of his lip from where he stood leaning against the wall, his arms folded.

Her eyes flicked to him, and then came back to Rusty. He stayed silent, his eyes boring into hers, and then he walked out, slamming the door.

"Rusty, wait!" she called after him.

Reno pushed off the wall and squatted down in front of her and advised, "Wouldn't be counting on any last minute reprieve if I were you, darlin'. Even if this guy does have the balls to show up, doesn't mean Rusty's lettin' you go. And as for the Dead, we'll kill every last rat-bastard one of 'em."

Skylar swallowed.

He stood and grinned down at her. "Just something to mull over. While you sit here waiting, pretty girl." Then he strode out.

Her eyes fell to the floor, her mind searching. The recording. The camera. It was the only proof he could have. But it was at Rusty's condo. Had he gone to get it? She'd told him about it. Apparently, he'd paid attention. Or was he bluffing? Her eyes slid closed. Either way, he'd be walking into the enemy's camp. Alone.

***

Shades pulled his cell away from his ear and looked over at Ghost who looked back at him with a what-the-fuck expression on his face.

"Shades, what the hell are you doing? You just promised to deliver proof she didn't do it! Proof we don't have yet."

"We're going to get it."

"Get it where?"

"Rusty's condo."

"A fucking DK's place?"

"Scene of the crime."

"You have got to be shitting me."

CHAPTER THIRTY-SEVEN

"Let's go," Shades said starting to rise from the dumpster they were crouched behind. Shades and Ghost had found the place that Skylar had told him about—Maple Hill Condominiums, unit 246. They'd scoped the place out. The first streaks of dawn were just breaking on the horizon, and there were no lights on in the place.

"Whoa, Captain America. What the hell's the plan here?"

"We bust the door in and get it."

"Okay, what's plan B? There is a plan B, right?"

"Ghost, the place is dark. Let's go."

"How about we scope it out first. Maybe I grab a red shirt and ball cap and pretend I'm delivering a pizza," Ghost strategized, pulling an empty pizza box off the top of the dumpster. "At least see if anybody is in there. And if there are, how many we're up against."

"Didn't you hear what I just said?"

"Yeah, but I think my idea is the less likely to get us killed."

"I don't have time for that shit, Ghost. They've got Skylar. Right now she's scared out of her mind. Locked up, tied up, fuck, who knows?"

"Okay, Brother. Calm down. Take a breath. We're gonna get her back."

"This has to work, Ghost, because failure isn't something I can live with. I need to get her back. I just…I need her, Ghost."

"Okay."

Shades pulled his piece from the small of his back where it was shoved in his waistband. He loaded a round in the chamber and took a breath. "Okay, I'm gonna tell you the plan one more time, and you'd better be fucking on board with it." Shades glared at him. "We're goin' in together, and we're comin' out together."

Ghost blew out a breath, giving in to Shades' insanity, knowing the man wasn't going to quit until he had Skylar back. So, he did the only thing he could. He nodded. "Good plan. I like it."

They moved toward the back of the building and climbed the exterior stairs to the second floor unit. They pressed their backs to either side of the door. Ghost bent down and peered into the darkened kitchen window and shook his head at Shades.

Shades tried the doorknob. It was locked. Ghost noticed the latch was not locked on the window. He dug his knife out and jimmied the screen off, setting it quietly on the porch.

Shades glanced around, keeping lookout. Ghost slid the window up an inch and listened. There were no sounds coming from the inside. He pushed it the rest of the way up and threw his leg over, ducking inside. A moment later, he opened the back door for Shades.

The two men crept quietly to the hall and glanced around. The place was dark. Shades flicked on a tiny flashlight and headed down the hall locating the bedroom. Shades eyes moved to the bookcase on the wall opposite the bed. It didn't look like anyone had messed with it. A line of books sat on the top shelf, the one on the end propped at a slight angle. He moved it, and there was the tiny camera.

"Got it, let's go."

They went out the way they came and got back to their bikes. They rode a couple of blocks and parked behind a church. Ghost took a laptop out of his saddlebag and booted it up. Shades grabbed the SD card out of the camera and inserted it in the laptop. A few moments later they had video pulled up and were scrolling quickly through it.

Rusty stumbling drunk and passing out in bed. Skylar leaving in the morning. Two figures in hooded jackets entering the room. One hits Rusty in the head with something, a big flashlight maybe, or a pipe, it was hard to tell. They look in the bag on the nightstand and pick it up. Taking it, they both leave the room. A moment later, one of them comes back in and stabs the dagger into Rusty's chest. As the man turns, he practically looks right at the camera.

Shades froze the video and turned to Ghost. "You recognize him?"

"Nope."

Shades played the rest.

Skylar comes back in, dropping the coffee, she slowly approaches the bed, obviously shaking.

"Fuck," Ghost murmured. "This is hard to watch. It's like watching her whole world fall apart."

They watched the rest of the video.

The DKs coming in, the paramedics and police arriving, them taking Rusty out.

"Wait a minute. Back up."

Ghost backed the video up.

"If the guy's dead, why didn't they pull the sheet over his head?"

"You're right. Check out the IV. Last I heard they don't hook up an IV to a dead guy."

"Fuck. He wasn't dead."

"At least not then."

"And maybe not now."

***

Twenty minutes later, Ghost and Shades quietly approached the DK clubhouse, staying out of sight.

"What's the plan here?" Ghost asked.

"I go in and I get her," Shades replied, studying the rundown warehouse in a sketchy side of town.

"You can't go in there alone," Ghost protested. "Wait for the guys. They're not that far out."

"I need to get to her. I need her to know I'm here. I just need to get inside, Ghost."

"Yeah, that's half the battle. Of course it's the getting

out part that's the really dangerous, bloody part."

"If I don't come out, if *we* don't come out…call the brothers and light this motherfucking place up."

"Shades, Christ, you don't know what you're up against."

"I am getting her back, if it's my last fucking act on this earth."

"Shades—"

"No matter how this ends, it ends today." He stood and began walking toward the gate. He wasn't waiting. Not one more minute. Not another minute of knowing Skylar was trapped inside with those monsters. Not another minute of wondering what she'd already endured because Shades hadn't fucking dealt with the fucking DKs weeks ago. Going in with an army took too long. He couldn't wait.

Ghost yanked his cell out and punched in some numbers, muttering, "Jesus H Christ. You stubborn motherfucker."

***

Rusty stared down at Skylar. "Your life means something to me, Skylar. But if I don't start getting the truth, that's gonna cease to be the case."

She'd given up trying to convince him and stubbornly stayed mute.

Rusty caught her chin and tipped her head back, but before he could say another word, there was a pounding at the door. His brow furrowed as he swiveled his head to glare behind him. "Go the fuck away!"

A low voice drifted through the door. "You're gonna want to see this."

"Fucking see what?" he snapped.

One of his brothers stuck his head in the door.

"We got a visitor."

Rusty lifted his chin to Reno. "Give me a few minutes and then bring her." With that he headed out the door.

Reno pulled a wicked-looking blade out and knelt behind her. A moment later, her wrists were cut free. She felt the blood returning to her hands and moaned. Her shoulders ached from being wrenched behind her all this time. She rotated them, trying to get feeling back in her arms. A bottle of water was pressed to her lips, and she drank thirstily.

She looked up at Reno as he capped the bottle. He'd been almost gentle with her this time.

"Thank you."

Reno's big hand closed over her upper arm and hauled her from the chair. She stumbled against him, her legs stiff from sitting for so long.

"Can you walk or do I need to carry you?"

"Please, just give me a minute."

Surprisingly, he hesitated, giving her time. But it only lasted a few moments before he was pulling her out the door. She stumbled along into a dimly lit hallway, all very industrial in feel. He dragged her down to the left, and then down another hall to the right, finally coming out in a big open room. Skylar's eyes flashed around her. They must be in some kind of warehouse, just like she'd suspected. But there were DK symbols up on the walls, so maybe this *was* their clubhouse.

There were about a dozen leather-clad members gathered

around in a circle. They parted, turning to look as Reno pulled her forward. And there, in the middle of the circle stood Shades.

She gasped.

He looked like they'd already beaten the crap out of him, but he was still on his feet.

His eyes found her, and she saw the stricken look flash across his face as he took in her appearance. She knew she must look a sight. Her blouse was torn open revealing the camisole underneath, and it was stained with blood from where Reno had backhanded her mouth, splitting her lip. The side of her face was probably bruised and swollen, her hair hanging in tangles around her, and she was barefoot.

She tried to move toward Shades, but Reno yanked her back, pulling her against his side, his hand clamped tight over her upper arm.

"You okay, baby?" Shades asked her.

She nodded, tears in her eyes. "You shouldn't have come."

Rusty glanced back at her, and then back to Shades. "You got something for me?"

Skylar's eyes roamed over Shades. He'd come. He'd walked right into the Lion's den. For her.

Shades pulled something small out of his pocket.

Rusty reached out and took it, studying it. "What the fuck is this?"

"You got a laptop? Insert that in it. Pull up the video recorded on it."

Rusty looked over at Growler who turned and gave a

chin-lift to one of his guys. A moment later, a laptop was brought forward and handed to Rusty. He slid the SD card in and fiddled with it a moment, finally pulling up the video. Growler, Rat and Rusty all gathered around it, watching. Reno tugged Skylar closer, peering over their shoulders. Skylar watched the video as well.

As the image pulled up and Rusty recognized his bedroom, his eyes flicked up to Shades. "What the fuck is this? How the hell did you get this? You bug my place?"

Shades stared him down.

"I put that camera in your room," Skylar admitted softly.

Rusty's head swiveled around to her. "You what?"

"You wanted to film us. I was going to give it to you for your birthday."

One of his brothers snorted with laughter.

Rusty's head swung around, and he snapped at the man, "Shut the fuck up."

"Holy fuck!" Growler snapped, drawing everyone's attention back to the video. Two hooded men were on the screen. One of them hit Rusty in the head. Then they went for the bag and left. A moment later one returned.

Skylar winced and looked away as he plunged the dagger into Rusty's chest.

Rusty paused the video as the man turned and looked straight into the camera.

"Spawns," Growler muttered.

"Who the fuck are the Spawns?" Rat asked.

"Eastside street gang. Play the rest."

Rusty started the video again. It showed Skylar returning

and finding him, rushing to his side, feeling for a pulse, shaking him, crying over him. Then she left the room, returning with her cell and making the frantic 911 call.

Rusty closed the laptop and passed it to Growler. Then he turned, his eyes searching out Skylar's.

She met his look, her eyes filled with tears as she'd been forced to relive the entire event through the images in the video. "I told you the truth."

He nodded. "Yeah." Then he lifted his chin to Reno. "Let her go."

She felt Reno's hand instantly release her, and she ran to Shades, flinging herself at him. He caught her, wincing, one arm pulling her tight against him, but his eyes lifted to Rusty's.

Skylar could immediately feel the tension. This wasn't over yet. They still had to get out of here.

One of the DKs came through the door and rushed over to Growler. He said something low in his ear. There was a heated, whispered discussion.

Shades took advantage of the opportunity it gave him to speak to Skylar. Dipping his head low to hers, he whispered in her ear, "I'll get you out of here, I swear. No matter what gets in my way, I promise you."

"You came for me," Skylar whispered back brokenly.

"Of course I did, baby. I'd come for you no matter what."

"How did you find me?"

"Shh, baby."

They could overhear some of what the DKs where

saying to each other.

"They're amassed outside the gates. We don't send these two out, there's gonna be a bloodbath."

Growler murmured a low question she couldn't hear, to which the DK replied, "Dozens of them. Armed to the teeth. We're outnumbered and outgunned."

"Is this going to start a war?" Skylar whispered.

"I gotta start a war just to bring you home, I will."

"I'm afraid, Shades."

"Baby, as long as there's still life in me, no one's touching you again."

Rusty broke from the group, stepping over to them.

Shades and Rusty stared at each other. Then Rusty's gaze dropped to hers. "Take care of yourself, Skylar." His eyes returned to Shades, and he lifted his chin. "Get out of here. Don't fuckin' show your face in Georgia again."

Shades didn't waste a moment. He turned, his hold on her tight. He stood there waiting for the circle of Devil Kings to step back out of his way. Then together they started walking toward the door, her arms wrapped tight around his waist.

"Are you okay?" she whispered noticing the way he limped, his movements stiff, and she wondered if they'd broken his ribs.

"Yeah, babe. Just keep walking."

One of the DKs opened the door for them and whistled to the two at the chain link gate. They unlocked it and stood back as Shades and Skylar shuffled across the compound.

Skylar tugged on Shades' cut. "Baby, look."

His eyes lifted. There, lining the street were about thirty members of the Evil Dead, guns drawn. He tried to smile through the pain. "Nothing like having your brothers show up with lots of guns."

Ghost was running toward them. When he reached them, he looped Shades' arm around his shoulders, taking his weight as Shades almost collapsed.

"Motherfuckers busted my ribs," Shades hissed.

"You're fucking lucky that's all they did, you crazy son-of-a-bitch."

Skylar was suddenly surrounded by Shades' brothers. They were all there—Butcher, Boot, Slick, Hammer, Griz, Heavy, Spider, JJ, Gator, and a bunch of others that Shades would later tell her were his brothers from the Gulf Coast Chapter. And then another pack of bikes were pulling up and suddenly Blood was there in front of her.

"You okay, Princess?" he asked, taking her face in his hands, his eyes running over her.

"I'm fine. What are you doing here?" And then he was shoved to the side, and her father had her in a tight bear hug.

"Jesus Christ, girl. You nearly gave me heart failure."

Undertaker was here? Stunned, her arms clutched at him. "Daddy?"

"Baby."

She heard Blood growl at Shades. "You walked in there alone, dumbass?"

She smiled into her father's shoulder. He had. He'd walked in there alone. For her.

CHAPTER THIRTY-EIGHT

The long line of bikes rolled through the gates of the Birmingham clubhouse, followed by Slick driving the big blue Buick that carried Shades and Skylar in the backseat.

They climbed out of the car and moved inside the clubhouse. When Skylar saw how uncomfortable Shades was, she insisted he sit down on a couch against the wall. He slumped down in it, but pulled her to sit beside him.

"We need to get you to a hospital," she murmured.

He tried to smile. "If you ain't goin', I ain't goin'."

"I'm fine. I told you that."

His eyes moved over her face, and his hand lifted to gently cup her cheek. "You don't look fine."

"They just slapped me. That's all."

Undertaker came over and squatted down in front of Skylar. "Baby, are you okay?"

She nodded. "I'm fine."

He shook his head. "You should have stayed in Slidell. I

should never have let you leave."

"It was my fault," Shades admitted.

Skylar's head swiveled to him. "No, it wasn't. You saved me. You walked in there and saved me."

Butcher approached. "You need help getting up, Shades?"

Shades frowned up at him.

Butcher nodded toward the meeting room. "This won't take long."

Shades nodded and got to his feet.

"Mind if I sit in?" Undertaker asked Butcher.

Butcher stared at him for a moment, and then nodded. "All right, you got anything to say, you can say it, but you don't get a vote."

Shades looked over at Skylar. "Will you be okay for a few minutes?"

She nodded. "I'll be fine. Go." After Shades and the rest of the brothers trooped into the meeting room, she moved to the bar.

Tink reached over and laid her hand over Skylar's.

"You okay, doll?"

Skylar gave her a timid smile. "I'm fine."

"What can I get you?"

"Jack and Coke."

"You got it, honey." Tink quickly mixed her drink and set it before her.

Skylar felt someone sit down on the barstool next to her and looked over to find Blood.

"Crown," he told Tink.

Skylar sipped her drink as Tink poured him a couple inches in a short tumbler, setting it in front of him.

He looked over at Skylar. "You okay, darlin'?"

She nodded and gave him a halfhearted smile.

He nudged her with his shoulder. "You know I was gonna give Shades a run for his money, but I gotta say…you seem like a lotta work, Cupcake." He grinned at her, and she knew he was trying to make her laugh.

His words reminded her of everything that Shades had just done to get her free. She couldn't stop herself from thinking about how violent this MC life he had chosen was, and it gave her pause. *I can't do it*, she thought. This club meant everything to Shades. How could she ever compete with that?

Her mind was racing. And suddenly it was all too much. She couldn't breathe. The walls of the clubhouse were closing in on her. She couldn't think. Not here, not now. She needed time. She needed to *breathe*.

Panic overwhelmed her, and she pushed off the barstool. She noticed Blood's confused look as she whispered, "I can't do this."

She just had to get out of there. Out of this room, out of this clubhouse. She dashed toward the exit. By the time her tunnel vision cleared, she was out on the back stairs, leaning heavily on the railing. Blood must think she was insane the way she'd suddenly ran out.

Her eyes traveled around the lot at all the rows and rows of motorcycles.

She couldn't stay. She couldn't do this. Why had she

ever thought she could? Why had Ghost been so sure she could? She loved Shades. She did. But suddenly she was afraid that wouldn't be enough. Not for a man like him. He wasn't the same boy she'd fallen in love with years ago. Back then he'd been sweet and tender and loving. Until he'd shoved her aside, and he'd crushed her. Now he was a grown man, hardened into this life, everything about him spoke of his dedication and loyalty to the club. He had it in him to be VP, maybe even lead this club one day. He had the confidence, self-assurance, and street smarts. He was good at reading people, and he was smart at figuring out problems and diffusing situations.

He would need a woman just as strong, and she was afraid that would never be her. Maybe they could make it work for a while, but someday he'd see it, he'd realize…and then when he did, where would that leave her? If he tossed her aside again, she knew she wouldn't be able to survive it a second time.

Oh, God.

They were in there, right this minute, giving him that VP patch. She was sure of it. And she just didn't think she'd be strong enough for him, be the kind of woman he needed. Ghost had tried to tell her, hadn't he? Shades would make VP, and when he did he was going to need a strong woman at his side. Skylar just didn't think she could ever be that woman. How did one deal with a life like this? A life where your man came home with broken ribs? Or worse?

When Shades came out of that meeting, she knew she wouldn't be able to face him to tell him her fears. He'd talk her into staying. She knew he would. He wouldn't let her go. So, it had to be now. She knew he'd think that he'd done something wrong. Shit. *Why* couldn't she just be honest with him? Why couldn't she tell him what she was afraid of, instead of panicking and running away?

She hated her inability to confront this. The fear, the anxiety that *she wasn't good enough.* And that was what it all came down to. That's what it had *always* all come down to. Her whole life.

Suddenly, Blood was at her side.

"Skylar? You okay?"

She shook her head.

His hand reached up to slide a lock of hair over her shoulder. He was trying to see her face, she was sure. She tried to turn her head away, but he caught her chin and turned her to look at him. She knew her eyes were shimmering when she met his dark brown eyes.

"Babe." His eyes took in the bruising on the side of her face from when Reno had hit her. She watched his jaw tighten, saw the anger flash across his face, and then just as quickly he reined it in. His eyes skated down her body, taking in the torn buttons of her blouse, the stained camisole pulled halfway out of her skirt and her bare feet. They trailed back up, stopping at her crotch. "You should go to the hospital, sweetheart. Get checked out."

Oh, God. He thought she'd been raped. He was trying to be delicate about bringing it up, but that's what he meant. Maybe there was a soft spot under all that badass after all. Her throat constricted, and she shook her head. "It's not what you're thinking. They didn't touch me. Not like that."

"Whatever they did to you, it's got you shaking and on the verge of a panic attack. I should get Shades. You need your man." He turned to go, but she reached out and grabbed his arm. He looked down at it, her soft touch stopping him in his tracks.

"No. He's in that meeting. It's important."

"Fuck that meeting. You're more important right now."

"No. That's not what I need."

He frowned at her, studying her. "What do you need, Princess?"

"Will you…will you do something for me?"

"Anything." There was no hesitation in his answer, and that choked her up, closing her throat so she had to take a breath to speak again.

"I need to get out of here."

Suddenly his eyes were flicking around the yard. Anywhere but at her.

"Will you take me?" she whispered.

"Skylar, takin' a brother's ol' lady…" he broke off, shaking his head. "That's not allowed."

He was shaking his head, but in a way that made her think he was conflicted about his answer. "Please, Blood. I need to get my things. Then I…" Skylar paused, making a snap decision. "Then I want to go home…with my daddy."

Blood looked stunned, and he must be, she thought. That was quite a bomb she'd just dropped. He studied her a long time, then his eyes went to the horizon. She knew she was asking a lot. She was asking him to go against a brother. And in reality she was probably misleading him. If he thought he had a chance with her, he would be wrong.

His eyes came back to her. "Okay. Let's go."

He moved toward his bike, and she followed.

Twenty minutes later, Skylar gave him directions over his shoulder, pointing to the turn-off and then the drive. He pulled in and rolled to a stop at Shades' cabin.

Skylar got off the bike. She noticed Blood's eyes studying the place as he took his helmet off.

"Come on." She paused and looked back when she realized Blood was not following her. "Blood?"

"I'll wait out here."

She frowned. "Blood, it's like ninety-five degrees out here. Come inside."

He shook his head. "Givin' you a ride's one thing, babe. But goin' in a brother's house—with his ol' lady—when he's not here? That's a line even I won't cross."

Suddenly nervous, she nodded and said, "I'll just be a minute."

He nodded.

***

Blood leaned back on his bike, his ass in the seat, one boot on the ground, one on his foot-peg. His eyes went to the water visible beyond the cabin. He took in the quiet peacefulness of the lake. It was at complete odds with the turmoil rolling inside him. Riding off with Skylar was a big deal. Huge. If what she said about going back with them to Slidell—going home with her father—was true, then it was a game-changer.

If that's what she wanted, *really wanted,* then he'd take her. And maybe after the ordeal she'd just been through, that was exactly what she needed. But a part of him whispered in his ear that this was all wrong. Now more than ever, she needed her man.

And that man wasn't him. It was Shades.

Blood had seen the way the two of them were together. She loved Shades, and as hard as it was to admit it, Shades was a good guy, and he loved her. Blood saw it. Hell, anyone could see it.

His cell went off. Blood reached into his pocket, pulled it out and put it to his ear.

"Yeah?"

"Where the fuck are you?" Undertaker growled in his ear.

"Uh…your daughter is packing a bag. She says she wants to go home with you."

"Say what?"

"I think she's in some kind of shock or something. Got to be a knee-jerk reaction to what happened to her, I don't know. I was afraid she'd take off alone, so I took her."

Undertaker was quiet a long time, taking in the news. "Where are you?"

"Shades' place. She's inside packing a bag, like I said."

"All right. Call me before you head back."

"Right." Blood disconnected. Then he lit up a smoke.

CHAPTER THIRTY-NINE

"Where's Skylar?" Shades asked, glancing around the room as he approached the bar where Tink was loading bottles of beer into a cooler. She bit her lip. There was something she didn't want to tell him. His eyes narrowed on her. "Tink?"

He watched her eyes drop to the new VP patch on his vest. Butcher had tossed it to him, and they hadn't let him leave the room until he'd hastily stitched it on. He'd have to go back and do a better job later tonight, but for now, it was on his cut. At long fucking last. His chest would swell with pride if his ribs didn't hurt so fucking bad.

But now, all he could think about was Skylar. She'd been through a lot, and all he wanted to do was hold her. Butcher had insisted on having that stupid meeting the minute they got back. He'd only had the time alone with her in the car as they'd ridden from Atlanta. There'd been no way he could ride his bike, not with his ribs fucked up. Shit, the car ride had been bad enough. Thank God Slick and Boot had thought to bring the car, not sure what condition Skylar would be in. Slick drove them back, and Boot had ridden Shades' bike.

Shades and Skylar had climbed in the back. He'd pulled her close against his good side, his arms tight around her. Slick had gotten them out of there quickly, gunning the engine and spinning the tires of the big old Buick.

"Did they hurt you, baby?" Shades had asked her.

She'd pressed her face in his neck, and he'd felt her body shake with a sob.

"Slick, turn around. She needs to go to the hospital."

She'd looked up. "No. No hospitals."

"Babe, if they…" God, he couldn't bring himself to say the words. "If they hurt you—"

"They didn't. Not like that."

"Sky, you can tell me—"

"I know I can. They didn't rape me. Just slapped me. That's all."

He'd brushed the hair back from her face, his eyes going over the bruise. "I'm gonna kill the motherfucker that did this to you. I'll kill every last one of 'em for you."

She'd shaken her head. "No," she'd said sharply. "That's not what I want. That's not what I need."

Her angry outburst had brought his head back. Christ, he hadn't known what to say or how to make this better for her. "Okay, baby. Whatever you want."

"I just need you to hold me."

"Okay, Sky. I'm here. I've got you."

She'd sniffled. "You're the one they hurt. I'm so sorry, Shades. This is all my fault."

"Hey, listen to me." He'd squeezed her. "None of this is your fault. You did nothing to Rusty or his club, and you didn't deserve what they did."

"But they hurt you… because of me."

"They hurt me because I wear an Evil Dead patch, Sky. No other reason."

"But they think your club lied to them, hid me out and…and fucked them over."

"Skylar, shh, baby. Don't worry about any of that now. It's all over. It's all fucking over, baby."

"You came for me."

"Of course I did. You think I wouldn't?"

She'd sobbed.

"I love you, sweetheart. Couldn't live without you."

And now he was staring at Tink, and a bad fucking feeling skated down his spine. At Tink's continued hesitation, he prodded, "Tink?"

"I saw her ride off with Blood."

Shades brows shot up in shock. "What?"

Tink swallowed uncomfortably.

Ghost put a hand on his shoulder. "There's got to be an explanation, Brother. Maybe he took her to get checked out."

Shades was about to whirl on him, when Undertaker came up to him. "We need to talk."

"Not now. I have to find Skylar."

"She wants to come home."

Shades spun on him, frowning in disbelief. "Home?

What the fuck are you talking about? She is home."

Undertaker shook his head. "We need to talk." He grabbed a fistful of Shades cut and jerked him to the side. Shades was just confused enough to let him.

"What are you talking about?"

"I just talked to Blood. Skylar told him she wants to go back to Slidell with us. 'Wants to go home with her daddy,' she said."

Shades shook off his hold. "I don't fucking believe it."

"She's been through a lot. And if she wants my protection, she's got it. But I've seen the way you are with her. I know you walked in that fucking DK stronghold alone. For her. Goddamn, boy, I believe you'd walk through the fires of hell for that girl. My girl. So, I'm giving you a shot here. Givin' you a chance to talk her out of this. But mark my words, if when you're done talking, she still wants to go home with me, I'm takin' her, and you aren't stopping me."

"Where is she?" Shades growled.

"She asked Blood to take her to your place to pack a bag."

Undertaker barely got the words out before Shades was running out the door.

***

Blood heard the roar of the motorcycle before he saw it. One bike roaring up fast. Only one person that could be. Shades. The bike tore up the drive. Yup. One pissed off man, come to get his ol' lady.

Blood stood up and waited by his bike, he knew what was coming. He gave a quick glance up at the bedroom window. Skylar peered out. His eyes slid back to Shades as he dropped his kickstand. He hobbled a bit pulling his leg off the bike, and Blood knew what it cost him to ride that bike out here. He knew the pain of riding with cracked ribs. It hurt like a son-of-a-bitch.

Shades strode toward him, a bit of a limp in his gait. He didn't say a word before throwing his first punch, a brutal right hook that put Blood on the ground.

"Get the fuck out of here," Shades snarled down at him.

Blood rubbed his jaw, still on the ground, and looked up at Shades. "I let you have that one, 'cause I deserved it, but I get up I'm gonna hurt you."

"Then you better stay the fuck down."

"Shades—"

"You're fucking lucky I found you out here and not inside."

"Shades, I wouldn't do that. I just gave her a ride. She looked like she was about to lose it. She needed you. I wanted to break in that meeting and get you, but she wouldn't let me."

"Get out of here," Shades hissed, and Blood saw him reach a hand to his ribs, and he knew he was in some wicked pain.

"She's in there packing her shit. Maybe I'll stick around in case you can't change her mind."

"Get the fuck out or you'll be looking down the barrel of my gun."

"DKs took your piece," Blood reminded him with a grin.

"You think I don't have half a dozen more inside?"

"All right, Brother, but just so you know, you ever fuck up, I'll be right here for her, picking up the fucking pieces." Then he turned toward the window just quick enough to see her shadow pull back, and he knew she'd heard every word. He shouted, "You hear that, Princess? I'm just a phone call away."

Shades stood there a moment, clutching his side with one hand, his eyes drifting up to the window. And then his eyes returned to Blood. "She ain't ever gonna make that call."

Blood watched him hobble inside before climbing to his feet. He pulled his phone out, his thumb moving over the screen, and put it to his ear.

A moment later, Undertaker growled in his ear, "Yeah?"

"Thanks for the heads-up."

Undertaker's chuckle came through the phone. "Knew you could take care of yourself."

Blood moved his jaw back and forth. "He's got one hell of a right hook, I'll give him that. If I didn't have facial hair, there'd be an imprint of an Evil Dead ring visible on my jaw tomorrow."

Undertaker chuckled again. "She okay?"

"Haven't heard any screamin' yet. You want me to stay?"

"I want you to make sure she's okay. Knows if she needs me, I'm here for her."

"I made sure she knows I'm just a phone call away. And I ain't interested in stickin' around till I hear the bed springs squeak and the headboard hittin' the wall."

"Christ, Blood, that's my daughter. I don't want that image in my fucking head."

It was Blood's turn to chuckle. "Just sayin', that's where this is endin'. We both know it."

"Fine, get back here."

***

Shades limped inside and into the middle of the living room. He looked up toward the bedroom loft. "Skylar, get down here."

No response.

"Swear to Christ, you make me climb those fucking stairs—" He clutched at his ribs. Not that he'd get any sympathy from her, but fuck he could barely stand up straight.

She appeared at the top of the stairs, and then she was coming down them.

Shades eyed the duffle bags at the foot of the steps. Skylar pulled another one from her shoulder and set it down. She stood there, staring up at him.

"You're leaving?" When she didn't reply, he repeated himself. "What the fuck, babe, you're leaving? That's it? You're just walking out on us?"

She finally found her voice. "There's no 'us'."

"The hell there's not."

"There's you and your club. That's all that's important to you. That's all you care about." He knew the words coming out of her mouth were all lies, but she threw them up as a defense, guarding her heart. Hurting him before he could hurt her.

"Bullshit! Didn't I just walk through hell for you?"

"You did it to get your patch. Everything you did, coming for me, all of it...you did it all just to get VP, because you couldn't let Undertaker down, isn't that right?"

"No, it's not fucking right." Christ, she was grasping at straws now.

"You come back the conquering hero, and they make you their VP."

"Yeah, the club is my life, always will be, but that isn't all I care about. There's a place for you in my life. And if you're not in it, there'll always be a big piece missing. An empty place that won't ever be filled. I thought we worked all this shit out at the beach. Goddamn, Skylar. You're enough to drive a man crazy."

She made to move past him, but he stepped in front of her.

"Let me go."

"Like hell I will. Running again, babe? That your solution to everything? Hurt somebody before they have a chance to hurt you."

"I don't know what you're talking about." She tried to brush past him, but he grabbed her by the arm and turned her to face him.

"You're afraid this is going to end. You think I'm gonna leave, so you're gonna beat me to the punch. Hurt me before I hurt you." At least she had it in her to look ashamed, because she knew he was right. "Swear to God, babe, I'll toss every suitcase in this place out in that fuckin' lake, if that's the kind of statement I gotta make to you."

Her eyes lifted to his, giving him hope he was getting through to her.

"I'm not going anywhere, Sky."

She searched his eyes. He hoped she could see the resolve in his.

"And you're not going anywhere either. Not with your father and sure as hell not with Blood." He growled the last part, hoping to Christ she knew how bad of a fuck-up that move was. He huffed out a breath, trying to regain his temper. "Sky, you once told me you had no one. You want family? I'll be your family. Now you have your dad, the club, and me, if you want."

"Shades…" Her voice sounded shaky. Maybe she was starting to see.

"I'm here, Skylar. I'm standing right here in front of you."

Her eyes moved to the wall of windows and the lake beyond. He had her thinking, at least. "I know what this shit is about, Sky, and it's not about me choosing the club over you. It's about you being scared. You're scared, so you do what you do best. You run."

"That's not true," she whispered, her eyes still on the lake.

"Yeah, it is, sweetheart. You're afraid you can't let someone else hold the reins in your life again after having no control for most of your life. You're afraid to let me hold those reins."

Her eyes moved to his cut, the new VP patch.

"That's not it. I'm glad you got VP, Shades. I am. You

deserve it. It's what you wanted for so long. This is about me. Don't you see?"

"Babe…"

"I'm not what you need."

"Bullshit."

"You need a strong woman by your side. I'm not that woman. I never will be."

He shook his head and muttered, "How can such a smart woman be so Goddamned stupid?"

"What?"

"You're the strongest woman I've ever met. Are you kidding? All the shit you've been through in your life, you never let it stop you. You never let it hold you down. Every time life knocked you down, you got back up."

"Shades…" She broke off, shaking her head.

"And maybe you don't understand that about yourself. Maybe you don't get how strong you are. But not understanding something about yourself doesn't mean it's not who you are.

"Me getting VP, the absurd idea of yours that I went after you just to get that VP patch, that's bullshit, Sky and we both know it. I love you. I need you. Without you it all means nothing. How do you not get that?

"Yeah, that patch is what I've wanted for a long fucking time. Then I walked out of that meeting, and you were gone…" He ran his hand down his face in frustration. "I finally had everything I wanted for so long, but then I realized that without you, it isn't important, it means nothing if I lose you in the process. I realized that when the DKs took you. I finally got the position in the club, success, respect. But what I really need is your forgiveness and love."

He watched a tear roll down her cheek, and it tore at him. All he wanted to do was take her in his arms, but he knew this shit needed to be said. She needed to hear it.

"You've had to face so much, so young, all on your own. I get that, Sky. You know I get that. But what you don't get is that all that is over, sweetheart. You will never face anything alone again. Not as long as I live. Those fears you've been carrying all these years, hand them all over to me. I'll carry that load. All of it. You live free and easy, pretty girl. No more worrying about any of that shit."

Another tear rolled down her cheek, but he kept on.

"I know you think it's a risk you're taking…opening up to me and letting yourself love me, afraid I'm going to hurt you. I get that, too. But, baby, look at me. I am not going to hurt you. That is not going to happen. I'm not gonna tear us apart. And I'm not gonna let you tear us apart either.

"And maybe you don't get that now, but you will. Every year that passes, you'll get it more and more. Until finally one day, you'll just know, the way *I* know, that this is going to last forever."

"Oh, Shades." Her eyes brimmed over.

"Are you getting it yet, babe?"

She nodded.

His hand lifted, his thumb brushing the wetness off her cheek. "Good, 'cause my ribs are hurting like a bitch, and I think I gotta sit down." He collapsed on the couch with a groan.

"Shades, how did you get here?"

"I rode."

"Your *bike*?"

"Yeah. Quickest way to get here. See the pain I go through for you woman?" He tried to laugh, but winced as a jolt of pain jabbed through him.

She sat carefully on the couch next to him. "Baby, we should get you to the hospital."

"Nah. Slick taped 'em up. That's all the hospital would do anyway." He paused to look over at her, his hand reaching up to tuck a strand of hair behind her ear. "Did I make my point? You stayin'?"

She nodded. "I'm staying."

"Good." He smiled at her, his hand brushing down her cheek, his thumb stroking her lips. His eyes met hers. "I'd carry you up those stairs to the bed, but I don't think I'd make it with these ribs. But I want you."

"Baby."

"We got a couch right here."

"Shades, we can't. You're hurt."

"We can if you climb on top and do all the work," he suggested with half a grin. He didn't wait for her response; he was already pulling her leg across his lap, hiking her skirt up as he settled her on top of him. His fingertips skated up her thighs, sliding under her skirt, and his eyes stared into hers. "Do you want me, Sky?"

"Yes," she whispered, her breathing already accelerating.

He smiled, one hand going to the back of her neck and

pulling her face down to his until her mouth brushed softly over his.

"I love you, pretty girl." He searched her eyes. "I fell in love with you the night I gave you a ride home." That caught her interest.

"You did?" she asked, brows arched.

He nodded. "Um-hmm. I remember the exact moment it happened. Do you want me to tell you?"

She nodded.

"I was dropping you off. And just before you walked away, I hooked a finger in your belt loop and pulled you close for a kiss. Do you remember?"

She nodded again. "It was the first time you kissed me."

"Do you remember what you did after that?"

She put her hand over his beard. "I touched you. Like this."

Shades covered her hand, like he had that first time. "You'd been wondering about what it would feel like. When you touched me like that, all soft and gentle, it was like a mule kicked me in the chest."

"A mule, huh?" She grinned.

"Yep. *Bam.* I was in love." He grinned back at her. "And you've had my heart every day since."

She lowered her face, her mouth brushing his. "Hello, love," she whispered.

"Hello, love," he whispered back. His hand rose to cup her face, his thumb stroking over her lips, his eyes on her mouth a moment before they lifted to meet her soft gaze. "Every time we go through something, Sky, every time we make it to the other side of it, we're stronger for it. It makes us stronger, better. The couples who are meant to be are the ones who go through everything designed to tear them apart, and they come out even stronger. I've got no doubts about us, babe. None. No part of this road feels wrong."

She smiled.

"I'm sorry, Sky. I know how hard this has all been on you." His voice was soft, his tone tender. "I know you're afraid. I know it's scary, but I've got two strong arms to wrap around you when the world goes crazy. The only thing you need to know is *you are my world.* You get *that*, you feel that deep down? Everything else will follow; everything else will fall into place."

"I feel like I've been hit by a truck." She whispered the confession.

He grinned. "I know the feeling, Sky. When love comes along…sometimes it whispers in your ear. Sometimes it slams you against the fucking wall."

"I'm home." She said it almost in amazed wonder.

He wrapped his arms around her.

"You're home, baby. You're finally home."

EPILOGUE

Skylar—

I lay in our bed, naked, waiting for Shades to come home. After so many missed chances and screw ups, I was finally going to make his wish come true. I smiled as I realized how many times we'd tried to make it happen and had been waylaid.

But I was determined.

Most nights we went to bed at the same time, and that didn't count in my eyes. No, he had to come in and *find* me waiting for him.

I'd texted him a short time ago, telling him I was home from work early.

I immediately got a text back saying he was closing the shop.

I smiled. I knew my man. So well. And my baby knew me. So well.

I heard him come in. I heard him coming up the stairs. And then I turned to see him standing at the foot of the bed.

I was on my side turned away from him. I twisted, my shoulders pressing flat to the mattress, but my hips were still canted to the side. With one hand I slowly pushed the sheet down to my hips.

His eyes moved over my naked body.

"My pretty baby." His voice was soft.

Then he grabbed a handful of sheet in his fist and tugged it slowly the rest of the way off. The way the sheet glided across my skin—as well as the heat in his eyes—had tingles washing over me.

"You're home," I said in a breathy voice.

He gave a slight nod of his head.

"You're naked," he said in a growly voice.

I echoed his nod, the corners of my mouth pulling up.

God, how I loved this man.

Shades—

Damn. I felt my heart squeeze. My baby. Looking up at me with that shy little smile on her face—that shy little smile that I'd fallen for so many years ago. I didn't need to take in the rest of her gorgeous body; that smile and the look on her face was beautiful enough.

But, hey, I'm a guy, so yeah, I looked.

Perfection, from her head to her pretty pink polished toes.

Heaven all laid out for me.

I smiled back at her.

And then I pulled my shirt over my head, undid my belt, and let my pants drop to the floor. I heard the thud of the velvet box in the pocket hitting the carpet with a soft thud. The ring inside would have to wait until later tonight. My baby had a gift of her own for me and I intended to relish every moment of it.

She reached out with her foot, rubbing her sole up and down my abs seductively. I took it in my hand, wrapping my palm around the arch, squeezing, massaging, until she moaned in pleasure.

"Miss me?" I asked softly, my voice gravely with need.

She nodded. "I've been waiting for you."

"I see that."

I brought her foot to my mouth and kissed it. Then I wrapped her leg around me as I crawled over her, settling in the cradle of her thighs, sinking into her in one thrust. Her legs wrapped around me, pulling me close, right where I belonged.

God, how I loved this woman.

"Hello, love," I whispered against her mouth, stroking the hair back from her face.

She smiled, and her face lit up, *fucking lit up*, as she whispered back, "Hello, love."

The End

If you enjoyed reading SHADES, please review in on Amazon.

WOLF

An Evil Dead MC Story

The Evil Dead Motorcycle Club gave Wolf his nickname. They said it was because women stood about as much chance with him as Little Red Riding Hood stood against the Big Bad Wolf. And maybe that was true.

For Wolf, when it comes to his club, he's all about loyalty. He loves his brothers, he loves the freedom of the road, and he loves his independence. When it comes to women, Wolf is all about the chase. He likes the hunt, he likes the challenge, and he loves women. And for the hot-as-hell badass biker, they've always come too easily. But they never fully satisfy him.

That is, until he met Crystal.

Buried under that hard-edged sexy-as-sin tomboy with the smartass mouth that can put any brother in the MC in his place, is a feminine side she only reveals when pushed. And Wolf is just the man to push. Problem is she's the only woman to ever push back. Which only makes him more determined to have her.

Life in the Evil Dead MC isn't easy, and neither is loving one of them. It's a life that can leave a man scarred and bloody. And sometimes the fallout is far reaching and takes more than a man is willing to give.

It can be just as risky for any woman brave enough to love one of them.

The scars of life run deep, for both of them.

Sometimes life doesn't give you a fairytale, sometimes you have to make your own.

And sometimes it takes a spitfire to tame a hell-raiser.

THE EVIL DEAD MC SERIES

OUTLAW

CRASH

SHADES

WOLF

GHOST

Also by Nicole James…

RUBY FALLS

Made in the USA
Middletown, DE
06 July 2016